# Harley Quinn™

## RECKONING

# — DC ICONS —

# RECKONING

## -DC ICONS-

## RACHAEL ALLEN

Random House  New York

Copyright © 2022 DC Comics.
BATMAN and all related characters and elements © & ™ DC Comics.
WB SHIELD: ™ & © WBEI. (s22)

Harley Quinn created by Paul Dini and Bruce Timm

Cover art by Jen Bartel

All rights reserved. Published in the United States by Random House Children's Books, a division of Penguin Random House LLC, New York.

Random House and the colophon are registered trademarks of Penguin Random House LLC.

Visit us on the Web! GetUnderlined.com

Educators and librarians, for a variety of teaching tools, visit us at RHTeachersLibrarians.com

Library of Congress Cataloging-in-Publication Data is available upon request.
ISBN 978-0-593-42986-0 (trade)—ISBN 978-0-593-42989-1 (lib. bdg.)—
ISBN 978-0-593-42988-4 (ebook)

Printed in the United States of America
10 9 8 7 6 5 4 3 2 1
First Edition

To all the women and girls doing science:
Keep changing the world.

# PROLOGUE

WE'RE SUPPOSED TO LOCK THE DOOR WHEN WE LEAVE. IT'S one of Dr. Nelson's biggest Official Rules, along with keeping a detailed lab notebook and saving all your data on the Gotham U network. Today when I arrive, clutching a coffee I made at home and rubbing the sleep from my eyes, the door is open. Only halfway, which is another weird thing. It's always all the way open or all the way closed.

I can't explain why my shoulders tense. Why my hands clench into fists until my nails dig in.

I walk inside.

The table with the coffeepot looks just the way I left it, and the computer and the desks—everything is fine. Admittedly, I get kind of jumpy in the morning. Judge me if you want; I'm not reducing my caffeine intake. I set down my bag and my cup. Maybe a janitor came in early. People don't usually beat me here because (A) I'd rather die than see my hungover father in the morning, and (B) I am GOING to get the good thermocycler before that pissant Trent Bayers

1

comes in. Crap, is he here? Because there is no amount of coffee that could prepare me for that.

I step from the office space through the door into the main lab—without my coffee because having food and drink of any kind in the lab spaces is verboten. Trent's arrogant self isn't occupying the good machine. Thank. Goodness. I get my samples from the freezer, but I can't shake the feeling that someone's watching me. I wonder if Trent would do something as obnoxious as hide in the lab just to scare me. Actually, that is kind of a great idea.

I take a deep breath and try to focus on my work. The repetition of filling tiny tubes with even tinier amounts of liquid soothes me. As soon as I have my samples going, I make coffee and wash all the glassware that the undergrads and postdocs left in the sinks yesterday. According to Dr. Nelson's Unofficial Rules, these are my most important tasks as an intern. Then I double-check my thermocycler. (It's going! Which means the DNA in my samples is multiplying like rabbits!) And then I close a drawer that's open and grab an ice bucket that someone left on the counter. Water sloshes inside. Not just water. Little plastic tubes with fancy labels. Dr. Nelson is gonna be pissed. These antibodies cost six hundred dollars a pop, and somebody left three of them out overnight.

I slide over to the lab notebook on the counter to see who will be the next victim of his entirely deserved wrath. Bernice Watkins. Wait, what? Bernice is always so careful. It's something I noticed ever since August, when we started bonding over being in the same post–high school gap-year program. The uneasy feelings prick the back of my neck again.

I pull out my phone to text Bernice.

Harleen: Are you here?

Maybe she had some kind of emergency or something. Wouldn't she have texted me, though? *Not if she's mad at you.* I shake away the thought and go back to the office area, where I pour some fresh coffee in my travel mug and text again.

Harleen: Look, I'm not trying to be weird, but what time are you coming in today?

There's a vibrating noise from across the room. I text one more time.

Harleen: ??

I hit Send and wait. The drawer across from me vibrates again. The drawer in Bernice's desk.

I'm across the room in a second, opening it. Bernice's phone. Bernice's bag. These are things that should not be here without Bernice. I'm the early bird. She's the night owl, stumbling home exhausted after the rest of the lab is already gone.

Something's wrong.

There's a creak from the other room.

"Bernice?"

Maybe she got tired and slept in the lab. I'm not gonna lie—I've done it before, though it had a lot more to do with my dad than with my experiments.

I walk back into the main lab, where my thermocycler is still going, and the lab is as empty as it was before, but this time the emptiness feels sinister.

"Bernice?"

All these other rooms and hallways connect to the main

lab, stretching through the fifth floor like roots. Bernice could be in any of them, I tell myself. And so could anyone else. It'd be super easy to hide in— Nope. Not even gonna think about it. I check the cognitive-testing room, the surgery room, the cold room, even the bathroom. Empty, all empty. It does nothing to ease the sense that something bad is waiting, watching.

I go back to the main lab. Look at Bernice's notebook and the area where it seems she was working last night. There's a pipette with the plastic tip still on, as if she was just about to draw up her next chemical solution. *What the hell, Bernice?*

I stand in front of the benchtop. Pick up her pipette like it'll tell me the secret of where she is. Instead, I get this chill—like someone is watching me, hot breath on my neck. I shudder and look over my shoulder.

And then I see it.

The door to the darkroom is shut.

We never keep it closed unless we're actively working in there, but maybe Bernice is doing a really long exposure, or maybe she went in there at midnight and fell asleep while she was waiting, or maybe a hundred thousand other things, but when I touch the door handle, I don't want to open the door.

"Bernice, you in there?" If she *is* doing an experiment, I sure don't want to screw it up.

Nothing.

I have to go in, see what's going on. Otherwise I won't be able to shake this feeling of being watched. But my muscles won't move to turn the handle. I have to force them.

The door is locked.

My heart starts beating faster. I whip out my pocketknife,

wishing like anything I had my lockpick kit. I pull out the smallest tool and listen for all the right clicks. This lock is more complicated than the ones I'm used to, and every second feels important.

Finally, the door creaks open. A shape forms in the darkness—

Bernice, sitting in a chair, her torso flopped over a benchtop.

"Oh thank goodness. You scared the crap out of me."

I touch her shoulder at first, then shake it. "Bernice?"

Harder. "Bernice!"

Her mouth lolls open. Her eyes are glazed. *Don't be dead. Please, don't be dead.* I cup my hand in front of her mouth and wait for a breath that never comes.

"Oh crap, Bernice."

I unlock my phone with shaking fingers and dial the campus police.

"Hello? My friend needs help, and she's not breathing. I'm in the neurobiology building. Nelson Lab. I need you to get here *now.*"

A trickle of white foam leaks from the corner of her mouth, and her cheeks are so, so pale.

"You have to hurry, okay? She's . . . she's dying."

# OCTOBER

# CHAPTER 1

I WONDER IF I COULD FLICK THIS PAPER CLIP INTO TRENT'S mouth. If he doesn't stop talking, I just might. *Blah-blah, listen to me, all you peons, while I talk about my superior scientific intellect even though my western blots never work.*

I should really stop making out with him in the darkroom.

"It sounds like things are going well," says Dr. Nelson.

"Really well," says Trent. "I've already started writing my senior thesis, even though it's still two years away. I'll probably be the lead author on at least three papers this year."

My eyes meet Bernice's across the table, and I make a face, I can't help it. We both have to look down at our laps, quick, so we don't start laughing.

Finally, FINALLY, Trent is finished, and then Kijoon gives an update, and then Bernice.

"How about you, Harleen?"

"Yeah, Dr. N, it's going really well! I ran another batch of tests on the blood samples from the Arkham patients this week, and we're seeing genetic differences in this one too."

The Nelson Lab has blood samples from all the most dangerous criminals in Arkham, and I get to analyze them. Super badass, right? Interns don't usually get to do cool stuff like that, but my grad student mentor, Oliver, totally trusts me.

"That's fantastic news," says Dr. Nelson.

"I KNOW!" I think about saying something else—I actually have this Big Scientific Idea I was hoping to run by him, but Trent's got this annoying smirk plastered on his face that makes me want to wait for another time.

Dr. N opens a schedule on the electronic whiteboard. "Okay, gang, I've got meetings with Wayne Industries and Alston Pharmaceuticals next week. Alston just developed a new antidepressant. Does anyone have time to test it out in our models?"

It's so cool that he meets with all the heavy hitters. And that he's one of Gotham U's youngest full professors, at thirty-eight. I'm already pretty strapped, but I think about volunteering. He's the kind of person you want to say yes to.

Trent's hand shoots up. "I'm on it!"

Of course he is.

"Excellent," says Dr. N. "Who's next?"

"Actually," Michael says, "I've been meaning to bring up some trouble I'm having with my immunostaining. These brain sections should be lighting up like fireworks, but I'm just not seeing it."

"Have you tried upping your concentrations?" asks Oliver.

"Did you test a positive control?" asks Bernice.

Michael nods on both counts.

"Is it possible you're using too strong a detergent?" I say.

"Like, if you switched to one that's less stringent, maybe it wouldn't damage the cell membranes so much, but it would still poke enough holes to allow the immunostaining to happen. Because what if the protein you're trying to stain for is actually—"

"Have you tried embedding the brains in different ways before you make sections? Frozen versus wax?" asks a postdoc.

Michael shakes his head. "Yeah, I've tried everything."

"What if your protein is in the cell membrane?" says Trent. He gets some funny looks and throws up his hands. "Hear me out. Because it keeps disappearing on you, so maybe it's getting washed away during your detergent steps. Maybe if you used a weaker detergent . . ."

I wait for someone to gently break it to him that I proposed this plan fifteen seconds ago.

"A cell membrane protein. Interesting idea," says Michael.

"Quick thinking," says Dr. Nelson.

I smack my hand on the table, louder than I mean to. "I literally just said that."

And . . . silence. Every head turns to look at me, and I can see the judgment written in their eyes.

"Harleen." It's all Dr. Nelson says. It's all he has to say.

"Sorry," I mutter.

After lab meeting, when Trent and I are in the darkroom, I accidentally on purpose bite him on the ear a little too hard.

"Come *on*, Bernice. We're only in college once! Live a little."

"Um, we don't actually go to college here yet."

"*Exactly.* How many of the other gap-year students got invited to a frat party with college boys?" I put my hands on Bernice's shoulders, just grazing her strawberry-blond hair. She looks at me doubtfully through her black-rimmed glasses. "Your experiments will be here when you get back. I promise."

"But I didn't bring a costume." Bernice eyes my jean skirt and lifeguard tank and the Frankenstein stitches and neck bolts I drew on with eyeliner.

"You can totally wear jeans to a haunted beach party! What do you have on under that sweater?"

"A camisole?"

"Perfect!" I make a puppy face. "Pleeeease?"

Bernice gives a tiny shrug. "Okay, but just for a little bit."

"YAY!!!" I yell way too loudly for someone who is indoors. There's a happy fizzing in my veins, and I want the party to start NOW. I grab Bernice by the hands and swing her around in a circle while a Bunsen burner flares in the background. Trent gives us a dirty look because he's jealous AF.

Then Bernice and I skip across campus to the frat party of our dreams. I hope they play Lizzo.

"I'm so glad you came with me!" I tell her.

Bernice and I are both in the Gotham University Bridge Scholars program, wherein high school graduates who are outstanding in STEM (that's us), especially ones who aren't from the best neighborhoods or backgrounds (that's also us), get paid to intern in labs across campus during a gap year between high school and college, thus changing our futures and someday the world. That's the idea, anyway. I can't wait to go to college. Well, assuming I can afford it. There's a

Gotham U Presidential Scholarship I applied for that could actually make it a possibility for me, but they don't give it to many people.

"Won't it be so cool when we actually go here?" says Bernice.

"Yeah." I smile. "Hey, do you ever worry about how you're going to pay for it? Gotham U, I mean?"

Bernice blushes. "I'm doing okay. I've been trying to save most of the money they pay us in the Bridge program, and also I, um, make one-of-a-kind, creepy stuffed animals and sell them on Etsy."

"Wait. Seriously? Like what kind of stuff?"

She shrugs. "Like, gargoyles and zombie kittens and Cthulhu and stuff. Sometimes from scratch, but sometimes I repurpose things I find at estate sales. And now people know I do it, so I'm always getting a creepy old teddy bear that a friend's cousin's sister found in their dead grandma's attic."

That is . . . dark. But, like, cool dark? And delightfully unexpected.

"Okay, first of all, that is the weirdest thing ever. And second of all, you're about two hundred percent more mysterious than you were five minutes ago."

She blushes again. She's one of those people who are physically incapable of taking a compliment without turning red. Then her face grows serious. "Are you worried about it?"

Now I'm the one feeling flustered. "Paying for Gotham U? Oh. Well—" I guess it should have occurred to me when I asked the question that I was also going to have to answer it. I don't know why I feel the need to hide my poverty like a dark secret. Especially from Bernice. She wouldn't be in the program if she weren't poor like me, right? My high school is closer to Crime Alley, and hers is down by the docks, but it has just as bad a rep.

Bernice stops walking. "It's okay if you are," she says. Something about the firmness in her voice makes me stop walking too. "My stuffed-animal savings—it'll only be enough if I get all the financial aid my school counselor thought they'll give me. And even then, I'm not sure if it's enough to fill in the gaps for the entire four years. Anyway, sometimes I say everything's okay when really it's not. Because I want this so badly that I'm going to do whatever it takes to make it okay." She fixes me with eyes that can see right through me. "You know?"

My breath catches in my chest. Somehow I manage to choke out the word *yes*. Bernice waits like she can tell there's more. I look around at the gleaming buildings that surround us, stretching to the sky, bursting with ideas and opportunities and things just out of reach. "I want this so much, the wanting feels like a fire that's going to eat me alive."

Bernice's eyes flash, passion recognizing passion. "Yes."

It feels like such a powerful word coming out of her mouth that I want to say it too.

"Yes."

I shiver and pull my coat tighter around me.

The spell breaks.

"Oh, gosh, you must be freezing. We should get to the party," says Bernice.

"Right. The party."

We start walking again. Double time, because wearing a jean skirt on an October night in Gotham City is no joke. We don't say anything else, and I know we're both lost in thoughts of the future and how we'll get there.

But then we get to the party, and you can feel the bass

14

from outside, and there are cute boys on the front porch sitting in rocking chairs, and I feel like the living embodiment of an exclamation point. I touch up my lip gloss, and then I put some on Bernice too because I'm a really good friend, and then we go inside.

I heard the haunted beach party was supposed to be the fraternity's big event of the year—a Thursday-Friday-Saturday rager for Halloween weekend—but holy crap, I was not expecting this. There are a ton of people here. And sand. So much sand. They built an actual beach on the main floor of the frat house. With a tiki bar. And three hot tubs. Also: dudes drinking beer out of plastic cups, people doing body shots, and a guy in a *T. rex* costume who's carrying a box of wine on his shoulder like a boom box and yelling that he's about to complete the Tour de Franzia. But what I really want to do is dance.

I don't have to dance by myself for long before a boy materializes in front of me. He's doing that awkward I-only-dance-with-my-shoulders thing. He shuffles closer but tries to pretend that's not what he's doing until—oops, look at that—we're dancing together.

He clearly wants to make out with me.

And, okay, maybe I want to make out with him too. He's hot, ya know?

I brush my lips against his, and he's actually a pretty good kisser for a boy wearing mid-thigh khaki shorts and boat shoes. The song ends, and he pulls away so we can catch our breath.

"Hey, I have to go check on something in my room. You wanna come with me?"

I give him an extremely suspicious look. "Um . . ."

But he just laughs. "A puppy. I have a puppy in my room."

"OMG, are you serious?!" I. Love. Puppies. Well, all baby animals, really. Even (especially?) the ugly ones.

"Yep. She's gonna be our house dog. I have to keep her in my room during parties for now because she gets scared of the loud music. You wanna meet her?"

*Do I?*

I walk over to where Bernice is dancing and touch her elbow. "Be right back."

I follow him upstairs.

"I haven't seen you before," he says. "Are you a freshman?"

"Nah. I don't go here. *Yet.* I'm hoping to next year."

He shrinks away from me. "Wait, are you in high school? How old are you?"

"Eighteen," I say, standing taller, as if that'll prove I'm not just some kid. "I'm doing a gap year right now. I live around here, though."

He waggles his eyebrows. "A townie, huh? What part of the city are you from?"

I could lie. Say I live in Gotham Heights or the Fashion District. But—

"The East End." It just kind of comes out.

"Oh." His eyes flick up and down my body. Like I'm a different person now that he knows. But maybe I'm just imagining it, because in the next second, he throws on a smile and says, "Well, that's cool."

He opens the door to his room. It has a bar painted with his fraternity letters, and the walls display his questionable taste in posters (here's hoping those belong to his roommate). Also: the most adorable German shepherd puppy I've ever seen is curled up on a blanket inside a crate.

"Oh my goodness, she's perfect!" I squeal.

He laughs, and it almost covers the sound of him locking the door behind us. It's amazing how such a small sound can make you feel as if someone has raised all your monsters from the dead.

My chest goes tight. My fists clench.

*Door swinging shut. Pop-Tarts box on the towel rack.*

But I take a deep breath and force my hands to open.

Then I tuck the dark thoughts back in so he can't see them, and I walk over to the door and flip the lock. "I'd rather leave it unlocked," I say brightly.

He gives me a boyish grin. "I'm sorry. I just wanted to kiss you some more, and I didn't want anyone to walk in on us."

He goes to the crate and starts scratching the puppy behind the ears like it doesn't matter to him either way. I bounce over so I can pet her too, and oh— She is so perfectly soft and snuggly.

"What's her name?"

"Jude."

"Hi there. Hi, Jude." I pet her some more, and then he stands up, and so do I.

"So, can I?" he says.

"What?"

"Kiss you some more."

"Ye-es." I draw the word out and make it two syllables. Taste it on my tongue. *Yes* is a hot word.

He wraps one hand around the back of my neck and brings his lips to mine. And it's not like I feel falling-in-love fireworks or something, but the boy really is a good kisser. I pull him closer, this college boy I am kissing at a college party. Just the thought of it feels exhilarating. He kisses a trail from my neck to my collarbone.

And then he grabs my jean skirt in one fluid motion.

I tense. "Hey, what—"

"Shh, c'mon." His mouth is on my neck again, near my ear. "I already know you want to. Just let me—"

And then it's all happening so fast.

Him, trying to pry my legs apart with his knee.

Me, kneeing him in the groin, yelling, "I freaking said no."

Him, crumpling in half.

And I'm thinking, *That's it, threat neutralized.*

And then *WHAM.*

A quick blur of motion.

So many stars.

And pain. First the tingly surface kind, and then something deeper.

I manage not to fall over from the force of his backhand, but just barely. I stumble away and make sure to get the bar between us, even though my face and eye are throbbing and my equilibrium's all jacked up.

As soon as the waves of wooziness stop, I stand up straight and ready myself for another attack. Yank my clothes back into place protectively.

He narrows his eyes at me. "It's not like I was going to *rape* you."

I raise my chin. Try not to wince. "Sure felt like you were." I feel like my insides are on fire and I could incinerate him with my eyes. "I'm gonna go. See you around, puddin'."

I say the word *puddin'* so that it sounds like a double middle finger.

Then I walk out of his room without waiting for a response. But before I get two steps down the hallway, I hear him mutter it under his breath. *Crazy East End Bitch.* I stop and grab the banister and squeeze. Hard.

The anger bleeds its way from my peripheral vision inward, until everything I see is tinged in red. I slide down the banister, fifty miles an hour, hair trailing behind me like streamers. I stick the landing. Half the eyes in the room turn toward me. It'll be all of them soon. I storm across the sand to the guy deejaying the party via his laptop. He doesn't think to yell until I've already ripped it away from him and thrown it into the nearest hot tub. *Hiss-crackle-spit.* Rest in peace, Drake. Then I beat the ever-loving slop out of every guy here and throw a TV through their stupid trophy case.

I pause to catch my breath. I want to do all that stuff. *Believe me.* But because I'm such a high-class lady, I calmly walk downstairs so I can tell Bernice it's time to blow this Popsicle stand.

I check the great room first. Still a bunch of dudes dressed as vampires and superheroes, wearing leis and drinking cheap beer. No Bernice.

I sigh. I feel like such an idiot for thinking that prick upstairs was one of the nice ones.

"Hey." I push a guy's shoulder maybe a little harder than I mean to. "Have you seen Bernice?"

"Huh?"

"Bernice Watkins? Red hair and hipster glasses and really teeny?"

"Oh, uh, yeah. I think that girl left. *Are you okay?*" He squints at my face and says it like an accusation.

My hand goes to my right eye like a reflex. That's the part of my face that took the worst of it.

"I'm fine," I say through clenched teeth.

I call Bernice, but she doesn't answer. And then I leave. I really wish she was still around—I'm kind of hurt that she left without me, if I'm being honest. It doesn't seem like something she'd normally do, but then, she was probably pretty miserable after I left her downstairs alone.

I walk to the subway and catch the train home. I get off a stop early because I need some time to think. It's probably not the best idea for a girl to walk around alone in this area at night, but I dare anyone to try and mess with me with the way I'm feeling right now. I'm almost hoping for it.

By the time I get back to our apartment, I've calmed down a lot. But when I go inside, I realize the Gotham U frat boys aren't the only ones who've been drinking tonight.

I close the door as quietly as I can. If I can just pretend to be a ghost as I slip behind the television and toward the hallway that leads to my room . . .

My father's recliner creaks. "Harleen."

I wince. "Yes?"

There are more than a few empty beer bottles on the coffee table (which is bad) and even more on the matted carpet underneath (which is worse). His eyes are hazy, but they still rake over me without missing a thing.

"What the hell happened? Are you okay?"

And I know better, I do, but he said the word *okay* so softly, and it unlocks a piece of my armor.

"There was a boy at a party. He tried to do things I didn't want him to do, and when I pushed him off, he hit me."

He stands. Sways.

*Hug me. Comfort me. Love me. Ask for his address and a list of any known phobias—I'm begging you.*

"Huh." He touches my shoulder.

I don't move, don't even breathe, because I don't want to screw it up.

"Guess that'll teach you not to wear such slutty clothes to parties."

He sits back down and unpauses the TV.

"Yeah," I say flatly.

I've known since I was a kid that my father deals in things that hurt worse than black eyes. I'm embarrassed that I hoped for anything else.

I go to the kitchen and open the freezer door just right so the handle stays on. My dad tore it off a couple months ago when he couldn't find his wallet. I stand there and let the cold air hit me as I look for something to ice my face. I am so sick of it. All of it. I'm sick of my dad and his it's-your-fault-for-wearing-a-skirt-that's-too-short BS. I'm sick of people acting like I'm crazy. Anytime a woman gets mad or sad or emotional, *boom*, let's put a big stamp on that feeling that says it isn't valid. That it's maybe even pathological. You know as many as 70 percent of women got diagnosed as hysterical by certain doctors back in the day? But what if none of them were Crazy Bitches? What if they were just tired? Tired of pretending everything was okay when it wasn't, and living in a world that was designed to be against them, and being told to smile through the knife wounds. Maybe pretending to be okay in the middle of a tornado is the truly crazy thing.

# CHAPTER 2

FROZEN BLUEBERRIES FEEL BETTER THAN ICE. I THINK IT'S because they're so small and round—there's more surface area to mold to your face. I hold the package of berries to my eye as I watch the city below. Well, the alley below, anyway. When I close my eyes, I can *feel* Gotham City's energy. Trains vibrating past and horns honking—everyone rushing to do something. Be someone. When I open them? Graffiti on brick walls and rivers of trash cascading out of dumpsters. And if I squint, I can just make out a woman (girl?) a couple blocks down in a rainbow scrunchie and sweatpants that are too short on her coltish legs meandering into the road to lean into a car window.

As I watch her, I pull the blueberries away from my face for a second and touch my cheekbone. I can already feel the bruises forming.

I live in an apartment building called Summit Place, which is a super-fancy code name for what it really is: the projects. The woman a couple blocks down gets into the car.

I can't see the man inside, but I know he's there, sure as I know his sleek black Mercedes is too nice for this neighborhood. And I think, *What if he hurts her? Will anyone care?* I already know the answer. Doesn't make it right, though.

I find myself thinking about everything that happened today—Trent acting like an intolerable crap wafer at lab meeting and that guy at the frat party and then, to top it all off, my dad. For one freaking second, I thought he might stand up for me. That's the part of the world that I just don't get. There *should* be someone to stand up for me. For the girl with the rainbow scrunchie. For all women.

I'm readjusting my frozen blueberries when I hear it. Gunshots echo down the alleyway, which is nothing new, but the laughter that follows—that feels distinctive. It reminds me of the time my friend Alexa saw Dove Cameron in the airport. She knew it was somebody famous even before Dove took off her sunglasses and Alexa saw who she was.

I lean forward.

It's probably not him. Probably just some drunk guy doing an impression.

The laugh rings out again, and all the hairs on my arms stand up. Not just a drunk guy. I've only ever seen him on TV, but I know I'm right. The laugh is louder than it was the first time too. Closer.

I hear other voices. Shouting. Feet pounding pavement. A flash of purple to my lower right that turns out to be a jacket being thrown over the barbed wire capping a fence. He vaults over it like it's nothing.

The Joker.

He is standing in the alley, only a block away. Close enough that if I yelled, he'd look.

He sprints toward me. Well, away from the police, but it happens to be toward me. I'm too many floors up for him to notice me, so I don't even think before scooting my body to the edge of the fire escape.

The Joker's goons are over the fence now too. All except one. His clown pants get tangled in the barbed wire, and the police pull him down. They flood the alley from both sides, two blue waves ready to crash.

"End of the line, Joker."

He skids to a stop. Sees they've got him surrounded. It's quieter than you'd think. Every gun is trained on him. All the trigger-happy cops with beads of sweat dripping down the backs of their necks and into their polyester uniforms.

He stands there, white skin almost glowing in the moonlight. Ethereal. Magnetic. Like an angel bathed in hellfire. And he parts those brilliant red lips and he laughs. Loudly. Maniacally. Commandingly.

The cops become, if possible, even more twitchy. They're terrified. No one messes with him. No one says anything to him. No one approaches.

And I think, *There is power in becoming a persona.*

And I think, *There is power in laughter.*

And I think, *There's something darkly gorgeous about him.*

The cops inch forward, closing the circle. I shift the bag of blueberries to my other eye, the one that didn't take so much of the blow. I barely notice the cold anymore—I'm so focused on the scene below. There's dozens of them and only one of him. It doesn't seem fair.

Not one of them notices when he gives the tiniest flick of his wrist, though. Maybe it's because of the angle, but I see something black and red slip out of his sleeve and into his hand. He rears back like he's going to throw it, and they see it immediately.

"Bomb!" somebody yells, and they all hit the deck.

I hold my breath, fingers clenched tightly around the bag of frozen blueberries. I wonder if The Joker is going to kill them all, and I wonder why I feel a thrill of excitement about it. But, then, I always wanted the coyote to catch the roadrunner too. Maybe there's something wrong with me.

He gently sets the bomb down on the street in front of him. Only from here, it doesn't look like a bomb after all. The black-and-red object inches forward with choppy, robotic steps. A windup toy? Now doesn't seem the time for a prank, but The Joker's grin doesn't falter. His henchmen whoop. The police begin to stand up. Everyone is watching this toy as it trip-traps down the street, first rapidly and then slower, slower. . . .

*BOOM.*

The toy explodes in a thundercloud of smoke. The henchmen thrash against their restraints, hoping to wrestle away from their captors. The police try to keep some kind of order, but half of them are doubled over coughing. They can't see him as he slips right past one of them and escapes down a side street. But I can. I can't take my eyes off him as he retreats into the night.

And then a drop of red liquid splatters against my leg.

"What the hell? Is that blood?"

More droplets, slipping down my arm, falling like tiny crimson explosions onto my legs. I can feel something wet against my cheek too. More inkblot splatters hit my thigh. But really they're not the black-red of blood. It's more like—blueberry. It occurs to me that I might have clenched the bag a little too hard in my excitement.

"Aw, crapola."

I leap up and hurry to the bathroom so I don't ruin my skirt. Try to cup my hands around the bag so it doesn't stain the carpet. I leave the door open—always open—and I flip the bag into the sink and lean over the counter. I didn't do too badly, I think, surveying my clothes and the floor. Then I notice myself in the mirror.

One of my eyes is dripping with purple-red juice, the other black with bruises.

I laugh.

Loudly. Maniacally. Commandingly.

An idea begins to take shape inside my head. I just need to figure out how to use it.

# CHAPTER 3

I HOPE THE MAKEUP IS ENOUGH. NO ONE IN MY BRIDGE program classes really noticed, and it fooled Trent and Dr. N when I set my stuff down in the lab this afternoon. But no matter how much concealer I caked on in the mirror, my cheek is still puffy, and last night's bruises want to rise to the surface like secrets. I toss my head so my hair falls over that part of my face a bit.

"What's next?" I ask Bernice.

She moves some bottles around on the shelf in front of her. "Calcium carbonate, calcium hydroxide, calcium chloride, chlorobenzene, citric acid, and copper sulfate," she says.

I note them in the tablet I'm using as Bernice writes a *C* on a piece of lime-green lab tape and sticks it to the rim of the shelf. I try to keep the bad side of my face angled away from her at all times because if anyone's going to notice, she will. Especially since we have to work so closely together today reorganizing and cataloging the chemical shelves.

We make it through the *D*s, *E*s, and *F*s without incident.

"Gs are next," Bernice says. "Just a few of these."

I happen to remember seeing a white plastic container with a red lid on the counter. "Hang on, somebody left a bottle of glucose out."

I hold out the bottle to Bernice. I take a deep breath. She'll have to turn toward me to take it. If she's going to notice, it'll be now.

She quickly takes the glucose from me, never once looking up.

*Huh.*

We move on to the *H*s. I reach for a brown glass bottle way at the back. It's covered in dust, and the paper label is crumbling. I look at the date. "Holy crap, this hydrochloric acid is older than us."

Bernice doesn't laugh or say anything back. And after a few more letters of the alphabet, I realize something: she's avoiding me as much as I'm avoiding her.

Her eyes are glued to the bottles on the counter and shelves. I try to catch her gaze. Completely forget about hiding my face from her. She feels me looking, and for a split second her eyes flick to mine. They're red. She's been crying. Maybe still is.

"Bernice, are you okay?"

"Um." She gets this caged-animal, fear-flashing-in-her-eyes look. "No-oh-oh."

She immediately bursts into tears. Hunched over, sobbing. An emotional avalanche.

And at that exact moment, Dr. Nelson walks in.

He gives me this utterly baffled look, like, *There's no crying in science.*

Bernice manages to choke out "Excuse me" and rushes off in the direction of the girls' bathroom.

Dr. N turns to me, eyes wide. "Is she gonna be okay?" *I have no idea what I'm doing.* "Maybe you should go check on her." *Can you take care of that?*

I'd snicker at his discomfort if I wasn't so worried about Bernice. "Sure."

"Bernice?" I close the door to the bathroom behind me. "Are you in here?"

A sniffle from one of the stalls is my answer.

"Do you want to talk about it?"

Another sniffle.

"Okay, well, I'm just gonna hang out here, and you can talk if you want, but also it's okay if we're just quiet together."

I hop up on the counter between the bathroom sinks and sit cross-legged. I hope that's the right move. Bernice and I are friends, but we're more the kind of friends where you share lab gossip and help each other on projects and purposely try to take your lunch at the same time once you realize how much you like being around each other. She's the person in lab I'd ask if I needed a tampon, but other than that moment we had on the way to the frat party, we've never really talked about anything serious. For a few minutes we're quiet, but then something about the wall between us makes me feel like it's safe to tell her what happened to me last night. Who knows? Maybe my sharing will make her feel more comfortable about opening up too.

"I know we're in here because you're upset, so this might be kind of a jerk move, but is it okay if I talk to you about something?" Bernice sniffles in a way that makes me feel like it's okay. "Cool. So, you know that party we were at last night? Of course you do—you were at the party." I shake my head. *Your friend's in crisis mode, Harleen. Now is not the time to get mad that she ditched you.* "Something bad happened to me there."

Bernice is silent, the abrupt kind that feels like an absence. She's listening too hard to sniffle.

"Yeah, so I went up to that guy's room with him to see his new puppy, only afterward he got all handsy and I had to knee him in the groin. And then he backhanded me. Oh, and then when I got home, my dad pretty much told me it was my fault."

My hands grip the counter so hard it hurts. It isn't right what happened to me. None of it is right. And the worst part is it feels like there's nothing I can do about it.

"I wanted you to know that if something's going on, you can tell me. No matter how effed up it is."

I'm not really expecting her to say anything. It's totally fine if she doesn't. And then I hear her voice, so fragile, so desperate. "Harleen?"

I jump down to the floor, and I'm in front of her stall in a second. She doesn't open it, but I can't help pressing my hand against the door.

"Yes?"

"Something bad happened to me too."

The bottom falls out from under me. I'm kind of a hardcore chick. I can handle stuff like this. But Bernice? Even though she's from the East End too, she's soft. Kind. The sort of person you want to protect.

She tells me everything that happened after I went upstairs. She met a boy named Grady. He told her he liked her glasses.

And then he took her up to his room, and he assaulted her.

"I said no." Her voice almost cracks on the word *no*, and my heart almost cracks right along with it. "I know I could have tried to fight him off more, but he held me down, and he's a lot bigger than me, and I was really scared. But I said no a lot of times, okay?"

I press my hand against the door even harder. "Hey, I believe you. You didn't do anything wrong here, do you understand me? This was him. All him." I tell her everything I wish my dad had told me. I tell it to myself.

"I was crying," Bernice says softly. "What kind of person wants to do that with someone who's crying?"

"A terrible person," I say through gritted teeth. "The absolute worst kind of person."

"The only reason he even stopped was because his roommate came in. I ran away as fast as I could."

I could kill him. I could seriously, actually kill this guy. There's a big part of me that wants to. The other part feels guilty.

I shouldn't have left her there. She never would have left without me. I should have known that. This is all my fault. I should have checked.

"I'm so sorry," I tell her. "What do you want to do? I'll support you however you want."

The door swings open. Bernice stands in front of me, tears streaming down her cheeks, bird shoulders hunched. She lifts her chin. "I want to make him pay."

The anger inside me swells like a living thing. "Then that's what we'll do."

She nods rapidly and falls into me, and I hug her tight and whisper, "It'll be okay. I've got you," into her hair.

I wasn't expecting her to say that at all, the part about

making him pay, but something about those words resonates so deeply with what happened to me last night—hell, what's been happening to me my whole life—that I feel SO SEEN. My mind goes back to my reflection in the mirror last night, one black eye and one red, and the idea to do *something*. To take a stand. I decide Bernice's frat-boy douchebag is my first target. *Our* first target.

By the time Bernice stops crying and pulls away, I've put it all together in my head. I try to keep my face from looking too wild when I tell her.

"This is going to sound totally bananas, but I think I have a plan."

The circular saw whirs as I slice through another length of PVC pipe. Beautiful. I set it with the others. I haven't started assembling anything yet. I'm mostly hoping to keep it looking like a mess because—

"Hey, how's it going over here?" The girl who runs the physics machine shop on Fridays—Bianca, I've learned her name is—has come over to check on Bernice and me. She has long brown hair that's shaved on one side, and Bernice says she grew up on an island in the Caribbean. Today she's dressed like she's about to lead a kickboxing class.

"Great!" I smile at her brightly. "I'm all finished with the sawing. I just need to 3D-print something."

She surveys the bits and pieces on the counter. "What is it you're making again?" she asks, a hint of suspicion creeping into her voice.

Bernice's eyes get big.

"Blast tube," I say quickly. "We're looking to replicate military injuries from IEDs. We still need to print the holder and put everything together, though."

"Right." She adjusts one of the straps of her workout top and checks her phone. It makes the muscles in her arms ripple—the girl is jacked. "Listen, I hate to do this to you, but we close in about five minutes, so you may have to finish up on Monday. I'd stay with you, but I'm babysitting tonight, and I can't be late because I'm taking her trick-or-treating."

I already know Bianca babysits for a neighbor on Friday nights. And that she's a second-year grad student at Gotham U. And that she wants to be a physics professor someday. (This is all thanks to my A-plus-plus flirting abilities.)

"Yeah, I understand. It's just that our principal investigator said we *have* to have something by Monday. If we could just stay another half hour, I could take all the pieces home with me and put them together over the weekend." I look up at her through my eyelashes.

Bianca hesitates, lips twisting as she sizes me up. "You're all done using the saw?"

I nod. Try not to smile too hard.

"You promise to lock up afterward? And you're not gonna steal anything?"

"Scout's honor," I say, hoping she doesn't notice the sprinkler parts I already liberated from one of the campus flower beds.

Her eyes shift to Bernice. "I guess it's okay. Bernice has come in a few times before, so I know she's responsible. Just be careful, okay? I'll hunt you down if you screw anything up."

"Totally!"

Harleen's Genius Plan, step 1: Charm the physics machine-shop girl so I can stay late and use the shop for my own devices. Completed.

As soon as Bianca leaves, I cement the pipe pieces together to form a couple air tanks, and I attach the barrel I made to the sprinkler valve. Spoiler alert: we're not actually making lab equipment here. I do an air-pressure test on my tanks and then wire up a detonator. We'll probably have to wait twenty-four hours to make sure the cement is fully dry before we can use it. Then Bernice and I move to the 3D printer.

"Do you have the design ready?" I ask Bernice.

"Yep." She grins and hands it over.

"This is gonna be so perfect," I say as the printer buzzes to life.

It heats the end of a spool of red plastic, turning it into a liquid that builds our design layer by paper-thin layer. I was hoping they'd have pink, but this'll do. It's too early to make out the objects being printed, but it won't be long. It's almost time to go hunting.

# CHAPTER 4

### MONDAY, APRIL 4

IT'S WEIRD BEING IN DR. NELSON'S OFFICE WITHOUT DR. Nelson. The cops across from me are nice, though, especially the one who wrapped a blanket around me. I don't know why they do that in trauma situations, even indoors, but it does kind of make me feel better.

Blanket Cop moves his hand under the table, and I lean forward in my chair. "Is it Bernice?"

"What?"

"I saw you check your phone? Is it about Bernice? Is she going to be okay?" I found a faint pulse eventually, but I can't shake the image of her face, so pale and lifeless.

"We don't know yet," he says in a clipped voice.

A pit opens in my stomach. I start torturing myself with what-ifs. *What if she doesn't make it? What if I found her sooner? What if last Friday night I didn't—*

Blanket Cop seems to think better of it and gives me a kind pat on the hand. "I'll let you know as soon as we hear."

The cop next to him, a woman, clears her throat. Pointedly. Somewhat disdainfully.

He sits up straight. "I'd like to ask you a few more questions about what happened with Ms. Watkins."

We've been through this. When are they gonna let me go so I can go see her?

"I already told ya everything I know."

He raises his eyebrows, and he and the lady cop exchange glances, and I wish I had said it quieter, more like how a good girl is supposed to talk. I hate how my voice jumps straight to wrong-side-of-the-tracks mode whenever I'm annoyed.

"About how you found Ms. Watkins, yes. How did you get in again?"

There's nothing wrong with what I did. In fact, it's how I saved her. But somehow being asked about it multiple times has a way of making me feel guilty. *Calm, Harleen. Stay calm.*

"I picked the lock, as I mentioned before," I say primly.

"That's an interesting skill. How did you learn to do that?"

I bristle. "A lot of kids from the East End know how to do it. You gonna charge me with being poor or something?"

He doesn't answer me. Just takes a long sip of his coffee.

I reach my hand into my pocket and close my fingers around my pocketknife. I always carry it, starting when I was seven. Ever since—

*Door swinging shut. Pop-Tarts box on the towel rack.*

I don't like to think about it. But I taught myself to pick locks with a pocketknife, after.

I realize the police haven't asked me any more questions.

"Is it okay if I go?" I ask, all sweetness and light.

Blanket Cop leans forward in his chair. "Ms. Quinzel, what do you know about a group called the Reckoning?"

"The Reckoning?" My voice cracks like a teenage boy's. The cop's eyebrows rise again. Dammit. I take a second to steady myself before answering. "I've seen their symbols around campus. I was actually working in the lab the day Bayers's office got flooded." (Airtight alibi, so go ahead and dig.)

"Did you ever have reason to think Ms. Watkins was part of the Reckoning?"

"*Bernice?*" I say it with two parts surprise and one part disbelief and not a bit of fear. "You think Bernice is that women's rights vigilante?" I look back and forth between them.

It is the woman—Officer Montoya, I see from her name tag—who answers. "I think the Reckoning is most likely a *them*, but I think Ms. Watkins is part of it, yes."

I get this feeling—like she can see right through to my insides and sift out every bad thing I've ever done.

I force myself to keep talking. "Wow, that's unbelievable. I mean, Bernice is so quiet. She watches Saturday-morning cartoons, ya know? I think you're barking up the wrong tree. You should maybe start looking into—"

"We found evidence in Ms. Watkins's bag that suggests otherwise," says Montoya. "I think there's a good chance she may have been involved in the terrorist group."

*Terrorist group?*

"And that she may have been targeted because of it. So I'm going to ask you again: Are you sure you don't have anything you want to tell me about the Reckoning?"

Any number of things could betray me in this moment: heartbeat, breathing, eye movements, the trickle of sweat down my back. *Get it together, Harleen.*

"No, ma'am," I finally say, calmly and everything.

She scribbles something in a notebook and goes back to

watching me with narrowed eyes. I don't think she believes me. It's a tense moment, but luckily the door opens and another cop comes in and whispers something to them. I catch a glimpse of Trent through the open door.

The cop—the man, not Officer Montoya—frowns.

"Ms. Quinzel, did you and Ms. Watkins have a relationship beyond being just friends?"

*How did they find out about*—? Freaking Trent. He looks like someone who'd snitch.

"We were kind of dating," I say. "It wasn't official or anything. We were friends for a while before that, but a couple months ago everything just sort of . . . changed."

This is the truth. It's also the truth that the last time I saw Bernice before this morning, we were having a fight, but I don't tell them that.

Officer Montoya tilts her head to the side, like a bird of prey that's about to strike. "You didn't think to offer that information?"

I shrug. "I didn't think it was relevant."

Okay, I did, but I've seen the TV movies. The boyfriend always did it. Or, in this case, the quasi girlfriend.

Officer Montoya stands. "Yeah, I think you'd better come with us."

"Wait, seriously?" How long is that going to take? By the time they're done with me, Bernice could be— She could be— I can't even bring myself to think the word.

"We'll take you downtown for fingerprinting," the other cop says. "It's just a formality."

But I know better. Officer Montoya thinks I tried to kill Bernice.

_potential girl gang members_

_Bernice Watkins_
_Harleen Quinzel?_

# NOVEMBER

# CHAPTER 5

BERNICE AND I SIT ON A TOWEL IN FRONT OF THE LIBRARY and have a picnic. *Pretend* to have a picnic. Our books and snacks and flat-top sunglasses say we're just two students studying outside on a beautiful day, surprisingly warm for November. There's nothing to see here.

My light jacket mostly covers an old black gymnastics leotard that I cut up and spray-painted red in places (Harleen's Genius Plan, step 2). Bernice opted for plain black from head to toe. We rushed over as soon as I was sure the cement was dry, but apparently our target isn't home. Now all we need to do is wait for this disgusting SOB to get home from his Saturday-afternoon-hangover Pancake Palace run. (Thanks, social media!) His frat house is conveniently down the hill from the library, and his tricked-out silver SUV is unmissable.

It peels into the parking lot.

"Harleen!" Bernice pushes my arm.

"I know."

I stand and grab the towel corners in one fluid motion, books and snacks rolling to the center as I help Bernice stuff it into her backpack. Then I whip off my jacket as we dash across the grass and down the hill. He's parking the car. Bernice and I crouch in the bushes where we stashed our stuff as soon as we saw his roommate's video of him cramming his face with pancakes and then downing a cup of syrup because someone gave him five dollars. We're only about thirty feet away now. We pull our masks over our heads.

He and his friends get out, and he slams the door, sun gleaming off his face like he's a living, breathing frat-boy action figure. I bet his hair doesn't even move when the wind blows.

"That's the one," whispers Bernice, pointing to the guy in the green T-shirt. "Grady."

My anger is a monster that wants to eat this kid alive. It's chained to a post. Starving.

I pick up the handheld pneumatic cannon we spent all of Friday night making and step out of the bushes.

And I unclip the leash.

"Hey! Rich boy!"

All three of the guys turn. Grady takes in my outfit and the PVC monstrosity/wonder I'm holding.

"The hell," he mutters.

"I GOTTA TALK TO YOU ABOUT SOMETHING." I yell it, all caps. It's an all-caps kinda day.

He gives me this hassled, puzzled look, like he's really too busy for whatever brand of crazy I'm peddling. His friends snicker.

"Did you assault my friend a couple nights ago?"

The snickering stops.

"I don't know what you're talking about." Again with that hassled freaking voice that is like a screwdriver twisting under my skin.

"Oh really?" I yell even louder. "You didn't tell her you liked her glasses and then take her up to your room? You didn't ignore her when she said no?"

There's a crowd forming now. Probably waiting to see what comes out of this cannon—T-shirts? Pies? Hamsters? The way he squares his shoulders tells me he's acutely aware of his growing audience.

"Pretty sure she was into it."

My head snaps to the side. "WRONG ANSWER."

I brace myself and click the detonator button.

*BOOM.*

The sound is utterly ridiculous, like something you'd hear at a circus. The blast knocks me back, but I'm able to stay standing. The cannon explodes, candy-colored shrapnel shooting out of the barrel, whizzing through the air. The chunks of red plastic find their way to his skin, and he squeals like the pig he is.

Some people duck. Some yelp and laugh uncomfortably.

"Oh, chill out. We're not gonna kill him. We're just gonna shoot him with the word *no.* Repeatedly." I turn back to Grady. "Do you know what consent is, bruh?"

"Um, yes?"

At this point it has clicked for the growing crowd that they're witnessing a spectacle, and everyone whips out their phones now instead of just the 20 percent who are horrible people.

"You sure? 'Cause you sound a little confused. Consent," I say as Bernice reloads the cannon with another round of

3D-printed *No*s, "is when you don't do things with a person unless they're okay with it."

He ducks low and tries to run around the side of his car, but I follow him. I hit the detonator, and the *No*s go flying, pelting him in the arms and jeans and chest and leaving some very satisfying *No*-shaped welts on his face and forearms. And okay, some of the *No*s look like *oN*s because I can't exactly control how they hit him, but I'm still really stoked.

He runs for the stairs of the frat house, but I shift so he's still in my line of sight.

"Is it sinking in yet?"

*BLAM!*

"I'm not sure he's got it."

*BLAM!*

"When a lady says no, she means it. Got it, creep show?"

*KA-BLAM!*

*No*s explode out of the cannon like fireworks. Fill the sky like vicious confetti. Pepper Grady's skin like a meteor shower of dissent. Then they fall to the ground, brave soldiers having done their job, destined to find their way to a nearby gutter.

He reaches the door, but just as he's going in, another guy comes out. My dance partner with the five-inch inseams.

"Grady, are you okay? What the shit is happening out here?" he says as he's pushed out of the way and into the doorframe by his frantic friend.

I grin. "Oh, good! I'm so glad you're here."

I fire a round at him too, and he rushes back inside and slams the door. "*No*s don't have to be a painful thing as long as you listen the first time!" I call after him cheerfully.

I pan my Dissent Cannon from one side of the crowd to the other.

"Is anyone else having any kind of trouble understanding the word *no*?" I yell.

No one says anything. They are like frightened mice. The power is delicious, but knowing the effect we're having right now—the changes we could make—that's the really intoxicating part.

"Well, good." I shrug. "I guess we're done here." I turn to Bernice. "Hey, you wanna go get cupcakes?"

"OMG, HOW ARE THESE CUPCAKES SO DELICIOUS?" I laugh and push Bernice's arm, high on sugar and life and being the kind of girl who shoots holes through misogyny with a cannon of her own science-ing.

Bernice laughs. "Victory cupcakes taste three hundred percent better than regular cupcakes. It is known."

She takes another bite of the cinnamon nut crunch cupcake. We got a six-pack sampler because neither of us could make up our minds when confronted with this much sheer deliciousness. Maple and bacon, raspberry-lemon, Mexican hot chocolate, Nutella and roasted marshmallow, and the crowning glory: a unicorn cupcake with rainbow sprinkles and a shimmery gold horn. (Not made with real unicorns. DON'T WORRY, I CHECKED.)

"That was exhilarating," I say. "Like, exceeded all my expectations. A-plus, one hundred percent best revenge in the herstory of all revenges." It occurs to me that Bernice may not feel quite so jubilant. "Um, so how are you doing?"

"I'm okay." She smiles. "Really. I know there's a lot of stuff I haven't even begun working through, and I know what we did today doesn't erase what happened, but feeling like we were in it together? That helped."

I feel exactly the same way, but to hear her say it makes my heart squeeze.

"Yeah," I say. It's like the perfect inverse of how I felt after that guy assaulted me, when I thought she'd left the party without me. And she's right. It's not like what happened magically goes away, but I feel different with her beside me. Stronger. Cared for.

She eyes me slyly. "Plus, that amount of power was pretty awesome."

"RIGHT?" I clink my cupcake against hers. "WE ARE UNSTOPPABLE!" I yell.

The entire cupcake shop stares at me. Oops. I'm usually pretty hyperactive and impulsive, but sugar takes it to a whole different level.

"Just thought you ought to know," I call out, this time at a more reasonable volume.

One time in first grade I ate two chocolate chip cookies and was seized with the idea that it would be a stellar plan to moon the entire cafeteria. When my mom asked me why I did it, I told her I thought it would be a funny joke.

*Did anyone else think it was a funny joke?* I remember her asking.

*No,* I replied, shocked. *No, they didn't at all.*

This was an important life moment for a couple reasons. (1) I realized for the first time that most people don't have the same sense of humor as me. (2) It led to me getting diagnosed with ADHD.

I remember sitting outside the principal's office as she explained to my mom that based on all the data she had gotten from my teachers, she would recommend having me evaluated by an educational psychologist. My mom fought like a gladiator to make sure the state paid for it. Anyway, the ed psych said I definitely had ADHD but also that I was a genius (she called it twice exceptional, or 2e) and that the public-school system would be doing me a grave disservice if they didn't provide accommodations for both. So my mom made sure they did. (Again, gladiator.)

And speaking of gladiators . . .

I wish we could do it all over again. I can't get enough of this feeling. I'm staring blankly at the cupcake display, daydreaming, when Bernice sighs and pushes away from the table.

"If I eat one more bite, I'll disappear into a sugar vortex," she groans. "Plus, I have to work on my scholarship applications. And it's impossible to focus at my apartment because my little brothers are the loudest children on the planet, and I have *so many essays* left to do."

I do some quick mental calculations. Dad at work. Not supposed to be home for three more hours.

"Want to work on them at my place?"

She blinks, surprised. "Sure."

Sure good or sure bad? Eh, if she doesn't want to be my friend anymore after seeing my crappy apartment, she's probably not the right friend for me anyway.

"Let's go!" I tell her. We throw away our cupcake wreckage and take the subway to my apartment.

The whole way there, I'm still buzzing off cupcake icing and unmitigated success. But when we get to my door, I pause. Is she still going to like me once she sees what my life is like?

Before I can think too much about it, I swing open the door to our humble home, which honestly doesn't look as bad as usual, because I picked up yesterday when I was bored.

"We can go to my room," I say, hoping her eyes don't linger on that weird stain on the ceiling or the duct tape on my dad's recliner or all the things he's "accidentally" broken in a fit of drunken rage.

It's easy to ignore these things when it's just me. They fade into the background of me living my life. The apartment becomes just a place to sleep. A temporary space between the past and all my dreams for the future. But now that Bernice is here? It's like having a filter where all the bad or embarrassing things are outlined in neon.

"Cool," says Bernice in a voice that totally doesn't sound terrified at all.

But I can't help wondering if she notices the fist-sized craters in the walls leading to my bedroom and if she's putting together how they got there.

We spread out our books in my room on the colorful DIY rug I made when I was twelve, and since I'm trying to be a good friend, we get right to work on studying, and I only interrupt half a dozen times to talk about how awesome we were today. I'm just finishing up some tweaks to one of my essays when I hear it.

The apartment door slamming open. Two hours too early.

I jump up.

"Is everything okay?" asks Bernice.

"Uh-huh," I say quietly. Urgently. "I'll be right back."

I hurry out to the hallway. Close the door, obviously. Tip-toe to the kitchen. If I can just keep him from getting mad at me. Just today. Just while she's here.

"Hey." I say it in my calmest, most nonthreatening voice. I throw on a smile for good measure because sometimes he gets mad at me for thinking he's going to get mad at me.

He paws through the cabinet, face flushed. Angry? Drunk. Both? "You ate the last Cosmic Brownie," he says accusingly. Definitely angry.

Pretty sure he ate that last night when he was inebri-ated, but is eating the last brownie really going to make him angrier than reminding him he was drunk (which he was) or implying that he's a liar (which he is)? He's growing im-patient with my mental gymnastics, so I land on "Yeah, I'm really sorry."

He turns to face me, eyes darkening the way they do on the very worst days. I glance over my shoulder at my bed-room door. *No, no, no, please not today.*

"I told you to save me the last one of everything in case I want it," he says in a voice so dangerously calm it pulls the walls closer all around, boxing me in.

"I know. I'm really sorry." I say it quickly, hoping to put out this fire before the smoke reaches my bedroom. I hate myself a little bit for it. Every time I apologize when I'm not wrong, every time I walk on eggshells instead of just living, a piece of me curls up and dies. If I can just get out of here before there are no pieces left . . .

He slams the cabinet door shut, and I jump. "Well, if you know, then why did you do it?"

Louder this time. I check my bedroom door again. I thought I heard a creak.

"There are conditions, you know. You're lucky I let you stay here. Most people would have kicked you out by now."

I take a deep breath and tell myself that the ceiling isn't really shrinking in on me. It's only my imagination. "I'm sorry, okay? Next time I'm at the store, I'll buy some with my own money."

He grunts and goes back to the cabinets, and I think I'm safe, but then he starts rattling handles and banging boxes around with increasing intensity and muttering under his breath.

"Nothing to snack on . . . nothing good at all . . . and you eat everything."

He slams a cereal box on the counter, and Rice Krispies go flying into the air like feathers. And then he screams.

"NEXT TIME YOU DON'T EAT MY DAMN FOOD!"

He smacks the front of the refrigerator, hand close enough to my face that it makes me grind my teeth together.

I hear a gasp behind me, and my heart sinks. The only thing worse than taking an emotional beating is having someone else witness it.

Dad at least has the decency to look embarrassed. "Oh. Hey. Why didn't you tell me you had a friend over?"

*Because that shouldn't change how you treat me? Because I was trying to hide the two of you from each other?*

"Bernice has to get home," I tell him.

Luckily, she takes the cue and goes to my bedroom to pack up all our stuff. My dad starts making himself some scrambled eggs. Tells me he's sorry he lost his temper but that I'd better come home with groceries. I just stare at him. Hating him.

I don't know how long it is before Bernice touches my shoulder. "C'mon."

I grab my backpack from her, and we leave, neither of us saying anything much as we walk down the streets of Gotham City without an idea of where to go. I wish I could will him out of existence with just my mind. I don't care that it's awful—I do.

Bernice clears her throat. "Hey, Harleen?"

I wince. "Yeah?"

"Are you ever scared by how much darkness there is inside you?"

That . . . is not what I thought she was going to say. Considering what I was just thinking, and all the times my mind goes somewhere violent and I'm only just able to pull it back from the edge . . .

"Yeah," I say. "Yeah, I am."

"Me too." She nods fiercely. "Like, when we were in your apartment just now—I could barely stop myself. If he ever— If you ever— I would help you hide the body. Heck, I'd help you do it. And I don't mean that the way wine moms do when they've had too much to drink and they're all up in their friendship feels. What you did for me today was huge. I'd do anything for you."

"Thank you," I manage to say, even though I'm kind of stunned by her soft voice saying those words. By having someone care about me so ferociously.

First the Dissent Cannon, and now this speech. She's not who I thought she was. She's still sweet as hell, but she's also bold and fearless, and now that I've had this realization, I can't stop looking at her eyes that are blue with a gold ring around them or her delicate hands or this freckle she has on her cheek just under her left eye.

I feel like I've been whacked in the heart with a croquet mallet. And I hope like anything she feels the same way.

# CHAPTER 6

I CAN'T WAIT TO GET TO THE LAB AND SEE BERNICE. UN-
fortunately, we have our Bridge Scholars small groups today,
and Bernice and I aren't in the same one. Also—it's the
Monday-est Monday in the history of humanity, *especially*
considering I forgot to take my ADHD meds this morning,
so I try really hard to take notes on what makes an outstanding college application essay instead of replaying our weekend shenanigans in my head on repeat.

Honestly? The classes aren't so bad, and I'm lucky to be
here. We have the big seminar with all of us scholars where
we talk about ethics in science and how to make a scientific
poster and things like that. And then in the small groups, we
get mentorship on what colleges might be a good fit for us,
and we get help with our college applications and essays and
coaching on scholarship interviews. Dr. N is actually one of
the mentors, but unfortunately not for my group.

I try to think of who *is* in his group. (That girl Sloane,
maybe? And this obnoxious kid named Graham?) And

then I'm trying to think of who is in Bernice's group and what Bernice might be doing right now and how bright her eyes looked when we were eating cupcakes and how cool it would be to do something like that again, to feel that high again, and— *Focus, Harleen! College essays!*

My phone vibrates in my pocket. (This does not help with the focus.)

> Trent: You coming into lab today? I could use your
> help with something in the darkroom.

I roll my eyes, but it doesn't stop my stomach from doing a double twisting backflip. I tuck my phone into my pocket. I can text him back later.

When I finally (FINALLY!) get to the neurobiology building, I'm rushing to lab so fast that I take the elevator instead of the stairs, even though I'm the only person on it, and being trapped in an enclosed space like that kind of makes me feel like my throat is closing up. (Someday I'm gonna work on that.) But for now, I close my eyes and wait for the elevator to do its thing while I tap my fingers against my leg, like, *hurry hurry hurry.* When the elevator doors ding open, I practically leap off . . . almost running into Morgan, who is getting off the other elevator.

"Sorry," I say. And then I notice her face. It's all red and splotchy. "Are you okay?"

"Yeah," she replies, flustered, sweeping her bangs out of her face. "I mean, no. No, this professor just said something *really* creepy to me on the elevator."

She whispers it in my ear because one of the guys from our lab is walking by.

"Ex*cuse* me? That is really messed up." For a second, I'm

just stunned. I look around like he'll be lurking, watching us. "Do you know who it was?"

She shakes her head. "He looked familiar, though. He was older? And he had on a tie with a gold tie clip."

I am sorely tempted to stalk through the building till I find him, but Morgan puts a hand on my shoulder. "Hey. I can handle this." She smiles. "I appreciate you letting me vent, though."

"Of course," I tell her, definitely not still thinking of hunting him down.

But then I remember Bernice, and I hurry into lab, and sure enough, there she is. She's doing dishes, and she smirks at me in a way that is entirely too satisfied for someone scrubbing glassware.

"What?" I ask.

She passes me a flask to rinse. "I saw him at Nighthawk's this morning getting a coffee."

I suck in a breath. "Oh no, are you okay?"

She nods. "Yeah." And then the smirk comes back. "He still has the imprint of the word *No* on his forehead."

I bust out laughing. "Are you serious?"

"Yep."

"Wow. Two days later. That's impressive."

I can't get the image out of my head—the idea of us making an imprint. Both in the literal, skin-on-his-face way and in the metaphorical, maybe-the-next-guy-will-think-twice way.

Bernice nods again, but this time she's not smirking. She acts like putting glassware on the drying rack is an all-consuming task.

"I talked to that counselor you told me about," she says quietly.

"I'm so glad." I say it in my absolute gentlest voice. "Did it go okay?"

"Yeah. I mean, it was really hard. Talking about everything. But I think I'm gonna go back."

I squeeze her shoulder. "I'm really proud of you."

"Thanks." She smiles shyly. "Are you doing okay?"

I was actually just thinking I should probably go talk to that counselor too. She's the one my mom set me up to do grief counseling with, for after she passed. Even after she was gone, she was still trying to look out for me. I'm thinking about whether to tell Bernice that, but then Bernice's grad student mentor, Michael, comes in, and we both act like we weren't talking about anything serious. Bernice moves to get started on her ELISA (enzyme-linked immunosorbent assay—for detecting protein levels in blood and tissue and stuff) while I keep putting beakers and flasks on the drying rack.

Michael leans against the counter. "Hey, Bernice, what are you doing?"

Bernice makes a note in her lab notebook. "Oh, hey. I was just about to start an ELISA."

"Perfect," says Michael. "I really need you to run these samples of mine before my next committee meeting."

She bites her lip. "Oh. But I really need to get my samples done so I'll have enough data for my project. Plus, I already thawed them."

He waves her off. "The symposium isn't till January. My committee meeting is *next week*. You have to learn to prioritize things that are urgent if you want to be a scientist."

My head turns around on my body like an owl's. I saunter over and step directly between them. Put my hands to his chest and push him against the counter. His eyes widen because he's never been this close to a girl before, and he thinks something's about to happen. Something is. I uncap the permanent marker on the counter next to him, and I write the words *Poor planning on my part does not constitute an emergency on her part* across his face in bold, swirly letters.

That's what I was going to do, anyway, but Bernice is already piping up.

"But my samples—"

He interrupts her. "Will be fine. And if you're really concerned, you can always stay late and run yours after you finish mine, okay?"

"I—"

"Thanks, kiddo." He makes finger guns at her and barrels out of the room before either of us can point out any of the eighty-seven things wrong with this scenario.

"Are you effing kidding me?" I finally say.

"Right?" Bernice rolls her eyes and gets started on Michael's ELISA. "I just spent half an hour washing up his glassware from yesterday, and I'm pretty sure he's leaving to go to a kickball game right now."

I'm about to tell her where Michael can shove his kickball when I hear someone behind us.

"Hey, Trent," I say.

"Hey." Bernice says it without looking up from her pipetting.

"'Sup." Trent pointedly clears his throat before heading into the darkroom. I don't know if I'm imagining it, but I'd almost swear Bernice glares at him. I suddenly feel warm all over. Do I want her to be glaring at him? I watch her try to blow a strand of hair out of her face so she doesn't have to touch it with gloves on. I think I do. Because glaring means she's jealous, and jealous means there's a chance she likes me or, at the very least, thinks about kissing me.

I toss my gloves into the trash and go back to the office area for a couple minutes so it won't be too obvious when I go to the darkroom. And for a fraction of a second, I allow myself to imagine what it would be like if I were meeting Bernice there instead of Trent.

"Hey, Harleen, can you come in here for a sec?" Dr. N calls from his office.

"Sure thing." I stop thinking about kissing (*Is my face red? I hope it's not red!*) and go inside and sit in one of the chairs in front of his big wooden desk. One wall of his office is painted with whiteboard paint and covered in diagrams and notes. Another is filled with framed pictures of him and his students at conferences, at lab parties, at the pub around the corner where he goes drinking with the grad students and postdocs on Wednesdays.

"Hey, how's everything going?" he asks.

I smile. "Good. It's really good."

He smiles back. "Good. Everything going okay with your Bridge classes? You have to tell us if we're ever working you too hard here. Your studies come first, so when midterms or finals come up, it's okay to tell us you need a little time."

Oliver told me pretty much the same thing. They are seriously the best.

"Awesome. Thank you so much. Yeah, everything's going pretty well, and I'm not really worried about my grades or anything."

"Cool, cool. So, there's actually something else I wanted to ask you about."

I sit up straighter. Something about his tone makes me excited.

"I have a colleague—a woman—and she's founded a campus organization I think you and Bernice might be interested in. It's called Gotham U Women in STEM. They have meetings, and there's a faculty-student mentor-mentee program. I've actually volunteered to be one of the faculty mentors. Anyway, it's meant for Gotham U students and faculty, but I told her I had a couple Bridge Scholars who might be interested, and—"

"Yes. Yes, I would definitely be interested. Like, sign me up! When's the first meeting? Doesn't matter, I'm in." I say all this in one breath.

Dr. N grins. "I thought you might be. I'll do an email introduction so you can get to know each other. I think she'd make a great mentor for you."

I frown. "But aren't you my mentor?"

"Absolutely." He holds up his hands. "And I'll always be your mentor. I tell that to all my students. No matter where your career path takes you, my door and my inbox are always open. But what I mean is, I'm not unaware of how difficult it is to be a woman in the sciences, and strong female mentorship can make all the difference. I'm happy to do everything I can as an ally to advance women in STEM, and that includes exposing you to every opportunity I can so you can be our scientific future."

"Wow, thank you," I say. And then I just kind of stare at my hands for a minute because I'm so struck by what he's offering.

He cares about my future. Hell, he just said I *am* the future. I don't know if I've ever had someone believe in me so much in my whole life. I mean, probably my mom, but I was so much younger then. I stammer another awestruck thank-you and walk—no, *float*—out of his office. I'm going to paint the words *our scientific future* on my ceiling.

♦

Trent grabs me by the loops of my jeans even as I'm pushing the darkroom door closed.

"What took you so long?" he growls into my ear.

I press my lips to his. Answer him between kisses.

"Oh, you know. Just meeting with Dr. N. Having him tell me I'm 'our scientific future.'" I'm glowing just thinking about it.

"He really called you that?"

I pull myself away. I don't think I like his tone. "Um, *yeah*. And he recommended me for this Women in STEM organization on campus."

"Ohhh," says Trent, like now the pieces finally fit together. "Yeah, he really likes to do all that 'women and minorities in science' stuff. Makes him look good for when they do faculty reviews."

"Um, pretty sure we don't say 'minorities' anymore. Also, did you really just diminish my accomplishment like that?" I say it all sassy, but there's a part of me that worries.

The sickly feeling sticks with me even as I'm taking the subway back from lab. I try to shake it off. At least I have gymnastics tonight! The sliding doors open, and I leap off the train and practically sprint to catch my next connection. The red line is down one level, so I get a good running start and slide all the way down the banister. I pluck a boy's hat from his head because I think it'd look better on me ("Hey!"), change my mind, and put it on someone else's head ("What?").

Then I hop on the train just in time and hurry to the building where my gym is and make a beeline to the vending machines at the back because that's where they keep the good candy bars. First chocolate, then vault practice. Crap, I'm gonna be late. I wolf down some chocolatey, peanut buttery goodness and plop down next to my friend Alexa right as class starts.

She gives me a sideways look. "You have chocolate on your face."

"What?" I laugh and lick at the corner of my mouth. "I don't know what you're talking about."

"Uh-huh."

We're about to begin our warm-up when Alexa's bag starts screaming.

I scrunch up my face. "Um, honey, if you don't stop whatever's doing that in the next five seconds, I WILL."

She pulls out a horrifyingly lifelike baby doll and cradles it in her arms. "Sorry," she says. "I think it wants milk. Or a diaper change. Or to be burped. It always wants something, and it's always screaming. Do you think it knows it was in my bag and now it's mad at me? They said there's sensors inside that keep track of everything I do."

She shoves a pretend bottle into its mouth, and thank freaking goodness it stops, because I thought I was going to have to remove my own ears.

"Definitely mad at you. Probably gonna come for you in the night." I shake my head. "I always forget you're a sophomore."

Alexa forces a grin. "Yeah, health class is awesome."

"Remind me why that school has mad-expensive robot babies but can't afford a properly working HVAC system?"

"They're going to lower our teen pregnancy rate," Alexa says dryly.

I snort. "Yeah, okay." (Have I mentioned how glad I am to be out of high school?)

"Right?" She rolls her eyes. "Shea Hyatt wants to keep hers."

A thought occurs to me. "You bringing that thing to the meet on Saturday?"

She sighs. "I have to. My mom says she can't watch it. What am I supposed to do?"

"Strap it in a BabyBjörn and hope it doesn't pop out during the uneven bars?"

"Ugh. That's definitely going to set off the sensors."

I'm just excited I still get to compete now that I've graduated. Luckily, the Greater Gotham Gymnastics League doesn't put an upper age limit on being awesome. We move over to the vault after finishing our warm-up, but my mind keeps going back to the conversation I had with Dr. N and then with Trent afterward.

A professor wouldn't say those things unless they meant them. I really do have potential. Right?

# CHAPTER 7

TODAY I DON'T HAVE ANY BRIDGE SCHOLAR CLASSES, SO I get to work with Oliver on immunostaining some slides so we can make ultrathin slices of brain tissue light up with fluorescent colors like modern art—I mean, learn important stuff about neurons and mental illness.

"Where are we getting free food this week?" I ask Oliver as I carefully suck the liquid off my slides with a vacuum tube without removing the tissue.

Oliver rubs his gloved hands together. (Grad students get extremely excited about free food.) "Well," he says, "there's a biology lunch-and-learn tomorrow that has decent gyro wraps, but you'll be at your Bridge Scholars class. Grad Student Alliance is having a social on Friday night with free pizza—Sara and I both RSVP'd, so you can be one of our plus-ones. And best of all, there's a neuroscience seminar this Monday morning"—he pauses for effect—"with breakfast sandwiches."

I whip my head around. "What kind of breakfast sandwiches? Are we talking eggs? Bacon? Bagels? Ciabatta bread? Do you think they'll have hot sauce? You know what, I'm just gonna bring my own."

Oliver laughs. "A, I have no idea. And B, share with me if you do."

His phone goes off in his lab coat pocket. He pulls off a glove so he can grab it and see who's calling.

"It's my mom. Hey, do you mind finishing the rinses?"

"Sure thing."

I keep working, putting a check mark in my lab notebook each time I do a rinse. This is one of my favorite parts about working in a lab—so much of what we do is hands-on, body and brain both active. It's so much easier for me to focus than when I was trapped at a desk at school. As long as I use little tricks like checking off each step, I can do a thirty-seven-step protocol without messing up once.

Oliver and his mom are still talking. I try not to listen in, but other people's conversations are *so* interesting, and I just want to figure out how they relate to each other and what makes them tick, and before I know it, I'm tuned in like it's a daytime soap opera.

"Yeah, I'm, like, one year away from graduating," Oliver is saying. "Yeah, Ma, I know I said that last year."

I try to hold in a snicker.

"Yes, and the year before too. You can't control how your experiments turn out. . . . You can tell Dad I'll be getting a real job anytime now. Look, can we not talk about this anymore? . . . It's okay. . . . I'm doing fine. I'm eating fine."

At this point, I can't hold back anymore—the guy is wasting away to practically nothing—so I lean toward the phone and yell, "HE LIES. HE NEEDS YOU TO SEND HIM AN-OTHER CARE PACKAGE. WITH COOKIES."

Oliver glares at me and mouths the word *traitor*. I can just hear his mom saying, "Is that that Harleen?"

"Yes, Ma."

"Well, tell her I said hi."

He rolls his eyes. "Mom says hi."

"HI, MRS. ROSS," I call back.

And because I'm leaning toward the phone again, I hear, "Tell her she can come have Thanksgiving with us if she needs somewhere to go."

Oliver winces and turns the phone farther away from me. "I'll tell her later."

I don't hear the rest of what they talk about, even though the conversation doesn't last much longer. I'm too fixated on what Oliver must have told her. About me. About my home life. It's nice of her to invite me over for Thanksgiving. And she's right that I won't have anything at home. It's nice, and it hurts at the same time.

"Sorry," Oliver says, and I realize he's hung up.

"It's okay. It's really nice of her to invite me."

"You don't have to come." He realizes how that sounds and then rushes to add, "But it's totally cool if you do! We'd be happy to have you. Sara and my sisters and everybody'll be there."

"Thanks," I say softly.

That stuff about making people tick? Well. My emotional baggage surrounding holidays alone could keep a therapist in business for years.

We finish the staining, so I go back to the office to check my email. I'm about to sit down at my desk when I see what's waiting for me on top of it and nearly swallow my tongue. I turn to Kijoon—he's the only other person in the office area right now.

"Did you see anybody come in here?"

He gives me his best WTF face. "No. Why?"

"Nothing," I say without meeting his eyes. I sit down in my rolling chair and try not to panic.

In front of me, resting innocently on the desk next to my keyboard, is one of the red plastic *No*s Bernice and I pelted that overgrown creep with. Underneath it is a piece of paper, the word *No* holding it down like a paperweight. I pick up the plastic and close my fingers around it. The paper is folded over once, so I open it.

> I know it was you. Meet me in the student center at noon.
> Sit at a table near the panini place.

I look around. Is this real? I guess it must be.

The note makes me feel vulnerable, like there's someone watching me, maybe even right now. I look again, but of course no one's there, and I instantly feel sheepish.

I wonder who wrote it. Probably one of those boys from the frat. Is he going to try to press charges? Blackmail me? I don't have any money.

I check my phone. It won't be noon for another hour, which is just the worst news because I am seriously going to spontaneously combust if I don't figure out what's going on ASAP. I try to run some stats on my most recent batch of data, but it's a lost cause. All I can think about is the note and who wrote it.

Later, when Bernice plops down next to me and asks if I'm hungry, I nearly jump out of my skin.

"Not really," I say. Half-true—my stomach forgets to work when I'm freaking out. "I actually have to go run an errand during lunch. But I'll catch you later?"

"Okay," she says, grabbing her lunch bag from the mini fridge.

*Whew.* I slide the note and the plastic *No* into my bag and leave before anyone else can ask me any questions. I honestly don't know if the note was meant for me *and* Bernice or just me. It was on my desk, but does the person who left it really know where we sit? I don't want to give Bernice anything else to worry about right now, though. She's dealing with enough.

I power walk across campus to the student center. Find an empty table near the panini place, as requested. I look around for Grady, but he's not here. Not yet, anyway. I kind of figured he wouldn't go to the police about what we did, because it would mean admitting he assaulted someone.

I check my phone. 12:05. I don't know why them being late makes me so nervous. Because it feels like someone's watching me? Maybe.

I'm still searching for Grady or one of his friends and fretting internally at 12:14, when that girl Bianca from the physics machine shop sits down in front of me.

"Oh, actually, I'm waiting for someone," I say. Crap, what if they see her and decide not to show because I didn't "come alone"? Not that the note said that, but I'm filling in the gaps with lines from bad police shows.

"Yeah, sorry I'm late," she says.

She slides a panini across the table to me. I stare at it. *Wait, what?* "I don't understand."

She shrugs, embarrassed. "I stopped by my favorite

Cuban place on the way here. I brought you a Cubano in case you didn't have a lunch."

And then it clicks. "You? You're the one who left the note?"

"I am." She opens a tin container of chicken, black beans, and grilled onions and peppers that smells heavenly, taking a quick bite and washing it down with a gulp from the largest water bottle I've ever seen.

I just. I can't even. Of all the people. Like, what is happening here? I have so many questions.

"Are you usually in the habit of buying sandwiches for people you blackmail?" (Perhaps not the most important one to lead with.)

"Whoa, Harleen, I'm not blackmailing you." She says it with all this conviction, like she's a super-good person who just happens to leave people threatening notes. "Also, you can eat that sandwich. I didn't poison it."

"Well, what are you doing here, then?" I narrow my eyes at her. I also unwrap my sandwich because it looks like slow-cooked pork with ham, cheese, and pickles, and I'm no fool.

Bianca glances from left to right, like there are spies lurking behind the salad bar. I do the same thing. I can't help it. Then she leans forward and looks me right in the eye.

"I want in."

A part of me flares with excitement when she says it—the same part that went on a power-drunk cupcake spree with Bernice. But also? I didn't realize how terrifying it would feel to almost get caught. Or how easy it would be for someone to figure out who we are. Plus, this girl could be a snitch, for all I know.

I decide to play it cool. "In what? There's nothing to be

in. Maybe Bernice and I served a little justice to a guy who really deserved it, but now it's over—if it was even anything to begin with."

Bianca's eyes fill with passion. "It doesn't have to be over."

"What more do you want to do? Blow up his car?"

She can't help but grin. "I do love explosions, but I was thinking more along the lines of scope. It doesn't have to end with him. There are so many professors on this campus who are horrifically sexist. We're supposed to be telling little girls that they should do STEM and be scientists, but we also need to make science a place where it's okay to be a woman. I've heard more messed-up stories than I can count from women all around campus. We could shake things up. *Change* things. I thought of it when I saw the videos of you and Bernice going after that guy. I want the bad guys on campus to know what it's like to be scared."

That's kind of what I want too. Isn't that all the stuff I was thinking on the fire escape? And then again with Bernice in the bathroom? I'm tired of living in a world where women aren't safe. Of swallowing down all the ways that men and women still aren't equal. Of biting my tongue at sexist comments. I want to DO something about it. Something big. There are still so many things to figure out, though.

"How do we even know who to go after?" I ask.

She smiles. "I know just the professor to start with."

Bianca tells me that her best friend, Jasmin, is a computer science grad student and that she maybe just happens to have footage of an admissions committee meeting with a professor saying you can't let women into grad school because they have babies and cry all the time and are distractingly sexy.

"Well, that's some BS." I take an angry bite out of my sandwich. (It's ludicrously delicious.)

"Right? So I think we should get him like you and Bernice got that guy with the *No* cannon. I mean, not the exact same way. Something that fits what he did but also sends a message publicly, you know?"

I nod, but I'm a little bit caught off guard by all this—I don't even know these girls, not really. Can I trust them? I didn't exactly have the kind of upbringing that makes you want to hand over your heart to people. I'm used to trusting only myself. And then there's the matter of my dreams. If I keep doing this, I'll put all my college plans at risk. I'm pretty sure that (A) what Bianca is talking about doing is some kind of illegal, and (B) they don't exactly let felons join the Ultimate Frisbee team at Gotham U. And if there's no Gotham U, well . . . There goes med school and residency and solving complex biomedical problems to save the world and also my chances of hauling myself out of the East End and that awful apartment that is like a gallery of bad memories.

"Bernice and I are lucky we didn't get caught," I force myself to say. "I don't know if we can continue to keep that from happening."

Bianca waves me off. "Jasmin'll handle all that. She's got mad hacking skills. It'll be no problem for her to hack the school's security systems and make sure we're never caught on camera. And we'll be extremely careful. Masks for every mission."

It would be pretty cool—to have a group of friends to band together with, I mean. A girl gang that doles out justice to the most misogynistic men on campus.

I focus on how it felt to find her note on my desk. That moment of free-falling panic. I'm reminded of a study I read, about how two parts of your brain light up when you're assessing risk—fear versus reward—and they battle to the death. Or, well, the decision. Which, depending on your appetite for risk, could end in death. Girl gang versus college. Smashing the patriarchy versus safety. Stability. Keeping myself out of an orange jumpsuit.

I know she wants me to say yes, but I just can't. So much of what I've worked for is at stake—but if we can't level the playing field, do I even stand a chance of succeeding to begin with?

"I have to think about it."

# CHAPTER 8

MONDAY, APRIL 4

TWO OF THE BIG RED LETTERS ARE BURNED OUT IN THE emergency sign that presides over the ER at Gotham Memorial Hospital. An alleyway filled with run-down tents sits to its right. Memorial is where all the trauma cases go, the really bad ones. Motorcycle accidents and muggings gone bad and street brawls and shootings and knife wounds so grisly that half the doctors and nurses get PTSD while treating patients with PTSD. Across town is Gotham General, renowned, no expense spared, shining white (walls on the outside and people on the inside). The rich want to make sure they never breathe the same air as us, even—especially—if it's their last.

But the people at Memorial are kind—at least they were when my mom came here so many years ago.

I picture Mom's nurse, the one with the soft smile.

*I brought this for you. You like crossword puzzles, don't you?*

I focus on that kindness and tell the universe to please give Bernice a nurse just like that. It's been seven hours, and she still hasn't woken up.

The man at the front desk directs me to Bernice's room. I'm headed down the chipped tiles of the eighth floor—this one's supposed to be hers—when I see a familiar face walking toward me. She has dark skin and flawless eyebrows that underscore the fact that she is the master of the one-eyebrow raise. Her hair is in crochet braids, like usual, pulled back into a high bun, which is how she does it when she wants to be laser focused (which is most of the time). Everything about her body language says not to talk to her: crossed arms, tight mouth, eyes that follow the wall rather than look at me. I wave my arms and call out anyway.

"Jasmin. Hey, Jasmin!"

She stops. (Okay, possibly because I am standing in front of her and she can't pass.)

"I don't really want to talk to you," she says, attempting to sidestep me.

"Aw, c'mon—"

She holds up a hand, feigning disgust. Her eyes tell the truth. She's hurt.

"We thought you were one of us," she says.

It cuts so deep that it takes me a couple seconds to remember how to speak. Long enough for Jasmin to slip around me.

"I am one of you. Jasmin, you know me. I—"

"I really don't have time for this." She doesn't even stop walking.

I chase after her because she needs to know.

"Wait!" I finally get close enough to touch her shoulder. "This is important. We have to figure out who did this. The police were asking all these questions, and I'm scared they'll think it's me, and—"

She turns on her heel. "You didn't tell them anything,

did you?" Narrows her eyes like it'll help her see if I'm lying. "About—?"

"Of course not. Are you kidding me?" It's one thing for her to be angry. Completely another for her to think I'd ever . . . That I *could* ever. I shake my head. "You can trust me."

"Can I? Can I really?" She looks me up and down, eyes cold. And then she says it. "You and B were pretty heated the other night. Any chance you're the reason she's in there?"

I take a step back like she's punched me. She can't mean that. She's just trying to hurt me. And damn, she might as well have reached into my chest and pulled out my still-beating heart so she could grind it into the floor with the heel of her ankle boot. Just because a person does one bad thing doesn't mean they'd do all of them. I try to tell myself that Jasmin doesn't really believe I could hurt Bernice. She's just angry.

I shake my head and shove past her into the hospital room.

I gasp when I see Bernice. Except no, that isn't quite right, because a gasp is pulling air into your body, and this feels like everything being sucked out of me all at once. She looks so tiny surrounded by all those machines. Her eyelids are shut, and her face is so pale, but in a delicate way that makes me think of women in Victorian times dying of consumption, whatever that is.

"Bernice," I breathe.

I sit in the chair by her bedside. There's a jacket draped over the chairback—one of her parents must be around here somewhere. I take Bernice's hand in mine, carefully, because of the tube giving her IV fluids.

"I really screwed up," I tell her.

*You and B were pretty heated the other night.*

I remember the betrayed look on Bernice's face. Her tears falling, hot and angry.

*Maybe I was lying to myself, okay? Maybe I had to lie to myself about a lot of things to be with you—*

*You want to know what else I was lying about?*

I rest my head on her blanket next to our clasped hands.

*Told myself it'd only be a matter of time until I destroyed her.*

"I'm so sorry," I whisper. "I wish you could wake up and tell me who did this to you."

there's got to be a hacker.

best hackers at Gotham U

Jasmin Jones ?
Ada Sinclair
Whitney Sanzero
Angela Pham
Marianna Palmour
Anya Babenko

# DECEMBER

# CHAPTER 9

I SHIMMY THROUGH THE OPEN WINDOW AFTER BIANCA. WE waited until after midnight to break into the computer science building, but there's still a chance someone could walk by and see half of me hanging out a window, so I need to work fast.

I know, I know, when she asked me about forming a girl gang, I said I had to think about it. But you know what? I thought about it. And you know what else? I'M IN.

(So is Bernice. It's possible her joining gave me that final nudge.)

Yes, I want to go to college. Yes, I want to be a doctor. But I feel like the decks are so stacked against me. Against all women in STEM. The fight for baseline levels of respect and having to prove that you're competent instead of people just assuming that you are. The ginormous gap in salary. The razor-thin line between being a boss and people hating you. And being a woman plus being from the East End and having the kind of childhood I had? It's like a one-two punch.

So, today? I'm ready to burn the whole system down. Starting with Professor Bayers.

And that vomit-y feeling I get in my stomach when I think about how quickly my future could disappear if we get caught? I'LL JUST IGNORE IT.

My feet hit the basement floor with a thud. Jasmin and Bernice thud in after me.

"Ow!"

"You okay?"

"Yeah, I just ran into something."

"That was my butt."

"Oops. Sorry."

"Can someone turn on a light?"

Bianca's flashlight flares bright in the darkness.

"Ow, it's like the surface of the sun!" I try to shield my eyes. "Bianca, are you trying to make us all go blind?"

(Honestly, though? I'm pretty relieved to know we're in a sprawling storage area and not, like, a closet or something.)

"Seriously, what is that thing?" Bernice asks, wincing.

Bianca scoffs. "It is a *tactical* flashlight. It has solar panels and a glass breaker and a seat belt cutter. Oh, and it can blast anything with two hundred lumens of light."

Jasmin throws a hand up. "Can you try blasting it somewhere other than at my face?"

Even though Bianca only introduced us to Jasmin a few weeks ago, I'm already obsessed with her expertly deployed eyebrow raises and the way she uses sarcasm like a paintbrush.

Bianca lets out a long-suffering sigh and shifts her beam of pure energy to a dark corner of the room. Jasmin pulls up her mask and wipes her face.

"I didn't realize ski masks got so sweaty on the inside. Don't worry," she adds when she sees Bernice's concerned expression. "There aren't any cameras in the basement."

"I can make you a mask for the next mission," Bernice says, pulling up hers too. "One that breathes better."

Turns out Bernice's creepy-stuffed-animal-making skills translate really well into making badass costumes. She actually made me a new one for today because the cut-up gymnastics thing I wore for the last mission was a "fabric abomination."

"She does a really great job too. I'm obsessed with my new costume."

Bernice turns bright red when I say it. Making her blush is just the best.

The costume Bernice made me really does fit like a dream, though. Black and red fabric pieces stitched together into a bodysuit that feels like a second skin. Glittery rhinestones crisscrossing to make a diamond pattern. A red-and-black hood that hides my blond hair and keeps most of my face in shadow. I'm the only one not wearing a full mask. But I painted one eye red and one eye black the way my mirror told me to.

Jasmin's too busy firing up her laptop to notice. She's wearing all black, just like the other girls, but it's funny how different that can look on different people. For Bianca, it's a pair of sleek, black moisture-wicking pants paired with a long-sleeved workout top with cool cutouts. For Jasmin, black jeans and a Neil deGrasse Tyson T-shirt. For Bernice, buttery-soft leggings and a turtleneck embroidered with an RBG dissent collar.

Jasmin looks up from her screen. "Cool. So I'm gonna

take out the camera system and card access now. We'll still need to get into his office, though."

"I can do that part, easy," I say.

"And I've got everything else we need," says Bianca, tugging on her backpack straps.

I eye her backpack, which (A) looks like something the military would issue and (B) is the size of a golden retriever. "Yeah, what is in that thing, by the way?"

Her face lights up. "In my tactical pack?"

"Is anything you own not tactical?" Jasmin asks dryly without looking up from her laptop.

Bianca ignores her. "Check it out. I've got cable-wire cutters, water-purification tabs, zip-tie handcuffs, hemostatic bandages, a Ka-Bar knife, seventy-five feet of Kevlar trip wire—I think that speaks for itself in terms of usefulness. Plus an eighteen-in-one survival kit with a compass and a fire starter and a device that opens any kind of can!"

"Are you expecting to encounter a lot of canned goods on this mission?" I ask, smirking.

"Ha-ha. What's in that sparkly fanny pack, if you're so smart?"

"Oh, just the essentials." I unzip it with a flourish. "My lockpick kit. Some lip gloss. Oh, and, um, gummy raspberries. You just never know."

Jasmin snorts. "Yeah, you don't get to judge her for the tactical flashlight anymore. And, by the way, I'm finished."

A hush sweeps over us. *Are we doing this? I think we're doing this!* We pull our masks back down. Fling open the basement door. And we're off! Slithering, slinking, slipping through the dark hallways. Giddy with our own cleverness. Blood pumping. Laughter pinging off the walls. This is the other reason I couldn't say no to Bianca. Right from the jump, I was sucked in by her intensity and the way she cares so much about other people. By Jasmin's dry sarcasm and big, change-the-world ideas. And I certainly don't mind spending more time with Bernice. . . .

But, tonight? So far, it's more than I ever could have dreamed. I can't contain it all. I have to blow off steam by doing a roundoff double back handspring down the hallway. I land with my arms outstretched, like a spy holding a gun.

We sneak along walls, peer around corners. It's physically impossible for us to stop giggling. We're talking three-a.m.-at-a-middle-school-sleepover levels of delirium.

But when we reach the door to the office suite, we fall silent.

"What if we get caught?" whispers Bernice.

"We won't." I throw my arm around her shoulders, like you do when you're friends, except the act of me touching her makes us both stop breathing, so I retract my arm, quick, and say, "Jasmin's a genius."

I don't look at Bernice. My eyes would give too much away.

"You don't have to worry about the cameras," says Jasmin.

"See?" says Bianca. "So we're not gonna get caught unless one of you tells. In which case, I'll be forced to kill you." She jumps up and slaps her hands against the top of the door-frame. "Woo! We're gonna blow up the patriarchy!"

"But there could still be a security guard or something." Jasmin nudges her.

"Right. My bad. I'll do my smashing in an indoor voice."

Our eyes dart in every direction, like the mere mention of a security guard will make one appear. That rattling noise—was it just the heater clicking on or something more sinister? We wait, listening. Sweating. When the tension threatens to strangle us, I reach out my hand and turn the door handle, the one right next to the card swipe box. It clicks and the door opens.

"Card access, bypassed," Jasmin says in a coolly robotic voice.

The office suite is dark but for a couple dim emergency lights and a red exit sign. Desks dot the carpeted floor in front of us—that's where the administrative assistants sit. And in the offices behind them are Gotham U's finest computer science professors. The first one on our left has a shiny nameplate that reads DR. FRANK BAYERS.

"So. Where do we start?" I ask.

"Luckily, he's right next to the break room. Jasmin and I can start there. Can you and Bernice work on getting us into his office?"

"Easy as pie."

Jasmin and Bianca disappear, and Bernice kneels and shines her phone's flashlight onto the lock so I can pick it. We are extremelyclosetogether, but we don't touch each other. It feels like it's on purpose. In a good way or a bad way? *Focus, Harleen. This lock isn't gonna pick itself.* I brought a lockpick kit and everything because I was worried my knife wouldn't cut it, but it's honestly less complicated than I was expecting. I insert a tension wrench, and then I fidget the correct-sized pick into the lock. I work it back and forth, going by feel. The lock clicks in a satisfying way that can mean only one thing.

"Victory." I grin at Bernice. I expect her to look away, but she doesn't. She holds my gaze as she pushes down on the door handle. *Does this mean she likes me or just that she's feeling intense about the mission?*

The door swings open, flashlight app cutting through the darkness, lighting up a desk, a computer, some file cabinets. But never all at once. Something is always left in the shadows.

Bernice's face changes in the ghostly light of her phone, glows with a new emotion. Her lips try to hide it, disguise her smile, keep her face from confessing the truth—she's as excited as I am. She takes a step forward, joining me in the doorway.

"We're really doing this."

The intensity in her voice makes my stomach flip, like it's going down that first drop on a roller coaster.

"Yep."

I take a step backward so we're not right-right next to each other under the doorframe.

"Let's go see how they're doing next door," I tell her.

Jasmin sits at a table checking something on her laptop while Bianca presides over an impressive selection of drill bits rolled out on the counter in a black canvas holder.

"Office is open!" I say.

"Damn, that was fast." She passes Bernice a set of plastic bolt-looking things. "Here, check which one of these valves fits the sink over there." And then to me: "Can you go back to his office and let me know if I'm drilling in a good spot? I don't want to try to punch through a metal filing cabinet or something."

"Sure."

I head next door and turn on my phone light. Yeah, Bianca is definitely about to drill into a giant bookshelf. But next to that, just a few feet over, is a clear expanse of drywall where Professor Bayers has hung his degrees.

"Sorry," I tell his PhD in computer science. "You're in the way."

I tap on the wall where his accomplishment used to be. "Right here," I call to Bianca.

"Here?" She taps back.

"Yep! You're good to go."

She fires up the drill, and it is LOUD. We're talking a-thousand-bees-buzzing, Weedwacker-outside-your-window-while-you're-studying-for-finals loud. For the first time I actually worry about getting caught. If anyone else is in this building, they're bound to hear. I should be scared. And I am. But a bigger part of me feels alive.

The silver drill bit punctures the wall in front of me, and I laugh.

The drill stops. "That was it, right?" calls Bianca.

I answer in the affirmative.

I hear the clinking sounds of her doing something on the other side of the wall, and then the drill starts again. This time it's a bigger bore, hollowing things out, scraping around the sides of the caterpillar-sized tunnel she's creating.

"I'm going to try threading you the tubing, okay?"

The hole left by the drill is about the size of a nickel now. If I peer into it, I can just see the skinny plastic tubing poking through Bianca's end. She tries to thread it through the insulation and empty space between us. Once. Twice.

"I will explode this whole wall if I have to!" she yells, and I snicker.

The clear tube finally pokes through my end of the wall, and I grab it, quick, before it goes away.

"Got it!" I call.

"Sweeeet!"

The girls rush over. Bernice holds up a can of spray paint. Bianca secures the tube to the wall so that it won't pull back through. I'm feeling weirdly tense as I watch, waiting for Bernice to do this. I can tell she's feeling it too—her hands are shaking. And then Bianca grins. "You ready to make waves?"

We nod, wild-eyed.

Well, all except Jasmin. She turns to Bianca with an eyebrow arched. "Did you just say that because—"

Bianca interrupts her, her grin even wider. "Well, c'mon. *Water* you waiting for?"

"Wow. Wowwwwww." Jasmin shakes her head, but she's laughing.

Bernice and I crack up too. Even if they're just some dad jokes, the act of laughing feels really good right now. Bernice isn't quite so stiff and scared as she holds a stencil against the wall, and the paint can hisses and spits inky blackness. She pulls the stencil away. In its place are the words *The Reckoning* in this really cool design she made. Bianca thought of the name. Said we'd be bringing judgment down on people who think they're above the rules. I like it. I mean, I think it's cool and everything. I'm not sure it fits me exactly, but maybe that's the way it's supposed to be. Like an aspirational name. Something I'll grow into.

I stare at the symbol and the four inches of clear plastic tubing hanging out of the wall like a wilted flower. Something's missing, though. With a sudden burst of inspiration, I replace the framed degree so that it covers the Reckoning symbol and the tubing.

I grin at the other girls. "Might as well not make it easy on him."

Then we sneak out of his office and close the door and tiptoe back to the break room. Bianca connects the other end of the clear plastic tubing to the valve she had Bernice install. She goes to turn on the faucet.

"Wait!"

We all turn to stare at Jasmin. I don't think I've ever heard her speak with such urgency.

"I . . . thought we could watch the video first," she says sheepishly. "To remind ourselves why we're doing this."

"I think that's a great idea!" I say it fast and a little too loud, like it'll diffuse her embarrassment.

She pulls up the video on her laptop and clicks Play. Professor Bayers's face appears on the screen. He sits at the end of a massive table—the kind that's, like, two inches thick and probably made of some rich-people wood, like teak or mahogany. There are a bunch of other white dudes at the table, all older than him, a white woman, an Asian man, and one really young white man who has to be a graduate student.

"This is the computer science grad school admissions committee," explains Jasmin. "I'm one of the student reps. Also the only Black person."

"How did you film this without them seeing you?" breathes Bernice.

"I had my tablet open anyway to take notes. And then I just kind of opened my camera app and clicked Record."

"Damn, you're brave," says Bianca.

The committee discusses one particular woman. They're on the fence about letting her in.

"Look, it's not that I'm against having women in computer science," begins Professor Bayers.

"Here comes some bullshit," I mutter. We all lean closer in spite of ourselves.

"But we have to think of the incoming class as a whole. We can't have a class that's seventy percent women. They're a lot more likely to drop out of the program. They take longer to graduate because they have babies. They don't convert to faculty." He grins and spreads his hands, the universal gesture for *Oops, not my problem.*

He's met with mostly silence, a few nods.

Video Jasmin speaks up. We can't see her on-screen, but I know her voice. "This woman is way more qualified than the last two candidates we glowingly discussed, both of whom were men, I might add."

"Well, they were both such a great fit for the program," says the old white dude with the most ear hair. "I just don't have a good feeling about this one. And, like Frank said, wouldn't it be fairer to have a class that's fifty-fifty?"

I don't have to be able to see Video Jasmin to know she is talking through her teeth. "I'm all for diversity and inclusion, but I didn't realize white males were a marginalized group."

The white woman's lips twitch, but she doesn't say anything.

Ear Hair jumps in. "Whoa, whoa, whoa. There's no need to get angry."

Real Jasmin's hands curl into fists in her lap.

"Pendejos," hisses Bianca.

"Excuse me. I need to go get a drink of water," says Video Jasmin. We hear the opening and closing of a door.

The committee releases a collective sigh of relief.

"That right there is exactly what I'm talking about," says Dr. Bayers, pointing at the door. "They're so emotional. Have you ever had one in your lab? They're distractingly sexy—

it's impossible to get any work done, and they cry *all* the time."

Jasmin hits Pause.

"That's the worst of it," she says.

THANK FREAKING GOODNESS because I'm pretty sure my microaggression bingo card is already full.

"It's so messed up," says Bernice.

"Disgusting," says Bianca.

"You're such a badass for standing up to them," I tell her. She gives me a half smile. "Thanks." And then she starts shifting in her chair and twisting her fingers together. "Also, there's something I need to tell y'all. I, uh, haven't been totally honest with you."

Oh crap, is this some kind of elaborate setup? The fear in Bernice's eyes mirrors mine. Bianca grips the chairback in front of her.

Jasmin—cool, sarcastic, even-keeled Jasmin—is breathing like there are hummingbirds in her lungs. "Getting Professor Bayers back isn't just about what happened at the meeting. It's personal."

We're all surprised by this, I can tell, but nobody says anything because (A) Jasmin looks terrified, and (B) we're nosy AF and want her to keep talking.

"I really badly wanted to work in his lab, but he wouldn't take me. Apparently, he hasn't hired a woman in the past ten years, but I didn't know that at the time. I just felt really worthless. He's a brilliant computer scientist . . . despite being the worst person on the planet. And I know now that working in his lab would have staked my love of coding right through the heart, but at the time, it was terrible." She looks down at her lap. "I spent that whole semester thinking

I didn't deserve to be here. That the school was trying to hit a quota or something. Another Brown body to make the numbers look good. You know?"

I hug her so hard I practically jump into her chair with her. She seems only mildly alarmed, which I'll count as a win.

"I'm so sorry they made you feel that way. And, also? We are happy to do this. For you. For the video. Because it's really freaking fun. For all the reasons, okay?"

Her stiff posture relaxes, and she actually hugs me back.

"Means a lot, Harleen," she says.

Bernice takes Jasmin's hand, and Bianca squeezes her shoulder.

"We're in this together. And that means looking out for each other, always," says Bianca. "From now on, we'll be honest no matter what."

"And we'll take care of each other," says Bernice.

Something inside me cracks, and I almost start to cry. Partly because her words struck something in me, and partly because I've never felt this way before. Looked after. Soup when you're sick and somebody in your corner, even when you're wrong, and an arm around your shoulders on the most terrible day. I like to think I'd have that with my mom if she was still here. And now that I have this good thing, I don't want to let it go. Can't. I'll do whatever it takes to keep it. I'll fight to be worthy of it.

I shake off the mushy feelings, quick. "So, that video's going in his presentation tomorrow, huh?"

"Yep." Jasmin smiles. "Professor Bayers has been invited to give the Tashwood E. Worthington Distinguished Computer Science Lecture at nine a.m. tomorrow. I scammed him last week by creating a fake Gotham U website that he

93

had to log in to for the details of his latest pay increase. All I have to do is enter his password and add the video to his presentation on the Gotham U cloud tomorrow while he's on his way to work. He'll put on his best suit. Go straight to the auditorium from his house. And—"

"BOOM!" yells Bianca, smacking her fist against her hand and making us all jump out of our skin.

"Sorry," she says. "I get excited."

But I'm already laughing. "You never have to apologize for being awesome."

"Or for having emotions," Jasmin says seriously.

"Thanks." Bianca pauses like she's unsure whether she wants to say this next part. "It's a whole thing. About being Latina. People—usually white people—are always telling us we're too loud or we need to calm down. But I *do* feel calm. For me. I'm just being my real self. Everything on the islands is loud: colors, music, conversation, food. That's my normal. It's only 'loud' when it's through the white gaze, you know?"

Bernice squeezes Bianca's hand. "I feel like everything you say on the outside is everything I'm feeling on the inside. It's one of my favorite things about you."

"Thank you." Bianca's eyes mist up. (Bernice's unbridled sincerity will do that to you.)

I am unequipped to deal with all capital *F* Feelings, so I yell, "Okay! Let's flood this office!"

Jasmin closes her computer, and we all walk over to the sink.

"I think Jasmin should do it," I say, even though my fingers are itching to touch the faucet.

Jasmin turns both the cold and hot handles at once. Water sweeps down the tube, threads along the counter, and

94

passes into the hole in the wall that leads to Dr. Bayers's office. By the time he sees his office tomorrow, it'll be flooded.

"Woo-hoo!" I yell.

We jump up and down and high-five each other, dizzy with our own genius.

"Last thing," says Bernice.

She pulls a label from her bag and attaches it to the tube:

## LADY SCIENTIST TEARS

# CHAPTER 10

RECKONING SECURE CHAT:

Bianca: When/where are we meeting tonight?

Harleen: When—as soon as humanly possible because I am high-key psyched to do another mission

Harleen: Where—idk

Jasmin: Somewhere public. But with a low risk of people we know seeing us.

Bianca: Hmmm

Harleen: OMG, y'all, my stomach is eating itself. I gave my breakfast sandwich to my Bridge group facilitator so she wouldn't mark me late for the meeting, and I REGRET MY CHOICES

Jasmin: I'm sorry for your loss.

Harleen: Also, how bout 6?

Harleen: And thanks. It had the thick-cut bacon and herb butter and everything

Harleen: I'll just be over here sobbing quietly

Bianca: Did you hear the rumor about butter?

Harleen: If it's gonna give me cancer, I DO NOT WANT TO KNOW

Bianca: Well, I'm not going to spread it.

Jasmin: Someone stop her. Please.

Bianca: HAHAHA Because butter!

Bernice: how bout the zoo? it's public and off campus.

Bernice: plus, i love animals.

I want to type something back, like, "OMG, how are you the cutest person ever?!" or "Me too! Soul mates!!" But instead I put my phone in my backpack and zip it shut. For my own protection.

I watch as the last few stragglers trickle into the arena-style classroom, where Dr. Catrambone stands at the front, hooking up her laptop to the school's system. As Bridge Scholars, we got to pick one real, official Gotham U course to attend out of a handful of options. (Naturally, I chose Intro to Psych.) Sitting here, pretending I'm one of them for the next fifty minutes—it's the best. Dr. Catrambone clears her throat and starts lecturing about exposure therapy.

"This type of therapy involves exposing a person to whatever caused their trauma. That could mean something as simple as reliving it in their imagination while taking slow, controlled breaths. Or holding a nonpoisonous spider in their hand. Or standing in an elevator without actually taking it up or down. It depends what things trigger that person."

Exposure therapy sounds . . . unpleasant. It makes me think of arctic climbers getting trapped in a storm and dying of *exposure*.

"It's extremely effective in treating PTSD and phobias."

*Huh*. I raise my hand.

"Ms. Quinzel?"

"So a person would just, like, do this exposure stuff and try not to be afraid?"

Dr. Catrambone takes a sip of her coffee. "That's the general idea. With a trained therapist, of course."

I nod seriously. "Oh, of course."

Who's thinking of trying this at home by themselves? CERTAINLY NOT ME.

I take detailed notes on everything she says about exposure therapy for the rest of class, purely for academic purposes, definitely just to feed my relentless pursuit of knowledge, no other reason. It's surprising how easy it is to focus when I'm interested in something. It's like everything else around me disappears. Like when I'd get sucked into a really good book as a kid, and my mom would tap me on the shoulder—it felt like I was somewhere else and I had to come up for air. When I was little, I liked to pretend hyperfocus was one of my ADHD superpowers.

Anyway, exposure therapy. I'd need a small space—my closet would probably work. I'd have to clean it out, of course, but at least it wouldn't involve buying anything.

And by the end of class, even though I haven't tried anything yet, I feel a little braver. I pull out my phone and text Bernice, just her, not the group chat.

Harleen: Want to meet at the zoo early and walk
around?

♦

Bernice and I sip pink lattes and watch the goats. Two of
them frolic around the children's area at Gotham Zoo,
inseparable, while a third watches forlornly after several
(failed) attempts to be included. The spurned goat stomps
over to one of the staff members and begins to gnaw on the
bottom of her shirt.

"Apparently, he has a lot of complicated goat feelings to
work out," I tell Bernice, and she giggles.

I don't know why making her laugh feels like such a
victory.

We leave the melodramatic goats and meander past the
elephant exhibit and the lions. At first I was walking around
all intense, pretending I was a spy and cursing myself for
not having a trench coat, but now I'm more chill. Talking,
laughing, walking with our heads angled toward each other.
It almost feels like a date. Does *she* feel like it's a date? Nah.
Forget it.

And the very next second, I actually do forget it because
the hyena exhibit appears on our left, and have you ever
seen a more perfect animal?! (No. No, you have not.) I run
over to watch them, all tan and spotted with messy manes
like little kids who just woke up, and faces so ugly you can't
help but want to snuggle them.

Bernice catches up to me.

"Sorry," I say. "I really love hyenas. Did you know they
have sideways birth canals that their babies have to fight

their way out of, and they always have twins who battle to the death at birth?"

Bernice responds with an extremely slow head turn. "Um, that is the most disturbing thing I have ever heard."

"I know, right? Aren't they cute?!" I wiggle my fingers at the hyenas. The one with the ripped ear sniffs in my direction and snaps at the air happily. "Hi. Hi there. I wish I could take you home with me. Yes, I do."

Bernice smiles, bemused. "I think it's cool that you can find the good in them."

I brush it off by saying, "Are you kidding? What's not to love?" But I'm secretly pleased.

It's almost time to meet Jasmin and Bianca, so we head to the sea lion exhibit. There's a big glass window with a half-circle arena around it where they do shows on the hour. A crowd of tired parents and sticky children files out, which is perfect. The show just ended, and the next one doesn't start for thirty minutes. The arena is empty.

Bernice and I grab a seat near the middle, like, *Hi, we're just super passionate about sea lions balancing balls on their noses and wanted to lock our seats down half an hour early.* A few minutes later, Jasmin and Bianca sit down behind us, all nonchalant. We're definitely not together. Nope. Just two sets of friends who independently happen to love sea lions and coincidentally chose these particular seats.

"Bianca. Jasmin." I say it while keeping my face pointed straight ahead.

Bianca matches my even tone. "Harleen."

"You know there is no one around to see us," says Jasmin.

"THAT WE KNOW OF."

Bernice elbows me.

"Oops."

"So." Bianca leans forward and puts her elbows on her knees. "It's time to brainstorm who's next."

"I think we have a more pressing concern," says Bernice, and something about her quiet confidence sets us all on edge. Whatever threat she's registered—it's real.

"Did they catch us?" I have a future, and it does not involve going to jail for office flooding.

Bernice shakes her head. "No. But—" She whips out her phone. Pulls up an Instagram account. "People have been posting pictures of us. Well, not *us* us," she rushes to add when we all panic. "But the stuff that we did."

There are about a billion reposted videos of me and Bernice taking down that Grady guy with the Dissent Cannon— we're lucky we thought to wear masks. And then there's a video that was clearly taken during Dr. Bayers's distinguished lecture. The quality is so high, it must be a clip from the official stream the school links to for all the big lectures. At first it's just a slide about quantum computing, and Dr. Bayers talking like he's God's gift to computer science. But then he clicks the advance button. Only the presentation doesn't progress to the next slide. A video pops up and begins playing. *The* video.

It only takes a couple seconds for him to realize what it is. For his face to crumble the way his world is about to.

"YES."

"Holy crap!"

"Did you see his face?!"

We bust out laughing, and a zookeeper peers around the corner to check that we're not some unruly teen hooligans. We immediately fall silent and go back to pretending we don't know each other.

This is amazing. I mean, I knew it would be, but I never

actually got to see it in person because we decided it would be a lot less suspicious if the three of us who aren't computer science students had alibis during his lecture.

"Here's the ones they posted of his office," Bernice whispers.

She flips through shots of the waterlogged office and the plastic tubing labeled LADY SCIENTIST TEARS.

I sigh. "I could not be prouder about how that turned out."

And then she shows us the next photo.

It's a close-up shot of the Reckoning symbol with a simple caption: *Anyone know who the Reckoning is?*

We all agreed we wanted a symbol. Something that would strike fear into the hearts of douchebags everywhere. I guess it didn't occur to me until now that it could make it easier to find us. We'll probably be fine, though. I don't think anyone—

"So, this girl DMed me on my Insta and says she knows who we are," says Bernice.

*"What?!"* The zoo starts to spin around me. I've got so much to lose. I picture my future, evaporating. Not getting into Gotham U. Staying at home and going to community college. Living in that apartment with my dad for so much longer than the days currently marked off on my calendar.

"It's okay." Bernice puts a hand on my shoulder. "I don't think she wants to turn us in or anything. But she has asked to meet with us. I think we need to do something."

"Break her kneecaps?" Bianca pipes up.

Jasmin gives her a Look.

"What? I was kidding. *Obviously.* That's the complete opposite of everything we stand for."

"I never can tell with you." Jasmin shakes her head, but she's smiling. "What exactly did she say?"

Bernice pulls up her DMs. "She says she figured out who we are, and she wants to arrange a meeting because her dad is a big donor to the school and she has some information that could help us. It's about the investigation they're doing into who vandalized Dr. Bayers's office."

An idea fireworks in my head. "Okay, okay, maybe we don't Tonya Harding her, but what about this?"

## CHAPTER 11

JASMIN TURNS OFF HER LIGHTS BEFORE SHE PULLS INTO the alley. Something about this feels even scarier than when we broke into Dr. Bayers's office. At least that night we could tell ourselves we weren't going to run into another person—tonight, that's kind of the point. This girl sending Bernice DMs about the Reckoning—Kylie, we know from her Instagram—is an unknown variable. She could help us. She could betray us. She could bring an army of police officers and/or sorority girls down on us because this whole thing could be a bait and switch. Any number of things could go right or very wrong. I try to suppress the thrill in my stomach.

"She just DMed me to say she'd be here soon. But she also posted a picture with her coconut cold brew thirteen minutes ago, so we may be waiting a while," says Bernice. "At least we know which direction she'll be coming from?"

The Greek parking deck is on the other side of the alley. All we have to do is wait for the girl with the caramel-blond balayage to skip across the street and into the backyard of the house with the big columns. I study the building curiously. I've never had one sister, let alone a hundred. I wonder if they feel about each other the way I've been feeling about the girls in this car.

"Good," says Bianca. "Because I am not about to get put in prison again because of this girl."

She says the words so bluntly, owning them, but her shoulders give her away. They creep up somewhere near her ears, like they're trying to protect her.

"Again?" I ask. Bianca almost never talks about her life before Gotham U. I want her to know she can. If she wants to.

She just shrugs. "I had a rough childhood."

I know how that goes. "In and out of juvie?"

"Something like that."

She doesn't explain further, and I don't want to pry. Who am I kidding? I totally want to pry, but her face absolutely says not to, and I don't want the other girls in the car thinking I'm a jerk.

So, I sit there. Silently. For many minutes.

"Ugh, I'm starving. This is taking forever." Bianca rips the wrapper off a protein bar like it has personally offended her and shoves a big bite in her mouth.

Jasmin's lips quirk. "Do you ever eat anything besides whey protein?"

"*Yes,*" says Bianca indignantly. "I eat chicken and broccoli and fish too. It's hard to hit two hundred grams a day if you're not careful. I've worked way too hard for these gains." She flexes a bicep, which, I have to say, is pretty impressive.

"Are you training for something?" I ask.

Her face lights up. "Yeah, there's this triathlon I'm doing. The Ironman 70.3 Puerto Rico? It's during the school year, so there's probably not time to fly home and visit my family, but it'll be great to get back to the islands for a little bit. As soon as I finish my race, I'm having tostones and pastelitos de guayaba and conch ceviche and fish stew with dumplings and a piña colada." She sighs just thinking about it. "Plus, the race I'm doing has qualifying slots for the Ironman World Championship. I know it's a long shot, but I'm hoping I can make it. Someday."

"That's so cool. I would love to try a triathlon one day," I say. "Well, maybe one of the shorter ones."

"Oh! We could train together! And you know, it's not a bad idea to do at least some kind of training all the time. It's part of my five pillars of fitness. Have I told you about my five pillars of fitness?"

Jasmin groans. "DO NOT get her started on the five pillars of fitness."

But it's too late. Bianca is already telling us about how if we don't drink 160 ounces of water a day, we'll be dried-up old ladies before we hit thirty. That goes double for us white girls who don't have the benefit of Bianca's Caribeña glow. She and Jasmin bicker in the front seat. In the back seat, Bernice sits next to me quietly, closer than you do if you're just friends. I don't know why I just thought that. *Don't you?* says the voice in my head. I mean, sure, Bernice is my favorite, and I get this happy feeling whenever I'm around her, but that's not enough. Because she's such a nice person, way nicer than me. And if I screw things up, I lose her. That right there is reason enough not to act.

I find myself brushing my knee against hers anyway. The

goose bumps on my legs and the pounding in my chest tell me it's a good idea.

It's only a matter of time until I hurt her somehow.

### An (Abridged) History of Harleen's Ruined Relationships:

**Age 7:** Trey Matthews gives me a store-bought Valentine's Day card and a bouquet of wild-flowers because I'm his girlfriend. I don't like how all the grown-ups are staring at us and say-ing, "Awww," so even though I think he's dreamy, I tell him my other boyfriend gave me a gold bracelet and run away.

**Age 11:** Jason Kim holds my hand at lunch, and for two-tenths of a second I think maybe I am his girlfriend. Then his best friend tells everyone I'm so poor I have fleas, so I whack him upside the head with my lunch tray. His tooth lands in Jason's applesauce. I get an in-school suspension, and Jason never looks at me again.

**Age 13:** Ellie Martinez invites me to her birth-day sleepover. (I do not realize I am deeply in love with her until three years later.) I want to impress her so badly that during Truth or Dare, when the other girls tell me to set all our ex-boyfriends' pictures on fire, I accidentally use too much lighter fluid. Her hair mostly grew back.

**Age 14:** I show up at the eighth-grade dance. With a mullet. My date pretends not to know me. I don't even blame him.

**Age 15:** I get my first restraining order. I DON'T WANT TO TALK ABOUT IT.

**Age 16:** I go out to the fire escape at a party to get some air. Ellie is there, sitting alone. We talk for two hours, and she gives me a kiss that makes me sprout butterfly wings. At school the next day, I catch her flirting with Trey Matthews. I tell her to go to hell because I can't stand looking at her stupid face. Turns out she was breaking up with him to be with me.

Bianca pops up in her seat. "There she is! Grab her!"

Bernice sets down her phone with approximately zero sense of urgency. "That is what you said about the last eleven blond girls."

"It's not my fault they're all blond!"

"Wait, no, this one's really her!" Bernice's eyes go all big, and she freezes like she's not sure what's supposed to happen now.

Bianca and I pull down our masks and fling open our doors in unison, striding toward the girl like we're two parts of the same creature. She's white and slender and wearing a cornflower-blue peacoat. Her high heels *click click click* across the pavement. She hasn't seen us yet. We creep closer.

She perches on the edge of a picnic table, her back to us. "Is it you?" she calls in a clear, calm voice.

Bianca and I flinch. Apparently, we aren't as quiet as we thought.

"Yes," I answer.

"We're going to put a pillowcase over your head until we get to the location. Okay?" says Bianca.

The girl nods and straightens her spine, waiting.

Bianca drapes a black pillowcase over her head, surprisingly gentle for someone with all those muscles.

"You're okay, honey," I tell her, because this whole thing feels a little too much like a kidnapping, and I don't want her to think she's being Taken or something.

We lead her to the car and help her maneuver into the back seat, where she sits pinned between me and Bernice. Jasmin drives us around erratically for a little while, doing laps around campus so it'll feel like we're much farther away. Then she parks at the physics building, which Bianca has all-hours access to, and I pull Kylie from the car, and we march her down to the basement. It's dark down here, and we keep it that way. Dusty pieces of ancient science equipment watch over us. In the middle, there's a circle that we cleared earlier and a small wooden chair. I sit her down.

"Best stay right where you are, honey." I pause. She doesn't answer—has been remarkably quiet this whole time actually. I have a horrible thought and lean forward, but no, she's definitely still breathing in there. I can hear it.

Bianca flicks the switch on a huge, bright-as-the-surface-of-the-sun light and shines it directly on Kylie's covered face. I get ready to remove the pillowcase, silently making eye contact with each of the girls first. *Are you ready? Can you do this?* Even Bernice looks back with steely-eyed resolve.

I pull off the pillowcase and step into the shadows.

So much light. Kylie blinks like a frightened mouse and struggles to get her bearings, but the light keeps her from making much progress.

"We know you've been looking into the Reckoning," I say in my most threatening voice.

"You're going to tell us what you know about the Bayers investigation," says Bernice fiercely.

Damn. Shy girl came ready.

"And when we let you go . . ." Bianca leaps down from her perch on a table, and Kylie flinches at the smack her feet make when they hit the floor. "You're not going to come looking for us again."

We wait.

She's probably terrified.

Gonna spill everything she knows about the investigation and maybe her darkest secrets while she's at it.

I hope she doesn't cry. That would be awkward.

Instead, her face splits into this dazzling smile. She claps her hands together. "I'm SO excited to join your crew! This is even better than sorority initiation! Also, we really need to talk about your brand!"

Jasmin gives me a sideways look.

"Um . . . ," I say stupidly.

Kylie keeps going, chattering like we're at brunch, her turquoise nails flashing in the light. "Social media can absolutely be the difference between whether you're perceived as a hero or a villain. On Twitter, you could flip from one to the other in a single day! Do we have a designated person who brings pumpkin spice lattes to meetings? Because I could do that and also make us super famous."

Jasmin snorts. "So, your superpower is being basic?"

Kylie shrugs. "I think the concept of 'basic' is just another way the patriarchy tells us that things women and girls like or are interested in are less than."

"Yep. She can stay." I throw my hands up in the air. Why the hell not? I like the fiery look she gets when she says the word *patriarchy*.

"Squeeeee!!!" Kylie actually says *squee*. I did not know that was a thing people said out loud.

"Hang on," cuts in Bianca. "We did not all agree to that."

Oops. Mom's definitely glaring at me.

"And I thought you had things to tell us about the Bayers investigation," she adds. "Or was that just so we'd meet with you?"

"Oh, no, that's totally real," chirps Kylie. "See, my dad had Gotham U's president over for dinner this week, and when they were in the library having small-batch bourbon, I was pretending to paint my nails but actually eavesdropping, and I heard them say they were starting a review committee to investigate Dr. Bayers *and* the computer science graduate admissions program as a whole."

Jasmin lights up from the inside out. "Wait, are you serious?"

Kylie nods.

Ohmygosh, we did it. Pranked him with the water, sure. Publicly humiliated him with the video. But, also? We *changed* things.

"This is amazing," I say. "This was the whole point. Of everything." I bump my shoulder against Bianca's. "We did it. Can you believe it?"

She looks moved almost to the point of tears. And Bernice is standing so tall, so proud.

But then it hits her.

"I thought you said the investigation was about us."

Kylie cringes. "Yeah, so that part isn't the best. They've also launched an investigation to find out who the Reckoning is."

Bianca lets out a swear in Spanish just as I say the same one in English. Despite the predicament we're in, we can't help but smirk at each other.

"But it's going to be okay!" Kylie continues. "This is where the branding comes in. I think it's really unlikely that they figure out who y'all are. But on the off chance that they someday do, we need to control the narrative. Build a story where the Reckoning are women's rights heroes. Valiant whistleblowers. Role models for girls everywhere. We do that, and it doesn't matter if they catch you. You'll be untouchable."

I mean, that all sounds pretty freaking great to me. I shrug my shoulders at Bianca, like, *Please? Can we keep her?*

"Give us a minute," Bianca says to Kylie. She's still acting tough, but her rough interrogator voice from before has softened.

"Sure thing!"

Kylie folds her hands in her lap and sits staring blankly into space because she still can't see a damn thing. The rest of us go to the other side of the basement and form a huddle near the boiler room.

"What do you guys think?" I whisper. "She seems pretty cool."

"She *seems* like a good way to get caught." Bianca crosses her muscular arms.

"I like her," says Bernice.

"You like everyone," says Jasmin, not unkindly.

"Pleeeeeeease. Think of the feminist pumpkin spice lattes. Plus, she's right. The more we control our own narrative and the more people know about us *in a secure way*"—I add that last part when I see Jasmin's face—"the more we can change things."

Bianca is going to say yes. I can see it even though her arms are still crossed and her brow is still furrowed. She can't walk away from the chance to make a bigger impact.

"Okay, fine."

"Knew it!"

She snaps her head up to look at me.

"I mean, I think that is an absolutely great decision. Very sound. So, we'll tell her?"

"Yes," says Bianca. "But if she rats us out, I really will make her sorry she ever heard of us."

"I'm sure she'll be very happy to hear that. Let's go give her the news before that light completely burns away what's left of her retinas."

We tell her.

There is much squealing.

Bianca lectures her about the importance of loyalty and honesty and having a full working knowledge of explosives.

Kylie responds with a serious nod followed by additional squealing.

Also, Jasmin finally turns that dang light off. (We're not monsters.)

Kylie says she's been a fan ever since she saw the Dissent Cannon video. She was at this campus dive bar called LuLu's one night when the guys were drunk and bemoaning what had happened. That was when she put the pieces together about who Bernice was. The fact that it was so easy for her to figure out makes me nervous, but before I can really think about it, Jasmin clears her throat.

"Hey, guys, can we talk about something serious?"

I smirk at her. "What could be more serious than a dope social media plan?"

"It's a rumor I've heard." She says it so simply, but a chill rolls through me. Through all five of us. We lean forward like we're sitting around a campfire and Jasmin's about to tell us a ghost story. Only we already know the monsters are real. "There's a professor on campus who's been taking girls."

I frown. "You mean he kidnaps them?"

Jasmin shakes her head. "That's the thing. He gives them back." She swallows, her eyes a mixture of hesitation and fear. "But he gives them back . . . different."

There's quiet as we try to make sense of what she's saying. I don't know where this is going, but I don't like it.

"Different how? What does he do to them?" Bianca asks, her look of disgust matching what I'm feeling.

"I don't know. None of them have ever said."

I pride myself on believing women, but my brain can't help pointing out the obvious. "Surely one of them would have—"

"They can't," says Bernice. Four heads whip toward her. "That's what I've heard, anyway. That they're— That he somehow keeps them from talking about it."

She sits, hunched, in her chair, hands clasped between her knees, eyes fixed on the floor.

"You know about it?" I say. It just comes out of my mouth. "I mean, I'm just surprised is all since we're not technically Gotham U students. I haven't heard anything about it."

"Oh, well, yeah." Bernice looks flustered. "You know, through the whisper network."

"People think he's kind of a serial assaulter. Or attacker. Or whatever it is he's doing," says Jasmin. "Apparently, it's been going back years. And Gotham U has been covering it up."

It takes us a minute for the words to fully sink in. I shake my head. "Wow." That is so incredibly messed up. Both that there's a professor who's such a sadistic trash fire of a human being and that the school is protecting him over its students.

"I can't believe this is happening on our campus," says Bianca.

"I think it's really important that we stop him. And guys like him," says Bernice.

She's staring down at the floor again, and I wonder if she's thinking about what happened to her at that party.

I jump in, wanting to make her feel better. "I'll do some digging. All of us will. And we'll report back at the next meeting."

"Do we have any leads?" asks Kylie. "How did you even find out about it?"

Jasmin shrugs. "Same as Bernice. Whisper network. All I know is that it's happening."

Bianca sweeps her brown hair out of her eyes. "This is exactly the reason I wanted to do this in the first place. To go after men like this."

"Same," I say. It's everything I've been thinking about. And then I can't help but sigh. "I still can't get over the fact that the school is just letting this happen."

Bianca nods. "It's not just individuals we need to go after. It's the whole messed-up system."

She's right. She's right, and we are not only going to kick the hornet's nest, we are going to set it on fire and maybe put a grenade inside for good measure.

"All right, then. We take down the system. And we start by figuring out who this guy is." I look around the circle. "We kick over rocks and talk to people and hack things, but we don't stop until we find out who is doing this and how. We do whatever it takes to end this." I think of the girls who have been hurt, who knows how many. We've got to do something to stop it.

"Promise?"

Five pairs of eyes meeting. Five jaws set with resolve.

"Promise."

# CHAPTER 12

KYLIE LEADS ME UP A STAIRCASE WITH MASSIVE PICTURE frames that have yearbook-style photos of, like, a hundred girls in them, each one in their own little circle. (Apparently, it's called a composite.) I've never been inside a sorority house before. I don't know what I was expecting. Catfights or pillow fights or some kind of fights.

"It's not like in the movies," says Kylie, as if she can read my thoughts. "Except maybe *Legally Blonde*."

There are girls. Everywhere. Giving each other emerald smokey eyes in the bathroom and studying for finals at a big giant table and draped over couches and each other, gossiping.

I just nod. "Thanks for letting me crash here. Especially since we've known each other all of a week." I lower my voice. "I don't really like to be at the apartment during poker night."

But Kylie just waves me off. "Any time. I'm just glad you said something about it or I wouldn't have known to ask you."

"Ask" is an interesting way to describe what happened. I made one teeny little comment about how I wasn't looking forward to my dad's poker night, and Kylie took one look at my face and told me that I had to come sleep over in her room at the sorority house. That I could consider it a Gotham U behind-the-scenes preview if I wanted to. The idea of spending a Friday night pretending to be a Gotham U student was almost more than I could handle. I completely forgot to feel weird about my dad and my situation and what Kylie might think. Well, until now. Now I have that uncomfy feeling you get when it seems like you're accepting a handout.

Kylie opens the door to a room decorated entirely in lavender and yellow and an inexplicable number of narwhals.

"They're our mascot," she says when she catches me looking at the stuffed animal on her bed.

"I'm obsessed. They're my second-favorite animal. Did you know their horn is really a *tooth*?"

"Please." Kylie throws up a hand. "I'm an Alpha Kappa Nu. Of course I know that."

Her room is seriously the coolest. There are all these amazing collages made of magazine cutouts—*National Geographic* photos pieced together to form a narwhal, pictures of makeup and flowers and macarons spelling Kylie's name in lavender letters, a piece made entirely of eyes cut from beauty magazines—just staring at you from the wall. And her desk. She has every kind of makeup in these clear plastic organizers, and a tiered cupcake tray offering a rainbow of nail polishes, and a pale-yellow vintage typewriter that I can't stop looking at.

She pats it gently. "She's my baby."

"You like to write?"

She gets this expression like her face is made of sunbeams. "I love it. I'm one of the only freshmen on the *Clocktower*'s staff this year, and I think I'm gonna add journalism as a double major, even though I'm already neurobio. Sometimes it's hard balancing science me and writing me, but I'm just not ready to let go of any of my dreams, you know?"

"Yeah." I swallow the lump that is suddenly in my throat.

Kylie looks at me for a minute, thoughtfully. "You know, it'd be really cool if you were a new member here when you come to Gotham U next year."

"Really?" I guess I always thought sororities were a rich-girl thing.

But Kylie just smiles. "Totally."

Something pings on her phone. "Oh! You gotta see this!" She jumps on the bed next to me. "My editor just forwarded me this article from the *Clocktower*. Someone did a think piece because the school just made a formal statement about the Bayers thing. Guess they got tired of getting dragged."

She scrolls down, and I read to myself. *Gotham University does not condone sexist or otherwise bigoted behavior . . . committed to equality . . . policy changes for graduate admissions committees campus-wide.*

"Holy crap! It's happening!" I squeal.

"Hells yeah, it is!" Kylie slaps me a high five and then makes me repeat it because our hands don't smack together satisfyingly enough the first time. And honestly, I can't help but appreciate someone who looks like a flawless superprincess while also showing a dorky level of devotion to proper high fives.

Maybe it's not so ridiculous to believe I could fit in here

after all. I start to unroll my sleeping bag. I hope I don't have any bad dreams while I'm here.

*Pop-Tarts on the towel rack, box getting emptier.*

My nightmares can be . . . intense. Waking up screaming in Kylie's room at two in the morning would probably not result in me being invited back.

"Oh, you can sleep in Madison's bed," says Kylie when she sees my sleeping bag. "She's shacking at her boyfriend's tonight."

"Awesome." I swing myself up, pommel horse–style.

Kylie laughs. "Where did you learn to do that?"

I grin. "I'm a gymnast."

"That's so cool! Like, with gold medals and saluting the judges and overzealous parents in the stands wearing T-shirts with your face on them?"

My grin slips. "Yeah. Sure," I say quickly, but it's no use. It's like she can see. How my mom's spot in the stands never got filled. How Coach started letting me work with the younger girls as an assistant in eighth grade to cover my tuition.

"There's no one to come to your meets, is there?" she asks gently.

"Well, my dad has to work a lot, and he—" I try to get a good lie going, but Kylie's onto me. And her persistent face is surprisingly intimidating.

"Harleen. Does anyone come to your meets?"

I hang my head. "No."

But she just smiles brightly and pulls her legs into a butterfly stretch. "Well, I'll come, then. When's your next meet?"

"Tomorrow. But you don't have to do that." I don't need a pity fan.

"I want to. I'll swing by if I finish my journalism essay in time, okay?"

I feel guilty and hopeful at the same time. "Okay."

When I get to my meet on Saturday, I change into my leotard and look for Kylie and do some warm-ups and look for Kylie and get a drink of water and look for Kylie and watch other people's parents start to fill the stands and look for Kylie. I don't find her. And even though I have a lot of practice searching the stands and finding no one, it still hurts. I've given up on my dad ever showing up, but I thought she'd be different.

Luckily, I've got vault up first, and there is no event more perfect for working out unresolved feels. I sprint toward the vaulting horse, arms pumping, legs pounding my aggression into the mats. Leap onto the springboard and punch down hard. And then I fly.

Hands pushing off, body twisting/flipping/slicing through the air. My feet hit the mat with a satisfying *thwack*. And I throw up my arms in victory because I just stuck the landing like a boss, and I don't need anyone else. Just me, myself, and—

ME.

There is my face. In the crowd. Staring back at me. (It's on a shirt—I don't have an evil twin or anything.) I look up at the person wearing the shirt, and, oh, it's Kylie, and she's cheering with a smile so big.

And not just Kylie. Bianca is doing one of those two-fingered whistles like she's hailing a cab in the 1930s. And

Jasmin is jumping up and down. And Bernice is ringing a cowbell. A COWBELL. My heart is so full, and I can feel myself turning bright red and giving them a little wave like—

Like how I used to do when my mom was still alive and would rearrange her work schedule so she could make it to every meet.

Alexa runs over and gives me a post-event hug. And then she frowns. "Hey, why are you crying?"

I shake my head and say, "I'm just really happy."

As soon as I can get away, I sneak over to the stands and tackle-hug all of them.

"I am completely obsessed with every last one of you!" I yell. I look at Kylie. "Did you really do all this?"

She gives me a bouncy shrug. "I wanted to see you compete. And I may have mentioned it to Bernice. And she may have mentioned it to Jasmin and Bianca. . . ."

Bianca jumps in like she just can't help herself. "You guys are amazing athletes. I have so many questions."

"You were incredible," breathes Bernice. She looks up at me through her eyelashes, and my heart collapses in on itself.

"Truly," agrees Jasmin.

It sets off the tears all over again. I swipe at my cheeks, and Kylie says, "Aw, Harleen." And before you know it, they are all hugging me at once, and I don't know how I became the luckiest person on the planet, but I'll take it.

This is love. Arms wrapped tight around you. And unconditional support. And someone screaming your name into the air like it's the most joyful word ever invented. And people who care about you enough to show up.

I forgot how wonderful it could feel.

# CHAPTER 13

## WEDNESDAY, APRIL 6

I TRY NOT TO THINK ABOUT HOW IT'S TWO DAYS LATER AND Bernice still hasn't woken up. Focus on the western blot I'm working on. I tip the little tray toward me so that the light reflects off the membrane. It looks like just a shiny piece of white paper. Photo paper, maybe. It's so strange that there's an entire universe of proteins on this thing that's smaller than a birthday card, but it just looks blank. For now.

Bernice's face, blank and white, in the hospital. Eyelids shut.

*You want to know what else I was lying about?*

Shake it off. Focus. This is my favorite part of the western blot.

*You and B were pretty heated the other night.*

Pour the tube of red liquid labeled PONCEAU STAIN over the blot. Gently rock the tray back and forth. Dozens of thin pink lines begin to emerge where before there was nothing. Bands of proteins. Neatly sorted by size. Getting darker by the second.

*Are you ever scared by how much darkness there is inside you?*

I tip the tray and pour the Ponceau stain back into the tube. Then I get out the destaining solution and pour it over the blot to make the reddish-pink lines disappear. It smells like dyeing Easter eggs. Like when my mom was still alive.

*You've got more on yourself than the eggs, Harleen.*

*Mommy, aren't they pretty?!*

*They're beautiful.*

Lungs working overtime. Kind nurse. Gotham Memorial.

*They're saying I've got a bad heart, baby.*

The last time someone I love went into that place, she didn't come out.

DON'T think about that.

The blot is white again. All traces of the dye have disappeared. That part of the experiment is just a test. You want to check whether your proteins ended up on the blot. You're making sure they're there. And mine were. And they are. Even after all the color is gone.

I am thinking there is something meta I could say about all this when a voice startles me.

"Harleen Quinzel."

I know I recognize the voice and that it scares me before I turn around and see that it belongs to Officer Montoya.

"You have the right to remain silent," she says all serious-like as she crosses the lab toward me.

"Wait, what?" I'm being arrested? Holy crap, I'm being arrested.

She recites the rest of my Miranda rights, but I can't seem to make it make sense inside my head.

"You're seriously arresting me right now?"

"I seriously am."

I hear shuffling in the office space next door.

A voice: *Was that the police?*

And another: *What's going on?*

A small crowd forms in the doorway. Oliver, Kijoon, and, because I am the unluckiest person on the face of the planet, Trent. I haven't hooked up with him since January, but he has the uncanny ability to materialize whenever things are going wrong for me, like he's the freaking ghost of hookups past.

It occurs to me that I would rather do just about anything than be arrested in front of Trent. It also occurs to me that I am still holding the tray with my blot in it. "Yeah, can it wait until I finish this western blot?"

Officer Montoya looks at me like I'm growing a third arm out of the middle of my forehead.

"Because Dr. Nelson is not gonna be happy."

Her side-eye only intensifies. "Um, *no.*"

"You've clearly never worked for a principal investigator."

I hear a jangling sound. Officer Montoya pulling a pair of handcuffs from her belt.

"Whoa, okay. Sorry! You don't have to do that. I'll come quietly. I've already told you everything anyway. I—"

"In this case, I think it's necessary." She continues with the handcuffing, and I can *feel* the joy Trent takes from this situation from clear across the room. It makes me look at him in spite of myself, and when I do, that waste of air actually smirks at me.

I lunge toward him, leaping ten feet in the air and twisting away from Montoya, handcuffs dangling. Grab Trent by his popped collar. Lift him to the ceiling. Watch the fear spark in his eyes as I—

Shake my head. He's not even worth it. I can't believe I

used to make out with that clown. I remain calm in front of Officer Montoya and allow her to finish fastening my handcuffs.

She doesn't clamp them tight, though, and I take it as a sign that maybe she doesn't think I'm an irredeemable lowlife after all.

I turn my head and look her directly in the eyes. Trent is still hovering like a freaking vulture, but I make myself say it anyway. "I know I was the one who found Bernice. And I know it looks bad that I didn't tell you we were dating. But I would never do anything to hurt her." I hesitate, and when I finally do say the words—ones I've only ever said to Bernice once—my voice is delicate. "I love her."

Officer Montoya's eyes soften for a moment. "This isn't about Bernice."

I'm so confused, I can't even piece together a question, but she answers anyway, her eyes steely again.

"A girl named Kylie Pearce is dead. And the coroner just found your name written on her ankle."

# JANUARY

# CHAPTER 14

"CAN YOU BELIEVE SOMEONE WE KNOW LIVES IN A HOUSE like this?" whispers Bernice.

Our shoes *clip-clop* on the brick pavers as we walk up to Dr. N's house. Mansion? House. I look up. And up. And up. Balconies and brass door knockers and plants perched happily in urns that probably cost more than our rents combined.

"It honestly feels criminal." I wrinkle my nose but force myself to stop it because Dr. N is really nice and never acts like an obnoxiously rich person.

Every January, he has a get-together at his house for all the Gotham U Bridge Scholars because he's the head of the program.

Neither of us has knocked yet. Bernice is looking up at the house like it might eat her.

"Hey," I say quietly. "We belong here just as much as anybody else. Got it?"

She gives me a firm nod. "Got it."

I adjust the poster tube on my shoulder like I'm walking into battle and rap my knuckles on the thick exposed-wood door. A woman with an aggressively wide smile opens it.

"Well, hellooooo. I'm Beverly. I handle all of the admin aspects of the Bridge Scholars program. We are *so* excited for you to be here tonight. Let me get you all signed in and show you where you can set up your posters."

She shoves some name tags at us, her smile growing, if possible, even bigger.

"I'm so proud to be a part of this program. And tonight is such a great opportunity to get to know you all and see your work."

I relax a bit. She wants to see our science. Yeah, she may be intense in a we're-shaping-the-scientific-future-of-the-world kind of way, but it's actually sorta cute.

"I know this isn't the type of thing you'd normally get to do, what with where you're *from*, and we're so happy to be able to do this for you. You've probably never even been to a party like this, huh?"

And . . . I retract my previous statement. Thanks for reminding me just how poor I am, you evil harpy. I hope you choke on some bad caviar, or whatever the eff it is they're serving. Bernice tries to put a hand on my shoulder, but we are already way past the point of no return. I fix Mommy Warbucks with a smile of my own.

"Thank you ever so much. And you're right. I hardly know what to do without the malt liquor and Doritos. I bet the roaches you guys have are, like, really small."

Her billion-kilowatt smile goes brittle. If I flicked my finger against her teeth, they'd shatter and fall to the floor in pieces.

"Think we can find our posterboards on our own, but let me know if you need someone to make a beer run." I flutter my fingers over my shoulder at her as we walk away.

Bernice and I weave past the grand spiral staircase and jacketed waitstaff serving crab cakes and stuffed mushrooms off silver trays. *We belong here. We belong here,* I tell myself. I'm wearing my usual smart-person disguise (secondhand pantsuit, sensible shoes, hair in bun, black-rimmed glasses that aren't even real), but I feel like people can see right through it to the East End girl underneath. I approach a couple of older men in suits—professors, I'm guessing, but way older than Dr. N—because despite what I told Mommy Warbucks at the door, I have no idea where our posters go. They don't notice me, so I clear my throat. Still nothing. Right, so, they do realize I'm here, they're just studiously ignoring me. I'm taking a deep breath and preparing myself to ask, when a familiar voice cuts in.

"Harleen! Bernice! I'm so glad you're here!"

Dr. N.

Thank. Goodness.

"Let me show you where to pin those posters. Did you get here okay?"

He leads us outside to a massive covered tent with lighting and heat pumping in and everything. There are rows and rows of what look almost like oversized easels, displaying posters with all kinds of research: flight patterns of Gotham City's eagles and fecal matter transplants and transgenic monkeys that glow in the dark. I heave a sigh of relief. I may not know how to recognize a salad fork, but I know when I'm among my people.

Dr. N grabs us a paper cup filled with pushpins and helps

Bernice and me hang our posters. He stretches his arms high next to me. He's taller than I realized.

"Is that level?" he asks Bernice. "We want them to be perfectly level."

"You're good!" she calls back.

"Excellent." He rubs his hands together. "I have to go make the rounds. As head of the program, I like to make it to everyone's poster. Anyway, you're both going to do great. Remember, people just want the gist of your work. Use your thirty-second speech on most of the people who come by, and save your full walk-through for the ones who are really interested."

I grin. "Got it."

I'm so excited. My first real scientific presentation. The beginning of my scientific career. I stare dopily up at my poster.

## THE ROLE OF SV1 GENE POLYMORPHISMS IN SUPER-VILLAIN PATHOGENESIS
### HARLEEN QUINZEL, OLIVER ROSS, BERNICE WATKINS, AARON NELSON

Bernice and I practice on each other a couple times to get our jitters out. Then some other students from the Bridge Scholars program come by, and some Gotham U faculty members, and before I know it, an hour has passed, and I keep saying the same thing over and over, but instead of being boring, it keeps getting better. *I* keep getting better. A clearer explanation here. A well-timed joke there. Bernice and I take pictures of each other whenever one of us has a lag in their audience. We want to remember this night.

An older professor approaches just as I'm finishing up and my listeners shuffle along to the next poster. I glance at his name tag. Dr. Jonathan Perry. Holy crap, his paper revolutionized the way we think about schizophrenia.

I throw out my hand confidently. "Hi, I'm Harleen Quinzel."

He has a smile that can only be described as jolly. "Nice to meet you. I'm Jonathan Perry."

"Would you like me to walk you through my poster?"

"Absolutely. I've had my eye on you. Been trying to get over here all evening to see your work."

"Really?"

This. Is. Awesome. I try to be animated but not too excited, because I've been told my excitement can come off as ditzy, which frankly seems pretty sexist, but I want to impress this professor so badly that I'll take any advice ever. I see Bernice snap a picture over his shoulder and give me a big thumbs-up. It's all the encouragement I need to dive in.

"So, I work in Dr. Nelson's lab, and we're very interested in the SV1 gene. We think differences in this gene could be responsible for determining how likely it is that someone becomes a Super-Villain. Here, I've genotyped the blood samples from Arkham patients and controls—" I point at the two sets of data on the graph. "And you can see that the Arkham inmates are much more likely to have the SV1-b version of the gene, while controls are more likely to have the SV1-a version."

I turn back to Dr. Perry to make sure I'm not losing him.

"Very nice," he says. Only he's not looking at my poster. He's staring directly at my breasts.

"Um, right, so. The SV1-b polymorphism. Well, this

graph shows that it's higher. In the Arkham patients." My clothes feel tighter, and the tent feels hotter. And oxygen. There's definitely less of it in the air right now.

A flash of gold catches the light. He's wearing a gold tie clip, I realize. Just like the professor who said that awful thing to Morgan.

"How many patients have you run?" he asks. His eyes don't move. Not even for a second.

Am I really supposed to answer him under these conditions? The Harleen that grew up in the East End and pumped a professor's office full of water a couple weeks ago screams that I should snap my fingers in front of me and tell him eyes up here, right before I knee him in the groin, rip the champagne flute from his hand, and smash it against the posterboard, only to use the jagged end to—

I calmly place my hands in the pockets of my pantsuit so he can't see them curl into fists. Calmly answer all of the questions, despite them being directed at my breasts.

But as soon as he walks away, I whisper to Bernice.

"When's our next Reckoning mission? I need to blow something up."

The way he made me feel in that moment isn't the worst part. The way I feel after is devastating.

*How stupid are you, Harleen?* To think an award-winning professor, a luminary in the field, could actually be interested in your little science project? OF COURSE he was only there to talk to your breasts.

*You may be going off to that fancy school every day, but that doesn't make you one of them.*

I watch Dr. Perry corner a pretty redhead across the room.

*Idiot. You can't even screw the lid on the peanut butter right. How are you gonna get a scholarship?*

I narrow my eyes like I'm trying to shoot lasers out of them.

"I'm going to go do some recon on Dr. Perry," I tell Bernice.

I walk up and down the aisles, scanning the titles of the posters and, more important, the author blocks.

Nope.

Nope.

Nope.

There. *Establishing a New Rodent Model of Schizophrenia. Sloane Garcia-Richardson.* And *Jonathan F. Perry.*

I throw on my most dazzling and disarming smile. "Hi!" I say to the girl with nut-brown hair and an ill-fitting pencil skirt. "I'm Harleen. Do you mind walking me through your poster?"

"Sure. You're in the Bridge Scholars program too, right?" She smiles and tugs at her skirt.

I nod. "Yep."

"I thought I saw you at one of our seminars."

I ask about a billion questions about her work and how she's liking the program so far. And then I drop the question I've really been wanting to ask.

"So, what's it like working with Dr. Perry?"

"Oh." Her face clouds, but she tries to hide it just as quickly.

I lean forward conspiratorially. "I've heard some stuff."

(Truth: I haven't. But I have a feeling I'm about to.)

"Well," she begins. Looks from left to right, tugs at her

skirt, and begins again. "He's kind of a creeper. Like, he's always making these skeevy jokes, and it's like he can't even see that everyone's so uncomfortable."

"I hate that! How can they not know?"

Sloane nods vigorously. "Right? Anyway, your professor seems pretty cool. Letting everyone come over to his house and stuff. He was really nice when he stopped by and asked me questions earlier."

"Yeah. Yeah, I really like Dr. N." How to get this back to Dr. Perry? "I'm really enjoying my project. And tonight has been really cool." Bingo. I force my face to fall like I'm embarrassed. "Actually, it hasn't. I was super excited about presenting my poster, and Dr. Perry came over, but he stared at my boobs. The. Whole. Time."

"Ohmygosh, he's always doing that," says Sloane. My confession really cracks the floodgates open. She talks about how he's always staring at the women in the lab. Putting a hand on a shoulder for a few seconds too long.

"Has he ever, like, done anything really bad?" I ask.

"Okay, you can't tell anyone I told you." She lowers her voice to a whisper. Whatever it is, it's gonna be big. "But we do a lot of optogenetics research, so he was one of the higher-ups in organizing this big annual optogenetics conference. And he named it Breaking Observations in Optogenetics and Brain Stimulation."

She waits like I'm supposed to get some big reveal.

"Ummm . . ."

"BOOBS. He named it BOOBS."

"Oh. *Seriously?*"

She nods. "Uh-huh. And at first maybe people didn't notice or maybe they thought it was funny, but then the men at the conference started making the women uncomfortable by basically turning the entire meeting into a three-day-long boob joke. He even made a half-day preconference called JUGS."

(Apparently, it stands for Journey to Understanding next-Generation Stimulation. Clearly, they were reaching.)

"Dude. That is so messed up."

"I know!"

After Sloane and I finish talking, I go back to my poster and finish off the presentation portion of the evening. Then there's time for mingling, but Bernice and I are kind of over it, so even though I know it would behoove me to chat up more creepy old dudes in hopes of getting a scholarship, we snag an entire tray of fancy snacks and hide in the mudroom, which is the name for this whole separate room that rich people have just for taking off your jacket.

"What do you think? You think Dr. Perry could be the guy we're looking for?" I pop another mini-quiche into my mouth. With Bernice in here with me, I could almost forget I hate enclosed spaces.

"Maybe." Bernice picks at her cuticle.

"Hey, are you okay? Did something happen tonight?"

"No." She freezes like a captured animal. "Actually, yeah."

Oh crap. If Perry got to her too—

"I was hanging out with this really cool girl, and we snuck away from this phony-posh party, and it was so great. But then she started eating all the mini-quiches."

"I did not!"

Bernice pointedly directs her eyes at the tray that now contains exactly one mini-quiche.

"Oh."

She grabs the quiche and stuffs it in her mouth like a

cartoon character, only she can barely chew it because she can't stop giggling, and then I start giggling, and then it's all over. She ends up spray-laughing crumbs down the front of her dress.

She swats at the crumbs. "Damn mini-quiches."

It only makes me laugh harder.

Now that our snack tray is empty, we should probably get back to the party. We don't, though.

I am very acutely aware of how alone we are. Of what it might mean that neither of us moves to get up. After a minute, Bernice shifts the way she's sitting on the bench and her wrist bumps against mine. I don't think much of it. Until I realize she's not pulling it away. Our wrists are just sitting there, canoodling. Bernice. Is making a move. On me.

And I like it.

I am about two seconds away from leaping over this quiche tray and kissing her (with consent, obvs), but I try to focus on the Reckoning and how I don't want to do anything stupid that will cause me to lose them. Like making out with someone else in our girl gang. Bernice moves her arm so that her wrist isn't just touching mine. It is rubbing along the entire length of my forearm. *When did she become a wanton seductress?*

I try not to return her arm brushing. (Fail.)

Try not to turn toward her. (Fail.)

Try not to think about how her eyes are searing into mine and that her lips are parted ever so—

The partially open door to the mudroom opens all the way with a *thwack*, and I nearly fall off the bench because I am just that cool.

A girl wearing all black—shirt, pants, apron—narrows her eyes at us. "What are you doing in here?"

"Nothing!" I blurt out. Cool as you please.

Why is it so hard to breathe right now, and what in the actual eff was that?

Bernice giggles into the back of her hand.

The waitstaff girl only eyes us harder. Can she tell that we're from the East End? Can she smell it on us? "Um, okay."

She watches us leave the mudroom and inspects the empty quiche tray suspiciously. We dissolve into laughter as soon as we round the corner.

"Do you think she knows we ate them all?" asks Bernice.

"She is the quiche police. Of course she knows."

It really is about time we get back to the party, though. People have started trickling out the door now.

"You want to head out?" asks Bernice.

I scan the party until I find Dr. N laughing in his study with a couple other investigators. "I was hoping to talk to Dr. Nelson," I say.

I keep telling myself there are too many people. That the whole point of tonight was to try to catch a minute alone with him to go over some of my ideas without guys from the lab like Trent trying to mock me, and if I can just wait for a few more people to drift out that door, I can make it happen. So I stick around. Bernice lags behind too. Eventually, we're among the last few people left at the party.

"It's okay, really," I tell her.

"Are you sure? I feel bad about leaving you to get home by yourself."

"I'll be fine. I promise. I'll catch up with you in lab tomorrow."

Bernice nods, but there's a hint of something in her face. Disappointment?

I shake it off, and just as I'm turning back toward Dr. N

and the last couple stragglers, opportunity strikes. Dr. N steps away from the two profs talking heatedly about whether $p$ values really are the best metric for determining meaningful results. He's filling up his wineglass. Perfect!

"Hi, Dr. N!"

He jumps. I guess that's a thing that happens when people appear at your elbow. "Harleen, I didn't know you were still here."

He seems surprised, but definitely not annoyed, so I go for it. "I was hoping to talk to you about some ideas I have. About the SV1 gene. If it's not too late," I add.

I wait for his answer, fingers crossed behind my back, eyes tracing over the display of antique knives and throwing stars on the wall behind him. He is seriously the coolest professor I know.

"Of course. Of course. I always have time for my students." He tops off his red and goes to put the bottle down.

He sits and I sit too, both literally and metaphorically taking a seat at the table. I wish little East End Harleen could see me now.

"What did you want to talk about?" he says kindly.

"I—" My breath seizes in my lungs. C'mon, Harleen, this is your Big Scientific Idea, and this may be your only chance to pitch it without the peanut gallery. "I've been thinking about your work with the SV1 gene. I think the idea of a potential Super-Villain gene is fascinating—it's why I wanted to work with you so badly."

I hesitate. Is this going to sound like I'm saying my ideas are better than his?

"But you have your own take," he says, rescuing me. "That's okay. It's good. I want to hear about it."

I heave a sigh of relief, but it's still hard to get the words out. "I was thinking, well, what if it's not simply a matter of having a different version or polymorphism of the SV1 gene that makes someone a Super-Villain? What if we also looked at epigenetics? What if every time a person experiences trauma, it causes a posttranslational modification to the gene, and if a person accumulates enough life trauma, it increases their chances of becoming a Super-Villain?"

I did it. I put it all out there. I have never been this terrified. A lifetime of my dad telling me I'm worthless is working against me.

"It's an interesting idea," says Dr. N, rubbing his close-cropped beard that is all brown with just a few white flecks. "But not everyone who experiences trauma becomes a Super-Villain."

"Right," I say. "Because not everyone has a dangerous version of the SV1 gene, like you talked about in that *Science* paper. But what if it's a combination of a bad SV1 gene *and* traumatic life experiences? Or what if some people experience trauma and their genes are like, 'Yeah, okay,' but other people experience trauma and their genes are like, 'Holy crap, imma modify a million things right now'?"

I realize I'm totally talking like a ditzy high schooler, and also that my hands are vibrating from all the coffee I've had this evening. It is possible these two things are related.

But Dr. N just grins. "I think you might have something there."

I feel like I could float right out the window and into the Milky Way.

He holds up his glass. "To new ideas and scientific discovery. Oops, I need a refill."

He pours more wine into his empty glass. He asks me more questions, and I talk and talk and talk. So does he. I don't even know how much time has gone by. The other two professors say their goodbyes, but we barely notice. The words and ideas are flying, and we plan and we scheme, digging into a flourless chocolate cake leftover from the party and spouting off outlandish theories. I feel like my scholarship dreams are closer than ever. I can barely believe it. To be talked to like an equal, by such a prominent scientist. To talk to a man who doesn't belittle me.

And then he says it. Well past midnight. Cheeks red. Eyes bright.

"You know," he says. "You know, I think you might be the most brilliant scientific mind I've seen in a long time."

I'm so overcome with emotion that I squeeze his hand impulsively. This is the best day of my entire life.

# CHAPTER 15

*DAY HARLEEN:* GOES TO LAB AT THE CRACK OF DAWN. DOES her experiments on epigenetics in the SV1 gene. Attends Abnormal Psych and the Bridge Scholars courses.

*Night Harleen:* Is the Reckoning.

*Day Harleen:* Preps for her scholarship interviews. Goes to gymnastics practice. (And teaches the younger girls so as to afford gymnastics practice.) Checks her mailbox four times a day and her email four times a minute, hoping/dreaming/wishing for an acceptance.

*Night Harleen:* Checks the virtual suggestion box Jasmin made for women to submit names and stories. (Well, not just women. Bianca amended the fight to include anyone who has been a victim of the patriarchy. Don't want to exclude people who might need our help.)

*Day Harleen:* Ponders how a sample from The Joker might compare with her samples from the Arkham patients.

*Night Harleen:* Combs social media, hoping to race to a crime scene and collect a rogue drop of blood or a stray green hair.

*Day Harleen:* Hears a rumor about a chemistry professor who bullied a grad student out of his lab for daring to have a child.

*Night Harleen:* Sneaks twenty-three screaming robot babies into Jack McKinnon's lab.

*Day Harleen:* Gasps over her turkey sandwich at the very idea.

"I heard they had on real diapers," says Kijoon.

"No way," says Michael.

But Kijoon just nods all the more fervently. "With real poop! It got all over him!"

"EWWW."

"Nah, that's nasty."

(Look, it was actually only guacamole, and Kylie only put it on the robot baby in his desk drawer.)

"And . . . now my lunch is ruined." Morgan pushes Kijoon's shoulder, and he grabs one of her chicken nuggets and pops it into his mouth.

"Hey!"

"You said it was ruined!"

I pretend their bickering is the only reason I'm smiling.

*Everyone* is talking about us. Not just in my lab—all around campus. It was even in the news.

*The Reckoning,* they say to each other.

A girl.

No, not a girl. Multiple girls.

They're terrorists. No, activists. No, feminists. Some kind of -ist who makes cishet men look over their shoulders.

"I heard he told her, 'You know, I only took one week off after I had a baby,'" says Kijoon. "And that she was like, 'Oh really? Was there stuff leaking out of you?' And then she walked out and never looked back."

Wrong.

"No, no, no. I heard from a friend in the chem department who's friends with her best friend that he told her 'This really isn't a good time to have a baby,'" says Morgan, suddenly serious. "And then he boxed her out. Like, created a hostile work environment and stuff."

It's true. It's also true that he grilled her about "whether or not it was planned."

I splay my hands in front of me like a showman. "You know what I heard?" I pause dramatically until someone asks what. "I heard he made her come in and go to a seminar even though her cervix was already dilated. She practically had her baby on her chair."

Complete and total lie.

Makes them squeal, though.

Also makes me seem like I have no idea what I'm talking about when it comes to the Reckoning.

For example, I definitely don't know that the words spray-painted on the wall across from Dr. McKinnon's desk are *Since we know you're going to ask, these babies were definitely planned—hope you find all 24!* and not *I hope you catch gonorrhea in hell*, like Kijoon is trying to convince Morgan.

I wouldn't know a thing about sneaking into a person's lab and office at night (too easy) or where to procure a robot army of infant simulators formerly used to teach high school sophomores about the seriousness of parenthood (the supply closet in Alexa's health class).

And I haven't the faintest clue what it feels like to imagine Dr. McKinnon coming into his office this morning, seeing the words and wondering what they mean, and at some point, after the screams registered, spending the rest of the day finding wailing cybernetic newborns in cabinets and under benchtops and above ceiling tiles. I hope he's still searching for that nonexistent twenty-fourth one.

Bernice, on the other hand? She has not said a word this entire lunch AND her face is the color of her spaghetti sauce AND she's making a weird expression like she's trying to eat her lips. Bernice "Zero Chill" Watkins. Yep, that's her. I tap my foot against hers under the table so she'll stop looking so damn stricken, and her eyes go big and she shovels another bite of spaghetti in her mouth.

And then there's Trent. He's making that smug face he gets whenever he's about to say something "radical" to show what a "freethinker" he is, when really he's about to be sexist or racist or some other kind of -ist that makes my blood boil.

He clears his throat. "Here's my take on it. Who's to say that this Reckoning chick is right? I mean, for all we know, this lady stopped doing her job well after she had a baby. My dad says he's seen it tons of times since he started as a professor."

"Wait, your dad's a professor?" says Morgan. "Here?"

Yes, Morgan, that's the part to latch on to in that whole entire steaming pile of horse manure.

But when Trent says, "Yeah," I can't help but blurt out, "What department?"

He sits up in his chair stiffly. "Computer Science."

Trent. Trent *Bayers.*

"HOLY CRAP, YOUR DAD IS *THAT* DR. BAYERS?!"

Oops. Guess I didn't need to shout that. In the break room. In front of half the lab.

Trent gets all red-faced.

"Yeah. He is. And now he's been asked to resign from two national foundations and he's facing an inquiry because of that Reckoning person." Only he doesn't say *person*. He calls her/us/whatever a word that makes Bernice gasp.

Oliver starts to say, "Hey—," but Trent is already slamming his lunch into the trash and walking out the door.

At the last second, he looks over his shoulder and fixes me with the coldest stare. "Wish I knew who it was. I'd definitely pay her a visit."

I swallow and pretend to look innocent.

It's harder than it was a few minutes ago.

*Day Harleen:* Ditches Trent. Look, I was just standing in the darkroom, alone, and trying not to let my throat close up over the fact that I was in the darkroom (alone!!), when he waltzes in like I gave him a personal invitation to kiss my neck. And as he was slobbering his way from my collarbone to my earlobe, I realized . . . I didn't want him to anymore. And I told him as much. (He took it about as well as you'd expect.) Exhibit #357 that Harleen Quinzel has a cold black heart that is incapable of loving others and will always end up hurting people, including beautiful strawberry-haired girls who are passionate about women's rights and making art out of horrifying stuffed animals.

*Night Harleen:* Can't stop daydreaming about Bernice when she's supposed to be blasting people with Dissent Cannons and ridding the world of injustice.

# CHAPTER 16

I WAS GOING TO DO IT ALONE.

I had it all planned out and everything, based on papers I found on PubMed. Ten sessions of exposure therapy spread over eight weeks. Audio that I listened to in between sessions. I was going to conquer my fears. Change my brain and my life and my choices. Put a stop to the nightmares and intrusive memories and the waves of panic I feel when a trigger hits me just right.

I'm still going to do all that. But after the girls showed up at my gymnastics meet, I realized something.

I don't have to do this by myself.

The hardest part was figuring out who to ask. I knew I didn't want to have a whole audience, but how do you pick between four people who are that awesome? I eventually settled on texting Bianca. I felt like I could be honest with her about my childhood and she wouldn't judge me. That maybe she'd even understand.

I hope I'm right because I just heard a knock at the door.

"Hey." I open the door to find a smiling Bianca on the other side. I try not to feel nervous for all the same reasons I was nervous for Bernice to see my place.

Bianca's smile is so big I completely forget. "Hey!" She holds up a big Ziploc bag. "I brought you these guava pastries my abuelita taught me how to make when I was little. Victory pastries, you know?"

I give her an extra-long hug because just having her here makes me less anxious about what I have to do. "Thank you so much," I tell her hair.

"So, how does this work?"

"Yeah, so." I lead her to my room. My dad is *definitely* gone all day today. I checked and double-checked. "I'm doing this thing called exposure therapy, where I try to expose myself to the thing I'm scared of. Which for me is being in small spaces."

Bianca nods. "I didn't know you were claustrophobic."

"It's kinda like that," I say. "But only if I'm alone. And especially if the door is shut or I'm locked in. But also, it's kind of like PTSD? It's from some stuff that happened when I was little."

I can tell Bianca wants to ask me more about what happened, but she doesn't, and I really appreciate it. I don't think I'm ready to talk about it yet.

"So, okay. Maybe you could just sit on the bed and wait, and I'll go into my closet and try to slay some dragons?"

Bianca shrugs. "Sounds good to me. I'm here for you, whatever you need."

"Thanks." Have I mentioned lately how lucky I am?

I go to my closet and take a deep breath. And then another. It was easy to be brave twenty minutes ago when

I was shoving all my shoes from the floor of my closet to the floor of my bedroom. But now I'm eyeing my closet floor like the crappy carpet is going to eat me and spit out my bones. I would rather do just about anything than go inside that dark, stuffy coffin right now. But I promised myself I'd give it a shot, trained professional or no. I'm sick of having an uncontrollable adrenaline spike every time I hear a door lock, and it would be really nice to be able to be in an enclosed space without feeling like I'm having a heart attack.

So, okay. Let's do this.

I place an old blanket on the floor. Squish my clothes to one side as far as they'll go. Brush my fingers against the back wall. It's close—it's not like we have the biggest closets in the East End—but honestly, that's probably better for what I'm doing. I step inside, feeling the soft blanket against my feet, telling myself that Bianca will be there this whole time. I'm not really alone. The walls are close to my shoulders on both sides, but I try not to let that get to me.

The old memories try to tug at my brain, send my cortisol and hormones through the roof so my pulse will race and my skin will crackle and my throat will close up entirely.

I don't let them.

I am in control right now. I am safe in this closet with one of my best friends waiting outside. I can get out anytime I like, and she will be there.

I take slow, yoga instructor breaths until my heartbeat settles down and armpits stop sweating. (Feeling glad I didn't ask Bernice now.) I'm able to wrestle my fear into a coffin and tack nails in all around. Keep it contained. I focus on that as I sink to the floor, sitting cross-legged. My knees bump the wall, but it's okay. I am in control. This closet may be dark and small, but I am safe.

More yoga breaths. Relax my muscles. Elongate my spine. I think I'm ready to try closing the door. I reach out my arm, hear it shut with a snap—that's when everything falls apart.

*Door swinging shut. Pop-Tarts box on the towel rack. Pillow in the bathtub.*

The coffin springs open, and my fear flies out like a monster, wrapping its sharp, bony arms around me and pulling me back back back into the darkness. The walls shrink. Time winds backward.

*I'm gonna die. I'm gonna die. I'm gonna die.* I crab-walk/fall out of my closet and onto the floor.

But even as I'm bursting into tears, there are strong arms lifting me up. Holding me together.

"You're okay. You've got this. You did great," Bianca tells me, her voice soft and firm and reassuring.

I hug her tight and sob against her and say unintelligible things. She doesn't mind.

And when the tears stop, she reminds me that there are still pastries made of guava paste and soft white cheese, except she calls them pastelitos de guayaba y queso this time. I take a bite, and they taste like love.

"I'm here for you," she says. "I know what it's like to climb out of a really dark place."

"Thank you," I tell her. I will never be able to thank her enough.

# CHAPTER 17

## WEDNESDAY, APRIL 6

IT'S HARD TO BELIEVE THAT KYLIE'S REALLY DEAD UNTIL they show me the pictures. Officer Montoya slaps the stack down on the table in front of me—I think she's getting tired of my nonanswers. Or maybe she's hoping this'll be like one of those old cop movies, where she squeezes me until I finally crack and pour out a tearful confession. That's honestly what this whole experience has felt like up until now. But seeing Kylie's lifeless body spread out in front of me, dozens of photographs forming a grotesque collage—it's real.

Her empty eyes stare out of the photo nearest me. Cold. No sparkle. I'll never get to hear her laugh again or get bubble tea with her at SunO. She had so many plans—to be editor in chief of a magazine, to backpack through New Zealand, to meet Timothée Chalamet—and now they're just . . . gone.

A tear slides down my cheek and lands on the metal table that is bolted to the floor.

"I'm sorry to upset you." Officer Montoya moves to gather the photos.

"No." I hold my hands over Kylie's picture. "It's okay. It's important to figure out who did this."

A single decisive nod. "It seems like you were very close to her."

And . . . I guess the empathy portion of this interrogation is over. Make no mistake: when Montoya says things like that, she's needling. Hoping to pry something out of you.

"I told you I was friends with her," I say tightly.

"Yes, and that's interesting in and of itself. How did you get to be such good friends with a college student from the other side of town?"

I shrug as nonchalantly as possible. "People tend to become friends when they have similar interests." Like smashing the patriarchy. And colorful mascara.

"Do you think she was in the Reckoning with Miss Watkins?" Montoya presses.

Why does this woman care so much about the Reckoning? "No."

She nods—in a way that suggests she actually believes me for once. "It was a long shot. She's in a sorority. Seems like she's one of those Instagram influencers. Doesn't really fit the type."

I bristle but don't say anything. I'm all too familiar with what it's like to be a woman and have people assume they know things about you because your hair is too blond or too bouncy and you're not afraid to want things. Another thing I loved about Kylie: she didn't think the measure of a woman's soul was found in the distance between her skirt and her kneecaps.

And then I realize something about the pictures in front of me. Kylie doesn't have any wounds. I search her neck for signs of bruising, her slender legs for lacerations, her clothes for blood.

My brows knit together. "How did she die?"

"Excuse me?"

"She doesn't have any injuries—not that I can see, anyway." I scrutinize the photos again, hoping for something I missed the first time.

It is then that I realize Officer Montoya has a photo clasped to her chest, blank side facing me.

"It's interesting that you would notice that," she says in a way that's meant to sound calm but is actually accusatory.

"I already told you I didn't do it!"

The caged-animal feeling flares up in me again. I can feel the target on my back. I have to figure out who did this. It's the only way to convince her that it wasn't me.

"You did," she says carefully. "But then why does Kylie Pearce's ankle say 'Don't trust Harleen'?"

The bottom drops out of my stomach. I have no idea. This is bad. Very incredibly bad. If I didn't know me, I'd be certain I was the one who murdered her.

A glimmer of an idea. "Could I see the picture? I want to check the writing."

Officer Montoya flips the photo, her money shot. She passes it across the table, and I touch it with hesitant fingers like it might set me on fire. Relief flares in my chest when I see that it's written in the blue swirls of an ink pen. I guess there's a small part of me that worried it might be scratched in blood or something. I wonder why she wrote it. And why she decided to put it on her skin and not, like, the floor or the walls. Were there floors or walls where it happened?

"It definitely is her handwriting and not, like, the killer's or something." I frown at the photo of her ghostly ankle.

Harleen
Don't trust

"What if it's a warning?"

Officer Montoya cocks her head to the side. "Yes, that is exactly what I think it is." She looks pointedly at me until it clicks.

I roll my eyes. "I don't mean about me. I mean *for* me. What if she was trying to warn me about someone, but before she could finish, someone . . . you know." I look down at the table. I hate to even think about it.

"That's a really nice story, Harleen. But I can tell you're lying to me about something." Montoya slams her palms against the table out of nowhere, and I jump. She leans forward until we're so close I can feel her breath against my cheeks, her eyes boring into me. "So, why don't you tell me what it is, so we can—"

The door opens behind her. OH THANK GOODNESS. I am so incredibly relieved because (A) Officer Montoya's eye-boring techniques could give Wonder Woman's Lasso of Truth a run for its money, and (B) I'm pretty sure she had pastrami for lunch.

A heavyset male cop stands in the doorway, the retired football player type. "We have some new information from the coroner," he says, eyes dark.

"Stay here," Montoya tells me, as if I have a choice.

She crosses the room, and the football cop talks to her in a hushed voice. I don't dare breathe—that's how hard I'm straining to hear. I can't make out a damn word he's saying, but I can see from her expression that whatever it is, it's bad enough to make her stomach turn.

"That could be consistent with the abrasions on her knuckles," she finally whispers.

Knuckles? I snatch a photo of Kylie's hands from the corner of the table. Sure enough, they're scraped and red like she was hitting them against something or someone.

Montoya frowns. "But I don't get it. Why didn't we find skin under her fingernails?"

He whispers something else. Looks like the words *I don't know* from over here.

He leaves, and Officer Montoya is back in front of me. I drop the scraped-knuckles photo and rest my elbows on top of it, hoping she won't realize I was eavesdropping.

"You're free to go," she says briskly.

It should make me feel good. But. "What did the coroner say? What did he find out about Kylie?"

Montoya narrows her eyes, I think, but it's honestly hard to tell because her default facial expression is ornery. "Something that suggests the killer is someone other than you."

"But—"

"I am not going to share the details of an official police investigation with you."

I gesture at the spread of grisly photos in front of me. "Ummm . . ."

"Why don't you go home and try to stay out of trouble."

She frog-marches me to the door. Clearly, she doesn't know me as well as she thinks.

I am going to figure out what happened to Kylie. And I'm going to find out who she was trying to warn me about.

I text Jasmin and Bianca on the way home. I mean to text Sophie and some of Kylie's other sorority sisters next, but instead I find myself looking through my phone for pictures of her. There's this one of all five of us Reckoning girls, right after that gymnastics meet where Kylie showed up wearing my face on a T-shirt. We are piled together, laughing, in a giant group hug. I remember how wonderful that day felt.

We'll never be a family like that again. Not without Kylie. When I get home, I crawl into bed and pull the covers over my head and call her number a dozen times just so I can hear her voice tell me she's not there.

Kylie Pearce

neurobiology major
sorority girl (Alpha Kappa Nu)
instagram influencer
libra
gorgeous but appears to have a soul
posts social justice things all the time
but also bikinis and colorful eyeliner and standing-
    in-front-of-the-mirror selfies and snuggles
    with her dog, Fendi
has a coconut cold brew on IV drip
never closes her blinds

# FEBRUARY

# CHAPTER 18

SOME DAYS DON'T FEEL LIKE BIG DAYS UNTIL YOU'RE IN them. Like, maybe you think the day you get a life-changing piece of news or meet the person you're going to marry would start out with bluebirds chirping you awake and hyenas making your bed for you, but in real life, it's different. You roll out of bed and burn your toast, but luckily the apartment is empty, so your dad isn't there to yell at you about the burning smell. So, you're happily scraping the burnt layer off your toast and into the trash can and daydreaming about the thick swath of peanut butter you're about to slather on, and you don't even notice your phone vibrate against the counter.

It's not until you're sitting at the kitchen table with your peanut butter toast and a cup of coffee that you realize you have an email.

YOU HAVE AN EMAIL.

Holy geez, it's from Gotham U. And it's an email!!! What if it's The Email?!

I shove the rest of my toast in my mouth in one bite and suck the peanut butter off my fingers so I can properly touch my phone. I unlock my screen with shaking hands. Barely able to breathe. Certainly not able to chew.

Click on the notification.

IT'S THE EMAIL!!! It says *Dear Harleen Quinzel*, so there's no way my brain can trick me into thinking they sent it to the wrong person by mistake, and in the next sentence, I am accepted. And by the one after that, I am crying.

I did it. I got into Gotham U. A lifetime of dreams and schemes made real.

The first thing I do is call Bernice.

"Gueff whuh! Gueff whuh! I gomf Gofam OO ack-fwompence!"

"Um, hello?"

I take a huge gulp of coffee (not that I need it now!!!!) and chew as fast as I can.

"Harleen?"

I force down my food, peanut butter sticking to the sides of my throat. That's better.

"Guess what! Guess what! I got my Gotham U acceptance!"

Bernice emits a high-pitched squeal on the other end of the phone.

"OMG, this is the best news! Congratulations!! I didn't realize they were sending out acceptances yet!"

"Yeah! You should check for yours too!"

"Ahhh!! You're right! Let me check it and call you back!"

We hang up, and I sigh and stare dopily at my acceptance email. I wonder if my mom can see this. She'd be so proud.

I finish the rest of my coffee. Bernice still hasn't called. Huh. Kind of figured I'd hear from her by now.

I wash my breakfast dishes, but there's still no call.

Oh no. Does this mean she got rejected? A dark cloud forms in my sunshiny landscape of a future. I'd hoped we were going to do this together.

My phone rings. Bernice!

"Hey! Did you find out yet?" I try to ask it softly, like any answer is okay.

"Come look out your window!" she squeals back.

"What?"

"Just do it!"

"Um, okay." I walk into the living area and peer through the blinds. Standing on the sidewalk underneath my apartment is a girl waving furiously and wearing a black-and-yellow scarf and beanie. Gotham U colors.

"AHHHHHHHH!!!!!!"

It is one long squeal that carries me out of my apartment, down seven flights of stairs, and onto the street. I don't remove my phone from my ear until I see her.

"Hey!" I say.

She hugs me around the neck, and we jump up and down, and I'm so excited I almost forget to notice how warm she feels against me.

"Congratulations," she says. "I'm so proud of you!"

"Thank you!!" (More jumping.)

"I got you something."

"Really?!" I! Love! Presents!

"Mm-hmm. These are actually for you." She pulls off the beanie and hands it to me, and it squeezes perfectly over my low pigtails.

"Aw, thanks. You're the sweetest."

She blushes a little as she unwraps the scarf from her neck and drapes it around mine, accidentally on purpose touching my collarbone. This is what our life could be like. Sharing a dorm room. Helping each other in and out of clothes. Making Bernice blush 24/7.

"I can't believe we're going to school together next year," I breathe.

"Oh."

Bernice's face falls.

I feel my eyebrows crinkle together. "Didn't you get in too?"

She kind of half shrugs. Can't look me directly in the face. "I haven't heard yet. I'm sure it's fine." She tries to force a smile.

I try to keep my jaw from hitting the sidewalk.

"Wait. You came all the way over here, with presents and stuff, and you're being all happy for me, even though I've gotten in and you still don't know yet?"

"Um, well, yeah."

Even as she's saying the words, it feels impossible for me to believe them. "That's the nicest thing anyone's ever done for me."

I stand there, staring at her—this person who cares so much about me. How did I get so lucky?

She blinks, dark eyelashes against pale skin.

Is it weird to be almost crying while simultaneously thinking about kissing someone? My eyes flick to her lips, and I have to dig my fingernails into my jeans to stop myself.

She leans forward on her front foot, pretending to shift her weight but really taking a step closer.

Maybe she doesn't want me to stop myself.

I take a step forward too.

I could ask her. It's important to check first, especially

when you're as impulsive as I am. Double especially when the girl you're in like with is a survivor and you want to make sure she's comfortable because you care about her so much you feel like your heart might burst.

She smiles this little smile like she knows everything I'm thinking. Like her brain has already fast-forwarded to the part where we kiss and it's a foregone conclusion. I reach out my hand for hers. Who am I to argue with time travel?

"Oh!" she yells, suddenly and directly into my face.

"WHATIDIDN'TMEANTO." I retract my hand, quick.

"Sorry! My phone." She pulls it out of her pocket. "It's Gotham U! Oh my goodness, I can't read it! You read it! No, wait! I'll read it!"

I watch her eye movements. Come on. Come on. Come on.

Back and forth. Back and forth. A tiny furrow in her brow. And then.

The Smile.

The one that holds all your dreams up until now and all the ones you'll dream in the future.

I know because I was smiling it earlier this morning.

"Congratulations," I tell her. "This is, like, the very best news."

"We did it. I can't believe we get to go together," she says.

"I know." I'm giddy as I take off the scarf she gave me. "I think you should wear this," I say.

I drape it around her neck. Only I don't let go of the ends.

We both watch my hands, holding us together. I don't want to let go. Ever. And I don't just want to be her friend, and before I can stop myself, I'm asking, "Can I kiss you?"

She leans forward and says, "Yes." Only she says the last

half of the word into my mouth because as soon as I know what her answer is, I kiss her.

And, oh. I am not sure how it took me so long to see her. But now she's here, and her lips are soft against mine, and this is the best day of all possible days, and—

No.

This isn't right. Bernice is really sweet, and I need to make sure I don't lead her on.

I pull away.

Her face falls. "What's wrong?"

She tucks a strand of strawberry-blond hair behind her ear so it stops flying around.

"If we do this," I say, hating myself already, "are you gonna want to be my girlfriend or something? Because I was kind of already seeing someone off and on, and I'm not sure I'm ready for being exclusive." I technically broke things off with Trent already, but he's still texting me all the time, and what if I slip? And if not with him, then someone else. Or maybe it's not another person. Maybe the awful rage inside me will explode on her instead of the bad guys. Maybe over time I get tired and I fall out of the habit of talking to her with kindness in my voice. There are a million ways I could screw this up. I'm not ready for all the things that come after a kiss with someone like her.

Her mouth makes the shape of the word *Oh* even though she doesn't say it, but she recovers quickly, turning it into a soft smile.

She squeezes my hands. "No, it's cool."

"Okay."

"Okay."

And a part of me knows she's lying to me, and I should

stop this, here and now, before I destroy her. But then she wraps her arms around my neck and kisses me so ferociously that I forget. And the wind is whipping our hair around us, and we are wrapped up together in the scarf, and she tastes like peppermint hot chocolate and hope, and she believes in me in a way that makes me feel like I'm better than I am.

I can't seem to make myself pull away.

After Bernice leaves, I walk to this free clinic so I can pick up more ADHD meds. I've actually noticed an improvement in my symptoms since I started doing the exposure therapy. My ADHD ones, I mean. Probably because of the better sleep quality and feeling less stressed and stuff. That reminds me. I pull out my phone and put in earbuds so I can listen to my script-driven imagery as I go. It's part of my exposure therapy. I've been keeping up my closet sessions for two weeks now. At first with Bianca's help, and eventually by myself.

I hit Play on the recording.

*I'm seven years old, and my mom's already dead, and I'm crying,* I hear my voice say.

The recording goes on for one minute, describing the trauma. I can choose to listen to it wherever. Like, right now—out in the sunlight, taking a shortcut through the park. Whatever I want.

I listen to the entire script and take deep breaths. Try to walk at the same pace. Just keep taking a step forward. And then another.

The script-driven imagery is becoming pretty manageable.

The exposure sessions are hard, but I can see myself getting better and better at it, and that's what stops me from giving up. The trick is to squash the fear cycle before it really gets going, because once that pattern of thoughts breaks loose, that's it. The train is off the rails. The toothpaste is not going back in the tube.

Sometimes I still have nightmares or get these intense, hypervigilant feelings when I'm faced with a tiny space, but I've made huge strides. I can choose to shower with the bathroom door locked or go in any room I want, no matter how dark or how small. I can stop spinning excuses, like, "I just really like showering with the door open because the steam makes my hair puffy." Or, "I don't feel like developing this western blot on my own because I get bored if I don't have a friend to talk to."

Because, truth? The only reason I asked Trent to come in that darkroom with me the first time is because I was scared to be in there alone.

And, now? I feel stronger than I ever have.

# CHAPTER 19

I GRIP THE KNIFE IN MY RIGHT HAND, WONDERING WHERE to stab first. Everything hinges on today. My entire future wobbling on the edge of a blade. I slice in with my knife. Deftly. Delicately. I hold my breath, but it cuts through like butter, bloody juice seeping out.

Knots in my stomach as I wait, watch. And . . . the meat has a red center that fades to pink at the edges. I feel like I can finally breathe again. See, today I went to the Gotham City meat market and spent 25 percent of my internship paycheck on a forty-five-day dry-aged New York strip that the guy at the counter assured me would "work better than a love potion to get any man to do what you want." And today I need dark magic and a miracle and a smile from destiny. I need it badly.

So I bought the steak, and potatoes and broccoli too, and I asked Mrs. Forester one floor down if I could have some fresh rosemary from her windowsill herb garden, and then I seasoned my cutting board, not my cooked steak. Did it feel weird sprinkling rosemary and cracked pepper and pats of butter onto an empty cutting board? Yes. But this guy on YouTube told me it would make the steak soak up moisture like a sponge, and I'm not taking any chances at this point. I cut the rest of the steak into slices and mix them with my cutting board deliciousness. Then I heat a plate using hot water from the kitchen sink, wipe it off, add mashed potatoes and broccoli, and arrange the steak slices like some kind of artisanal fan, and voilà!

Now for the hard part.

My mouth waters at the smell of caramelized meat as I carry the plate and a cold PBR to the coffee table.

"Hey!" I say brightly as my dad looks up from the TV. "Made ya dinner." And got into college. NBD. I'm pretty sure you don't have to have your parent's permission to go to college, but just in case there's a financial aid form or something I need him to sign, I want to be on his good side. And, okay, if I'm really being honest, there's a small part of me that hopes he'll be proud—getting into Gotham U is a really big deal. I try to keep myself from getting my hopes up as I pass him the steak.

And I wait. Because maybe this ends with him grunting approval as I skip off to college and maybe it ends with the plate shattering against the wall of our apartment, blood and dreams trickling down the drywall.

He hasn't taken a bite yet. WHY HASN'T HE TAKEN A BITE YET? MY HEART CAN'T TAKE IT.

He eyes the plate, mouth watering. And then he just can't help himself.

"What'd you do this for?"

And I . . . choke.

"I wanted to do something nice for you."

"Uh-huh." He grunts and grabs the plate. Shovels a bite of steak into his mouth with his eyes back on the TV.

I stand there, twisting my fingers together.

"It's not bad," he says, mouth full, as a way of dismissing me.

I continue to stand there and hope inspiration will strike.

"What?" He looks from me to the steak and back again like he's wondering if I've poisoned it.

"I've got some news," I tell him.

"Oh." His face changes, and he eyes the steak like it's a trick, sullen. Not that that stops him from eating it. But, still. It doesn't bode well for how this is going to end for me.

I try to hold the memory of me and Bernice on the sidewalk like a safeguard around my heart. I focus on saying it just right, not too happy, not too proud, eyes cast down at the floor.

"I got into Gotham U."

The left side of my mouth betrays me. It curls upward, the most joyful of all muscle flexes, while the right side remains a stoic and obedient soldier. Which basically means I look like I'm smirking.

The familiar meanness flashes behind his eyes. "How are you going to pay for all that?" He waits, letting the question hang in the air, preying on my deepest fear. "You get that scholarship yet?" he asks, all smooth, even though he can tell I didn't.

"Not yet." I hate how weak I sound when I say it. Hate how he can't hide his smile.

"Because I'm not gonna pay for it, I hope you know."

Like I needed him to tell me that. That wasn't even why

I brought it up. But maybe this is a good thing. He's pleased with himself, and when he's pleased, things don't turn ugly.

"I've been covering your food and rent for eighteen years. Clothes. Gymnastics."

He doesn't pay for gymnastics, not since I started assistant coaching, but I know better than to contradict him.

"You're lucky I let you keep living here, rent-free. You have a job now. You can start paying me."

"But once I'm in college—"

He waves me off. "Scholarships like that are a long shot. You really think you can get one?"

"Well—"

"I'll tell you, you can't. They don't give handouts like that to people like us." He twirls a particularly delicious-looking bite of steak around on his fork, then fixes me with his eyes. "And you're not as smart as you think."

I take the words like a punch. The worst part? He's right. The likelihood of getting a full ride is astronomically small, and I probably will end up having to live here while I save up. So, I let him tell me I won't be going in the fall, and I let myself feel further away than ever from the scholarship, and I let the joy I felt at getting that acceptance letter die inside my chest. Wilt like an abandoned doll.

Why can I fight everyone's monsters except mine?

# CHAPTER 20

THERE ARE SHADOWS, BUT I DON'T HIDE IN THEM. TONIGHT I am brazen. The streetlights wink and glimmer off the sparklers in my hands as I twirl my arms in graceful swoops, left and right and up and down and around, pretending they are lit. I stake them into the grass in front of me in just the right shape.

Across the quad, Bianca wires chain fuses, some slow, some split-second quick—she's the brains of this operation. She hunches over as she works, squatting low on muscular legs, like being just a couple feet off the ground will render her invisible. Jasmin moves with speed and precision (but mostly speed), securing box after box of fireworks to the ground. Bernice alternates between carefully arranging the fireworks and sparklers and overseeing us all, so she can make sure the design will be just right when all of our individual efforts come together. Kylie is primarily concerned with not getting anything on her calfskin boots.

I finish the section I'm on. "Where next?" I whisper across the quad to Bernice.

She points to a patch of grass about five feet away and draws a shape in the sky with her finger. Got it. I nod seriously and then make some hand signals back at her: two fingers walking, little horns on my head, a surprisingly lifelike turtle. She giggles into the back of her hand, and my chest swells with the tiny victory.

I could walk the few steps to my next spot, but Bernice is still watching, so instead I set my box of sparklers on the ground without letting go of it, stake a sparkler with my other hand while doing a one-handed cartwheel, and stand up again holding the sparkler box. All in one fluid motion, I might add.

Jasmin eyes me from her spot next to a statue of one of Gotham U's founders. "Harleen. *What* are you doing?"

"Dancing the ballet of revolution, obviously."

"Hell yeah, we are." Kylie joins in, and I can't tell if she's doing the worst-ever TikTok dance or the best-ever dad dance. I'm, like, 90 percent sure I just saw her wax a car AND crank a mower.

I start giggling and then Bianca starts giggling and then Bernice snort-laughs and we lose all sense of composure.

Jasmin shakes her head. "We are taking way longer than I think is wise." But even she is smiling.

I'm just finishing up my last section when I hear the footsteps.

"You guys!" I hiss.

Jasmin ducks behind the statue. The rest of the girls freeze because there's nowhere to hide. The quad is open space. Only a few trees here and there, and only at the edges.

The footsteps get louder.

We knew it'd be a risk, but we figured two a.m. would be safe enough. We were wrong.

Out from the sidewalk between the psychology building and the financial aid offices pops a lanky guy with a blue L.L.Bean backpack. At first I'm thinking he may never look up from his phone. As long as none of us breathes—

His head darts up, almost like it's being pulled by invisible hooks, that sense you get when someone or five is watching you.

"Wha—?" His eyes grow big, start to piece together what is happening.

"Keep walking, pretty boy." (Side note: He's not actually that pretty—I've just always wanted to say that to someone.)

He does. Backward. Then he trips over the sidewalk and tries to pretend that isn't what happened, even though we all literally just saw him do it.

"You don't have to worry about me! I'm an ally!" he calls, voice cracking. Then he claps his fist to his chest twice and flings his hand in the air with his fingers contorted into an indecipherable mess. "Girl power!" he yells before turning the corner of the theology school.

I cock my head to the side. "Did he just—?"

"Try to coin his own Reckoning gang symbol and fail miserably? Yes, that is exactly what happened," says Jasmin, deadpan.

I realize everyone has kind of stopped working, and Bernice is scanning the quad.

"Hey, I think we're done," she says, a satisfied smile on her lips. "How 'bout the fuses, Bianca?"

"Yep! Just chain-fused the last set of fireworks." Bianca punches her fist in the air. "This is gonna be the greatest. Are you sure we don't need more firepower?"

Jasmin puts a hand on her shoulder. "Step away from the flammables."

They snicker.

Kylie and Bernice stuff our leftovers into a big black trash bag—we'll stash it somewhere far from campus. Then they help Jasmin unroll a banner and stake it into the ground. Meanwhile, Bianca and I go around to the back of the admissions building so we can get onto the roof. We look up at the ladder that leads to a fire escape.

"Can you reach it?" she asks.

"Even I can't jump that high."

"Hmmm." She looks around. There's not much back here except a couple dumpsters. She looks from the ladder to a dumpster and back again. "Yep." She gets behind the dumpster, and it takes me way too long to realize that she's actually going to try to push it.

"Do you need h—" Before I can even finish my sentence, she's done it. I shake my head. "You're a beast."

She grins. "Thanks. Think you can get that ladder now?"

I grin back. "Piece of cake." I climb on top of the dumpster. Years of uneven bars have prepared me for this. I leap off the side and grasp the bottom rung of the ladder, pulling it partway down before I let go.

"Nice," says Bianca. She reaches up to grab the ladder and pull it down the rest of the way. Her shirt rides up when she stretches, revealing an electrical device clipped to her waistband and a spaghetti-like tube feeding into her abdomen.

She pulls her shirt down when she sees me looking.

"My friend has one of those. For diabetes," I say, not wanting her to feel uncomfortable.

"Oh, um, yeah." She tugs at her shirt again, even though her insulin pump isn't showing anymore, and then the other girls appear from the corner of the building, and there's no time to think about it anymore because we have to sneak up to the roof.

The stars wink through the smog overhead, and the quad is dark. Peaceful. It looks just like it did a few hours ago. Well, for the next couple minutes anyway.

"Y'all ready for this?" I'm smiling in that way I have that makes people want to take a step back, but I don't even care. This excitement feels too good to contain.

Bianca flings back the corner of a tarp to reveal the cross-bow she hid earlier today, when you could still access the roof from the inside.

"Made it myself," she says proudly as she passes it to me.

"It's amazing," I proclaim. But seriously, I look like some kind of medieval assassin/goddess of war/every badass broad who ever dared to change the world. I stand strong, legs apart, chest out, and nock an arrow. Queen of everything I survey. I feel Bernice looking at me, and I break character for a sec to wink at her, but then I'm back to being a warrior princess.

Bianca flicks a lighter. "Ready?"

I nod.

She touches it to the arrow and the gasoline-doused cloth covering the tip catches, crackling. I aim it at the far corner of the quad. We decided I'd be the one to do it because I'm the best shot. I try not to think about how embarrassing it'd be if I screwed up.

I take a deep breath.

Exhale.

And let it fly.

The ball of fire whisks through the night sky like a meteor in the snow globe version of Armageddon, planting itself in the grass fifty feet away. At first, it seems like nothing is going to happen. And then—

WHOOSH.

We gasp collectively. Rush to the edge of the roof. The fire spreads slowly down the fuses, licking across the grass like snakes, slithering, curling, hissing, spitting. And then it appears to consume the whole quad—cones shooting up fountains of sparks, Roman candles popping off colorful balls of fire, sparklers glittering like stars. The fireworks blaze so strong that we can feel the heat of it on our flushed faces. The banner Bernice made takes shape in the glow. I can just make out the words *Average salaries for men and women professors at Gotham University*. After another second, you can see that it isn't just one big, random mess of fireworks. On the left side burns the average salary for a male professor at Gotham U, and on the right side is the average for a woman. You can guess which one is substantially lower.

Kylie snaps a dozen photos for our Insta before the sparklers wink out. We roll out a few towels while we watch because the show's not over yet. Bianca has it wired like dominoes. Bernice sits next to me on mine, closer than she should, but I can't make myself move. I should. We haven't told the other girls about us yet, aren't sure if we're going to. There's something about it being a secret that makes it exciting. Dangerous. Even if it is the sweetest girl I know making Bambi eyes at me while we watch an incandescent act of vandalism. Plus, the other girls wouldn't like it. They'd take one look and tell me what I already know—I'm not good enough for her.

I shake away the thought before it can take root. Focus on the mission. "I can't believe you got them all to light up in sequence like that," I tell Bianca. "It's beautiful."

"Yeah," breathes Bernice.

For a second, we just sit there, peaceful, like a couple sitting on a towel on the beach to watch the sunset. We forget we're sitting on top of a building and our sunset is less actual and more metaphorical (See ya, patriarchy!). I'm just trying to conjure the salty sea air of the harbor when Kylie whips out a giant thermos and a pink cooler filled with hot-chocolate bombs because of course she does.

I about bust a gut laughing. "Kylie, have I told you you're my favorite person?"

Bernice frowns beside me. Oops. I didn't mean it like that.

Kylie doesn't seem to notice, just passes around the mugs filled with different bombs. "Cinnamon roll for Bernice, salted caramel for Jasmin, red velvet with black sprinkles for Harleen."

Bianca snorts. "Where did you even get these?"

Kylie gives her a bouncy shrug. "I may have stashed them up here earlier today. Here's a cookie dough one for you."

Bianca looks touched. "That's my favorite flavor of protein shake."

Kylie smiles. "I know."

"Oh man, that is really sweet of you. I feel so bad I can't drink this, but abs are made in the kitchen, not the gym," Bianca says seriously.

"I did bring you an electrolyte water, just in case. But you still have to drink it in a victory mug!"

"I CALL BIANCA'S!" I yell.

Kylie practically tackles me, trying to cover my mouth. "You are going to get us arrested," she hisses, but she's laughing.

Bernice isn't. She narrows her eyes at where Kylie's arm is flung across me. I need to fix this. Stat.

I wiggle out of Kylie's grasp.

"HEY, YOU GUYS, LOOK, MORE FIREWORKS ARE STARTING!" What? Isn't that how you do a seamless distraction?

"Ohhhh!" says Kylie as she pours steaming milk from her thermos.

The other girls watch too, even Bernice. Whatever tension was there before is forgotten.

We sit there laughing on top of this building, stars overhead, faces drenched in the flickering light of the fireworks exploding all around us. This whole night is just the best. I take a gulp of my hot chocolate and feel the warmth spread to my fingers and toes, sizzle in the ends of my hair. I look around at the four girls on this roof with me. Think about what we've accomplished. Together. For the first time in my life, I feel like I have a family. And power. The only lingering negativity is my father, who just today punched a new hole in the living room wall. But it only makes me want to work that much harder in hopes of getting away from him.

Because that's the absolute best part about having a group like the Reckoning. The things in your life that would push you down into the dark and never let you leave—they're not as scary when you have friends like this.

Bianca claps her hands together. "Okay! We have serious things to discuss. There's been some fallout from our missions."

"Yeah," says Jasmin. "Remember Dr. McKinnon? Apparently, our stunt with the robot babies led to some increased scrutiny. His wife left him after it got out that he slept with multiple grad students. I heard she's trying to take him for everything he's worth."

Part of me is thinking, *Big yikes*, and the other part of me is thinking he's literally a grown-up and he made his choices.

"Dr. Bayers too," I add. "We work with his son, and apparently he's been kicked off foundations, and he was asked to resign as editor of one of the big computer science journals."

Jasmin smirks. "Can't say I'm all that sad about it."

Kylie sets down her hot chocolate and bounces up on her knees. "It's not just the consequences for the bad guys, though. It's the positive changes too. Policy changes on admissions committees. Whole departments rethinking the way they do things. It's been different on the Greek side of campus too."

"Really?" I can't help but think about that sleepover I had at her sorority house.

She smiles. "Yeah. I feel like so many girls are speaking up now. And the way people are receiving it—that's different too."

I flush, proud to be part of making that happen.

"Twice this month, guys have been arrested for assaulting women. And one of them, he's the son of a big donor. That never would have happened before."

I catch Bianca giving Bernice's shoulder a squeeze, and my heart feels so full. We're really doing this.

Jasmin's smile flickers first. "Is anyone worried? The bigger we get, the bigger the consequences get, the bigger the chance that we get caught or someone tries to take us down."

I try to feel worried, I really do, but honestly, I just want to keep flying directly at the sun.

"Have you heard anything else from your sources?" Bianca asks Kylie.

She winces. "Yeah, there are definitely people calling for our heads. Privately, of course, so they don't ruin their reps, but a lot of people are really angry, and the president's been pressured to create a task force dedicated to finding and stopping us. We could think about taking a break?"

"No way," says Bianca. "I say we go even bigger this time. Really blow the lid off things. It's time to figure out who's next."

I sit straight up because I have just the guy and I'm 200 percent with Bianca on this one. "Have you guys heard about this professor in the neurobiology department? Dr. Perry?"

Bianca and Jasmin shake their heads, but Kylie nods. She's double majoring in journalism and neurobio. I tell them all about how the women in his lab think he's a big, giant creeper. And then I get to the part about BOOBS and how he couldn't stop staring at mine.

"*No.*"

"Ewww."

"What the eff?"

"Right? I don't know that he's the one taking girls, but he's definitely awful. He said something really creepy to one of the undergrads in our lab too."

Bianca nods. "Oh yeah, I feel comfortable aligning as his enemy. So, what are we gonna do? Blow up his house?"

"Dude." Jasmin gives her a Look.

"I didn't mean like while he was in it. What? Still too much? I'm kidding!"

I narrow my eyes, thinking back to how small he made me feel at the symposium. "Nothing's too much for this guy."

Bianca squeezes my shoulder. "Don't worry. We're gonna

get him." Something sparks behind her eyes. "Hey, Harleen, what happens when you put a bomb in a perfume plant?"

I glance at her suspiciously. "I don't know. What?"

"It blows up the olfactory!" She slaps her leg, and I can't help but smile. "What happens when you put a bomb in a cheese shop in France?"

"I don't know."

"Da Brie goes everywhere!"

I laugh in spite of everything. Not gonna lie, there's a big part of me that wants to go with Bianca on this one, joking or no, because I just have this *feeling* about him. But Jasmin is right. That amount of violence and destruction would bring the GCPD down on us in a big way. We can still find a way to hurt him. We just need to be more creative—less emotional, more strategic.

"I think we should hold off on him," says Bernice quietly.

I turn and stare at her. "What?"

"No, really. I think we should confirm first whether he's the monster taking girls, so we know exactly how hard to hit him. Also, I don't know, I like the idea of us going after other profs while he watches—if he is our main target after all." Her eyes go sharp. "Someday we're definitely going to take him down. But I like to imagine him sitting there in his office, seeing these other guys fall all around him. And wondering when the other shoe is going to drop."

For a moment we are stunned into silence. I've never heard Bernice sound so hard. But, no, not just hard. Calculating. Like not only does she stay up late imagining ways to hurt the bad guys, but also she's eleven steps ahead of the rest of us.

I recover first. "Oh-ho-ho, that is dark." I throw my arm

around Bernice's neck. "What other ideas are you hiding in there?"

Bernice makes a face like her heart skipped a beat. Because I'm touching her neck? "Nothing."

"Hold up, though." Kylie has her caramel-blond hair wrapped around her finger like she is literally trying to pull the thought from her head. "If we have some idea of who this monster might be—people like Dr. Perry or whoever—can't we just, like, make a suspect list and meet with them and cross them off one by one?"

Jasmin raises The Eyebrow. "What, you're just going to go to their offices and ask them if they attacked a bunch of people?"

"No," says Kylie. "I'm going to use myself as bait."

*That is such a great idea.*

"Whoa, okay, that is really brave of you, but I don't feel good about you doing that." Jasmin clearly sees the same determined look in Kylie's eyes that I do because she adds, "Please don't do that."

*I mean, dangerous idea. Very dangerous and unwise.*

"Jasmin's probably right," I say reluctantly, even as my brain is spinning visions of me slinking into his office wearing an earpiece and a wire and secret hidden weapons that slide out of my boots and bra and intricate updo.

"Okay, but if we're not making big moves to figure out who it is right now, that still means we need a new target," says Bianca. "I'm not ready to slow down."

I'm not either.

# CHAPTER 21

## WEDNESDAY, APRIL 6

RECKONING SECURE CHAT:

> Harleen: Can we meet? I just found out a bunch of stuff about Kylie from the police

> Bianca: Sure, want to meet at my apartment at 5:30? I should be back from work by then.

At least she replied to my text. That has to mean something.

*She doesn't hate you,* I tell myself as I climb the steps. Neither of them does. They feel angry and betrayed because I unleashed the fire of a thousand suns on them. I'll just explain and apologize (again) and hope it sticks this time.

Take a deep breath. Knock on the door.

I wait several agonizing seconds. Watch a reflection flicker in the peephole. The doorknob turns. Someone opens it, just a crack. Jasmin's face appears in the sliver of light.

"Hi," I say. It's just one word, but it feels like diving off a cliff and hoping there aren't rocks under the water.

The door opens wider. That's probably a good thing, right? I try to find the answer in Jasmin's eyes, but I can't tell what she's feeling. Only that whatever it is, it's seismic. The seconds stretch between us like a rubber band pulled too tight.

"I didn't do it," I blurt out.

"I know." Jasmin's face crumples, and she collapses into me, and we both dissolve into a puddle on Bianca's welcome mat.

It feels so good to wrap my arms around her and cry into her shoulder. For Kylie. For Bernice. For all of it.

The door creaks behind her, and Bianca shoos us inside.

"Did anyone follow you here?" she asks. "It's probably not a good idea for the three of us to be seen together, especially now."

I shake my head and half smile at the fact that Bianca's intensity is dialed up to eleven, even now.

As soon as the door is shut, she gives me a hug. "I can't believe she's gone."

It's all she can get out before she starts sobbing. Seeing her break down like that sets me off again. Jasmin too. For a while, we just stay that way. Wrapped up together like we're in an extremely devasted football huddle. Crying. Thinking about Kylie.

Then the teapot whistles from the kitchen, and Bianca motions for us to sit down. She returns with three cups of lavender chamomile.

"How are you doing, Harleen?"

She hands us each a mug.

I'm struck that this is the first time I've seen her since what I did at the last Reckoning meeting.

"I'm so sorry," I tell her. "About what happened the last

time we were all together. This group is the best thing that's ever happened to me."

"Me too, kid. Look, Jasmin and I are—*were*—pretty mad at you, but this is bigger than all that. We need to stick together. That's what Kylie would want."

She swallows, hard, and we nearly start crying all over again.

"What did the police say?" asks Jasmin gently.

I clutch my steaming mug in front of me. "They showed me a lot of pictures of Kylie." I blink and I can see them all again, wallpapering the inside of my eyelids.

Jasmin squeezes my wrist. "I'm sorry."

It feels so good to hear her say that. To feel like we're on the same side again.

"They asked me if I thought she was a member of the Reckoning." I take a nervous gulp of my tea.

Bianca scooches forward in her chair. "What did you say?"

I attempt to pull off a shrug. "I said no. And I'm pretty sure they believed me."

And, okay, technically I lied to the police, but it's Montoya's own fault for not believing that women contain multitudes.

Bianca lets out a long sigh through pursed lips.

"We're okay," she finally says.

Jasmin wrinkles her nose. "If you define okay as having two of our members attacked in the past three days, then sure." She turns to me. "Did they say anything about who they think did it?"

I try not to flinch. She may have said she believes me that I didn't do it, but is that going to change when she finds out what was written on Kylie's ankle?

"It was really weird," I say slowly. "At first, they were acting like they thought I did it."

Jasmin rolls her eyes. "Someone needs to defund them, like yesterday."

"How'd they even know you were friends with her?" asks Bianca.

"Oh." I take another gulp of lavender chamomile. "Kylie wrote my name on her ankle."

Jasmin nearly spits out her tea. *"What?"*

"Yeah, it said, 'Harleen, don't trust,' like she was trying to send me a message, only the police were trying to act like it meant 'Don't trust Harleen,' and I was kind of freaking out, but then this other cop pulls Officer Montoya out of the room and whispers a bunch of stuff, and suddenly she's like, 'Oh, sorry for handcuffing you in front of all your co-workers, we actually think it was someone else.' "

Bianca sits up straighter. "Did they say who?"

I shake my head. "All I heard Montoya say was that it was consistent with the scrapes on Kylie's knuckles. I don't even know how she died. I couldn't see anything physically wrong with her in any of the pictures except for those scrapes."

Bianca and Jasmin share a glance.

"It doesn't make any sense," says Jasmin.

"Yeah," says Bianca. "People are saying it's a mugging, and that Kylie's body was found in the East End without a purse or wallet or phone or anything."

There are so many things wrong with that scenario: (1) Kylie is one of Gotham City's elite. She wouldn't so much as drive through the East End in her town car, with the windows rolled up and the doors locked. (2) How did they mug her without giving her a single bruise? Because seventy-dollar gel mani aside, Kylie's a fighter. (3) The scrapes on her hands. If someone dragged her across the sidewalk against her will or something, how is it that only her knuckles are scratched? And, oh! Her fingernails.

"Kylie didn't have any skin under her fingernails," I say. "If she was mugged, wouldn't she have at least scratched the guy?"

"She definitely strikes me as a scratcher," says Bianca.

Jasmin doesn't say anything. Her eyes are drifting all around the room like they do before she solves a big coding problem. Her mouth falls open in the shape of an O.

"What if someone dropped her in the East End to make it look like a mugging?"

I shrug. "It's more believable than her actually being in the East End."

Jasmin nods. Apparently, that was all the momentum she needed. "I bet Kylie was trying to tell you who's hunting us."

Hunting *us*? "Wait, you think Kylie and Bernice are connected and that whoever did it is after all of us?"

Jasmin and Bianca exchange a glance.

"There's something we need to tell you too," says Jasmin.

"Someone's been leaving really creepy comments on the Reckoning Insta account that Kylie was running," says Bianca. "I mean, we get a lot of creepy and inappropriate stuff on there, but these are different. They're more . . . threatening."

"And they're all from the same person, and they're weirdly specific," jumps in Jasmin. "Here, I got receipts just in case."

She opens her phone and passes it to me. I scroll through

the screen caps of different pics from the Reckoning account and the comments from one particular follower underneath.

> **@Voyeur679:** I bet you think you're really cool, wrecking people's lives, you [extremely colorful and expletive-filled description of the female anatomy].

And then a few days later:

> **@Voyeur679:** How come you alone are qualified to decide who's good and who isn't? Who made you God?

> **@Voyeur679:** Hey, I'm talking to you. What, you too scared I might beat you in an argument?

I frown. "Isn't this pretty standard for that account?"

"Yeah, but they don't usually claim to know who we are," says Jasmin. "And they don't say 'can't wait to meet' on the same day that Kylie went missing."

A shiver of dread runs through me. "Are you serious?"

Jasmin nods, and I keep reading.

> **@Voyeur679:** I know who you are, you know. One of you, anyway. But you just keep sipping your coconut cold brew. It's only a matter of time until I figure out who the rest of you are, too.

There's another comment, a week later:

> **@Voyeur679:** I know who two more of you are. I know where you live. I know when your classes are. I know what you eat for lunch and when you take the back alley home. You're gonna stop ruining people's lives now, or I might just have to pay you a visit.

And then a single message that I'm assuming was written by Kylie:

**@TheReckoning:** There is no way in hell we're stopping. But have fun living in your mom's basement, you neckbeard.

**@Voyeur679:** Can't wait till we meet :)

I have never felt such a visceral reaction to a smiley face. "And you think this is the same guy who hurt Bernice?"

Jasmin puts her hand on my shoulder. "I mean, yeah. He says he knows who at least three of us are, and he said that thing about coconut cold brew, so it sounds like he definitely knew about Kylie." She bites her lip. "I think he's trying to pick us off one by one."

"How are we supposed to find this guy?" Bianca smacks her hand on the arm of her chair. "We don't even know how he found out about us or how he killed Kylie. We should set off all the leftover fireworks outside the police station so we can sneak in and steal her file!"

A smile forms on my mouth in spite of everything. "Yeah, how 'bout we try calling Kylie's mom first? I can get her number from one of the Alpha Kappa Nu girls."

Bianca pretend-pouts. "I guess that works too, if you want to be boring about it."

"But should we even be going after that kind of information?" says Jasmin, and the fear in her voice sends a shiver down my spine. "What if he finds out? What if it makes him even madder? He killed Kylie. He put Bernice in the hospital. He wouldn't think twice about doing the same to any of us."

I shake my head. "Bernice and Kylie would want us to keep going."

"Would they? Even if it gets us killed? Think about it. If Kylie hadn't been in the Reckoning, she'd still be alive. Something we did got her killed. Does it honor her more to keep doing the same thing? Or to stop?"

"I really think she would want us to find him," Bianca says quietly.

Jasmin deflates.

"We just, we have to be more careful, okay?" she finally says.

"Done," says Bianca. "We absolutely will be. But until then, who do you think did it?"

I read back over the screen caps. *You're gonna stop ruining people's lives.* A thought pings in my brain. "Do we think this is more than some rando on the internet?"

"You mean one of the guys we hit with the Dissent Cannon?" says Bianca. "Or one of the professors?"

"Yeah. I mean, it's hard for me to picture a person who wears tweed jackets with elbow patches killing someone, but—"

Jasmin looks thoughtful. "Could be. And if they didn't want to get their hands dirty, maybe they hired someone. We've really messed with people's lives this year. People murder each other in Gotham City for less. Do you think it's someone we've already gotten? I guess it could also be someone who has a lot to lose if we go after them."

I hadn't even thought of that, but now that she mentions it, it makes sense.

"Oh!" Jasmin's eyes go wide. "Do you think he could be the same person as the guy who's been taking girls?"

Holy. Crap. "I didn't even think about that. Maybe?"

What if he's, like, onto us or something?

Bianca throws her hands in the air. "It could be anyone. We've taken down seven professors so far, and more creepy frat guys than I can count."

Jasmin nods. "I could see it being Dr. Hawley. I heard he had to move back home to Central City after they fired him."

"Or Dr. McKinnon," I chime in. "Apparently his wife got the house AND the boat, and he's real sore about it."

"It could be Dr. Bayers," says Bianca. "I've never seen anybody look that pissed."

"People won't even talk to him at conferences now," says Jasmin. "He's toxic."

We go round and round for over an hour, but we're still no closer to figuring it out. That's the scariest thing about this. It could be anyone.

We make plans. Bianca talks about how we're going to find out who it is. Take him down just like all the others. But, honestly? It feels like empty words. He could be watching us right now outside her apartment. Waiting for one of us in an alley. And if he attacked me or Bianca, we could probably take him, or at least escape relatively unscathed. But that's if it's hand-to-hand. What if he has a gun? What if he goes after Jasmin?

For the first time since we started this thing, I'm scared. We've done something worth killing for. And one of us is already dead.

mwf schedule:
Bianca Alejandra Narvaez-Espinosa

7:00 am—leaves her apartment to go running
7:40 am—goes back inside
8:40 am—leaves apartment to go to class
9:00 am—quantum mechanics II
10:00 am—drinks a cookie dough—flavored protein
shake while lifting at the campus gym
11:00 am—condensed matter physics I
12:00 pm—lunch
1:00 pm—statistical mechanics I
2:00 pm—works at the physics machine shop
5:00 pm—leaves to go back to apartment
5:00 pm+ sometimes runs errands, rarely out with
friends, usually has dinner alone (i'm assuming),
often see her doing homework at her desk by the
window (unless it's Friday and she's babysitting)
turns out her light between 10:00 pm and midnight

i wonder how hard it would be to get her alone.

# MARCH

# CHAPTER 22

*HIS EYES ARE ACTUALLY A NICE SHADE OF BLUE.* THE thought pops into my head, and I'm so annoyed by it that I aim another dart at Professor Perry's face. Not his actual face. Just a printed-out picture of him from his faculty profile on the neurobiology website.

The dart zings across the room and hits him directly on the nose.

"Nicely done," says Bernice, slapping me a high five.

"Sorry, I'll focus." I tear my eyes away from the bulletin board where we've tacked him. "I just need to stop looking at his face."

We're all camped out at Bianca's apartment, where we've dedicated a bulletin board that takes up almost an entire wall to bringing Professor Perry to his knees. The other girls are getting ready to handle the suggestion box—driving around campus pelting evil dudes with the Dissent Cannon and spray-painting the Reckoning tags on things. Normally, I'd be all over that sort of stuff, but then Bernice says, "I think I'm going to hang back and work on this Dr. Perry stuff."

And I find myself saying, "I'll stay too."

She gets this shy little smile on her face, and I feel myself turning red all over, and the words WE'RE GOING TO BE ALONE WE'RE GOING TO BE ALONE must be scrolling across my forehead because Jasmin gives me the most epic one-eyebrow raise of all time. No words, just The Eyebrow. But it's enough to make Kylie look back and forth between me and Bernice and Jasmin, and I can tell she's putting the pieces together, even before she squeals, "OMG, is Bernice your *girlfriend*? I *knew* it!"

She does not wait for an answer before she tackle-hugs both of us.

Bernice is smiling so big, but then Bianca is all, "Wait, is it true? How did I not notice this?"

And I shrug, grinning like a fool, and say, "We're talking. We haven't made it official yet or anything. But I think Bernice is pretty great."

Bernice's smile—it changes in that moment. Becomes forced. I don't know if the other girls can see it, but there's hurt behind her eyes. Because I wasn't ready to say she's my girlfriend yet? I just want to push through this moment and get to the other side before the girls realize something is up, so I say, loudly, "Are you mad?" Bernice's eyes flick to mine, surprised. Oops, didn't mean her. "That we didn't tell you sooner? Sorry, it was just so new, and—"

"Are you kidding?" Bianca gives me a hug that picks me all the way up off the ground. "I could not be happier. You're two of my favorite people."

She hugs Bernice next, spinning her around, and it

sends the hurt somewhere else, and I breathe a sigh of relief. But only for a second. I know I can't avoid The Talk much longer.

Jasmin hugs us too, and then Kylie hugs us again because she just can't help herself. So, yeah. Now the other girls know. And it's surprisingly okay?

After they leave, I fire off yet another email to a woman who worked in the Perry lab over a decade ago. Not that it's going to help. I put my head in my hands. "How do we keep coming up empty?"

"I know." Bernice waves her phone at me. "That was the third woman I've talked to. They keep saying the same thing. Sure, he says sexist stuff a lot, and sometimes people complain, but they all swear he's never touched them."

I purse my lips together. "Wonder what he did to get them to say that."

"I don't know," says Bernice. "I'm starting to wonder if it's really not him."

*"It's him,"* I say emphatically. He named a whole-ass conference BOOBS. He thinks he's untouchable. Exactly the type to attack a bunch of women and think he can get away with it. "Maybe we just need to look at it a different way." I tap my pencil against the table, thinking. "Didn't you say something about looking into the Gotham U Bridge Scholars program before?"

Bernice almost chokes on her water. "Sorry. Yes. Someone told me they were worried girls in the program were being targeted."

"How do they know that? Have girls in the program complained or—?"

"There have been instances of girls dropping out of the

program under mysterious circumstances. That's what I've heard, anyway."

I shake my head. It's bad enough this degenerate has gone after multiple women, but girls just out of high school, desperate to make something of themselves? Thinking of how none of them came forward, of how scared they must have been—it makes me sick. I wish I could figure out a way to help them.

But how can I when I don't even know who they are? Or how many of them there are? And then I get the biggest freaking epiphany.

"Have we lost anyone?"

Bernice blinks at me. "Huh?"

But I'm already pulling up my email. "From our class this year? Have any of the girls dropped out?"

I have to go all the way back to the beginning of the school year, but eventually I find it. A welcome email with a doc attached that has little profiles for each of the incoming Bridge Scholars. Bernice leans forward. We scroll through the entire thing. There are two girls we've never seen in our one-hour-a-week research seminar and one boy.

Bernice bites her lip, and I try not to stare. "Do you really think that's more than how many would have dropped out by chance?"

She's right. Crap. "Well, maybe there's a way we could check other years too. I don't know how, but—"

"I do!" she says.

"Wait, really?"

She puts her hands on her hips and mock glares at me. "Do not underestimate my detective abilities." She opens a browser on her computer. "Or my extreme dorkiness over being part of this program." She pulls up an article and turns her screen toward me. "At the end of the selection period each year, the list of Bridge Scholars gets published in the university newspaper, the *Clocktower.* I may have printed ours out and taped it to my wall. We should be able to go back to each year and find the list."

"That's perfect!" I clap my hands together. "I'm totally teasing you about that list later, by the way."

She pulls up the list for the previous year, and I frown.

"How are we going to figure out who made it to the end of the program, though?"

"I've got an idea for that too," she says, her eyes bright or glassy, it's hard to tell. "Go to the Bridge Scholars page on the Gotham U site."

I do. And then I see it. "They post a group photo from every certificate day!"

Bernice nods smugly.

The photos are perfect. The whole group at what is essentially Bridge Scholars graduation, so nobody misses it. All the names are listed underneath. The program's only been around for the past five years, but still, that's something.

We look at last year's photo and then the one before that. Bernice gets this look on her face. Wistful, or maybe like she's going to cry.

She shakes it off. "Here," she says. "I'll read you the names from the list, and you cross-reference them."

I love it when she says hot stuff like *cross-reference.* I'm tempted to tell her that just so I can see her blush, but she's already calling out names, and I have a very important job to do protecting women's rights and stuff.

Bernice reads each name from the campus paper, and

every time I find one missing from the end-of-year group photo, we social media stalk them and print out a photo. By the end of five years, we have twelve missing girls. And four boys.

"If four is the number that dropped out by chance," I say, "then the other eight . . ."

"I know," says Bernice. She looks as sick as I feel.

We tack them up all over the wall around the photo of Professor Perry, expecting to make a web of threads connecting to him, like in the police movies. One of the girls worked in his lab, but that's it. One sad teal thread winding from her blunt-cut bangs to his stupid face.

"Maybe we just need to do more research," I say.

"Yeah," says Bernice.

"I could kind of use a break, though."

"Me too."

Bernice heats some water in Bianca's teapot and grabs a couple cups from the cabinet. Bianca always says to help ourselves to whatever, but since her kitchen is mostly protein shakes and boneless skinless chicken breasts, we usually just drink tea. She has about a million varieties (and a million and one dad jokes about spilling the tea). Today, it's peach-ginger, and we blow on our cups before we go back over to our Crime Wall and sit on top of the table and stare at it.

Bernice takes a cautious sip of her tea. "How's your SV1 research going, anyway?"

"It's good. It's good." I tamp down my doubts and tell her about my epigenetics idea and how I want it to work more than I've ever wanted anything. "So far, the results look okay, though, really, I need to run it with more controls before I take it to Dr. N."

"That's so cool!" says Bernice.

I grin, feeling almost shy, which is so not me. I don't know why I have so much trouble believing in this part of myself. "Thank you."

We both go quiet, staring at the spiderweb of clues in front of us.

After a minute, I forget to think about clues because I remember that we're all alone in Bianca's apartment, and that almost never happens, and it feels like it's been entire years since the last time I kissed her, and I've never actually looked at her nose from this angle, and I didn't realize how adorable it is.

She turns toward me.

Whoa. We are looking at each other. Like, right in the face. It feels like an awful lot. Like, how long can you just sit there—right next to someone—staring them full in the eyes with your chests rising and falling in time like you're pieces of the same being?

"Can we talk?" says Bernice.

(Until someone says that. That's how long.)

"Okay." I feel walls go up all around my heart.

Bernice winces. She must be able to feel the walls too.

The seconds stretch, brittle and uncomfortable.

"Why don't you want to be my girlfriend?" she finally says.

It is a fair question. I was expecting this question. I still want to run out of the apartment screaming.

"I'm not good at this." I force the words out because she deserves an answer. "Like, really spectacularly bad at this. I've never had a real girlfriend. Or boyfriend." It's so embarrassing to admit that, especially knowing why. "I always seem to hurt people."

I hold my breath. Wait to see how she takes my confession.

Her mouth turns up in a half smile. "So, you're a heartbreaker?"

"Well, yeah, and one time I lit this girl's hair on fire."

Bernice's eyes goggle.

"But it was an accident!!" I cringe. "Probably should have kept that one to myself."

She smiles. "Hey, no. I want to know you. All of you. Fiery past and everything."

"Thanks." I scoot closer to her. "And just so you know, I can't stop thinking about you. I want to spend every day with you. I think you're the best person I know. I more than like you, Bernice. I'm just . . . scared."

I worry I've said too much. Put it all out there like dirty laundry. But Bernice's face lights up like she finally gets where I'm coming from.

"I want you to be comfortable. And if that means taking things slow and not using any labels for now, that's fine."

I feel a rush of warmth to my cheeks. What did I do to deserve someone as understanding as her? Someone who cares so much. That reminds me.

"I want you to be comfortable too," I say. "I know that after what happened at that party, boundaries are going to be extra, extra important, and I totally respect that. I never want to do anything you're not ready for."

"Thanks," she says quietly. "And me too. Like, for you."

And then she smiles, almost coyly. "I'm ready. Well, for some things. I'll let you know about the other things."

She puts her hand over mine.

Sweetly. Gently. Two of her fingers stroking the back of

my knuckles. *Would it be weird to make out in Bianca's apartment?*

She traces her fingers all the way up to my wristbone. *Screw it.*

I cradle her face in my hands and kiss her. Peach-ginger lips. Peach-ginger tongue. If I pushed her back against the table, would that be cool? If I—

*Bzzzzzzz.*

We jump apart like magnets pushed together at the wrong ends. Do magnets pant? Because I am doing a lot of panting.

*Bzzzzzzz.*

I recognize that it is my phone, but I am incapable of doing anything about it. I recognize that Bernice is breathing as hard as I am. I recognize the second realization makes me feel like I've just gulped an entire mug of peach-ginger tea.

*Bzzzzzzz.*

"I think it's your phone." Bernice states the obvious and holds it out to me, having recovered both the power of speech and the ability to move before I did. Show-off.

Does this mean I like her more than she likes me? *Don't think about that.*

The phone vibrates in Bernice's hands, and she frowns. "Do you . . . have alerts about The Joker set on your phone?"

*"No."* I snatch away my phone, but unfortunately not my dignity with it. "Maybe."

Bernice bursts into giggles at my expense.

"Hey!" I say, mock-angry.

This only makes her laugh harder.

I try to regain control. "So, there's something I should tell you."

"You write secret fanfic about The Joker? Have a shrine dedicated to him in your bedroom closet? Watch news footage of him while thinking about things you shouldn't? Make out with your hand and pretend it's him?"

"Ohmygosh, Bernice, *no*." Okay, look, only one of those things is true.

I unlock my phone. A few people are tweeting about The Joker's new heist. And it's really close!

"We gotta go!" I tell Bernice. I'm already pulling on my jacket.

Bernice does the same, even though she doesn't know what we're doing yet, which is exactly the kind of ride or die you want for this sort of thing.

"I've been trying to get a Joker sample for weeks," I tell her as we rush out of Bianca's apartment and lock the door. "Following any snippet of news. Going to crime scenes and hoping to find a strand of green hair or something. But the police always get there first, and they're always like, 'Crime scene integrity, yellow tape, blah-blah.'"

"How frustrating for you," says Bernice, lips quirking into a smile.

"Right?"

We hurry down the block and into the nearest subway station, swiping our Gotham U transit cards as we enter.

"Anyway, Frontonac's Jewelers is so close I think I might actually have a shot at beating them." I unlock my screen again. "Hot damn! He's still there."

We wait for the train to arrive.

"C'mon. C'mon. C'mon."

Bernice puts her hand on my shoulder. "Don't worry. We are going to do this."

It's really sweet of her to say, but I've been close too many times before.

I hear a train. "I hear a train!" I tell Bernice.

She nods, and we both go silent, listening. My face splits into a grin. The rumbling sounds are definitely for our side of the track. The black-and-silver train groans to a stop, brakes squeaking against metal rails. The sliding doors part, and I grab Bernice by the elbow and rush on, squeezing up against the other people on the train.

One stop. He's only one stop away.

My phone doesn't get signal in the subway tunnel, so I just have to hope he's still there when we surface. I scoot closer to Bernice because the train is packed, and the guy behind me is holding a bouquet of grocery store roses and clearly put on an entire bottle of cologne in preparation for this train ride. I actually don't mind all the people, though. It's being *alone* in small spaces that still kind of gets to me. Being locked in. And even that isn't nearly as bad as it used to be now that I've finished my eight weeks of exposure sessions and listening to scripts. It feels good to have set this big mental health goal and to achieve it, but it's also weird. Like, what do I do now? Keep doing the sessions? Only do them if I notice my symptoms getting worse? This is where I realize it would be helpful to have the input of an actual medical professional. Because people like to act like there are magic bullets and forever fixes, but real life is more complicated than that.

As soon as the train stops, Bernice and I take off through the terminal, running up the escalator and weaving between people and laughing. As it spits us out onto the street, my phone buzzes about a bajillion times.

"Oh no, he's been injured." I bite my lip.

"Is he okay?" asks Bernice, peering over my shoulder.

I scroll down, trying to ignore the dread I'm feeling. "Yes." A full-body sigh of relief. And then a realization. "He'll be bleeding!"

Bernice and I tear around the corner. *Please no police yet. Please no police. Please let there be a drop/streak/splatter of blood big enough to scrape into the serum tube I carry around with me at all times like a big creeping creeper.*

We skid to a stop in front of the jewelry store. No police! The Joker's long gone, of course, but if I listen close enough I can almost hear that laugh of his. The crowd of rubber-neckers only grows because there's still a giant glass window smashed out. A couple people have that shifty look, like they're thinking of darting in and trying to grab something. If they were alone here, would they?

I pull up a video of The Joker someone posted less than two minutes ago, so I can confirm that the blood dripping down the glass in front of me is his and not just some goon's. On my screen, he splashes through the window like it's nothing but a waterfall. It's his, all right.

I take a few steps closer and feel the crowd shift behind me, restless. They think I'm going to steal something. I make my steps bouncier, more innocent. Feel my pigtails swing against my neck. I cup a hand to my mouth in an exaggerated stage gesture.

"Are you okay in there? My friend's calling the police." I nod to Bernice, who is already pulling out her phone. Told you she was the best. I step closer, affecting a face of concern. "Does anyone need medical attention?"

The crowd behind me seems less interested in me helping people than in me stealing things, and it's easy to whip the tube out of my pocket, scrape it up the side of the glass, and watch the blood slide to the bottom. Lucky we got here so fast. It hasn't even coagulated yet.

I slip the tube back into my pocket without anyone noticing. The shop owner and his sawed-off shotgun seem fine, so Bernice and I back away "so as not to disturb the crime scene" (*ha!*) and walk calmly down the sidewalk in the direction of the lab, which also happens to be the direction The Joker took. I can't see him or his crew, but the occasional explosion lets us know they're there.

After we're a couple blocks away, I take out the sample again so I can look at it. Clear tube. Tan screw top. Gel in the bottom to help separate the serum from the red blood cells when you centrifuge it. And on top of that, a dark stripe of burgundy. Joker blood. Funny how you almost expect it to be green or something.

This is it. I've finally done it. My feet barely touch the ground, and I start laughing, full-on, flat-out.

"I can't believe it," I tell Bernice. "I am holding The Joker's blood. In my hands. All I have to do now is get to the lab and spin it down so I can take off the serum. HOLY CRAP, BERNICE, THIS IS THE JOKER'S BLOOD!"

I leap into the air as I yell it.

Bernice laughs with me. "It was amazing. No one even noticed."

I grin. "We just walked up to that window and took it. Like that." I snap my fingers. "I am doing this experiment, and I AM GOING TO TAKE THE SCIENCE WORLD BY STORM!"

"Give this girl a Nobel Prize!"

The sight of Bernice yelling and acting silly in the street completely undoes me, and I'm so excited that I grab her hands and we start jumping up and down, right on the corner of Fourth and Wayne. And I'm laughing, and she's laughing, and she looks so beautiful with her hair flying every which way that I lean forward and kiss her. The Joker bombs explode like fireworks in the background, and this moment is so perfect I feel like I could burst from it. When I pull away, I say it without thinking.

"I love you."

I've never said that to anyone outside my own family. Haven't said it to my dad in years. The words feel foreign on my tongue. But also right.

I stare at her, scared she won't say it back, terrified that she will. Already catastrophizing the ways this will change us.

"I love you too," she says.

I expect her to look fragile, on the verge of tears. But the fire that flares behind her eyes steals my breath.

She kisses me so hard it scares me.

# CHAPTER 23

THE NIGHTMARE ALWAYS ENDS THE SAME WAY. I'M IN SEC-
ond grade, and I'm banging on a giant door as the room gets
smaller, smaller. And I'm beating so hard with my little fists
and I'm screaming and I'm crying, but no one hears me. No
one is coming to save me.

I pound my fists against the door until the skin scrapes
off my knuckles and then the muscle. I look down at my
hands in horror and realize there's only bone left.

That's when I wake up screaming.

*BANG. BANG. BANG. BANG. BANG.*

I startle. How am I still knocking if I'm awake?

*BANG. BANG. BANG.* "Stop screaming in there. I'm
trying to sleep."

My dad.

My dad is banging on the wall between my bedroom
and his.

I try to calm my breathing. My shirt and sheets are soaked
in sweat, and I shiver. My phone says it's 5:38 a.m., but I can

never get back to sleep after a nightmare, so I get up. I take a shower—quietly, so as not to wake my dad (again)—and I get ready for lab. Tiptoe from my bedroom to the kitchen like a mouse. Make the quietest bowl of cereal in history. Slip on my jacket and backpack and ease open the front—

"Harleen?"

I jump. He is standing in the hallway in a stained T-shirt, rubbing the sleep from his eyes.

"Yes?"

He yawns. "I need you to get a couple hundred bucks over to Mr. Thompson. I was a little short on the rent this month."

Are you freaking kidding me? "But I—"

His eyes flash, sharp and angry. "You wanna live here or not?" He snarls, suddenly wide awake.

I grit my teeth and nod, but he's already walking back to his bedroom.

"Besides, it's the least you could do for waking me up."

He closes the door behind him.

I'm so angry, it feels like an explosion trapped inside of me with nowhere to go, but I swallow it down and pay our landlord two hundred hard-earned Gotham U dollars, and I get through all my classes like a model citizen, because of all the days he might have the power to ruin, I will not let him spoil today.

*Shake it off, Harleen.*

And I do. I blast music in my headphones and put everything that happened this morning behind me.

Today is the day I run The Joker's sample.

I skip down the sidewalks of Gotham U on my way to lab, and there are birds chirping like I'm a freaking fairy-tale princess and today is the day I get my prince. And okay, it's

Gotham City, so instead of darling little bluebirds, I have curmudgeonly pigeons. And, yes, they're probably carrying eleventy billion diseases, seeing as how they're essentially rats with wings, but I am a SUPERPRINCESS OF SCIENCE, y'all.

As soon as I get to the lab, I go to the minus 80 freezer to get my serum samples so they can start thawing. I put on a lab coat and these fluffy, padded blue gloves first because minus 80 freezers keep things at, well, minus 80 degrees. Celsius. So, basically, they're colder than Mr. Freeze in an ice storm. I pull out the metal freezer rack and find the white box with my initials on it. Then I place the samples in an ice bucket so they can thaw and I can start my life-changing experiment.

Did you know waiting for something to thaw is even worse than waiting for water to boil? Takes longer too. But you have to do it properly because, like, how do you know the sample froze evenly, and what if the part that thawed first isn't absolutely identical to the part that's still frozen, and I am not making any rookie mistakes on this, the cusp of my scientific triumph.

I make coffee. I wash glassware. I hide all of Trent's pens in various locations around the lab. Hell, I even dust everyone's desk because I am SUCH A NICE PERSON. I also check my samples every three to five minutes. I'm just pulling out a tube for what has to be the tenth time when I get this weird creeping feeling like someone is watching me. I whip my head around, but there's nobody there.

"Huh." I give the sample a shake even though it's clear there's still a chunk of frozen serum in the bottom.

Then I go back to my desk and do crossword puzzles and try to ignore the feeling that someone is standing behind me and sniffing my hair. Finally, *finally*, my samples are ready, and I can get started on my assay.

I can barely keep my hands from shaking as I pipette the Arkham samples, a fraction of a drop in each well, done in triplicate, even though I've totally run this assay with them before. I pipette in the control samples too. Lucky I took those new ones last week to increase our $n$, or sample size. It's funny, though. I could have sworn I had these tubes in a different order. Ah, well, I'm probably just jumpy because I'm so excited. I have no idea which of these samples I'm working with is The Joker's. For half a second, I pictured a pale-green tube on ice with the letter *J* marked on the lid in permanent marker. But it's important to code them by number so I'm not biased. Plus, it's kind of exciting. With every sample, I get to wonder, *Is this one it? Is this The Joker's?* Before I know it, there's only one sample remaining.

I push down the plunger on the pipette. Carefully draw up one hundred microliters of serum (his serum?) and expel it into the first of three wells. My entire body is made of electricity. In just a few hours, I'll know the answer to my question.

Am I really worthy of going to school here?

Ahem. I mean, do Arkham patients have higher levels of epigenetic modifications of the Super-Villain gene?

By the time things finish running, it's late, and everyone in the lab is gone except for Bernice and Dr. N and Oliver, who is nearly finished writing up his thesis and who (totally coincidentally, I'm sure) appears to have lost ten pounds and pulled out half an eyebrow.

Oliver raps on Dr. N's door, even though it's already open. "Hey, can I talk to you for a sec? I've been finding some inconsistencies in my data, and I'm freaking out. I don't know—it could be nothing? It's probably not nothing. Oh my gosh, it's going to ruin me."

Whelp. That's gonna be a while. I decide to make a game of seeing if I can finish analyzing my data before they finish meeting.

Bernice comes in yawning. "I hate how the darkroom makes me so sleepy. I have to watch my brothers, so I'm gonna go, but text me as soon as you know the results, okay?"

I grin. "Will do!"

She squeezes my shoulder. "Good luck, Harleen." And checks her phone. "Oh!"

"What's up?" I ask, one eye on exporting my data to an Excel spreadsheet so I can pull it up on my lab computer.

"Remember how two girls dropped out of the Bridge Scholars program this year, but they weren't in either of our small groups?"

"Yeah." My heart starts beating faster. This feels like it's going to be big.

"I just got a text from another friend in the program." She looks down at her phone again, like she's checking just to be sure. "They were in Dr. Perry's group."

"Oh!!!" I can't help but be loud right now. "I knew it! I knew if we looked hard enough, we'd uncover something on that creeper."

"It's starting to happen," Bernice says, the hint of a smile on her lips. "We might be able to catch him."

She has to rush off to get to her apartment in time before her mom leaves. I try to calm down enough to look at my data. Do some averages. Make some graphs. Just like before, the Arkham samples show much higher levels of methylation (epigenetic changes in DNA that might be due to trauma) than the control samples.

"Sweeeet!" I say out loud, and then check over my shoulder to make sure Oliver and Dr. N didn't hear me.

These are just the group averages, though. I still want to look at individual samples. I hold my breath as I check The Joker's. It's off the charts. Higher than any of the Arkham samples, and much higher than the set of controls I'm using. I am brilliant and powerful and my cells are full of magic, and if I was alone in the lab right now, I would absolutely be doing one of those mad scientist laughs.

I didn't realize it would feel this good—so satisfying, exhilarating—to have an idea that I dreamed up about the world turn out to be true. I am meant to be at Gotham University. I am meant to be a scientist. And every poisonous word my dad has ever spoken loses its teeth—they don't disappear exactly, but they can no longer hurt me.

I stare at my beautiful, freaking gorgeous graph like a proud parent or a dopey boyfriend. I always thought it was weird when scientists called experiments elegant or sexy because, hi, we are not talking about a lady in a couture gown. But my experiment is sexy as hell and elegant as a claw-foot bathtub filled with Chanel N°5. I cock my head to the side. Huh. The error bars on the control graph are really big, though, which is kind of like my sexy, elegant experiment having a big, giant pimple.

I bet there's an outlier throwing things off, probably from the new controls—the ones I just added from people in the lab, because the controls I ran earlier were fine. I scroll up to check the individual values. A couple people are higher than you might expect for controls, one even showing Arkham levels, but nothing too terribly alarming. And then I see it.

Someone is twice as high as The Joker.

# CHAPTER 24

IT'S PROBABLY A MISTAKE. I CAN RUN IT AGAIN TOMORROW. But the fact that each of the triplicate wells is spitting out the same value makes me nervous. I rush back to the lab and grab my notebook so I can check the sample IDs against the names I wrote down when we did the blood draws.

Ugh, something smells terrible in here. It only takes a second to find the source—Oliver left a glass beaker on the hot plate, and now it's boiling over. Poor guy. He's really breaking down. Because he secretly has epigenetic changes in SV1 that are twice as high as The Joker's?! I laugh the second I think it. It's not Oliver.

It's someone, though. Someone I know.

I put on the lab equivalent of oven mitts and move the boiling beaker to the sink. Turn off the hot plate. Is it Kijoon? Bernice? Trent? Ha-ha-ha, Trent wishes. I put on nitrile gloves and clean up the mess with paper towels, being extra careful since I don't actually know what was boiling in here.

I discard my gloves in the biohazard trash. Should I tell the person when I find out? What if they take it badly? What if it's that last little push they needed, and it sends them on a Gotham City crime spree or murder spree or other kind of nefarious spree?

What if they try to hurt me to keep it quiet?

The thought sends a shiver down my spine. Not that I'd tell anyone else. That'd be unethical. I check my notebook against the numbers and find out who among us could rival The Joker.

The name hits me like an adrenaline shot to the heart.

For several seconds, I just stare, like the letters are playing a trick on me and they're about to magically rearrange themselves.

*Aaron Nelson.*

I check it and check again, hoping I've somehow got it wrong.

Then I panic.

What does this mean? He seems like such a nice guy. Is my hypothesis about the SV1 gene completely wrong? Maybe there's no actual connection after all between villainous qualities and high levels of epigenetic changes in the Super-Villain gene? Was I so totally off base? Or . . . what if I was right? And there *is* a connection . . . meaning Dr. Nelson isn't who I think he is?

I am not at all ready to answer these big questions, so instead, I furiously text Bernice. (Avoidance. Excellent strategy, Quinzel.)

Harleen: OMG WTF

Harleen: I just finished my assay and you would not BELIEVE it. Dr. N IS A SUPER-VILLAIN. Like, twice as bad as The Joker, according to Science. THIS IS CRAZYPANTS. Do you think he'd have a psychotic break and turn evil if I told him?

I am nothing if not professional. Luckily, Bernice texts back almost immediately. Someone needs to save me from myself.

Bernice: OMG

Bernice: also, no!!!!

Bernice: just because someone has high levels doesn't mean they're definitely a villain or even a bad person

Bernice: also, did it work out with the joker's sample?

Bernice: because I'm planning victory cupcakes just in case

All the muscles in my neck relax. Of course she's right. A lot of people could have this Super-Villain gene and also have past trauma that caused changes to the gene, and just because a person has both of those things, I mean, they could still make good choices that go against both their DNA and their life experiences. I remember this article I read—about a scientist who used brain scans from psychopaths and controls to develop a way of identifying what a typical psychopath brain looks like. And then the scientist TURNED OUT to have a psychopath brain. (But, like, he wasn't a serial killer or anything.)

This doesn't have to mean Dr. N's a bad guy.

There's a loud *thwack* behind me, and I nearly jump out of my skin. I turn to see that (A) Oliver is leaving Dr. N's office, and (B) he just tripped over the copy of Kandel's *Principles of Neural Science* that Dr. N uses as a doorstop because it's so mammoth. Dr. N holds on to Oliver's elbow.

"Easy," he says. "This'll all work out. Why don't you go home. Get some rest. You can have another look at the data tomorrow." He pauses, nostrils flaring. "And maybe take a shower."

Oliver nods, triple-speed. Eek, how much coffee has he had today? "Right, right. I can do that. Yeah."

He stumbles out of the lab with glazed eyes and one twitching eyelid.

As soon as he's gone, I rush into Dr. N's office.

"Hey, I know you're leaving, but guess what! I was able to get a sample of The Joker's blood from a crime scene—don't ask me how—and I just ran it, and I'm so excited, and it can't wait till tomorrow!" I bounce on my heels and make my best pleading face.

Dr. N laughs. "Okay, let's see it. I don't have anywhere better to be."

I have him pull up the graphs on his computer. Scoot my chair around to his side of the desk so I can dramatically gesture at the data.

"He's off the charts," I tell Dr. N. "Way higher than the Arkham patients, who are way higher than the controls."

I conveniently leave out the part about his own results.

Dr. N is shaking his head like he can't believe how amazing I am. "This is fantastic. The Arkham results alone would have warranted a high-impact paper. But this piece with The Joker—he's captivated society with his violence and chaos. The press is going to eat this up. I'm friendly with an editor at *PGAS*. I can reach out and have him expedite the process."

I grin like I've swallowed the sun, like everything in my past doesn't exist. *Proceedings of the Gotham Academy of Sciences*—that journal's a huge deal.

"Of course, I'll have to figure out a way around the informed-consent issues, but that'll be no trouble," he says, almost talking to himself. He snaps out of it and turns back to me. "This is going to be huge, do you know that? You should come over for dinner tonight so we can celebrate."

He grins and squeezes my leg. The biggest rush radiates through me. People are going to know my name. They're going to respect me. My eyes meet his. And Dr. N thinks I'm brilliant.

"It's incredibly exciting, isn't it?" I don't want to stop talking about it, ever. I want to feel this way and stretch this moment for as long as I possibly can. I'll definitely go to dinner with him—people probably have dinner with their professors all the time, right? I lean forward, so drunk off it all that I don't hear the footsteps behind me.

"Dr. Nelson?"

We freeze. Me, leaning toward Dr. Nelson. Oliver, slack-jawed in the doorway. And Dr. N, with his hand still resting on the inside of my leg. The hand that Oliver is currently staring at.

I was so excited, I kind of forgot it was there.

Dr. N recovers his wits first and removes his fingers from my person.

The air gets stuffy and tense and unbearable. Dr. N shifts

his eyes away from me and stands up. And it slowly starts to dawn on me what Oliver must think he's walked in on—what it must look like.

I start. Why didn't I see this before?

"Why don't you go on home, Harleen," Oliver tells me quietly.

My head nods without me realizing I'm doing it, like a puppet master's pulling the strings. I stand slowly and turn toward the door, but it feels like I'm swimming through fog. I don't know how I get outside of Dr. Nelson's office, but the next thing I know, Oliver is closing the door behind me.

I gather my things and leave the lab, walking to the subway, thoughts rushing through my head. Two minutes ago, I couldn't have been prouder of what I'd discovered. But now? I feel so grimy. Like I could take a dozen showers and I'd still feel ashamed.

This whole time, I've been telling myself pretty stories about who Dr. Nelson is and how he's *such* a good guy and a great professor and how much he helps promote women in science. I'd probably just imagined it when he looked at me *that* way, right? He only put his hand on my leg because he got caught up in the moment today! He paid me special attention because he knew I was worthy of it—because I was smart and ambitious and *promising.*

But now? Seeing Oliver look at us, so shocked, so concerned, with Nelson's hand on my thigh and an invitation to dinner resting in the air between us, the uncomfortable truth I've been hiding from myself becomes clear: grown men don't let themselves get caught up in moments with teenage girls. Every flicker of doubt I doused and every moment of suspicion I smothered were real all along.

The betrayal hurts more when I realize now I have to ask myself about the motivation behind every good thing he ever said to me. Did he say it because it was true? Or because he wanted something from me, something he had no right to want? That's the part that stings the most. The wondering. You shouldn't be allowed to call someone *our scientific future* and not mean it. You shouldn't be allowed to use someone's hopes that way.

Harleen Quinzel

blond
brilliant
smoking hot
a gymnast—i bet she can do all kinds of things

there's a look that she gets. like there's an animal
inside her—just waiting to get out.

of all the girls, harleen's the one i want the most.

# APRIL

# CHAPTER 25

I SEE IT ALL DIFFERENTLY NOW. ESPECIALLY THAT NIGHT AT his house, after the party.

We talk and talk and talk about science. And he keeps pouring more wine for himself, sometime before the other two professors leave. No, after they're already gone.

"How 'bout you stay and have some dessert?"

He's smiling, and I want to do what he says. He's the kind of person you can't say no to, his students flocking around him like he's the leader of a cult.

When he goes to the kitchen to get us some dessert, I wait in my chair patiently. And when he comes back with the flourless chocolate cake and sits back down next to me, I pretend the only reason he scoots his chair closer is so it'll be easier to share the cake. I ignore how he gets this flash of hunger in his eyes when I accidentally moan over my first bite (it really was a damn good cake). Because he's talking to me like I'm an equal. And I want him to keep talking to me like I'm an equal. I want to BE an equal.

And then he says it. Well past midnight. Cheeks red. Eyes bright.

"You know," he says. "You know, I think you might be the most brilliant scientific mind I've seen in a long time."

I'm so overcome with emotion that I squeeze his hand impulsively. Our eyes meet. The moment stretches and sharpens and sizzles.

"Hey, it's getting late." He looks up from his glass with a sleepy grin. He even stretches. "Are you sure you don't want to spend the night? In the guest bedroom, of course. I just want to make sure you get home safely, even if that means tomorrow morning."

On the train ride home, I repeat the words *most brilliant scientific mind* in my head, over and over and over and over and the doors to the train open and the doors to the train close.

I tell myself he was only offering for me to stay over to be nice. He didn't mean it the way I think he meant it.

I tell myself it is the best day of my entire life.

Kijoon sets his backpack down behind me, and I almost choke on my own spit.

I'm back at lab twelve hours, one sleepless night, and three cups of coffee later. I decide to analyze my data all over again because of that one weird, off-the-charts sample and because it squeezes some normal out of a day that feels anything but. I open my spreadsheet. Does Oliver think something happened, like, *really happened*? Is he going to report it? What's going to happen to me? Is everyone going to know?

I pour another cup of coffee, which may or may not induce a heart explosion. I fill my travel mug, and just as I'm putting the coffeepot back, Dr. Nelson sweeps in. I bobble my travel mug and almost drop it. Speaking of heart explosions.

I try to get out the word *Hi*, but it sticks in my throat. He gives me a tight nod and slips past me into his office. Shuts the door brusquely even though he always keeps it open.

Right. It hurts more than I thought it would. Somehow I shuffle over to my desk and sit down. My computer is on and my hands are on the keyboard, but all I can do is stare at the blank cells of my spreadsheet and try not to cry. Time passes. Hours? Minutes?

I hear footsteps in the hallway again, and this time it's Morgan. She says hi, but she gets right to work. Does she know? Does everybody know? Do people think we've done stuff together? Do they think I slept with him? That I slept my way into the Bridge program?

*Don't think about that. Just try to get through the next few hours of work so you can go to your Reckoning meeting and finally feel some release.*

I move like a robot. The numbers in my spreadsheet barely make sense, which is not surprising given my mental state. I decide to check the sink for glassware to wash so at least I can feel like I'm doing something. Oliver walks into the lab as I'm cleaning up.

"Hi." This time I do manage to get the word out.

"Hi." His eyes slide to the door like he wishes he could escape.

I'm thinking he'll do the same as Dr. Nelson—lock himself away and pretend I don't exist, but instead, he moves closer and lowers his voice.

"Are you doing okay?"

My eyes narrow. "I don't know. Am I?"

I feel a sudden flash of anger. I can take care of myself. I didn't need him to step in like that, without even asking me what happened or what I wanted.

He sighs, but not unkindly. "Look, I don't want you to be hurt by this, but also, what Dr. Nelson did is absolutely not okay." His arm twitches like he wants to put his hand on my shoulder but he thinks better of it. *Do not touch the eighteen-year-old girl.* He kind of hugs me with his eyes, though. "I've filed a complaint with the university, and I've warned him to stay away from you. If anything else happens, if you need anything else at all, you let me know."

"But nothing *did* happen," I say. Nothing big enough for him to get in trouble for, anyway. I can see myself in front of the ethics board, like I'm the one on trial. Because I will be if this story gets out. *Are you* sure *he put his hand on your leg? Are you certain you want to ruin a man's career over this?* I know how this goes for girls like me.

Oliver just gives me a pity smile and walks away.

I'm grateful to him for looking out for me. I am. But I'm terrified about what this might mean for my scholarship. I don't have another way to pay for school without it. I'd probably have to defer acceptance and get a job. Save up. Live at home with my dad for so many months, I can't even bring myself to do the calculations. I already postponed once because the Bridge program seemed like my best chance at landing a scholarship to a college (so, *actually* being able to go), but I can't do it again. I don't have another year in me. I wish I could get some kind of sign from Dr. Nelson, but he keeps the door to his office shut for the rest of the day, working furiously on his computer. I try to ignore the voice in my head—my father's—that digs in like a rusty nail at every turn, at lunch, as I grab my bag and leave for the zoo.

*How are you going to pay for all that?*

I know something is wrong the instant I enter the sea lion exhibit. It's something about the way Bianca's hand is tapping an angry beat against her leg. The way Bernice has her arms hugged around her midsection like she's trying to hold herself together. The way all four girls are leaning over, looking at something. No pretending like they don't know each other today.

The very first stair creaks when I step on it, and four heads swivel in my direction like they're being pulled by the same string.

And now I know whatever it is that's making their faces go so tight has to do with me.

"What's going on, babes?" I force the bright words from my mouth, and they fall like bricks.

The way their eyes slide back and forth makes my heartbeat quicken. If no one wants to tell me, it really must be bad. When I reach the top of the stairs, Bianca thrusts her tablet at me. The girls stare at me as I read, watching the knowledge hit me with critical force.

To: ReckoningSuggestionBox@reckoningmail.com
From: oliver.ross7@gothamu.edu
Date: Thursday, March 31, 11:38 p.m.
Subject: Aaron Nelson, PhD

Hello,

My name is Oliver Ross, and I'm a graduate student in Dr. Aaron Nelson's lab in the Neurobiology Department. I need to report an instance of sexual harassment. I've filed a formal complaint with the university too, but honestly, that feels like it's too good for him.

I'm so sorry. I feel responsible because she's my student mentee and because this has happened again, and I didn't do anything the other time he did something like this. The last time this happened, the girl was a grad student, and it seemed consensual, so I kept quiet. But this girl is only 18, and she's like my little sister, and I feel sick.

I found them in his office tonight, and I saw enough to know there's something going on. There was this time a couple weeks ago too. It was late and I saw him in the parking deck, making out with a blond girl against his car. I should have checked to see if it was her. I shouldn't have been such a coward. If you need any help, please let me know.

Oliver
Oliver J. Ross
PhD candidate and senior graduate student
Nelson Laboratory
Neurobiology Department
Gotham University

I don't want to look up from this email and see their faces. It takes more courage than anything I've ever done. I take a deep breath and lift my chin. Their expressions are worse than I could have guessed. Shock, concern. Horror. All played out in their eyes and the stretch of the skin around their mouths and jaws. I don't even know what to say, but it doesn't matter because they all start talking at once.

"Are you okay?" (Kylie)

"He better get fired." (Bianca)

"It's not okay that he did this to you." (Jasmin)

"I will do whatever it takes to make him pay." (Bianca)

"How could you do this to me?"

That last one comes from Bernice, and when I see the way she's got tears pooling in her eyes, the way she's trying to hold them back—it breaks me.

*Told you it'd only be a matter of time until you destroyed her.*

"I didn't—" I try to say, but my voice cracks, and the words die in my throat.

Bernice's jaw works like she's trying to gather the courage to say something else. "I think we need to be open to the possibility that Dr. Nelson is the serial assaulter," she says, never taking her eyes off mine.

My jaw drops, but Jasmin and Bianca are nodding.

"Absolutely." Bianca's fist clenches and unclenches. "If he'd do something like this— With a student! Who knows what else he'd do?"

"Whoa, whoa, whoa. Are you guys kidding me right now?" I shove Bianca's tablet right back at her. "Nothing actually happened."

Jasmin puts her hand on my shoulder. "It's okay if it did."

I appreciate that she's trying to be supportive, but she's not hearing me. "I'm serious. This whole thing—it was just him putting his hand on my leg for a second. Which, yes, is sketchy. I know how it looks, but nothing *else* happened, okay? And I definitely don't think he's the one taking girls. I mean, hello, Dr. Perry? Anyone remember him?"

My voice is rising now, and I can't help it. I can't stop myself from defending Dr. Nelson, despite everything that's happened. Maybe it's just my stupid unending loyalty coming to the surface, but I don't want to burn this bridge down all the way. I'm not ready to. He thought I was brilliant, and I can't let that go. Salem the Sea Lion gives me a knowing look before going back to her herring.

"Yeah, I met with Perry, and he was pretty gross," says Kylie, bringing me back to the surface.

And now everyone is looking at her.

"Wait, you did?" says Bernice.

*"Alone?"* adds Jasmin. "That's *so* dangerous. I thought we agreed you weren't going to do that."

Bianca makes a face like we're all missing the point. "Also, we're not supposed to KEEP SECRETS FROM EACH OTHER."

Kylie just shrugs. "We need to know who's doing this."

"Exactly. And it looks like it's Dr. Perry," I say. "And even if it's not, that doesn't mean it's Dr. Nelson."

I have to make them see. I can't handle the alternative. That the first person to ever see anything in me is a monster.

*But his samples were twice The Joker's,* a voice in the back of my mind whispers.

*Don't* think about that.

"Look, I think Perry is probably our guy too, but that doesn't change what happened to you. Harleen, you know this is not okay, right?" Jasmin says. I hate the sympathy in her voice.

"Yeah, I mean, he's thirtysomething," chimes in Kylie. "And you're eighteen. He's a professor, and you're his intern. That kind of power differential is *messed* up."

Bianca cracks her neck and rolls her shoulders, like she's physically incapable of holding still. "Yeah, I'm comfortable digging up every skeleton in this guy's closet. And you need to come forward, Harleen. I can't believe you're protecting him right now."

"Whoa." Jasmin puts a hand on Bianca's arm. "I'm every bit as mad as you, but assault survivors should never have to come forward if they choose not to."

Anger flares in my chest. Now I'm an assault survivor?! They're saying they're angry at him, but it sure as hell feels like they're coming after me.

Bianca sighs. "You're right. I got so caught up in wanting to stop other girls from getting hurt. It's your choice, Harleen. We're with you either way."

But they're NOT with me either way. They're only with me if I confirm the narrative they clearly all believe.

"I already told you!" I shout. "I can't come forward because there's nothing to come forward *about*. I mean, yes, okay, some of this is weird or not the best or whatever. But—"

"Like him making out with you against his car?" asks Bernice, the hurt clear in her voice.

"That wasn't even me, I *swear*. The only time we've ever really been alone was at his house party, and I was the one who waited until everyone left so I could talk to him, not the other way around. And okay, maybe he asked if I wanted to crash there, but he didn't try anything and he was totally cool when I said I was going to take the train home. If he wanted to take advantage of me, he wouldn't have been that nice, right? He's not the big bad we've been looking for, I know it." I am pleading now. It feels so important that I make them understand. This person I've been idolizing isn't— I could never—

Bernice shakes her head. "But he still asked you to stay

the night. And he kept scooting all close to you over chocolate cake and stuff."

Something about her words flips a switch inside my head and I start. "How do you know we had chocolate cake?"

And now four sets of eyes are on Bernice.

She gulps like a cartoon character. "I was worried. Well, and I guess I was right to be, right? So, when I left that night, I might have stayed and watched you through the window." Her cheeks go red. "I mean, I didn't *watch you*. I just, you know, hung around long enough to make sure he wasn't going to drug you or attack you or anything. I just wanted to make sure you were okay."

Now it is my turn to feel betrayed.

"YOU SPIED ON ME?"

The other girls are shocked, but I still get the impression that they don't believe me that we didn't do anything. Which means they're on her side and not mine. Something about that undoes me. Drives cracks into the glass case that keeps my darkness contained.

"At least Dr. Nelson thinks I'm brilliant! He supported me." I circle closer to Bernice. "Maybe you're jealous," I say in a low voice. "Because he never thought you had as much promise as me."

"That is not it!" Bernice shoots back. But she has red splotches on her neck now.

"*Really?*" I jut my chin out. Really get in her face. Feel the darkness uncoiling itself in my brain. "Then, why'd you do it?"

She flinches away from whatever she sees in my eyes. Won't answer. It only makes me madder.

"You won't even trust me to be alone with a man without spying on me. And you're not even my girlfriend!" Bernice glares at me, tears welling in her eyes, but I don't stop there. I turn on the rest of the girls. "And you. All of you are supposed to be these *literal* social justice warriors—you're supposed to be my *family*—and you can't even support me. What happened to believing women? Or does that only count for women who aren't like me?" They stare at me, stunned, and I don't wait for an answer. I will burn them down before they burn me. "You know what? I'm done. And you're gonna stay away from me. You're gonna stay away from Dr. Nelson too. And if you don't? I'll call that Reckoning task force myself."

Jasmin takes a couple slow steps backward, and Kylie has her hands up like she doesn't want to touch this situation. Bianca looks horrified. Everything I've said sinks in all at once, but I can't take it back, so I just stand there with my mouth open.

"This. Is a whole lot of mess I did not sign up for," says Kylie, picking up her Fendi clutch and turning to leave. "I'm gonna go and let y'all work this out."

"You're right. Screw this. The Reckoning was supposed to be about loyalty and honesty." Bianca grabs her backpack and stomps after Kylie.

"Yeah, I have a paper due tomorrow." Jasmin starts to follow them down the stairs but stops when she passes me. "I can't believe you'd say something like that," she says quietly.

They wind past Salem and exit toward the penguins. I watch them walk away with a lump the size of a grenade lodged in my throat.

Bernice and I stand there. We don't say anything at all, but her eyes are so accusing.

I know I'm getting defensive, but I can't help it. Just because I'm this morally gray, chaotic neutral explosion of a person doesn't mean I'm lying right now. I may like the sizzling feeling I get when I cross a line, but there are lines I won't cross. I would never betray the people I love. Not really. "I'm sorry I said all that. But I'm telling the truth. Nothing happened."

"When you said you were seeing someone else and didn't want to be exclusive, I thought you meant Trent," Bernice shoots back.

"I broke up with him weeks ago! And anyway, you just said you saw me through the window with Nelson. You *know* we didn't do anything. What are you playing at?"

"Maybe not that night. But how do I know about all the other nights? I see the way you look at him all the time."

She really thinks I actually did it. Of course she does. When you're hot and blond and spontaneous, and someone says you slept with someone, no one is ever going to believe you didn't. I want to be angry, but instead there's this ache so deep, it has to be terminal. "Why did you even want to date me, then?"

Bernice's tears, the ones she's held in so carefully up until now, start falling, hot and angry. "Maybe I was lying to myself, okay? Maybe I had to lie to myself about a lot of things to be with you because I like you so damn much."

My heart flips and I realize the pain all this must have caused her. "Bernice—" I try to touch her shoulder, but she jerks away.

"No! You don't get to do that." And then she gets this look—all calculation and sharpness. "You want to know what else I was lying about?"

Based on the fire in her eyes, I don't think I do.

"Dr. Nelson."

No. She can't—

"I've *always* thought he could be a potential for our serial assaulter. That it was between him and Dr. Perry. And you know what?"

I make myself say it. "What?"

"I'm going to figure out who it is if it kills me."

I don't know what that means, but I'm scared to find out. Scared I'm losing her.

Losing everything.

Bernice leaves too, and I'm left standing there. Alone.

I find myself wandering to the hyena exhibit, but even they can't cheer me up today. Everything I care about— the Reckoning, my relationship with Bernice, my academic future—is falling apart.

I know I should be thinking about how to pick up the pieces of my life plan and cement them back together, and about whether the Nelson drama affects my chance at a scholarship at Gotham U, especially now that Oliver has reported it. But instead, there's a terrible drumbeat of emptiness and loss: The Reckoning. Bernice. The Reckoning. Bernice.

The sorrow threatens to drown me. When we started the Reckoning, I never could have imagined what it would become. That it would be more than just vengeance and justice and fun. I trusted those girls, and they trusted me. They saw the best in me. Believed in me. Saw something more than the garbage reflected in the mirror. They were my family. And now I've set the whole house on fire.

And Bernice. . . . My brain skitters away from thoughts of her like they'll burn me, because they do. I thought I knew myself well enough to know I'd hurt her. I thought I had set the bar low enough. But of course I can always go lower.

Even when I'm trying harder than I've ever tried before. Even when I'm expecting to wreck things and doing everything I can to prepare for the storm. I felt like I was ready for my first real girlfriend. And now I'll never get the chance.

My life plan, the Reckoning, Bernice? I've lost them all. And I don't know who I am without them.

# CHAPTER 26

### Thursday, April 7

HER FACE ALMOST LOOKS LIKE KYLIE'S. BUT DEAD KYLIE doesn't have on nearly enough eye makeup, and her hands are folded just a little too sweetly, and something about her skin looks . . . odd. Like she's the upscale department store mannequin version of Alive Kylie. I tilt my head down so I can glance behind me to make sure no one is within earshot. Then I lean closer.

"I will find out who did this to you. I promise," I whisper. I think about what this fall at Gotham U would have been like if she were still here. "I miss you already."

Bianca and Jasmin didn't come with me because we didn't want to look too suspicious as a group, but I know they're planning to visit her gravesite later and bring her a coconut cold brew. I move to the receiving line and tell Kylie's parents how wonderful she was and hope they don't know I'm the girl whose name was written on her ankle. Her mom is crying so hard I don't think she'd notice if I were Batman. There's no way I can ask her any questions without looking like a coldhearted bottom-feeder. But maybe one of Kylie's sorority sisters knows something that could help?

About a hundred of them showed up. A hundred black linen dresses. A hundred pairs of classy black shoes. Across the funeral home, I see a cluster of the ones who were closest to Kylie. Her roommate, Madison, and her Little Sis, Sophie, and a couple other girls I've actually met before. Tall, sophisticated. Shiny hair and understated jewelry and heads full of dreams. I remember being so intimidated by them. Until Kylie announced I was coming with them to their vampires-versus-werewolves crush party, and then Sophie did my makeup, and Kate plunked a pair of wolf ears on my head, and no one cared that I was from the East End, and in two minutes I belonged. Kylie could do things like that.

"Hey," I say to Sophie, a lump swelling in my throat.

"Hey, c'mere." She pulls me into a hug, and it feels so good just to cry.

We tell our favorite Kylie stories, and they offer me a ride back to campus. They're going to get their overnight bags so they can have a sleepover with Kylie's younger sister. Meanwhile, I've somehow been talked into going into the lab, even though I took a bereavement absence from my Bridge classes and I just went to a funeral.

I'm glad to have a chance to be alone with them, though. I hope they'll have the answers I need.

I sit in the back seat, and I squeeze the hem of my dress before I ask it.

"Does anyone know what happened to her?"

The car goes silent. They know. They know, and I shouldn't have pushed so early.

I squeeze my dress tighter.

Wait.

Wait for the silence to become so big it looms like a monster that someone must stake through the heart by filling it.

"She had a heart attack," Sophie finally says.

Kate bows her head beside me, staring down at her black eyelet skirt.

"But she's so young." It just slips out. *Is*, not *was*.

More silence. And then:

"There was some kind of weird toxin in her system."

"Not a drug," Kate says sharply. And then she looks sheepish at her outburst. "Some people are saying she OD'd."

I frown. "But Kylie never does drugs. She only drinks." Something sinister grasps at my heart. "Do you think someone drugged her?"

Sophie looks stricken. "Yes. But they don't think that's what made her have the heart attack. The medical examiner found fatal levels of adrenaline in her bloodstream."

"Adrenaline?"

"Whoever killed her literally scared her to death."

The words hit me like a sandbag to the chest. How scared does a person have to be to die from it? I try to picture Kylie's final hours. How terrified she must have been. Also, how in the world did she manage to write a warning to me while she was having a heart attack? We're quiet as the car pulls in front of the neurobiology building, caught up in a shared nightmare.

I put my hand on the door handle. And then I pause. "I'm going to find out who did this. I don't think the GCPD is up to it, and I'm not letting this monster get away." I glance around the car, but not one of these girls is looking at me like I'm ridiculous. "Anyway, if you hear anything, let me know."

Kate nods, and Sophie squeezes my hand, and Madison turns around in the driver's seat to give me an awkward one-armed hug.

I walk into the building, still wearing my black dress and tights, trying to make sense of everything I've just learned. There's something about it that doesn't make sense. It nags at me like a splinter in your finger that you know is there but you can't find with the tweezers. And then it hits me. The police. None of this information would have made them release me. There must be something else I don't know.

My phone buzzes as I wait for the elevator. It's Bianca, which is great because hearing the sound of her voice would make me feel a lot better right now, and also because I need to update her on this Kylie stuff.

"Hey," I say.

"Hi."

It's weird how much you can tell from a single word. For instance, I can tell that Bianca is the most scared I've ever heard her, but she's trying hard to pretend she's not.

"Hon, are you okay?"

There's a fraught pause on the other end of the line. And then her voice, even smaller than before.

"I think I'm next."

The bottom drops out from under me. "What are you talking about?"

The elevator pings open in front of me, but I don't move. Have the elevators in this building always been this small? There's no way I'm hopping in that airless death box alone when I'm feeling this freaked. I'll take the stairs, thanks. I wait for Bianca to answer, keeping my cell phone pressed against my ear like my life depends on it. And maybe it does.

"It's that Voyeur guy," says Bianca. "I was scrolling through the Reckoning Insta again while I was in between sets, and there was a new comment, and it said, 'I'm at the campus gym too, watching you do your squats. Your form's not bad, by the way.' So, I'm freaking out and looking all over the place, and then another comment pops up. 'You don't have to panic. If I wanted to put something in your water bottle when you went to the bathroom, I would have done it.' And I had JUST gone to the bathroom and of course left my water bottle unattended at my station like an idiot!"

Her voice takes on a desperate tone, and I get it. Hearing her say those words sends me into a cold sweat. I look around even though I have no reason to believe someone's watching me.

"Holy crap, Bianca, that's terrifying."

"It gets worse."

Oh no, *did* he put something in her water bottle?

"When I was leaving the gym, I couldn't find my straps—the ones I use to do pull-ups. Which wasn't a big deal because I wasn't planning to do pull-ups today anyway, but the thing is, I could have sworn they were in my bag. I never take them out except to wash them.

"So, I check all around where I was working out and in the locker room, and I ask the guy at the front desk, but he hasn't seen them. And then I get home, and—" She swallows. "They were on the kitchen table."

That should be a good thing, but something about her tone tells me it isn't.

"There was a note, Harleen. Signed by the Voyeur. It said, 'I wanted to show you that I could.'"

No, no, no, no, no. This cannot be happening. "Do you

need me to come over? Because I can be there in a minute."
I don't care what I supposedly have to do in lab today. This
is an emergency.

"Jasmin said she'd come hang out with me in a few hours.
But, Harleen?"

"Yeah?"

"Be careful, okay?"

After I end my call with Bianca, I take a sharp detour to the
girls' bathroom, which is, mercifully, much larger than the
elevator. Between Kylie's funeral and what Bianca just told
me about the Voyeur, I need a minute or sixty to collect
myself before going to the lab. It's almost like I can pinpoint
the day my entire life started to disintegrate—the day of the
Reckoning blowup. Three days after that, I found Bernice
passed out in the lab, barely breathing.

*I'm going to figure out who it is if it kills me.*

Two days after that, Kylie wound up dead.

*Harleen*

*Don't trust*

I'm terrified about what might happen tomorrow. Or
today. Because I'm not figuring this out fast enough, and
everything keeps getting worse, and this Voyeur guy is closing in on us, but how fast? And who's next?

I splash cold water on my face because people are always
doing that in the movies and it looks like it helps. I'm not
convinced it actually does anything other than get water on
my dress, but the act of trying makes me feel a little bit better, and I'll take whatever placebo effect I can get. I should

probably do a few more exposure therapy sessions this week too—I don't like that I couldn't get in that elevator. And the nightmares have definitely been happening more often since Kylie was killed.

When I get to the lab, I'm glad I took the time to emotionally prepare myself. Because things are falling apart here too.

There are men in the lab. Strong men. Surly in their efficiency. Menacing in their silence. Men seizing computers and manila folders like the lab is a crime scene.

Oliver hovers by the coffee maker protectively.

"What's going on?" I whisper. The panic rises in my chest. Honestly, I shouldn't even be here, still in my black dress, eyes still red from Kylie's service—I said I had to go to a funeral. But Dr. Nelson told me he really needed me to come in because he was hoping to have me make some "critical tweaks" to my figures for the epigenetics work to make them publication ready, and could I come in after? I'm not about to let anything get in the way of my work being published, even if it means having to work with Nelson while I'm still trying to figure out my thoughts.

I shoot a nervous glance at the man pawing through the file cabinet next to my desk. Who do they think I killed this time? Did they find out something new about Kylie? "Are they here . . . for me?" I whisper to Oliver.

He shakes his head. "The investigation isn't about you. It's about Dr. Nelson."

A rush of relief. And then I notice Oliver can't quite meet my eyes. Is he the reason they're here?

*Why don't you go on home, Harleen.*

But before I can ask him anything else, Dr. Nelson sweeps in, all grandiose hand gestures.

"Hey, everybody, can I have your attention, please?"

The lab goes so silent so fast, you can hear a centrifuge whirring two rooms away. I don't think any of us were expecting him to face this head-on.

"I need you all to know that I'm under investigation for some ethical concerns." He smiles. Openly. Widely. The way you do when you're trying to calm a small child.

We are nowhere near calm. Trent looks like he's swallowed his tongue, and one of the graduate students appears to be mentally calculating the number of years this will add to her PhD.

"What kind of ethical concerns?" asks a postdoc.

Dr. Nelson grins even more broadly, only now he's crossed the line from calm to fractured. "Some people who are jealous want to make sure I'm not getting illegal kickbacks from drug companies."

Oliver's jaw tightens.

"I'm giving them my full cooperation." Dr. Nelson spreads his arms wide. "I have nothing to hide."

The man carrying Dr. N's desktop past us makes a face that says otherwise. I scan the faces of the other lab members—do they think he did something? Dr. Nelson's smile falters, and he heads out of the room at a brisk clip.

We are quiet.

The sound of his footsteps echoes down the hallway.

Frenzied quiet.

The door opens with a creak.

The loudest freaking quiet you have ever heard.

The door closes.

And we explode.

*Did you know?*

*No, did you?*

*Do you think he really did it?*
*He didn't look so good.*

Oliver fills his coffee mug and makes a quick exit.

I slip across the office and stand next to Trent.

"Hey," I say. "Unbelievable, right?"

He manages to pull himself out of his shell-shocked stupor. "I hope this doesn't affect how people will view his letter of recommendation for med school. It probably won't. And I'll be getting three other strong ones. Extremely strong." It occurs to him that I am witnessing this display of floundering vulnerability.

I grin. "Don't worry. I'm sure you'll still be facing multiple medical malpractice suits before you're thirty."

His eyes narrow as they go from my shoes to the top of my head. "What are you, goth now?"

I stare him right in the face. "I went to Kylie Pearce's funeral today."

A flinch! I saw a flinch! Because he's hiding something? Because my eyes are boring into him? Or because he actually feels bad that a girl has been murdered?

"Oh, uh, sorry." He scuffs his loafers against the floor. "That's right. I think I knew you two were, uh, friends."

"Did you know her?" I narrow my eyes at him.

"I've heard of her," he says. Again with the flinching. Huh. "Listen, I've gotta get going. I have, uh, class."

"Sure you do," I say, cool as you please. Montoya's got nothing on me.

He hurries away, and I make a mental note to check his schedule and see if he really has class right now. But before I can do it, I get a text.

Jasmin: Bernice is awake.

# CHAPTER 27

WHEN YOU'VE JUST RUN UP EIGHT FLIGHTS OF STAIRS BE-
cause elevators take too long (and, okay, maybe you're still
scared of them) and your favorite person, your Bernice, is
awake, and who knows if she's asked for you and how many
times, running face-first into Officer Montoya is the last
thing you're expecting. I attempt to extricate my limbs as
gracefully as possible.

"Hi," I say, heart beating like a hummingbird's. I hate
how my face has a way of looking guilty whenever she's
around.

Montoya crosses her arms over her chest, calm and confident, even though I just bulldozed into her like a football
player. "Ms. Quinzel, what are you doing here?"

"I'm visiting my friend." There's the slightest pause between the words *my* and *friend*, where my breath catches,
and I can feel myself blushing. I feel like a chicken for not
saying *girlfriend*. We're *together*, but we never settled on
a label before all this happened because I wasn't ready,

and now? Who knows if she'll still want me? She didn't answer a single one of my texts after our fight. It was getting to the point where I was going to show up at her apartment with flowers and art supplies and tell her that I couldn't live without her, but then I found her in the lab that morning, and I almost really did have to live without her.

"Mmmm," says Montoya, still blocking the door. She waits, like how teachers or therapists do because the silence can make you spill answers and secrets and the whole truth and nothing but the truth. I make a mental note to put The Long Pause in my arsenal should I ever become a psychiatrist.

And then it occurs to me that there are things I want out of her too.

"Do you know what caused Kylie's heart attack yet?" I ask in a low voice.

Officer Montoya's chill slips for a fraction of a second, and there is something so satisfying about that. "How did you—?"

I slide by her and into the hospital room. "Let me know when you do."

I know she's still watching me—I can feel her eyes—but Bernice is sitting right there, propped up in bed under a thin hospital blanket and smiling at me so big. I don't know what I did to deserve that smile, but I rush to her side like we're the only two people in the world.

"Are you okay?" I grab her hand, brush her hair out of her face. And then I stop abruptly. We might be broken up. She might not want me to do that. "Sorry. Um. Are you okay, though?" I wait for her to say something. She looks okay, but she was out for three days, and that can cause residual brain damage and stuff, right?

She nods.

"Can you . . . talk?"

It's just a fraction of a second, but it stretches out like an eternity as I spin worst-case scenarios in my head.

"Yes." She smiles again, and my heart, it can continue beating. "Tired, though."

"Of course you are." My eyes go all glassy. I want to kiss her on the forehead so very badly, but I don't. "I'm so glad you're okay. And I'm really sorry about our fight. If I didn't get to— If something had happened before—"

But Bernice just picks up my hand and kisses it, and it makes me feel so okay that I do my best not to cry all over her.

"Come here," she says, scooching over.

I climb into the hospital bed with her and lay my head on her shoulder, and we sit like that for a long time.

"Hey, Bernice?" I say after a while. "Do you remember what happened? In the darkroom?"

She shakes her head. "The police already asked. I felt someone grab me." She touches her neck like a reflex. "And I remember running to the darkroom and locking the door." She fidgets with the edge of her hospital blanket. "I never saw the guy's face."

"Oh." It's too bad. I was hoping Bernice waking up could be the answer to everything. I'd find out who did this, and then I'd hunt them down and make them pay. And this time, I'd let the darkest parts of my imagination do whatever they wanted. I shake off the thought. "Did they say what was in your bloodstream? Was it some kind of weird toxin?" Did he dose her with the same stuff that killed Kylie? Oh, gosh.

Kylie. Bernice doesn't know. How am I supposed to tell her something like that?

She frowns. "No."

"Are you sure?" Maybe her mind isn't entirely right yet. It's probably hard for her to remember everything they've told her.

"Not a toxin," she says. "An anesthetic." She says the word *anesthetic* as one big yawn.

I think about asking her what kind of anesthetic knocks a person out for three days. I also think about breaking the news about Kylie and what we've learned about the Voyeur, but then she yawns again, and I decide it can wait. Just for a day or two. Just till she gets her strength back.

"I'm sorry, I should let you get your rest. I could stay here and read a book or study for Abnormal Psych or something, if you don't want to be alone, though. Of course I didn't bring my backpack with me. I could go home and get it super quick, though."

I stand up.

"Wait," says Bernice, so firmly that I freeze. "I need you to do something for me."

"Anything."

And I mean it. I would hang glide off a building. Break into the GCPD evidence locker. Jump into a pit of boiling acid.

"I need you to search my bedroom for a beaver and read the notes inside."

That . . . was not where I was expecting this to go.

"That's where the truth is," she insists.

"Okay, sweetie, I think you've had too much happy juice. I'm just going to—"

Bernice grabs my arm, stronger than you'd expect. "Promise me," she says.

So I do.

The dread settles into my stomach the minute I walk out of the hospital. Is it safe to leave her in that room all alone? I know she has a buzzer to call the nurses and everything, but in the movies, the bad guys are always able to slip in and smother you with a pillow before you can reach it.

I'm pulling out my phone, debating whether I should call Officer Montoya and ask her to come back, when a text from a restricted number comes through.

I know you're in the Reckoning.

I look around like I'm expecting to see someone hiding behind the Gotham Memorial sign or inside a decorative planter, but I'm alone. A GCPD squad car *harrumphs* over the speed bumps in front of me. I narrow my eyes.

Harleen: Is this Officer Montoya?

I wait, smirking. I wonder if she'll keep up her bluff now that I've called her—

Guess again.

The words send a chill through me, and I know, even as I type his name, what the answer will be.

Harleen: The Voyeur?

Yes.

I suck in my breath. Those three little dots appear, letting me know he's not finished with me.

> I want you to stop what you're doing with the Reckoning. And if you don't? Well, I've been paying little visits to your friends, and I've got something special in mind for you.

A photo comes through immediately after. It's of me, just a couple hours earlier, leaving the neurobiology building right after I got the news about Bernice. There are Xs slashed across my eyes and a caption at the bottom:

> You're next, Harleen.

I squeeze my phone tight. Can't take my eyes off the photo. First Bernice. Then Kylie. One girl in a hospital bed, having clawed her way back to the land of the living. One girl dead, her exuberance snuffed out, her body in a box under six feet of dirt, perfect blond waves still glossy. I don't want to be either of those girls, but he knows who I am. He knows who I am, and he's coming for me.

# CHAPTER 28

I SLINK THROUGH THE ALLEY NEAR BERNICE'S BUILDING, still jarred from my texting session with the Voyeur. *Officer Montoya promised to send someone back to Bernice's room,* I tell myself. *You can stop imagining all the different ways he could come back and "finish the job."*

Bernice's neighborhood is about as rough as mine, aka really rough. Not I'm-going-to-slum-it-on-the-West-Side-and-buy-a-boho-dress-and-then-drink-a-café-crème-while-I-pen-some-intensely-emo-poetry rough. Rough like the rats here could eat a poodle.

But as I walk along the cracked sidewalk, two guys wave at me from a stoop, and a kind-looking grandfatherly man sits in a lawn chair, sipping from a bottle wrapped with a paper bag, and someone's nosy aunt peers through the blinds, and four little girls play hopscotch. There are good people here. That's what the people from the shiny parts of Gotham City can't ever seem to see. I wave at the girls as I enter the apartment building and slip through the hallways until I reach the door to Bernice's apartment. I stand there for a second, wondering whether to knock or whip out my pocketknife. (I decide to go with knocking, even though it involves WAY less intrigue.) The door swings open, and a woman who has to be Bernice's mom answers.

"Harleen!" She has a grin that lights up the entire doorway.

I try to say something back, but the words get stuck. She doesn't even notice. She's too busy hugging me like a long-lost daughter.

"I am so excited to meet Bernice's girlfriend," she says, squeezing me tighter. She smells like laundry detergent and fresh-baked bread. Like what I'd imagine the perfect movie mom would smell like. Hugs like her too.

I'm stunned. At her kindness. At what she just said. Bernice calls me her girlfriend to her family? Something about that makes me blush all over.

She lets me go too soon. "Look at me! What am I doing? Come on in. Come on in."

Mrs. Watkins mothers me into the apartment, where there are two little boys playing an ancient video game system and the smell of chili drifts from the stove. And it's clear they don't have money, and it's not like the place is decorated all fancy, like out of a magazine, but it's clean and there are family pictures smiling from the wall. There is love in this apartment. You can tell. Somewhere in the most secret part of my heart, I ache to know what that's like.

"Would you like some orange juice?" she asks.

"Sure thing," I say, even though I don't want any, really. I think I just want to keep pretending I have a mother.

She places a glass in my hands, and I remember why I'm really here.

"Oh! Bernice wanted me to come by and get a few things for her. Is that okay?"

She squeezes my shoulder. "Of course, honey. I meant to go by the hospital again today, but . . . the boys."

She moves like she's going to show me Bernice's room, but then Bernice's brothers start playing a game of what appears to be "how hard can I pull your hair before it hurts," which quickly and decisively goes south, and she seems pretty occupied with that, so I start down the hallway alone. I'm just about to go into what has to be Bernice's room when her mother hurries inside ahead of me. She pulls a curtain to close off half the room, even though it looked like all that was in there was another twin bed.

She turns toward me with a smile that is apologetic and a little bit broken. "This side of the room is Bernice's."

I want to ask about the other side of the room—the one that isn't Bernice's—but her eyes say not to.

And then a flurry of shouts from the living room breaks the silence, and she runs out, saying, "Feel free to grab what she needs," over her shoulder.

The room is . . . odd.

There's the pretty bedspread and the desk with coffee mugs filled with buttons and snaps and thread and beads and every kind of art supply you can imagine. One of those little jewelry boxes with a ballet dancer inside sits on a dresser next to a sewing machine and colorful bolts of fabric. But then there are the stuffed animals. Only they're not like what you'd see in a toy store. On Bernice's dresser, there's a jaunty raccoon eating from a box of Cracker Jack. On her bookshelf, a duckling with two heads holds court over crocheted versions of basically every major horror movie villain from the past five decades. On the shelf above it is a series of the creepiest teddy bears I've ever seen next to a squirrel dressed like the queen of England. And on her nightstand, the taxidermized beaver, gazing watchfully at her pillow like some kind of demented guardian angel. Apparently, she found it at a flea market and fell in love.

"Gotcha!"

I expect it to feel like a stuffed animal, but underneath all the fur, it's a lot harder and sturdier. I turn the beaver around, inspecting it on all sides for some kind of opening.

"Ummm."

Is this hidden-compartment thing even real? A figment of Bernice's drug-addled imagination? I shake off those thoughts and try to get in the right frame of mind. If I was a superspy, and there were secret military plans hidden inside a taxidermized animal, how would I get at them? I look the beaver directly in its shiny black eyes, and I press its nose like a button. It stares back judgmentally.

"Well, if you're so smart, where would you hide the notes?"

I turn it all around one more time, this time feeling along its fur carefully with my fingers. And then I find it. A small latch hidden between its shoulder blades, perfectly covered by fur. Seriously, who designed this thing? I twist the latch, and a hatch falls open. Inside is a journal and some loose papers. I ease them out so I don't rip anything. And then my stomach does a backflip. There's a Post-it sticking out of the journal, two words written in Bernice's handwriting:

*for harleen*

I flip the pages of the journal until I get to the one marked with the Post-it.

*april 3*

*dear harleen,*

*if you're reading this, things have gone terribly, irrevocably wrong. i hope i'm still alive. i hope you don't hate me too much. but there's something i need you to know.*
    *it was me.*
    *i planned the reckoning from the beginning. i mean, i didn't actually know it was going to be called that—the name was bianca's idea—but i was the one who wanted to organize a girl gang.*
    *i hope when you read this journal, you'll understand why i had to do it.*
    *i love you.*
    *and i love her.*
    *please don't stop until you get the truth.*

*love, bernice*

There's a coldness slipping into my stomach. A frenzied, jittery, dizzy feeling spreading from my head to my finger-tips. Is this really happening? Bernice is a sweetheart whose interests include science and weird art projects and cup-cakes. How could she have organized the Reckoning? I keep running my fingers over the words, especially the part where she says she loves me. Even after everything that went down, she loves me. But then, *her.* Who is *her?* I may be reeling with confusion, but I can still feel hot jealousy licking at the back of my neck. I flip through the journal, closer to the beginning, looking at a page here and there at random.

october 1

women's rights vigilante girl gang

Bernice Watkins

Harleen Quinzel

Bianca Narvaez-Espinosa

Jasmin Jones

Kylie Pearce

Kylie? She even knew she wanted Kylie way back at the beginning? My mind is blown, and there is no putting it back together again. Bernice had the whole entire thing planned before I ever even met with Bianca in the student center. I am stunned. And a little creeped out, if I'm being honest. It's weird to know that someone you care about was watching you and making plans about you. But I'm also kind of impressed because, hi, this is me we're talking about.

I flip back even farther.

september 15

we'd need girls with all kinds of abilities. hacking, fighting. safecracking? i don't even know. but how am i going to get all these amazing women to listen to me?

*maybe if they don't know i'm the leader. but there's still the matter of approaching people and asking them. there's actually a girl i met in lab who's really cool. she could be a potential.*

*Harleen Quinzel*

*blond*
*brilliant*
*smoking hot*
*a gymnast—i bet she can do all kinds of things*

*there's a look that she gets. like there's an animal inside her—just waiting to get out.*

*of all the girls, harleen's the one i want the most.*

Bernice's mom appears in the doorway, and I snap the journal shut, quick.

"Did you find everything you need, hon?"

"Yep. Totally. She, uh, really wanted me to bring this beaver here, so, yeah, I'm just gonna take it. To the hospital."

*Smooth, Harleen, real smooth.*

But Mrs. Watkins's face breaks into a smile. "She sure does love that thing."

As I walk past, Mrs. Watkins actually rubs behind his ears like he's alive.

"Say hi to my girl for me, will you, Bernie?"

And . . . his name's Bernie. Nothing weird about this at all. Nope.

But I just roll with it because all I want to do is get out of this apartment so I can keep reading Bernice's journal.

> *i love you.*
> *and i love her.*
>
> *of all the girls, harleen's the one i want the most.*

# CHAPTER 29

*sophomore year*

*april 15*

> *guess what!!! Stella got picked for the Gotham University Bridge Scholars program! mom is so proud. dad too. i can't wait for her to tell me everything about it! she's going to work in an aerospace engineering lab and meet college boys and everything!*
>
> *i'm 95% happy and only 5% jealous, so i feel like that means i'm a really good sister.*

I'M IN THE BREAK ROOM, READING BERNICE'S JOURNAL ENtries from three years ago while I eat my sandwich and banana, trying to piece together the girl I fell in love with and the girl she kept from me. At least I know who *her* is now. Bernice's sister. Stella. I flip ahead to a different part.

september 23

*Stella got to play in a wind tunnel today, and learn how to design airplane wings. i got to take a pop quiz on <u>A Farewell to Arms</u> while sitting in my assigned seat behind Mark Edwards, whose farts smell like jalapeño poppers, BUT IT'S ALMOST THE SAME THING, RIGHT? i won't be old enough to apply to Bridge Scholars till a year from now, but the countdown is starting today, PERIODT.*

Is Stella who the other half of Bernice's room belongs to? Belonged to? I still don't understand what happened to her, but it sure didn't look like her half of the room had someone living there. I imagine what it must have been like for Bernice, sharing a room with her sister's ghost. I flip ahead again, searching for the part where things get bad, knowing that it's coming.

*junior year*

april 3

*Stella didn't come home from campus tonight. mom and dad are freaking out. the police said she probably went to a party or something and to check back in the morning, but i know something's wrong. she may not have told mom or dad or anyone else if she was going somewhere. but i know she would have told me.*

This is it. I turn the page to keep reading. And at that exact moment, Trent strolls in to microwave some poached salmon prepared by his family's chef until the entire room reeks of fish and privilege. He sits down next to me with his dish and nudges me.

"Did you see?"

"See what?" I don't care how many pictures of baby hyenas he has on his phone, I already told him we're never making out again. (The best part? I'm not even tempted anymore.)

Trent smirks at me. No joke, he could not look any more smug if he was standing on a yacht and holding a golf trophy. "The new paper the lab just put out."

The combination of those words and his expression doesn't bode well.

"I assume it's one of yours?" I say in a tone that suggests I give zero effs.

His smile grows—if possible—even bigger and even smugger. "Nope. One of yours."

"Wait, what? Gimme that." I snatch his phone. Read over the title and the abstract.

There it is. My work on epigenetics and the Super-Villain gene and Arkham patients and The Joker.

With Dr. Nelson as the lead author. Not me.

"*Proceedings of the Gotham Academy of Sciences*," Trent says over my shoulder. Ugh. I had forgotten he was there for one glorious second. He goes on in an oily, irritating voice. "Impact factor of 9.58. Not too shabby, though I'm planning to shoot for *JAMA* or *Nature* with my own—"

I slap his phone against his chest. "Bite me, Trust Fund."

I stalk out of the break room, half-eaten sandwich on

the table. Then I print out the paper and storm Dr. Nelson's office.

I throw it on his desk. "How could you do this to me?"

Several people in the office area turn to look, and I feel my face flush. I didn't mean to say it that loud.

I lower my voice and ask again. "How could you?"

He nods his head at the door. "Can you close the—?" Shakes his head. "No. Better to leave it open." He leans across his desk. Talks in a low voice just above a whisper. "I really needed this."

I take a seat and cross my arms, waiting.

He looks from side to side, like there's someone hiding in the two hundred square feet of office space, takes a breath, and begins. "I've decided to resign. I've already got some bites at Metropolis University. But I needed a big win to make the offer happen."

I try to make sense of his words, to grapple with the feeling of the hours I've spent, the ideas I've had, being ripped away from me. "But this is my work. We agreed I would be first author."

Dr. Nelson sweeps my worries aside with a wave of his hand. "I made you a coauthor. You're going to get the scholarship. Don't worry."

There's a part of me that flares with happiness over hearing him say that. But it's a tiny matchstick flame in a dark storm. And the matchstick just fizzled out. "I could prove to *PGAS* that it was my work and that I deserve to be lead author," I say, straightening my back. Trying to be strong. And hard. Like granite. "It's all in my lab notebook."

"You don't want to do that. These are the kinds of complaints that get out." He's still smiling, still calm.

There's no scary music or menacing lighting change. But somehow I know to register his words as a threat. "Especially if the investigation proceedings continue and they start deposing students. Do you really want the scholarship committee thinking you're the kind of person who makes waves?"

And suddenly it clicks for me.

He's been using me, manipulating me, grooming me, this entire time. Squeezing every last drop out of me—and then squeezing 10 percent more. Making me feel like if I don't do everything he says—by the end of the week, tomorrow, today, now—I'm an impostor. Not dedicated enough. To science. To him. He somehow makes them the same. And maybe he wasn't lying about me being brilliant, but he saw my intelligence and found a way to use it against me.

Another realization: the other girls in the Reckoning knew it all along. I can't believe I ever defended him to them.

*If he wanted to take advantage of me, he wouldn't have been that nice, right?*

How am I ever going to get them to trust me again?

Hot shame rises in my throat, but I don't cry. In one fluid motion, I am rising from my chair and closing the door to the office so no one can see us. His eyebrows lift, surprised. Not for long. I dart around his desk and I tie him to his chair with his own lab coat. Tight, like a straitjacket. And I tear the paper into bite-sized pieces and force him to eat every last word.

I shake away the image and swallow down the shame. Bite the inside of my mouth until I taste blood. I stop myself from saying another word to him, from wasting another breath. And I walk out of his office impassively.

When I hear Trent whisper "Lover's quarrel" under his breath, I don't crack him over the head with a bottle of sulfuric acid like I do in the scene that plays in my mind. But I do make a mental note to shake all his energy drinks when he's not looking.

# CHAPTER 30

*junior year*

*april 4*

they found her in the bathroom.

cheek pressed against the cold floor. limbs lifeless.

the man who cleans the aerospace building in the morning and a grad student who had to be in early for an experiment.

my sister's cheeks were pale as milk, and she didn't move when they shook her arms.

the grad student called 911 while the man checked to see if she was breathing.

the police showed up minutes later. EMTs too.

not that they were any help.

april 29

i was hopeful.

after all, Stella woke up. she was alive. that was all i
needed. anything else we could fix. together.

a few days in Gotham Memorial. some interviews
with the police. they'd get to the bottom of it all, and
she'd be right as rain.

how'd she end up in the bathroom?

she didn't know.

there were drugs in her system. a toxic compound
they were still working to identify. did she ever do
drugs?

no. definitely not.

remember taking anything? maybe someone gave
her a drink?

no, she didn't think so.

who was the last person she saw before it all went
dark?

that was when the screaming started.

one psych evaluation later and we knew.

someone had tortured my sister.

drugged her and assaulted her mind (and her
body too? they weren't sure) and dumped her on the
bathroom floor of the lab where she worked.

which meant it couldn't be just anyone. whoever it
was had to know that was where she worked. maybe even
worked there with her.

she won't say.

can't.

every time someone tries to ask her questions about that night, most specifically the who-did-it part, she screams and she screams and she screams.

### junior year

may 22

mom and dad are mad at me because i made Stella have a screaming fit again. they say we should just keep her as calm as possible. try not to do anything to upset her.

i love them, but they don't understand. Stella's grades have slipped. she stopped going to class weeks ago. her eyelids look permanently bruised from the night terrors. the only way to unbreak her is to figure out who did this and put them somewhere they can't hurt her.

so, i ask her questions. i already know i can't ask her who, but if i can ask things that circle around it, play chicken with her terror, i might be able to help her.

today, i was going through her calendar with her again, the date that it happened pulled up on my phone. i already know i can't ask her what was the last thing she saw (screams) or where was the last place she remembers being (screams) or who did this to her (so much screaming).

instead, we talk about what she did in the lab that day.

*who she had lunch with.*

*she is fine. happy, even.*

*then I get to the part of her schedule that says only "Coffee."*

*her breath quickens.*

*there is no use asking who she was meeting with. i've tried a dozen times. but today i try again. i've printed out pictures of all the boys who work in her lab and all the other labs in the building. i had to scour every lab's website to get them.*

*did you see him that day? how about him? this guy?*

*no.*

*no.*

*no.*

*all of them, nos.*

*and then it hits me. i've printed out pictures of STUDENTS.*

*Stella, was it a professor?*

*my sister screams until she passes out.*

My phone rings, and I practically have a heart attack.

"Bernice," I breathe. "Are you okay?"

No answer.

"Bernice?"

"Sorry. I forget you can't hear me nodding through the phone." There's a pause. "So. Did you read it?"

I tuck the journal into my gym bag. All around me in the locker room, girls are getting ready for tonight's meet. "I'm still reading it. I've read enough, though."

I can hear her suck in air through her teeth.

"I'm so sorry this happened to your sister." I'm still trying to process it. The monster we've been looking for—Bernice must think he was the one who drugged her sister and hurt her. Why didn't she tell us that before—that Stella was one of the girls he took? I try to remember if she's the one who told us about him in the first place.

And the entries in Bernice's journal—they're chilling. Is that what it was like for all the other girls? The thought of it almost breaks me.

Bernice lets out a huge sigh of relief. "Thanks. It's— Well, it's been really hard. I miss her so much."

"I can't even imagine."

And I can't. Losing Kylie has been unbelievably hard, and so was losing my mom, but they're hard in different ways. Grief means battling a different beast every time.

That reminds me. "Bernice, there's something I need to tell you. About Kylie."

"Oh," she says in a way that tells me beyond a shadow of a doubt that she already knows. "Jasmin told me."

There's a pause on the other end of the line, like maybe she's trying not to cry or maybe she's already crying.

I hate that she feels this way. And that she's in a hospital room right now, probably alone, as she sorts through her grief over Kylie.

"I'm sorry I can't come see you tonight. My meet's starting pretty soon."

"It's okay. My mom just brought me dinner. And Officer Montoya's been having someone check in on me twice a day."

"Right." I move so the girl next to me can get to her stuff. "Did Jasmin tell you about the Voyeur too?"

"She did. Harleen, I'm scared. Whoever killed Kylie and drugged Stella, I really think it's the same person."

My mind snaps back to what I just read.

*There were drugs in her system. A toxic compound they were still working to identify.*

"Oh my gosh, the toxin. You think the Voyeur and the serial assaulter and Kylie's killer are all the same guy?"

"Yeah," says Bernice quietly. "And I think they're really dangerous. Promise me you'll be careful, okay?"

"*Me?* You're the one in the hospital."

"I know. But I'm worried about *you.*"

"Thank you." I say it almost shyly, which is so not a word I'd ever use to describe myself. It's funny how she can make me that way.

Just then, Alexa pokes her head in the locker room and motions for me to hurry it up already.

"Listen, I better go. We're about to start warm-ups."

"Wait! I, um, I actually have a favor to ask you."

I laugh. "You want me to go to your room and retrieve another taxidermized animal? What do you have in this one? Passports? C-4? A map to the lost city of El Dorado?"

"I was hoping you'd go talk to Stella for me."

Now it's my turn to suck in air. I guess I just assumed, with her mental health, and Bernice's mom pulling that curtain across the room— I shake my head. "She's alive?"

"She's at Arkham Acres," Bernice says quietly. "It's like the noncriminal sister facility of Arkham Asylum. My parents sent her away to get help. Since she went there, I've kind of stopped trying to ask her about what happened. I ran out of ideas, and it seemed to really upset her when I said I was applying to the Bridge Scholars program, so I never really talked to her about it. I thought if you went, maybe you'd be able to think of a way to ask her that I couldn't. You're the smartest person I know, Harleen."

I'm still reeling from all this information—Bernice's sister is alive and she's the reason Bernice dreamed up the Reckoning. But one thing is clear: we need these answers. There's no doubt in my mind that whoever did this to Stella is our monster. And that he isn't done with us yet. Girls are still in danger. We need any information we can get from Stella. And I might be the only person who can get it.

"I'll do it," I hear myself say.

Bernice thanks me about a million times before we hang up. I'm so floored by finding out that Stella's alive and that her attack is connected to Kylie's that I forget to ask about certain similarities between Stella's story and Bernice's. A girl passed out and drugged up. Found in the lab where she works. And not just any girl, a Gotham U Bridge Scholar. A teenager. Young and beautiful and pale and lifeless. Gaps in her memory that you could sail a ship through. It's uncanny.

A lot of the girls on my team hate beam. Doing back tucks and aerials is hard. Doing them four feet off the ground while standing on a beam that's barely wider than a box of crayons? Nearly impossible. It's a nail-biter to watch. Every flaw, every bobble, every (heaven forbid) fall. It plays mind games with the best of gymnasts. I adore it.

All of our events take superhuman amounts of grace and power and flexibility. But this one—this one is a mental battle. My brain versus the boundaries of physics. And my secret? I'm not afraid. Of falling to the ground in shame, of smacking against the beam, of losing a point. All I'm focused on is the beam and where my center of mass is in relation to it. It's a good thing too. I'd probably die or get a concussion or something if I wasn't so freakishly focused. Coach says I lack basic self-preservation instincts.

Alexa and I finish our beam warm-up, and she's up first. I give her a hug and wish her good luck. My phone vibrates in my bag, so I check it, expecting a good luck message from Bernice.

Don't choke.

It's a restricted number again. I whip around. Is he here? Is he watching me? I search the stands, but that's the worst part. He could be anyone.

Before I know it, Alexa's routine is over, and I'm greeting the judges and standing by the beam, and this is it. My routine is starting. My heart isn't supposed to be beating this fast. Is this what nervous gymnasts feel like before every beam routine? I try to push everything else away and begin. My first few skills go fine, but they're easy. A scorpion, a split jump, a double turn. *You're okay, it's just ninety seconds,* I tell myself. Which is the first sign that I'm screwed. I shouldn't need to talk to myself right now.

I take a deep breath and step-step-launch myself into a front tuck. I flip through the air, legs tucked against my body. Front tucks are scarier than back ones because you can't see where your feet will land, so you just kind of have to launch and pray. *Thunk.* I land, and I have to jerk sideways to stay on the beam. It's ugly—I know without seeing it. I can hear the gasps from the stands. *Take it easy, Harleen.* I prance forward, setting up for my next combination, the hardest one. Point my toe. Stretch my arms over my head in prepara—

Everything freezes—the blood in my veins, me on the beam, time itself. I gaze across the arena, almost like I have tunnel vision. And in the stands is a white sign with a red symbol. The Reckoning symbol.

The moment stretches and then snaps. I'm back in my routine. Stretch my arms up one more time. Back hand-spring, layout step-out to Arabian—whoops, no Arabian. I don't even know what happens. My body just makes an executive decision to cut it from the routine. I somehow slog through the rest of the thing. It's all (relatively) easy (compared with the accidental Arabian skip). Even the dismount isn't so bad. But as soon as I stick it, I'm on the hunt.

My eyes rake over the stands where I saw the sign before, but it isn't there. What the—?

Alexa squeezes my shoulder as I exit the beam area. "Don't worry, you'll get the next one."

Coach claps me on the back. "Shake it off, Harleen."

I barely register them.

I'm already moving to the stands, searching them for a familiar face. Whose, I'm not sure, but I'm overcome with a certainty that the Voyeur will be someone I know. I don't see anyone in the stands that it could be, so I check under the stands and then behind them. Where did he go? People can't just vanish into thin air!

I peer all around the arena. There!

White sign, red labeling, going out one of the exit doors. I can't tell if it's the Reckoning symbol from here, but I race across the floor just in case.

"Harleen!" I hear my coach call out, but I keep running.

If I could catch this clown. If I could find out who he is.

I throw open the exit door—it leads to an alley.

"Hey!" I yell.

But the alley is empty.

I search around the dumpsters and fire escapes. He was here, right? I swear I saw him.

Just when I'm about to give up, I see it. A white bit of posterboard sticking out from under a dumpster.

I grab the corner and pull it out, and sure enough, it's the Reckoning symbol. I flip it over on a whim.

*I'm always watching.*

# CHAPTER 31

THE BUS FROM THE TRAIN STATION TO ARKHAM ACRES smells like broccoli and not in a good way. I press my nose against my sleeve as I curl against the window and read Bernice's journal. There's the day she applied to the Gotham University Bridge Scholars program.

> i always wanted to do it. but after what happened with Stella, i had to.

There's an entry about the night of the frat party where Bernice was assaulted that makes me sick to read. And another entry about the Dissent Cannon and us getting revenge.

> i knew i wanted to start this vigilante group for my sister. i never knew it would become so personal.

I grip the journal tight as Arkham Acres appears over the top of a hill. It's beautiful here. Totally different from the pictures I've seen of Arkham Asylum. A sweeping green lawn and tennis courts and wide curtained porches. The bus chugs to a stop between a goldfish pond and a wishing fountain. How in the world do Bernice's parents afford this place?

I sit on a park bench out front so I can formulate some kind of plan about what I'm going to ask Stella. I know from her journal that Bernice showed Stella photos of every faculty member in the aerospace engineering building and none of them got a reaction. I also know Bernice's parents caught her with the photos and forbade her from moving to the next step of her plan—showing Stella photos of literally every faculty member on campus and waiting till she screamed.

I try to work out a timeline in my head. Stella was pretty far into the program. She had already done the symposium. She'd finished her interviews for the Gotham U Presidential Scholarship. I try to think about how whoever it was would have gotten to her. How Professor Perry would have gotten to her, if I'm being honest.

I honestly haven't met that many professors outside of the Nelson Lab. I tick off the events on my fingers. Scholarship interviews. Collaborating professors. And the symposium. That was the most professors at the same time for sure.

All the professors on the scholarship committee could be suspects. Anyone listed on a paper with Stella's aerospace lab. Though not all collabs lead to a paper—damn. And then the symposium, hell, that could be any of the professors affiliated with the Bridge Scholars program. And some who aren't. So, okay. That's where I start. Narrow down the pool. Focus in on who could have done this to Stella. I know Bernice thinks Dr. Nelson is just as likely as Dr. Perry, but

I'm positive Perry is the one doing this. Maybe today I can prove it.

I'm nervous they'll put me right back on my bus, so I breeze inside and walk straight up to the front desk like I own the place and declare I'm here to visit Stella Watkins. I wait for the span of a held breath, but Bernice has called in advance (of course she has), and a woman in cheerful scrubs leads me to the rec room.

I know which girl is Stella even before the woman tells me. She's beautiful—in the way a faded photograph is beautiful. She looks a little like Bernice.

"Hi," I say, taking the seat across the coffee table from her. "I'm Harleen. I'm Bernice's girlfriend."

The word tastes unfamiliar on my lips. But good. Really good.

Stella smiles. "Bernice didn't tell me she had a girlfriend."

I blush so hard I'm sure it looks like I'm wearing clown makeup. "It's a recent development."

We play a board game that Stella likes called Labyrinth. You have to shift the tiles to change the shape of the maze so you can find treasure.

"Bernice said you went to Gotham U," I say, pushing a tile onto the column to my right so that my wizard can move to the space with the crown. "I'm really hoping to go there this fall. I've already gotten in, but I still have to see about scholarships and stuff."

"Congratulations," says Stella. Politely. Carefully.

"Hey, you were in an aerospace lab, right? How'd you like it?" I feel like a jerk for prying initially, but Stella lights up when she starts to talk about aerospace. She tells me all about the work she was doing, happily answers my questions about the different labs they were working with. Whoever did this to her, it definitely wasn't someone she worked with.

I shoot for talking about the symposium next.

"I'm working in a neurobiology lab," I tell her.

"Oh yeah? My sister really likes neuroscience too."

"I know." I grin at her, a real one, because how can I not be smiling when I'm talking about Bernice AND brain science. "I actually just presented at the Bridge Scholars symposium—did you ever do that?" I see her chest tighten, her eyes flash with fear, but I pretend I don't. "Hey, you wanna see my poster?"

I'm already scrolling through photos on my phone, looking for the ones of the symposium, but the shift to my science seems to relax her. I hate that I'm probably going to stress her out again. Hanging out with her, talking with her—it's actually pretty great. I imagine for just a moment how it would feel to have this be my job. To work in a place like Arkham Acres and help people like Stella. Maybe this is the kind of doctor I'm supposed to be.

I find a photo with her sister. "Here's one of me and Bernice," I say.

"Oh." She smiles and touches the case of my phone as a reflex, almost like she's trying to give her sister a hug.

"Here's one where you can see my poster better." I slide to the photo of me talking to Professor Perry, my poster looming huge in the background, the title and the coauthors from the lab stretching like a teleprompter over our heads.

Stella gasps and leans close to the picture. And then it's almost like she short-circuits. Her mouth tries to move, but she looks too terrified to form words.

"Stella, are you okay?" I flip my phone over and put it in my bag. Brace myself in case she starts screaming.

I feel terrible for bringing her to this point. But part of me is relieved. If it's Perry, then it isn't Dr. Nelson.

The moment passes, and Stella comes out of her haze of fear.

"You should quit the program," she tells me, eyes cutting through me like a hot knife. "I want you to quit, and I want you to make Bernice quit too, do you understand?"

She's talking about what happened, but she still seems lucid. This could be my chance.

"Stella, what happened to you?" I say it in the calmest, most reassuring voice.

"I can't." She grits her teeth. "Just make Bernice quit. Because he—" Her eyes go wide; it's like something I can't see is converging around her. Memories and monsters digging their claws into her brain. She darts her head from side to side, focusing on things that aren't there. But she's fighting it. I can see it in the way her hands grip the table. In the way her teeth are clenched so tightly.

She's fighting it for Bernice.

"I'll tell her to quit," I rush to say. "I'll quit, and I'll tell her to quit, and everything will be fine. You don't need to worry."

I say it, again and again and again, until Stella's breathing goes back to normal. My breathing does the same. I didn't realize my lungs were working overtime to match Stella's until now. It really was an intense reaction—almost scary. I can't help but think about how there's a whole spectrum of ways that people respond to things like rape and assault. Stella and Bernice are so different. And my response was different still. And we're different people, so of course we

284

respond differently to trauma, but with Stella, I wonder if part of that is the toxin. And if Kylie were still alive, would she be in here with Stella?

Bernice says she wants to unbreak her sister, but you can't take a survivor's journey for them. Maybe the person she's really trying to unbreak is herself. Maybe it's been that all along. It reminds me of when we built the Dissent Cannon—wasn't I so much more invested in avenging Bernice than myself? Sometimes fighting for all the women who come after you is the most powerful way to heal.

Because even if we do figure out who did this and bring down an entire universe of vengeance on him, is it really going to change anything for Stella? Or has the toxin somehow tweaked her sympathetic nervous system so that it's on high alert, fight or flight, adrenaline exploding like bombs when she least expects it—forever? I glance around at the doctors and nurses and staff. I really hope they can help her. She seems like such a good person, and also, whoever did this to her took a brilliant mind away from science. How many discoveries and breakthroughs have we lost out on because women were pushed out of science before they had the chance to make them?

Stella and I finish our game of Labyrinth and say our goodbyes.

I try not to feel guilty about lying to her when she hugs me.

# CHAPTER 32

I CALL BERNICE AS SOON AS I LEAVE ARKHAM ACRES. THEY finally let her out of the hospital, so I meet her at her apartment. She flings open the door and hugs me, kind of like her mom did a couple days ago.

"You look so much better!" I tell her.

"Thanks!"

I could seriously stand in her doorway and talk in exclamation points forever, but she grabs me by the hand and pulls me down the hallway to her room. Once the door is shut, though, we are quiet. Nervous. *Do you still like me and can you ever forgive me and are you sure you want to be together?*

"I'm so sorry," I tell her. "I should have believed you about Dr. Nelson. I can't believe I let him twist me around like that. I still don't know why I did it." *Daddy issues?* I shake my head. "Anyway, I get the kind of person he is now, and I'm really, really sorry for freaking out when I felt like everyone was against me and saying all those awful things and if

286

you could ever forgive me and want to be my girlfriend, like, my official, not-seeing-anyone-else girlfriend, I would really, really like that."

Bernice blushes. "I don't ever think I've seen you so nervous before."

"I've never asked anyone to be my girlfriend befo—"

"Yes." Bernice cuts in. She's smiling this sunshine-for-days smile and looking so damn beautiful.

"Yes?"

"Definitely yes."

My heart is one giant glitterbomb right now. That's how happy she's made me. I cross the room in two steps, ready to swing her around like we're having one of those sappy airport scenes.

She stops me.

"I'm sorry too," she says. "I should have believed you. It was really crappy of me not to. Also . . . I was hiding some really big things."

She was, and maybe I should be mad at her, maybe I would be, but any feelings I had about our fight and her hiding stuff got worked out real quick when I thought I was going to lose her.

Not that I have to let her know that . . .

I nod my head like I'm just remembering. "Yeah. You know what? Let's get back to the part where you planned the whole entire Reckoning."

Bernice winces. "Okay."

"You masterminded an entire vengeance girl gang, and you did it without any of us figuring it out."

I cross my arms, and Bernice bites her lip.

"Yes, I know. Super sorry about that."

I don't give away anything, really let the pause stretch between us, before I finally speak my truth.

"It's kind of hot."

She giggles. "What?"

"I don't know, I'm just saying. I fell in love with you because you're so damn sweet and wonderful, but now it turns out you're some evil genius, and . . . I'm into it." Seriously, I don't see how superheroes ever get anyone to fall in love with them. The villains are so much more interesting.

"You are?"

I pull her hips against mine. "Very."

Bernice gives me this sly grin. "I also created a fake online account and I've been spying on the personal activities of all the Gotham U professors people gave me dirt on."

My eyes widen. "Bernice!" I pretend to be scandalized, and she blushes so red. "You are a diabolical feminist."

She snorts. "Can I get that on a plaque?"

"No, I mean it. You're . . . dangerous." Just saying the word makes me feel hot all over, like I might just spontaneously combust if I don't get to kiss her right now, but also, I don't forget her history and my history, and no matter how much I want things—

"Can I kiss you?"

I register that she's the one who said it and not me and also that her voice is breathless, and we haven't even started doing any of the things. I can barely pull myself together to answer her.

"Yes, please."

And now if you'll excuse me, I'm going to kiss my hot vigilante girlfriend, and we will not be coming up for air for many hours, so don't wait up.

Eventually, we do decide that oxygen is important, so we lie on Bernice's floor with her head resting on my side like a pillow, just breathing.

My phone buzzes, and I drag myself away from her for a second. It's just Morgan from lab, asking me where some reagents are, but my heart skipped a beat when I unlocked my screen. Because I thought it'd be him. "Hey, I meant to tell you, he was at my gymnastics meet last night."

Bernice's eyes go wide. "The Voyeur?"

I nod and tell her the whole horrible story. Right down to losing beam to Kelsey Van Meter (ugh).

Bernice gets all fired up. "Okay, you know what, no. We are not letting him do this."

I grin because having her be mad on my behalf feels so damn good right now. "I maybe possibly have a plan for catching him, but A, I don't know if you're gonna like it, and B, it requires us getting him to follow me but also us *knowing* that he's following me, and I have no idea how we're gonna get him to do that."

"Oh!" Bernice pops up so she's bouncing on her knees. "I have an idea. But you're going to have to piss him off."

I throw up my hands. "I *excel* at pissing people off."

She explains how we could maybe engineer a meeting with him, and then I explain what I'd want to do if we did, and then we pull up my text messages with the Voyeur. The one from last night is still there, taunting me.

Don't choke.

I narrow my eyes and text him back.

Harleen: How'd you know where my gymnastics meet was?

He doesn't text back right away, which is super annoying, but at least Bernice has the foresight to get us cupcakes and milk while we wait. I'm about halfway through with mine (strawberry with sprinkles) when he replies.

"MMM!!!" I yell because my mouth is full.

> Followed you. It was only too easy. I know your entire schedule. I watch you walk to the subway from your lab every day.

I smirk at Bernice. This was exactly the kind of response we were hoping for.

> Harleen: Doubt it.

Wait for it. . . .

> Excuse me?

I ripple my shoulders excitedly and text back.

> Harleen: I think you're full of it. If you really followed me home from lab every day, and you're really as mad as you say, you would have done something about it already.

This time, there's an element of foreboding in the pause. I can barely contain myself.

> You're a stupid little girl. I could kill you if I wanted.

Bernice sucks in a breath, but I know we've got him.

> Harleen: Uh-huh. I'll believe it when you make contact.

The pause is so long, I worry we've lost him. And then those three beautiful dots appear.

Monday. Watch your back.

"We did it!" I squeal.

"You are a criminal mastermind boss lady," says Bernice, and the admiration in her eyes is like a drug.

I push her shoulder playfully. "No, you!"

We toast our victory for a while, and then as the sugar coma sets in, we go back to lying on her floor.

"I didn't succeed," says Bernice after a few minutes.

"Huh?"

"A real supergenius would have caught him already." She traces shapes on my palm with her finger. "I still don't have any proof that Professor Perry attacked her. Or any of the other girls. There's absolutely nothing out there. Not even in the whisper network."

Bernice pushes up on one elbow. "All we have is my sister who can't tell us anything and the suspiciousness of a bunch of girls dropping out of an elite STEM internship program and none of them being willing to talk about why. I really thought I'd have enough to go to the police by now."

"You know, you did just get out of the hospital," I say gently. "It's okay to give yourself a break."

But Bernice shakes her head. "No matter what happens, I can't fall apart. I have to keep fighting for Stella because she can't fight for herself right now. I feel so guilty all the time." She takes a deep, tense breath. "After what happened to me at that party, it's almost gotten worse. Because, like, I'm still walking free and I'm 'okay' or whatever, and she's still stuck in Arkham Acres. I said I'd do this for her, and I failed her. Kylie too. This is all my fault."

I grab her hand in mine. "Hey, no. Look at me. You've done so much. I'm so proud to be a part of this group you created. And you're right, we may not have all the answers yet, but we know something happened. You should have seen Stella's face when she saw that picture of me and Dr. Perry. If we keep digging, I know we'll find something eventually. We have the truth on our side, and eventually the truth always bubbles to the surface, no matter how ugly it is. I'm going to help you. And we're going to make things right for Stella and Kylie and all those other girls. But first, we need proof. We need the Reckoning."

# CHAPTER 33

BERNICE TAKES HER SEAT AT THE DESK NEXT TO MINE IN the lab office and gives me a meaningful look.

I raise my eyebrows.

She raises hers even more, and then rolls her eyes and writes a word on a sticky note and sticks it beside my keyboard. *Phone!*

Oh.

I get out my phone and find that I do indeed have a text from Bernice.

> Bernice: it's almost time.

I think about saying something like, "Yes, I'm aware," but I know she's just nervous (we are attempting to bait the Voyeur, after all), so instead I text back:

> Harleen: It's going to be okay. I promise.

She sighs. With relief? With resignation? She starts typing into her phone again.

Bernice: i'm gonna go now. but. be careful, harleen.

"See you," she says out loud.

"See ya," I echo back, trying not to smile my nefarious-things-are-afoot smile.

She leaves, but I stay a little longer, wrapping up a few last things. Stalling, if I'm being honest. I really should be more scared. I'm about to come face-to-face with a monster. This guy killed Kylie. Tried to kill Bernice. Probably spends his evenings dreaming up creative ways to torture me. I check my phone. Five o'clock. The time I usually leave lab if I want to make it to gymnastics practice on time. I find him in my text messages. Read the text he sent me this morning one last time.

See you tonight.

The dread finally sets in the way it should. This could go really badly—someone could end up dead. I have no idea how strong this Voyeur guy is. Only that he's violent enough to kill Kylie and he may be armed with some sort of super-toxin. I wonder if I should have told Montoya. Just in case. It's too late now, though. I sling my backpack over my shoulder like it weighs a million pounds. I wave bye to Morgan and head down the back stairwell like I always do. Only this time I may not make it home.

The girl with the blond pigtails pulls her jacket tighter against the wind. Keeps the neck flipped up high around her face. She *clip-clops* down the sidewalk with legs like a newborn colt. Scared? Unsure? Probably both.

He watches. There's a white van in the parking deck that hides him well enough.

And when she gets far enough away that he thinks she won't notice, he slinks out of the shadows.

Her pigtails bounce with each step.

She doesn't see him. Hear him. Doesn't know he's there. Yet.

He prowls closer, black ski mask over his face, navy jacket with no logos. He could be anyone.

She doesn't hear him and she doesn't hear him and then she does. A slight hunch of the shoulders gives her away. A speeding-up of steps.

He speeds up too.

The gap between them closes. He looms bigger on the sidewalk. She wobbles on her next step but doesn't fall.

He sucks in a breath.

There's something about the act of following another person—danger and power coursing through your veins, beating where your heart should be. A spark of something darkly sexy that threatens to set the whole volatile mix on fire.

She tries to break into a run, but he is chasing, stalking, hunting, and it's too late for her to get away.

He will catch her.

He knows it even as he's lunging forward to grab her around the waist.

He doesn't know I'm right behind him.

I lash out with my foot, and I kick—hard—right behind his kneecap. He falls to the ground in a heap of muffled swears. His voice sounds oddly familiar, but it's smothered by his ski mask, and I can't quite put my finger on it. He almost takes the girl down with him, but I rush forward and manage to keep her standing. She looks up at me, blond pigtails askew, a sliver of strawberry hair showing underneath.

In the second my eyes meet hers, he tries to make his escape. Crawling, obviously. Hopping, if I'm being generous. I really made a mess of his knee, and I might feel guilty about that, but (A) he killed one of my best friends, and (B) he's trying to get away. So, I tackle him. Knee to the back. No mercy. He goes down hard, head bouncing off the sidewalk. Good. I whip out a pair of Bianca's flex handcuffs, and I do his hands first and then his feet. Not that it's easy. Or quick. (He's a kicker.)

But eventually I get him hog-tied, and now it's time for the moment of truth.

I look up at Bernice. "You want to do the honors?"

She pulls off the blond wig and rakes her hand through her hair. "Okay."

I flip over the body, and we both go quiet. This is it. The Voyeur. The one who's been terrorizing our days and nights. The person who murdered Kylie and tortured Stella. We're finally going to find out who he is. Bernice pulls off his ski mask, and we stare into the face of evil.

"TRENT???"

"Bernice?"

Bernice and I are stunned. And weirded out. And stunned. Trent just doesn't seem like the kind of person capable of murder and attempted murder and masterminding an intimidation strategy, and did I mention how stunned we are?

Bernice stares at him in bewilderment, still clutching his ski mask. "Did we make a mistake?"

"I don't know. Search him." Could it be we got the wrong guy? That he was just messing around and the Voyeur is still at large?

I don't move from where I'm pinning him down because wrong guy or not, I wouldn't put it past him to try to caterpillar himself away.

Bernice wobbles over on her heels. "I can barely walk in these things."

I snicker. "Sorry. We had to make you as tall as me."

Trent glares at her as she goes through his pockets. "Of course I'm not the— Whoever you guys said you're looking for."

Bernice finds a phone in his jacket. "Here."

I turn it over, inspecting it. "It's not his. Must be a burner phone." I shove it at him. "Unlock it."

He has the nerve to smirk at me. "If you haven't noticed, my hands are a little tied up right now."

"Okay, cool, well, I guess I'll just call Officer Montoya down at GCPD. . . ."

"Wait!"

He tells me how to unlock the phone.

And inside—it's everything. Texts to me. *Don't choke.* The Finsta account he'd been using to scare Bianca and Kylie. He's him. Trent's the Voyeur. But if that's true—

*Can't wait till we meet :)*

"You killed Kylie?"

His face contorts in horror. "What? *No.*"

"But you commented on our Insta account about how you couldn't wait to meet her, and then she died the same day," says Bernice.

"Yeah, I know that looks bad." Trent winces. "But I swear I didn't do it. I was just trying to shake you guys up. Scare you. I was hoping I could get you to quit. You ruined my dad's life, you know."

What he's saying makes sense, but— "What about Bernice? Were you trying to scare her too?"

"I didn't even know Bernice was *in* the Reckoning! I only realized Kylie was in it because she got really drunk at our golf party, and her phone fell out of her bag with the Insta account pulled up. And then I thought it was weird that you and Bianca both spent so much time with her, so I started paying attention."

I turn to Bernice. "Do you believe him? That he's not the one who drugged you that night?"

She gulps like a cartoon character. "I mean, yeah."

Trent's face, which has been turning various degrees of pale during this encounter, suddenly spreads into a smirk. "You're going to stop being the Reckoning," he says.

"Like hell we are."

But he just keeps smirking. "You're going to stop, or I'm going to tell everyone who you are."

He waits, and we wait, and eventually his smug-ass expression slips a smidge.

I fix him with the most razor-sharp smile I can muster. "No. You're going to stop. Because I'm going to keep this burner phone, and if I hear anything about the Reckoning's identities getting out, or if there's so much as a peep from the Voyeur, I'm giving Montoya this phone and you're going down for the murder of Kylie Pearce."

He mumbles something, and I jerk him forward by his jacket collar. "Say it!"

"I won't tell."

A part of me feels relieved. Bernice and I made it through this ridiculous entrapment scheme alive. The Voyeur is just Trent, and he's not going to be messing with us anymore. But then it hits me. If Trent isn't the one who killed Kylie, who is?

# CHAPTER 34

BERNICE AND I CALL THE FIRST RECKONING MEETING SINCE before she went to the hospital. The door that was cautiously cracked when I needed to talk to them about Kylie and the police swings wide open now. Bernice and I are back together, and we may have caught the Voyeur, but whoever attacked Stella and Bernice and killed Kylie is still out there. It's time to make a plan. To catch this snake and to bring down vengeance on him in a way that makes everything else we've done seem like harmless pranks. We meet at Bianca's apartment, and we haven't even gotten inside all the way when she blurts out, "TRENT BAYERS?"

"I know," says Bernice.

"But he's so . . ."

"*I know,*" says Bernice.

Bianca shudders. Apparently, Trent and his arrogance have frequented the physics machine shop.

Bernice and I fill them in on the Trent stuff while Bianca makes us all paleo plantain-almond pancakes that are honestly delicious. We sit around her dining room table. You could almost pretend it's the old days. Until Kylie not being there hits you like a ton of bricks.

"Has anyone found out anything new about her?" asks Bianca around a mouthful of pancake.

"Not since the funeral," I say. "But Bernice and I did find out some new stuff about Professor Perry."

Jasmin and Bianca set down their forks.

"First, though, I wanted to apologize. Again."

Bianca waves her hand like it's water under the bridge, but I keep going.

"I understand now that family is more than a bunch of people you love unconditionally. It's a responsibility." I take a deep breath. "Anyway, if you want to make Dr. Nelson a target . . . I'm cool with that."

Jasmin's mouth curves up in a half smile. "Right on, Harleen."

"Yeah, we're cool," says Bianca. "But we screwed up too. I was so angry at Nelson that I didn't listen to you. And I should have."

"Same. We should have supported you," says Jasmin.

And the thing is, I kind of knew they were going to say that, but nothing prepared me for how good it feels now that it actually happened. Bernice squeezes my hand under the table.

"Thanks," I tell them, meeting Jasmin's eyes and then Bianca's and Bernice's. I wish Kylie was here. I'm sad that she never got to see us all reunited.

Bianca nods. "Anytime. Now tell us how we're gonna end Professor Perry! I'm talking take everything you're thinking and multiply it times one million. Kylie died for this. Give me all the dirt you've got on him."

Bernice and I explain what happened when I went to visit

Stella at Arkham Acres. Well, first Bernice has to explain who Stella is and what happened to her, but Jasmin and Bianca are really cool about it, despite Bianca's past declarations about liars. Then I tell them how we still don't have any conclusive evidence of any kind despite being 200 percent sure it's Perry.

We go round and round, rehashing previous ideas that lead to nothing. Then I think about how Dr. Nelson is undergoing an investigation and how it all started with someone filing a complaint against him.

"What if we search for past complaints? If Perry's preyed on so many women, there has to be a record somewhere of complaints made against him, right? Although, do you really think he'd still be teaching here if he had complaints against him?"

"Yes," say Jasmin, Bianca, and Bernice at the exact same time.

"Oh yeah. Right."

Jasmin's already got her laptop open. "Imma see if I can get into human resources," she says. "I remember a friend in Perry's lab filing a complaint about some disgusting joke he told at a department dinner. They told her that it would go in his file and that an ethics board would be notified."

She works furiously while we help Bianca clear the table and clean up the kitchen. I have to squeeze past the photo of Professor Perry on the wall in order to grab Jasmin's plate. I think about Stella at Arkham Acres, and I try to shoot laser beams through his face. Bernice notices.

"Actually," she says, "we should probably add a picture of Stella to the wall."

I glance at the different photos. She's right—Stella's not on here. "But—"

"When we were going through the names before and printing out the pictures, I kind of left Stella off." She winces like she hopes I'm not mad.

"It's okay." I squeeze her hand so she'll know I mean it. "I'll help you add her now, okay?"

She nods.

A couple hours later, the wall is updated, the kitchen is sparkling clean, Bianca is doing burpees because she's bored, and Jasmin's use of swear words is multiplying exponentially.

"I can't find anything," she says. "I've looked everywhere."

"Do you think they deleted them all?" I ask.

"How could they get away with that?" asks Bianca. "Whatever it is, it's got to be huge. Big enough to kill someone over."

"What if when it went in his file, it *literally* went in his file?" says Bernice. We all turn to look at her. "Like, in a file cabinet. Manila folders and alphabetized labels and all that."

Jasmin's upper lip curls at the thought. "That seems incredibly archaic. But it would explain why I haven't been able to find any evidence of any complaint on their system," she concedes.

"Holy crap, we've been looking in the wrong place."

Bianca looks stunned, but I am grinning. We are going to find out the truth about this waste of air once and for all. We are going to help Stella. And we are going to extract a vengeance the likes of which this campus has never seen.

"Any of y'all ever want to go night rappelling?"

# CHAPTER 35

*gap year*

*april 1*

i just did something. i waited in the hallway outside Dr. Perry's surgery room, and as soon as his lab tech took a break, i slipped inside and stole an entire bottle of anesthetic. i can't even tell you how much i was sweating. then I hid in the bathroom and i googled this particular anesthetic cocktail so i could try to figure out an appropriate dose for someone my size. i'm not even sure the information was accurate, but honestly, it doesn't matter. i'm taking it either way.

yesterday was a lot. i thought there was something going on with Harleen and Dr. Nelson, but having a worry at the back of your brain is one thing, and having the proof thrown right in your face? i can't even look at her right now.

*the most awful part is knowing that the person who hurt my sister and the person who's been harassing my girlfriend could be one and the same.*

*but i DON'T know. that's the thing. Dr. Perry. Dr. Nelson. as i sifted through gotham u's dark past, two names rose to the top. i need to know which one. definitively.*

*so, i stole the anesthetic from Perry's lab, and i'll dose myself in Nelson's lab. they'll find me. drugged. pale. unconscious. and they'll start digging.*

*i'll do it monday.*

*april 4th.*

*the anniversary of the day they found my sister.*

*seems like poetic justice that that's the day i make it all unravel for him.*

I should be paying attention in Abnormal Psych. I petitioned the program especially so I could take another course with Dr. Catrambone this semester after I liked her Intro to Psych class so much last fall. Plus, we're learning about schizophrenia this week, and I've been waiting for it all semester. But then there's reading the last few pages of Bernice's journal that I never noticed before because there were blank pages in between, and messaging the Reckoning Secure Chat under my desk because we're not allowed to have phones out in class, and—

"Ms. Quinzel."

I shove my phone under my leg, eyes on Dr. Catrambone. "Yes?"

"Can you tell us what made the methods in the Walker study so novel?" She crosses her arms, but she's smiling. She's not going to call me out for being on my phone, but she's also not going to let me get away with not paying attention. In high school, I always had an IEP (individualized education plan), but it doesn't travel with you to college. Instead, I had to go to the accessibility office and advocate for myself (LIKE A BOSS), and then they emailed my accommodations to my Bridge program professors but kept my diagnoses private. Anyway, one of my accommodations is that my teachers should redirect me if I'm not focusing the way I should be, but still. There's a whole range of ways to actually go about doing that, and I love that Dr. Catrambone never makes me feel stupid or embarrassed.

"Right. Well. The Walker study." *You read this paper last night. C'mon, Harleen.* "They used home videos from when people with schizophrenia were kids. And they found that the kids who were going to develop schizophrenia would do things like hold their hands in kind of a characteristic, contorted way, like how adults with schizophrenia do. And their siblings didn't so much."

Dr. Catrambone's smile widens. She really wants you to get the answer right. Even when she's sneak attacking you. "Correct. They show neuromotor abnormalities. But what makes the home video usage so important? Why should we care?"

This is her favorite thing to do. Assign a primary source journal article. Make us read critically. Ask us why we should care.

I'm on a roll now, despite Bernice's latest journal entry burning a hole in my brain, and I sit up straighter, more confident. "Because it's fast. Imagine how long it would take to follow kids until they were grown-ups, waiting to see if they got schizophrenia. And now that we know, you could assess kids when they're little. Watch the kids that show the neuromotor abnormalities and catch the onset of schizophrenia earlier. Maybe even treat it before it starts so that it never develops." My nerdy eyes are shining bright now. My geeky heart is bursting.

"You could." She nods thoughtfully. "But what if your child was one of the ones identified as at risk? Would you give them a medication—possibly one with lots of side effects—because of something they *might* develop?"

I falter. "I don't know."

"That's absolutely okay," she says quickly. "It's an extremely difficult question, and I'm not sure there's a right answer. But it's important for us to think about both the science and the ethics behind the science."

Huh. That is a really good point. It reminds me of how Oliver's always saying we need to consider the moral implications behind the SV1 gene because in the past, things like the "Warrior Gene" have been weaponized against people of color. I spend the last little bit of class turning the thought over and over in my mind. Then Dr. Catrambone dismisses us, and my mind snaps back to what I read in Bernice's journal.

I text her once I get outside.

> Harleen: I can't believe you put yourself in a coma for three days just to figure out if it was Dr. Perry or Dr. Nelson!!!!

She replies immediately.

Bernice: u got to that part, huh?

Bernice: and i didn't mean to! i was just trying to knock myself out, but apparently people can have bad reactions to anesthetics.

Bernice: like a small percentage of the time.

Bernice: i'm so lucky.

I shudder, thinking how much worse it could have been.

Harleen: I'm really glad you came back to us

She texts back.

Bernice: me too 🖤

What if she hadn't? I read over her journal entry again. It would have been because of me. I try to push away the guilt before it sinks into my stomach like a brick.

And then I realize something.

Harleen: Did it work? Did you find out which one of them did it?

I wait, fingers drumming against my leg, badly wanting her to type the words *Dr. Perry*.

Bernice: not exactly.

Bernice: i think it may have contributed to them opening that investigation against Dr. Nelson, but i don't think they're looking at Dr. Perry very hard, which is really annoying because it turns out that wasn't the first time drugs and anesthetics have gone missing from his lab.

Bernice: but of course they're not following up on that part properly. i'm actually worried i may have gotten some people in his lab in trouble.

Bernice: i feel awful.

Before I can reply, the Reckoning Secure Chat goes off again, so I dash out a quick You shouldn't! and switch over.

Jasmin and Bianca are finally answering the messages I sent in class.

RECKONING SECURE CHAT:

Harleen: I AM SO EXCITED TO GO NIGHT RAPPELLING!!!

Harleen: Does anyone actually have any night rappelling gear?

Harleen: Or day rappelling gear?

Harleen: Will take any kind of rappelling gear

Jasmin: No

Jasmin: That's not a thing people just have.

Bianca: OBVIOUSLY!!! In multiple sizes.

Jasmin: I stand corrected.

I message them back.

Harleen: Awesome!! Can't wait for tonight!

I see a message from Bernice pop up right after mine.

Bernice: me too!

I switch back to my conversation with her.

Harleen: Hey, have you told Bianca and Jasmin yet?

I wait. The three little dots appear. And disappear. And appear again. So, that's a no.

Bernice: not yet

(Told you.)

Bernice: i'm scared

I'd be scared to tell Bianca too. She's big on the honesty and loyalty. She's like the glue that holds the rest of us together, in that way.

Harleen: Let me know if you need help

Bernice: thanks

# CHAPTER 36

RAPPELLING DOWN THE SIDE OF THE HUMAN RESOURCES building is easier than you'd think. Well, if you're me. The scariest part is being on top of a seven-story building and having to jump backward off the edge and into the abyss with only a small cable for security. There's a brief moment of free fall when your brain and stomach are 99 percent certain you're going to die. I can't wait to do it again!

I lean back into the harness and kick with my legs to bounce-bounce-bounce my way down the side of the building. This is the easy part. I count the windows as I pass. Seventh floor. Sixth. Fifth. And . . . fourth. Bingo. Breaking into a fourth-story window is a little more complicated than picking a lock. Why we are lucky: the human resources offices are in one of the older, more historical buildings on campus, so at least they have windows that open. Why we are unlucky: even though the windows are those double windows that open outward, they aren't really designed to be opened from the outside, and also they have been painted once every few years since the beginning of Gotham City, so they might as well be sealed shut with epoxy.

I have to use a machete, a crowbar, and a battery-powered Dremel tool, and I almost lose a finger (once) and smash my arm through the glass (twice).

Finally, FINALLY, I get inside this blasted building without impaling myself with pieces of glass or plummeting to my death. I poke my head out and wave at the other girls to let them know it's safe to follow. Bianca goes first and spouts off muffled swears all the way down. Bernice is next, but after taking fifty eternities to coax herself over the edge, she's actually pretty good at daintily skipping down the wall. Jasmin stays on the roof so she can watch the rappelling equipment.

Once we're inside, Bianca's the lookout, and Bernice and I go through the file cabinets as fast as we can. I call the *P*s, and Bernice gets to work on some of the Bridge Scholars professors elsewhere in the alphabet. It's important to cover all our bases. Not that there'll be anything for her to find— I'm certain Professor Perry is who we're looking for.

I flip through the files.

Price.

Powell.

Peterson.

Perry!

I ease the file folder out of the metal cabinet drawer, being extra careful not to rip it, because this file, it is FAT. Barely closes. Probably'd be better as two separate folders. Chock-full of secrets and atrocities. I get that soft-drink-fizzing-through-my-veins feeling. This is our guy. I just know it. Professor Perry is Gotham University's serial assaulter, and now is the moment when I catch him.

Visions of vengeance bloom in my head. I am ready to dole out retribution like never before. For Kylie. For Stella. I may even let Bianca break out those homemade explosives she's always going on about.

I flip open his file and try to ignore the sense of relief that flickers in my stomach. Education, previous employment, teaching, research, service. A list of publications a mile long. And BOOM. A complaint filed on behalf of [name redacted]. Against Professor Perry. Dated three years ago.

Nature of complaint: sexual harassment.

HERE WE GO.

The professor in question made a joke stating that "women look sexiest barefoot and pregnant."

Okay, but a sexist joke is probably just the tip of the misogynistic iceberg. I flip to the next page. More highly inappropriate jokes. Another page. Commenting about the hotness levels of women at a particular scientific conference. Another. Making a woman feel uncomfortable at a faculty meeting. Another. Another. Another. Dirty jokes. Dirty jokes. Hostile work environment. What the eff? Where are the assault complaints? I flip faster. It's got to be him. Are they covering for him? Is that why nothing's in here? Do they keep the really bad complaints in a different folder? I pick up the next page and slam it down angrily, almost tearing the paper. It's got to be in here. It just has to. If I don't find it, we'll never be able to follow his trail to Kylie.

I flip another page. Here it is! One of the girls from the Bridge Scholars program—a girl who eventually dropped out—was in Perry's mentoring group, and she asked to be transferred to a different group *because of inappropriate touching.* I knew it. I freaking knew it. I keep reading, and I find two other girls from the Bridge program who asked to be transferred (why in the world did they allow him to continue being a Bridge mentor?!), and the details are vague, but—

"Psst," hisses Bianca.

We freeze.

A flashlight shines through the door and into the office, and we hit the floor, fast. The beam of light swoops over us menacingly, cutting just over our heads.

There are a few seconds where none of us so much as blink. Then the person with the light moves past, and we can all start breathing again.

I go back to Professor Perry's file with renewed zeal, but it's only a minute or so before Bernice appears beside me. She doesn't say anything, just waits for me to look at her, and when I do her eyes are so desolate, and all she can say is "Harleen?" in a voice that makes me feel like the walls are closing in on me.

She's holding Dr. Nelson's file.

# CHAPTER 37

SEVEN WOMEN.

Some with multiple complaints. My hands are shaking, but I force myself to read them.

Vanessa Park. An undergraduate doing her senior thesis in the lab when he was first starting out. Two complaints ignored and then an assault in the bathroom of a bar at lab happy hour. Filed after she graduated. After he gave her a B, he insists.

Lindsay Hernandez. Lab tech. A string of emails in which he very clearly invites her to go away with him to a bed-and-breakfast for the weekend. Only if she'd be comfortable with that, of course. She tells him she has a boyfriend, but she doesn't file a complaint until years later. Until she's safely in med school in Metropolis, I realize. The gap in filing is deemed "suspicious" by the university.

Amaya Reynolds. A grad student from about five years ago. He slipped his room key into her pocket at a conference. Later claimed it was a "huge misunderstanding." There aren't any other incidents with her even though she stayed on in the lab for a few more years, but it seems that she left without completing her PhD.

Cadence Brown. Another grad student—she graduated just a couple years before I started working in the lab. Woke up in his house, in his bed, without any idea of how she got there. He was able to convince HR that it was consensual.

And on.

And on.

And on.

He's just as bad as Dr. Perry—worse, even. There are multiple complaints for both of them—multiple arrows pointing to the fact that either of them could be the one taking girls. And this is only the women who weren't too scared to file a complaint. Stella isn't in either of their files, for sure, and she's just one person. How many others are there? And all of these girls who did speak up and out—they're all just sitting here in this stupid file cabinet, while more girls are out there getting hurt.

I can't stop crying. I feel like I'm going to be sick. And not the way people usually say it, all metaphorical and stuff. I think I actually might vomit up everything I've eaten for the past week. The complaints in Dr. Nelson's file hurt so much more personally than the ones in Dr. Perry's. How could I not have realized he was such a terrible person? How could I have let myself get caught up in someone this vile? I squeezed his hand. I thought he was a genius. I had him on a freaking pedestal.

Bernice and Bianca are trying to talk to me, but I feel like I'm underwater. If I hadn't been so enamored with him, would I have figured all of this out sooner? Soon enough to save Kylie?

*Don't think about that.*

I can only do what I can do. Now that I know. I slip out the window with both of their folders and ride the cable all the way down to the sidewalk below. The rope burns my hands, and I don't care.

I stay up all night. Take the subway to the GCPD as the sun comes up. There's a bagel shop a few blocks down, so I buy a big box of cheap coffee and pretend like I'm there to make a delivery. People don't ask too many questions when you come bearing caffeine. I ride that Trojan horse all the way over to one particular desk at the GCPD where I deposit the folders with a sticky note on top that reads: OFFICER MONTOYA.

## CHAPTER 38

I WONDER IF I COULD JUMP ONTO THIS TABLE AND PUT HIM in a choke hold before anyone stops me. If he doesn't stop talking, I just might. Blah-blah-blah-blah, listen to me, all you peons. I can't believe I ever idolized a man like that.

"I have a few other announcements to make." Dr. Nelson flashes a toothpaste-commercial smile from the head of the table.

You've been fired? The cops are on their way to arrest you right now?

"I've just been offered a new job at Metropolis University."

WHAT.

Stiff smiles and congratulations filter in from around the table. Most of the table. A few of us remain stone-faced. Oliver. Bernice. Me. Some people look nervous about what this will mean for their jobs in the lab, but he jumps in quickly.

"Everyone will have a position at Met U," he says. "I've already arranged all of it. We'll be able to take on a couple new postdocs. We'll have *a lot* of new space. This is really a great thing for all of us."

Bernice and I exchange glances that say, *Is this mother-effer seriously failing up right now?*

Oliver clears his throat. "What about those of us who are almost finished here?"

"Not to worry, not to worry," says Dr. Nelson. "You, Trent, and anyone who needs to finish up here will absolutely be able to do that. We'll have meetings to figure all that out. Also"—for the first time he looks like his tie is slowly choking him—"I might be taking an administrative leave until I start at Metropolis. It's nothing to worry about, and I may end up continuing in the lab after all. I just have to see how it goes.

"The other thing we need to talk about is Harleen."

All the blood rushes to my head at once. Where is he going with this? I shoot a glance at Oliver, but he has no idea either.

"Miss Quinzel," Dr. Nelson continues, really drawing it out, "has been awarded a Gotham University Presidential Scholarship. This is really a huge honor, the most prestigious scholarship awarded to our undergraduates here, and I hope you will all join me in congratulating her."

Another round of half-hearted smiles and clapping. Because I look like I'm going to faint right now? Because everyone in lab secretly hates me? I try to focus on Bernice's smile because it makes me remember that this news, even if it does come from his mouth, is life-changing. I don't have to worry about college. Books, tuition, room and board—all paid for. I will be able to alter the course of my entire future, shape it into whatever I want it to be. This is such a huge gift.

*Yeah, and what was the price?*

My silence? About the paper and the invitation to stay over and his hand on my leg. If I had come forward about any one of those things, would I still have gotten this scholarship? Is he pulling my strings even now? I'll never know if I earned this scholarship or if he swayed the committee somehow. I'll always have to wonder if I was enough. Of all the things he's done to me, that might be the worst one.

I don't really know what happens for the rest of lab meeting. Those two announcements have me ping-ponging back and forth between a rage blackout and euphoria. As soon as the meeting ends, Bernice runs over and gives me a hug.

"I'm so proud of you!" she squeals. "Do you know what this means? We get to go to school together. We could be roommates!"

"Holy crap, I can't wait!" Honestly, I kind of feel like I've been hit by two trains going in different directions, but in this moment, it starts to become real. I will be starting school at Gotham University this fall. My father will be at our apartment. Dr. Nelson will be at Metropolis. I don't have to see either of them ever again. And Bernice. I'll have Bernice. "Holy crap," I say again, only this time I'm smiling so big I might cry.

Oliver claps me on the back. "Congratulations," he says. Then he looks me directly in the eyes. "I want you to know that you deserve this. You're an outstanding student, Harleen."

I swallow, hard. "Thank you."

When he says it like that, even the darkest parts of my brain have to believe it.

I head to the office area to make a celebratory cup of coffee. There's usually a crowd fueling up after lab meeting, and their voices filter into the hallway as I walk.

"Are you kidding me? You've seen how close he gets to her when they're working."

"And the way she looks at him."

Oh snap, the gossip is good today. Is it Kijoon and Morgan? Because I've always kind of thought there was something there.

"But do you really think she'd do that?" asks Morgan. "He's thirty-eight. That's so *old*."

"Think we all know how she got that scholarship," says one of the postdocs.

"Daddy issues." Trent laughs at his own joke, but it turns into more of a whine as I enter the room.

Seven faces turn toward me. Seven jaws drop.

I turn right back around and run down the hallway. They know. *Everyone* knows. Everyone in the Nelson Lab? In the neurobiology department? The entire campus? I imagine they've been talking about me like this the whole time. Seeing him grooming me and watching all the stupid ways that I fell for it. Maybe they know about the complaint Oliver filed, and maybe they don't. Maybe it doesn't matter if I actually did anything with him or not as long as people can tell themselves I did. This is the way I will always be talked about, whether I'm sleeping with anybody or not. Because this is the kind of rumor that follows people forever, right?

I slip out the office door and then the bigger one, the one you have to have a keycard to get through. I'm lucky. I make it all the way to the stairwell before the first tears fall.

The cement stairs are hard and uncomfortable, but I hug my arms around myself and cry. I am a Gotham University

Presidential Scholar. I get to go to school here next year, and I don't have to worry about how to pay for it.

I thought it would feel a lot better than this.

The door behind me creaks, and I flinch. *Please don't let anyone see me this way.* I close my eyes like it'll make me disappear. Whoever it is shuffles over and sits down beside me. I open one eye. Bernice. If it was going to be anyone, I'm glad it's her.

She gives me a sympathetic smile, and for a minute, we're both quiet and still, except for the part where I try to wipe my nose on my sleeve without her noticing.

Then she says, quietly, thoughtfully, a bit philosophically, "They told Marie Curie not to accept her second Nobel Prize."

"Um, okay."

Not sure how that's relevant to my situation, but she just keeps going.

"After her husband died, she was having an affair with another scientist, who apparently had a 'thriving mustache,' and the Royal Swedish Academy of Sciences told her maybe she should just stay home from Stockholm so the king wouldn't have to shake hands with an adulteress."

That pulls a small smile out of me. "Oh yeah?"

Bernice grins. "Yep, and you know what she told them? 'Screw you, I'm coming anyway.'"

Wait. "WHAT?"

We both bust out laughing.

Bernice holds up both hands in surrender. "Okay, no, she said it really fancy, like, 'I thought this award was for my scientific work and not my personal life.' But she basically gave all those old scientist dudes the double middle finger."

I shake my head. "Madame Curie. Such a badass."

"Yep. There were duels fought in her honor and everything." Bernice puts her hand on top of mine. The way she's looking at me feels big. Important. Like she's seconds away from chickening out about whatever is in her brain right now. "I'd do it," she finally says. "If it came down to it, I'd kill for you, Harleen."

"I don't think that'll be necessary, but thanks." I smirk when I say it, but it feels really good to have her on my side again. *Really* on my side. Ride or die, preferably with more riding than dying. "I'm glad we're together again," I tell her. But even as I say it, my eyes are drawn in the direction of Dr. Nelson's office.

"But?" Her delicate face looks worried, so I lace my fingers in hers and squeeze, probably harder than I should.

"But the fact that Dr. Nelson is just going to walk out of Gotham U unscathed and get a shiny new job in Metropolis? Yeah, there is no way in hell I'm letting that happen."

# CHAPTER 39

BERNICE AND I ARE WALKING TO THE SUBWAY FROM LAB (Bernice went back inside and got my bag and stuff so I wouldn't have to AND she gave everybody the stink eye—she's a really good girlfriend) when we get the message from Jasmin.

RECKONING SECURE CHAT:

> Jasmin: I finally got into Dr. Nelson's calendar. You need to come over, quick.

"Oh wow," says Bernice.
"I know."
I message back:

> Emergency meeting at Bianca's? We can be there in 20.

I also look over my shoulder at the neurobiology building like I'm expecting to see Dr. Nelson glaring down at us from his office window, having telepathically received this info.

When we get to Bianca's, I knock on her door approximately seventy times before she can answer it. Not that she took a while. My thirst for vengeance has apparently turned me into a freaking woodpecker.

"All right, all right, geez, Harleen."

She lets us in and closes the door behind us.

"What do you know about Dr. Nelson?" I ask. "Please tell me we're taking that scumbag down!"

"It's bad," she says seriously, but I can't tell if she means bad-bad or bad-good.

She waits till we're all seated at Bianca's table to explain. Something about it makes me think of Kylie's funeral. Maybe the way Jasmin bows her head before she speaks.

"He's got one-on-one meetings with female students from the Bridge Scholars program dating back to when the program started five years ago," she finally tells us.

Bianca's jaw gets tight, and she has to get up and stalk around the apartment for a minute, even though I feel certain Jasmin would have told her before.

That parasite. That pond-scum-on-the-bottom-of-a-toilet-seat, horror show of a human being.

"Can we see them?" asks Bernice in a voice so fragile it shoots arrows through my heart.

"Sure." Jasmin squeezes her shoulder. "I didn't see her name in there, but I also didn't know what year she might be in."

Bernice sits down in front of Jasmin's laptop, and Jasmin shows her where to look.

Bianca shakes her head. "How did we not find this before?"

Jasmin shrugs. "I was looking for stuff on Perry, but after we found those files, I started looking for stuff on Nelson too."

Our eyes drift to the suspect wall at the mention of his name. I walk over and remove the pushpins.

"Will you print one of Dr. Nelson?" I ask Bianca quietly.

She nods, and by the time I've removed Perry and the teal thread that connected him to the photo of the girl with the bangs, and the other two threads that connected him to the two girls from our year, she's got it ready for me. I tack it to the bulletin board, trying not to look at his eyes for too long because if I do, I'll be sick.

"Can somebody hand me some darts?"

But I only launch a couple at his face before I'm interrupted.

"Stella has a meeting in here," Bernice says in a halting voice. "It's from the day before they found her in the bathroom."

I rush over and hold her tight, even though it's kind of awkward with me hunching over her chair. She doesn't seem to mind. She cries into my hair for a minute, but then she wipes her eyes and walks over to the suspect wall with a ramrod spine and stands directly in front of her sister.

"Can I have a piece of thread?" She holds out her hand without breaking eye contact.

Bianca hands her a purple one, and Bernice attaches one end to Stella's photograph and the other end to Dr. Nelson's. Jasmin searches for the next girl in the calendar after Stella, calling out name after name. Sometimes they're not on the wall, but every time they are, one of us adds another piece of thread. And suddenly all the connections that we couldn't force before are being made one by one by one. Nine girls. Nine faces on this wall of pain and fear had a meeting with Dr. Nelson.

I squeeze Bernice's hand. "You okay?"

She nods. "I'm glad we finally know for sure." And then she frowns at the wall. "You know what's weird, though?"

"What?" I ask, even though, honestly, what's not weird and warped about this?

"There weren't any complaints in his file in the last three years." She gestures to the wall. "And he's clearly been doing this still, so what's the deal?"

"You think it's because the complaints went digital?" I ask. I never noticed that three years were missing, but I was high-key emotionally distressed at the time.

"Negative," says Jasmin. "I scoured their server. If there were digital complaints, I'd know."

"Yeah, and Stella was in the last few years, but she wasn't in the complaint file," says Bernice.

"Right, but Stella never filed a complaint, did she?" I ask.

"Exactly," says Bernice. "She couldn't. Because she gets too scared whenever she so much as thinks about it. And she had that mystery toxin in her bloodstream when they found her."

Bianca gasps. "Like Kylie."

Jasmin nods sadly. "She's in here. I checked. The afternoon before they found her in that alley."

Bianca mutters a swear in Spanish. There's a part of me that figured as much the minute we found Dr. Nelson's file, but the knowing still twists like a knife.

"She's not a Bridge Scholar, though. Do you think she was meeting with him because she's a neurobio major, or do you think it's because she was using herself as bait to figure out if he was the serial assaulter?" asks Bianca.

"Could be either," I say. "Though if it was the second, that might explain why she never came back from the meeting. She must have uncovered something huge." I wish she had asked us to help her. I would have helped her.

*Would you, really? Before you read his file?*

It's not a question I want to answer.

"You're not in here, though, Bernice." Jasmin says it quietly, but she fixes Bernice with that puzzle-solving stare. Bernice has trouble meeting her eyes. "Maybe it's because you're already in his lab. Maybe he thought he didn't need to schedule a meeting." It's clear she doesn't actually think this is the solution. Her stare only intensifies.

I nod at Bernice. *You can do this*, I tell her with my eyes.

"Yes, well." Bernice's cheeks flush. "I may have drugged myself on the anniversary of my sister's attack and locked myself in the darkroom so the police would start investigating Dr. Nelson. And I may have stolen the anesthetic from Dr. Perry's lab so he would get investigated too. And also I may not have known I was allergic to that particular anesthetic cocktail."

Jasmin is stunned. Bianca looks like she is undergoing a rather painful werewolf transformation. (She does have a thing about lying.) But before she can explode or something, Jasmin leans closer to her computer screen and says, "You aren't going to believe this."

Bianca's eyes bulge. "Jasmin, I can't take a whole lot more."

"He has another coffee meeting with a student on the schedule for next week."

"Wait, WHAT?" Of course he does. Of course he freaking does.

"Although I guess it's impossible to know if it's a meeting or a *meeting*," says Jasmin.

"I think we have to proceed like it's the second kind," says Bernice.

"Anyone know a Sloane Garcia-Richardson?" asks Jasmin.

"Yep," I say, and my stomach drops. I gesture to myself and Bernice. "She's in the Bridge Scholars program with us."

"Of course she is. I can't believe he'd try something like this in the middle of an investigation. *Monster.*" Bianca pounds her fist against the table.

But I'm already shaking my head. "They're all the same. They think they're untouchable." I clench my jaw and meet the eyes of every girl at the table. "And I want to show him that they're not."

## CHAPTER 40

I'M SO SPENT WHEN I GET BACK TO THE APARTMENT THAT I forget to count beer bottles and read micro-disturbances in the air. It's a mistake. Big one. I make it when I throw my bag onto the chair, registering that he's watching TV but not seeing him. When I trudge toward the fridge, pinching the bridge of my nose between my fingers and praying there is something caffeinated and carbonated inside. In the bottom shelf of the door, there is a single Diet Mountain Dew, and I could just cry. Sometimes you so badly need one good thing to happen, even if it's just a small one.

I open the bottle. Hear the hiss, fizz. Take a sip.

*It's gonna be okay, Harleen.*

I turn around, and there he is. Waiting.

Eyes—red. Blood—boiling. Hands—gripping a piece of paper like a red flag.

"You weren't gonna tell me about this?" he slurs.

"What?" I say stupidly. Our shotgun kitchen just shrank by half. It can barely hold the two of us.

"You think you're so much better than me. That you can just run off to that fancy school and not tell me about it." He slaps the letter on the counter.

**Dear Ms. Quinzel, we are pleased to inform you . . .**

My scholarship letter. I hate that it's crinkled now, like that somehow compromises the message on the paper.

"You know, I could have gone to a school like that too. Not everybody has the opportunities you have." He puffs up his chest, but I can see even he doesn't believe the lie.

And I think,

*No, you couldn't.*

*You failed high school chemistry.*

*Have never held down a job longer than a year.*

*Lack the ambition/grit/IQ/creativity.*

*Take your pick.*

And I say,

Nothing.

But I don't say it fast enough.

He lunges closer. "You think I'm stupid?"

"I never said that," I fire back, annoyance in my voice, but just a hint. Anything else would be unsafe.

"You were thinking it!"

He's right. He doesn't have the ability. And not just the intellectual kind. The act of sending up your dreams like a fragile kite in a lightning storm, unspooling them higher and higher, despite the fear, despite having a brain that relentlessly calculates the probability of your own failure. It takes a kind of courage he will never know.

That courage flares up now, and I shrug, frustrated, and tell him, "Can't you see this is a good thing? I don't have to worry about how to pay for school. And I'll be out of the house. You're always saying I don't pull my weight around here. This *helps* you."

I said it all wrong. I know this. He knows this. It's his chance to really let loose on me and tell me it's all my fault. And he does.

He yells a garbled mess of obscenities, and his arm lashes out, and I think he's going to hit me, but instead, he snatches my scholarship letter from the counter.

"I DON'T HAVE TO LET YOU GO," he screams. He starts ripping it to pieces right in front of me.

His face is disgusted, like the very idea of it is a personal offense to him. Because that's a thing men like him do. They think the fact that you're intelligent or tough or funny or badass makes them small. They don't know they're small to begin with.

There was a time when him ruining the letter would have felt like him tearing apart my actual dreams. But I am so much more than a piece of paper. I am Harleen Freaking Quinzel, member of girl gangs, bringer of justice, Reckoning on the men of Gotham City.

*Why can I fight everyone's monsters except mine?*

That ends today. I feel the strength spreading through me like a current, and I could grab his head and slam it into the countertop or punch him in the face so hard his teeth rattle, but instead I say in the hardest, most sarcastic voice I can muster, "Go right ahead."

He freezes mid-tear. Like you hit pause on a cartoon. It's almost comical.

So, I laugh.

Loudly. Maniacally. Commandingly.

His anger swells like a living thing that fills the entire kitchen. "What the hell is so funny?"

There's barely room for air, but I take a deep breath.

"I just realized I'm not scared of you anymore."

I wait for him to do something. So I can retaliate? So I can show him how not scared I am? I'm not sure, but it doesn't matter because he can't really think of anything to say back.

I stand up straighter, the walls of the kitchen stretching on all sides to make room for me. "You can't take this away from me," I tell him. "I am leaving in August. And I am never coming back."

I stalk off to my room and lock the door.

# CHAPTER 41

I EXPECT HIM TO BREAK DOWN THE DOOR. WONDER IF today is the day the emotional violence turns physical. I hear him banging around the kitchen and living room, the sound of maybe a glass or a plate hitting the floor, of him punching things and then howling in pain, but his stomps and slams never carry down the hallway. After a few minutes, there is quiet. But I'm not sure if it's because he left or because he's melted all the way down in front of the TV.

I want some ice cream real bad. There's a street vendor who parks around the corner from us on Thursdays, and I can practically taste the fresh-baked waffle cones. Do I want one badly enough to risk tiptoeing into the living room and finding out my dad is still there? That seeing me is the trigger that really pushes him over the edge? I decide to sneak out the window.

I slip onto the fire escape and make my way down the stairs. When I get to the last platform, I have to climb down a ladder and hang off the last rung so I can drop to the ground.

It's not an insignificant fall, but I stick the landing. There's a shout from the other end of the alley, and I freeze.

My dad's voice.

Did he come after me?

I turn, wincing, but he's not yelling at me. A white guy in a leather jacket shoves him up against the faded brick of our apartment building. Eagle on the back with a branch clenched in its talons. Probably a goon sent by some small-time crime lord.

"Where's the money, Quinzel?"

This is not an unfamiliar sight. My father is no stranger to terrible gambling habits and even more terrible debts. Schemes and plans and "if I just had a little money to do this thing."

"Oof!"

I wince again at the characteristic sound of someone getting punched in the gut. My father. He's doubled over in pain. Another guy launches forward, knocks my dad to the ground. They surround him. Steel-toe boots into ribs and kidneys. Dad attempts to scramble away, spits blood onto the ground. As he tries to right himself, our eyes meet down the alley, and for the smallest fraction of a second, hope flickers in his.

*Guess that'll teach you not to wear such slutty clothes to parties.*

*I DON'T HAVE TO LET YOU GO.*

I'm probably strong enough to fight both of them off.

*Pop-Tarts on the towel rack, box getting emptier.*

*I'm seven years old, and I'm crying, and I'm telling him I'm scared of small spaces and please don't lock me in the bathroom again. I can take care of myself. I'll be good, I swear. There's a box of Pop-Tarts on the towel rack like usual. I try to scramble past him, but he picks me up by the back of my overalls and throws me in the bathtub.*

*I'll only be gone a few hours, he hollers through the door. Gonna meet some friends.*

*He's lying. If he was only going to be gone a few hours, he wouldn't have put the pillow and blanket in the bathtub.*

*That time—he didn't come back for three days.*

*I was down to half a Pop-Tart.*

*And I couldn't stop thinking that he had gotten into trouble— worse trouble than usual—and he wasn't coming home, and I was going to die in that bathroom. I remember banging on the door, crying, screaming, hoping somebody—anybody—would hear me.*

*I think I had a panic attack.*

*It's hard to say. I was only seven.*

My dad is still taking a beating at the other end of the alley, but I pretend I don't see him. There's ice cream waiting down the street.

There's a huge line at the ice cream cart, so I decide to go for a walk first. A delicate spring breeze rolls through the city as I make my way down cracked sidewalks, past ancient five- and six-story brick buildings, the bottom floor of each housing a pizza joint or a grocery store/deli or a dry cleaner. Some of the storefronts are closed and spray-painted, and sometimes I have to weave through a tunnel of plywood and metal posts because there's construction— always construction—but I don't mind. I let the breeze and the noise and the repetition of my steps soothe me.

I'm still a little in shock that my dad was so angry at the idea of me leaving. I thought he'd be happy to get rid of me. He's always saying how lucky I am that he lets me live here. Acts like I'm the biggest burden. Maybe he needs me more than I thought.

Not that it matters. Soon I'll be at Gotham U, and there's nothing he can do to stop me. I'll run away to college and I'll never come back. And if he's miserable or alone or drunk or furious or violent, it can't touch me. He'll be waking up in the morning, hungover, banging around the kitchen looking for food because I didn't make muffins for breakfast and leave them on the counter. And I'll be sipping coffee as I walk cobblestone pathways to class. He'll be late for work because he couldn't find a clean shirt because no one did his laundry, and I'll be opening my mind to neuroscience, art history, calculus, philosophy. He'll stop by the package store on the way home and drink in front of the TV until the bottle is empty, while I study in the shade of a hundred-year-old oak tree. And as he passes out on the couch, alone, I'll be dancing at a party with fifty of my newest friends, sweaty and exhilarated, until we pour out the doors and onto the grass, sneak up to the roof and talk until the sun rises, our heads resting on each other's shoulders, just because we can.

Only a few more months now. As conflicted as I feel about the circumstances of me getting my scholarship, I wouldn't trade it for anything. The hope that's been getting me through each day for the last I-don't-even-know-how-many years is here, and it's happening, and my future is closer than it's ever been before.

I think about Bernice. She's part of that future. A big part. And the other girls in the Reckoning—I'll be at Gotham U with them too.

*Not Kylie,* says a voice in my head, and an ache opens up inside me like a canyon. I miss her so much. Her silliness and her kindness and the way she noticed every little thing. If you got distracted by how beautiful and bubbly she was, you could miss that—her careful sense of observation. I think about how much closer we would have gotten, how much stronger our friendship would have grown, how much fun we would have had. If Dr. Nelson hadn't murdered her.

My hands clench into fists at my sides as I wait at a crosswalk for a walk signal.

"We're going to make him pay for what he did to you," I whisper at a passing taxi. "I promise."

The woman next to me gives me a sideways look and tugs her leash so that her dog isn't standing so close to me. It barely registers. All I can think of is how we're going to catch him in the act. Stake out his meeting. Stop him from hurting Sloane. Get all the proof we need about what he did to Kylie and Stella and all those other girls. I will break into his house and tear it apart piece by piece if I have to. Jasmin, Bianca, Bernice, we're all in agreement. We do whatever it takes.

Are we still going to be friends after? Or is this mission the kind of thing that destroys everything in its path like collateral damage? I like to think we'll still hang out. That I'll meet Jasmin for coffee or hit the gym with Bianca. Maybe we'll even do missions still. It's not like toxic misogyny is going anywhere. But I don't know. Something about this mission with Dr. Nelson—it feels final.

Final for me and Bernice too? I shake away the thought. Bernice and I are endgame. We're going to be roomies, and we're going to decorate our dorm room all cute so it doesn't look all sad and beige, and we're going to stay up till two in the morning quizzing each other on the Krebs cycle while we eat white cheddar popcorn and chocolate-covered pretzels, and then I'll go to med school and she'll go to grad school, and we'll live in an off-campus apartment and get a puppy with an underbite, and and and. It just keeps going. I can't imagine a future without her in it.

I know she feels the same way. Well, I hope she feels the same way. I guess we never talked about our future beyond being roommates this fall, but I feel like it's implied that she wants to spend the rest of her life with me. And, okay, yes, if I really think about it, she only approached me in the first place because she wanted me to join the Reckoning, not because she wanted to date me, but I've changed a lot since then too. I'm *finally* ready to say I have a girlfriend. I'm finally ready to *be* a girlfriend. That's huge. Something like a revenge plot that may or may not end in catastrophe doesn't just break that up.

I realize I've circled back around and I'm at the ice cream cart again. This time the line isn't so long, though. I order a soft-serve vanilla with Pop Rocks and rainbow sprinkles. And then I can't help but ask Abraham about each of his kids and whether JT is playing hockey and if Macy's landed her full yet. I know you're not supposed to have favorites when you coach, but I'm obsessed with that kid.

When I come back with my ice cream, I don't go down the alley. I go up to the main entrance and take the stairs, trying to eat my vanilla cone before it melts all over my fingers, even though it's only April. I bite off pieces of the cone, not caring that it makes it worse because I like to have a good ratio of ice cream to cone all the way down. The mess becomes almost unmanageable as I push through the door to my hallway. I'm laughing and trying to lick ice cream off the back of my hand when I see her. Officer Montoya.

Standing outside my door. Leaning against the wall in her police uniform. Something about the look on her face makes my heart catch in my chest.

But she's not whipping out the handcuffs this time. Does that mean I'm not in trouble? It feels like too much to hope for.

"Is this about Kylie? Did you get something on Dr. Nelson?" I ask.

Her eyes bulge. "How do you—? You know what, never mind. I can't discuss the details of a case. This is about something else."

Cold fear worms its way through my intestines. "Is it one of the other girls? Did he strike again?"

Her face reveals nothing. "Miss Quinzel, could we go inside, please?"

"S-sure." When I unlock the door, the keys shake in my hands, and I have to try once, twice, three times to get the key into the lock.

"You can have a seat on the couch," I tell Officer Montoya, suddenly acutely aware of the duct tape and beer bottles.

"Some of your neighbors said you and your father had an altercation today," says Montoya, all serious tone and folded hands.

Did someone really call the cops on us? People in our building fight way worse and nobody does a damn thing. Not even for gunshots.

"I mean, yeah?" I say, trying to put the pieces together.

Her eyes dig into me all steely. And then she lets the bomb drop. "Your father is dead."

The floor drops out from under me, and I free-fall all

the way to the basement. I don't understand the words that she's saying. Only that they make me feel like I'm a house with the foundation missing.

"*What?*"

Her eyes rove around the apartment, taking in the pieces of my scholarship letter confetti-ing the kitchen floor. Broken glass and the imprint of a fist in the wall—the aftermath of our fight.

It finally clicks in my brain.

"Whoa. Hey. I didn't do this." I'm still not even sure I believe the words she's saying. I *just* saw him.

"If there's a history of him hurting you—" begins Montoya, and I suddenly get why it felt like she was on my side this time.

"*No.* He didn't hurt me." My heart squeezes. "Well, not physically," I say quietly.

"What happened during the fight?" she asks. Gently.

I regurgitate it for her as best I can. The scholarship. Him raging. Me not being afraid. I hesitate when I get to the part about sneaking down the fire escape.

"I saw him in the alley with a couple of men. He . . . often has gambling debts." I look down at my hands. I could have intervened. I could have stopped this.

*You didn't know what was going to happen.*

Didn't I?

"Did you call anyone?" asks Officer Montoya.

"No," I say, still unable to meet her eyes. "I was angry. About our fight."

"I see." Officer Montoya doesn't say it. She doesn't have to.

This is all my fault.

His death is on my hands.

# CHAPTER 42

THIS IS THE SECOND TIME I'VE WORN THIS FUNERAL DRESS this month. Not that we had a real funeral for my dad. I didn't realize until now how expensive it is when someone dies. We had to cremate him because we couldn't afford to bury him. Some uncle I'd only ever met twice kept the ashes.

I lock the door to the apartment and pull out a chair. My feet are aching, so I flick off my shoes and flex my toes back and forth. Maybe I should burn it. The dress, I mean. I don't think I could wear it again without feeling weird. *Maybe I'll need it again, though,* says the dark voice in my head. Maybe I'm the kind of person people die around.

I lay my head on the table. I'm lucky the landlord was willing to sign a month-to-month lease with an eighteen-year-old. (Well. On the condition that he gets to fix up the place for the next tenant while I'm still living here.) Much as I hate this place, I'm a little panicked about how I'm going to keep it. It's just for the next few months until college.

Maybe if I teach summer day camp at the gym AND start giving private lessons on top of it. And get a job as a waitress on top of that? My dad didn't really leave me with a whole lot, and my savings from getting paid to do lab work only go so far.

There's a knock at the door. *Please don't be the police.*

I force myself to stand up and answer it, cringing as I wait to see a badge in the gap under the door chain. But it's just this girl from the building—Maggie Forester. She lives one floor down from me, and I've watched her a couple times when her mom had to work nights. Honestly, it's pretty easy work because she spends most of the time playing guitar, and she's not half bad. I close the door so I can unlock the chain and then open it again. She's holding a foil container.

"Hey," she says shyly. "My mom made you chicken parmesan."

She hands me the dish and waits like she's hoping I'll ask her to come in or something.

"Thanks." I try to inject some warmth into my voice so I don't sound like a robot. "Tell her that's really kind of her."

I close the door. Stick the chicken in the fridge.

I know I'll feel hungry again. Eventually.

I don't know how I expected to feel, but this isn't it. Shouldn't it feel like weights lifted and shadows vanquished to have a person like him out of your life? Instead, I pace the apartment like a restless cat. Angry. Unmoored. Even if someone's terrible, if they're your reference point for everything else that ever happens to you, how do you navigate the world without them? How do you run away from someone who's already gone?

I need to change something. Do something. I stalk to the

bathroom, parting my hair down the middle like a woman possessed. The girl that looks back at me has confidence blazing in her eyes. And longing. She dreams, and skyscrapers shoot into the air and butterflies leave their chrysalises and birds escape their cages all over the city and entire worlds materialize out of a cosmic soup. She is a girl with choices spreading out in front of her in every direction like roads. And she isn't afraid of fire because she already knows she comes out a phoenix on the other side.

I break out the dye—permanent. Whoever this is, I want to be her all the time. I dip-dye one side of my hair pink and the other blue. Tie my hair back in pigtails. Paint a red star over my right eye and a black diamond over my left. It's a start, but it's not enough.

So, I grab my Reckoning costume and my dad's old baseball bat that he keeps under his bed. And I take to the streets.

I stalk past the run-down park, past Thirty-Seventh and Low. I'm not sure what I'm looking for exactly. Some man being awful, so I can beat the crap out of him? My father's ghost, back to get me?

I walk for hours, but instead of making me tired, it only gives me more energy.

And then I see him.

Down the street. Causing mayhem.

The Joker.

He's dangerous. I know this. I should slink into a nearby alley. Pretend I never saw him. If I go now, I could still watch him through the crack between the wall and the dumpster. He'd never see me.

His laugh is getting closer. He's not facing my direction, but if he was—

I find myself picking up my bat and smashing it into a window.

The shatter is an explosion, violent and beautiful. The glass fills the air like glitter, falls like snow. Tinkles like bells when it hits the ground.

He turns.

My stomach flips. He's staring right at me. Hungry? Angry? Murderous.

He takes a few steps in my direction. I should run. Now.

I force myself to stand firm and meet his eyes. It is a terrifying kind of power.

Green hair. Ghostly skin. Like sugar and starlight. Or a drowning victim. And the wildest eyes I've ever seen. Walking toward me. A man runs out of the alley near The Joker. The Joker draws a bazooka from his coat without skipping a step. He pulls the trigger without taking his eyes off me.

Guns are so much louder than in the movies. I jump without meaning to. And when the smoke clears, I realize it wasn't a gun at all. Just a big red boxing glove, spring-loaded to really knock you on your butt. The Joker raises his eyebrows like I've just gotten the punch line. I answer him by smashing another window. Walking toward him too.

He smiles. Holy hell, that smile.

We get closer and closer and closer.

I wonder if he's going to kill me. Wonder if he's wondering it too.

But instead, he says, "Well, aren't you a cute little Harlequin?"

I tug at one of my blond pigtails, the blue-tipped one, and say, "Thanks, Mr. J," through painted eyes and blinking lashes.

And all the while, I'm thinking, *Harlequin. Harleen Quinzel. Harley Quinn.* Well, that fits like a glove.

One of his henchmen screams down the street in a car and stops just long enough for The Joker to get in.

The questions are right there, waiting for me to ask them. *Do I get to see you again? Do you know I stole a vial of your blood? What just happened here? Will you think about it tonight the way I will? What are all the things inside your brain that make you this savage and creative and volatile, and will you let me see them?*

The door slams shut.

"See ya around," I say to the night air as the car squeals away.

# CHAPTER 43

TODAY, WE BRING HIM DOWN. BERNICE AND I PRETEND TO study in an alcove of the neurobiology building that gives us a perfect view of the elevator Dr. Nelson takes when he leaves the lab. I'm reminded of that first time with the Dissent Cannon. How different am I from the girl I was then? How much have I changed because of this man? Because of all the men who have hurt me? I wish I had the cannon with me now.

Monday at four o'clock. Sloane Garcia-Richardson, the girl I met at the Bridge Scholars party. A tête-à-tête at one of the campus coffee shops. I don't get how he's going to pull this off, out in the open and everything, but I wouldn't put anything past him. I check my phone. 3:44. Bianca couldn't get anyone to cover for her at the physics machine shop, and Jasmin's proctoring an exam, but they're going to join us as soon as they can. Hopefully coffee will take a while. We're assuming there's a second location involved, but as long as he doesn't take her there for about an hour, we'll have reinforcements. The more of us that can be here, the better. Just in case things get ugly.

I check the elevator again and realize this time there's a girl standing in the lobby, fidgeting and checking her phone. A brunette in an ill-fitting pencil skirt. Weird that she's meeting him here at the neurobiology building and not at the coffee shop.

I nudge Bernice. "It's the girl. The Sloane girl."

She frowns. "How do you know?"

"I met her at Dr. Nelson's party. It's definitely her." I watch her tug at her skirt. The fact that she wore it both to the party and here today isn't a coincidence. Most of us only have one or two professional-type outfits. The skirt means she's treating this like a job interview, I realize with a sick feeling in my stomach.

The elevator dings open at 3:46. Dr. Nelson steps out and aims himself toward her. Bernice and I slump in our alcove, and I tuck my pink and blue pigtails into the collar of my shirt. Bernice picks up her phone and starts recording. Just in time too.

"Sloane!" Dr. Nelson beams at her and gives her shoulder a squeeze. "Thank you so much for meeting me here. I live just a few blocks from campus, so I figured we could walk. I could really use a coffee, and my espresso machine is so much better than that toxic sludge they serve in the student center."

I try not to throw up in my mouth. Bernice shoots me a frantic glance.

"No problem." Sloane grins back, and the unsuspecting excitement on her face makes me want to punch him directly in the crotch. "Thank you for taking the time to meet with me." Her eyes dart to the wall next to them. "I'm pretty nervous about how to pay for Gotham U now that I didn't get a presidential scholarship, so I was really relieved when I got your email."

"Of course, of course." He puts his hand on the small of her back and guides her to the door. "I've got some truly unique and exciting possibilities in mind. And you know, I think it's smarter that we decided to do this at my house instead. It's more intimate that way. It'll really give us the space to figure this out and do some exploration."

The wind pulls the door shut behind them with a snap.

"Harleen?" Bernice says it like I'm breakable or something. Her eyes flick to my hands. I look down and realize that the pen I'm holding has snapped in half, and that the ink is running onto my skin and my notebook, and also that I am bleeding.

"Oh."

And then I recover. "Crap. We don't have time for this." I rush to a nearby trash can and throw away the pen, rubbing the ink off as best I can with a sheet of notebook paper. The back of my hand still looks like it's covered in blue lightning.

Bernice appears at my elbow. "I already packed up our stuff. Here's a bandage. If we hurry, we can still follow them."

I sling my backpack over my shoulder, and we leave through the same door they did. Way down the sidewalk, I can see Dr. Nelson walking with Sloane to his house off campus.

"Oh thank goodness," whispers Bernice.

"I know," I reply. We've been to his house before, so it's not like we don't know where they're going, but I had this weird feeling that if we let her out of our sight we'd lose her completely.

Bernice's face goes tight. "What are we going to do? I

thought we were going to wait for Jasmin and Bianca and go after him together. He's not supposed to take her to the second location for at least an hour. All of our plans hinged on that."

"I don't know." I pick up my pace like it'll help fix the fact that our meticulous scheming is falling apart. Sloane and Dr. Nelson turn onto his street. "He's just one man. We can probably take him with you, me, *and* Sloane."

Bernice bites her lip. "But what if they really are just talking?"

I give her a look.

"At first, I mean. We're supposed to wait until we know for sure. That's the plan."

I jerk my arm in their direction. "He's already leading her to his house like some kind of storybook villain. How far are we supposed to let him go before we bust in and save her?"

"I don't know! I'm just asking!" says Bernice.

It's an echo of the argument I had with the rest of the Reckoning at our last meeting. They wanted to be sure we had enough to convict him, but after what happened to Kylie, I'm not willing to take any chances.

We're at his street now too. He's only the fourth house, so we hover by a stop sign as he opens the door and ushers Sloane inside. Bernice's chest is heaving up and down, and she's wearing her calculating face.

"Okay, you're right," she says. "We follow them inside the second things look bad. Reinforcements or not."

I nod. "Message them and tell them to hurry."

She has her phone out, texting furiously, as the door closes.

"C'mon," I tell her.

We race along the sidewalk and hide behind an oak tree in his neighbor's yard. I hope they're not home.

"Anything from Jasmin and Bianca yet?" I whisper.

She unlocks her phone, keeping it close to her chest. Shakes her head.

"There's no way we can wait," I say, peering around the tree trunk at Dr. Nelson's house. I see his head in a window and pull back, quick. "He's in the kitchen. I think I saw one of those fancy coffee machines."

"He said they were going to have coffee. Where do you think they'd drink it?"

"In the dining room? Or maybe the study?" How did I never notice his house has almost all the same rooms as Clue? And then it hits me. "Neither of which we can see from here."

Bernice points at a window over some bushes near Dr. Nelson's privacy fence. "If we stand over there, we can see them in the dining room. Maybe in the study too, depending on where they are."

I shake my head. "The window's too high."

"There's an air-conditioning unit we can stand on," says Bernice with so much certainty that I— Oh. "I may have used it last time," she says, embarrassed.

"It's fine." I rush to say it—I can figure out how I feel about it later.

We tiptoe across the manicured lawn and slip behind the bushes, lilacs, I think. I hop on top of the air conditioner like I'm doing a box jump and peek through the window. I can see them across the dining room, perched in a couple of chairs with spindly legs like the kind in *Mad Men*. They really are just sitting and talking. For now.

As soon as something happens, though. The minute he makes a move.

I'm ready.

We break in. We save her. We hold him until the police come, so we can show them the video Bernice is taking and anything else we find. We ruin him.

And maybe before the police come, I ask him some questions about Kylie and do whatever it takes to get the answers I need. But I don't tell Bernice that.

Sloane takes nervous sips of her coffee every few seconds. Laughs at whatever it is Dr. Nelson is saying. I can't tell if she's figured out enough to be scared yet, or if she's just nervous because of what an important meeting this is for her. Meanwhile, he couldn't be more relaxed. Legs slung wide. Gesturing with his coffee mug. Scooting his chair closer to her, but never all at once. He's sly about it. Calculated.

I feel like such an idiot watching it happen to someone else.

"No," says Bernice.

"What?" Did I say that part out loud?

"Whatever you're thinking, however you're blaming yourself right now, he is the predator. Now. Then. Every other time. Geez, look at him. He's like a natural. What kind of person is a natural at such a terrible thing?" Bernice's glare sizzles all the way through the windowpane and across the room, where it tickles the back of his neck.

He turns in our direction, and we duck, fast.

"You think he saw us?" I whisper.

"I don't know," she whispers back.

We wait, backs against the house, butts against the AC unit, chests heaving. It doesn't feel safe to try to look again.

I'm half expecting him to come around the side of the house with a shovel. After a few minutes, my heart stops racing like it's trying to break the sound barrier, and I put my hand on top of Bernice's.

"Thanks," I say. "I needed someone to tell me it wasn't my fault."

She puts her head on my shoulder. "Anytime."

"Hey, have you heard anything from Jasmin and Bianca?"

She checks her phone. "Not yet," she says apologetically.

"That's so weird. They're supposed to be on standby. Did the message go through? Maybe I should—"

"Harleen!" Before I can get out my phone, Bernice pulls me up carefully so I'm at eye level with the window again.

What I see makes me stop breathing. Dr. Nelson pulls something that looks like a miniature can of Lysol from behind his chair and sprays Sloane directly in the face with it. She coughs a couple times and shakes her head. Based on what Bernice has told me about Stella, I expect her to start screaming, but she doesn't. Her face seems calm, almost slack. But her chest. It rises and falls so quickly, her rib cage almost looks like it's glitching.

Dr. Nelson watches her, his head cocked to the side. Then he asks her a question.

Her eyes dart back and forth, but she doesn't move, doesn't even speak.

"We can't wait anymore," I tell Bernice, jumping out of the bushes before she can stop me.

I run around to the front of the house and knock on his door.

# CHAPTER 44

C'MON, C'MON, C'MON. I KNOCK AGAIN AND PULL A LIP-
stick from my bag, my most dangerous shade of red—might
as well really sell this. The door cracks open as I'm sliding it
across my bottom lip.

"Harleen?" he says, surprised.

I throw on a huge grin. "Caught me."

I press my lips together with a popping sound and tuck
the lipstick back in my bag, all demure, like I'm so embarrassed to be caught putting on lipstick, even though I know
it turns men on. (Have you ever seen the looks you get when
you do it on the subway?)

"I wasn't expecting you," he says, a touch nervous. He
doesn't open the door more than halfway either. Can't take
his eyes off my lips, though. (Told you.)

It makes me feel powerful. Being right. Flipping the narrative against him. The power threatens to consume me, but
I tamp it down so all he can see is my doe eyes.

"Right, I should have texted. Sorry." I shift my weight,

trying to see around him. The double doors to the dining room are open, but I can't see Sloane from here. "I've been thinking a lot about everything that's happened, and I'm sooo grateful for my scholarship, and I guess I wanted to come over and officially bury the hatchet about this Joker paper business."

I wait. Will he actually buy it? I could barely even say it without throwing up in my mouth.

A moment of hesitation, and then. His eyes grow hungry.

Of course he believes it. Men like him will never not believe it.

Then he glances over his shoulder, like, *Oops, I forgot about the* other *girl I have squirreled away in my house right now.* "This is not the best time. I was right in the middle of something," he says. He looks me up and down. "But you know what? Give me a second. I'll be right back."

He shuts the door, and there's the sound of him turning the lock. Footsteps. Some other sounds I can't make out. He's back sooner than I expect, though, opening the door wide this time.

"I'm really glad you came," he says.

"Me too."

He guides me inside, his hand on the small of my back, and I don't break all his fingers, so I'm pretty sure I deserve a major acting award. I try not to stare at the dining room doors as we pass. They're closed now. Is Sloane okay in there? Is she going to end up like Kylie?

And then I realize we're headed toward the kitchen and not upstairs.

"Why don't you stay for dinner?" he says. "I'll make us gnocchi."

He opens a door at the back of the kitchen. My first thought is that this is where he'll hide my body after he kills me.

"My wine cellar," he explains. "Do you mind picking a bottle of white for the sauce? I make a mean beurre blanc." He holds out a hand as if to say, *Ladies first*. Because that's the most annoying thing about this guy. He's always a model gentleman in none of the ways that matter.

"Sure," I say. Wine bottles make excellent weapons.

I head down the wooden stairs first, and he creaks along after me.

"You pick, and I'll be right back. I have something to take care of upstairs first."

He starts to leave.

But as I walk over to one of the racks, planning to grab the largest bottle and crack him over the head with it, I get this weird feeling and I turn my head. Just in time to see him lock the door behind me.

I sprint up the stairs, even though I know that sound better than any other. I twist the doorknob and find out what I already know. It's locked. Somehow I make it back down the stairs, even though my legs have gone all wobbly. I pull out my phone, but there's no signal down here.

The wine cellar is definitely smaller than it was before. Walls shrinking. Wine racks closing in all around me like a cage. I'm never getting out of here. This is where my life ends. In a dark, cold shoebox underneath a monster's house. I melt to the floor because I don't have real bones anymore. Curl my arms around my head protectively. Try to take calming breaths. Or any breaths. If I close my eyes, I can imagine I'm somewhere big. An open field. An auditorium. An ocean.

*Pop-Tarts on the towel rack, box getting emptier.*

My eyes snap open. I stifle a scream. The wine cellar is so small now that it's pressing in on my elbows and toes, squeezing the breath out of me. This is just like when I was a kid, only this time I probably really am going to die.

He'll kill me. Or the fear will kill me first. Walls squeezing smaller, heart beating faster. Until it just . . . gives out. Because there's no way it can keep going like this. That much is certain. I'm going to have a heart attack. I'm already having one, I must be. It can't go any faster. It can't get any worse.

The wine cellar swims in front of me, vision darkening from the edges inward. Maybe if I'm lucky I'll pass out first before my heart explodes.

*The heart has the only self-excitable cells in the body.*

The thought just pops into my head, but it takes me out of my fear for a fraction of a second. I lean into it. I tell myself everything I learned in AP Bio that I can remember. This particular cluster of cells—they fire again and again and again, automatically, without any stimulation from light or touch or pain. Without the brain telling them to. They create the current that makes your heart beat.

For a minute or two minutes or ten, every cell in my body is devoted to one task: trying not to hyperventilate. There's a part of me that wants to give up. Lie down on the floor of the wine cellar and close my eyes and let the fear have me. But then I remind myself that there's a girl upstairs who is even more scared than I am, and I need to get it together.

I pull out my pocketknife.

# CHAPTER 45

MY PHONE BUZZES IN MY POCKET JUST AS THE LOCK CLICKS. I have signal again! I turn the knob to confirm that I picked the lock, but for now, I leave the door shut and pull my phone from my pocket.

RECKONING SECURE CHAT:

> Bianca: Hello??
>
> Bianca: You doing okay with the stakeout?
>
> Jasmin: We're starting to get pretty worried that you haven't checked in.

What the . . . ? I scroll up, but there's no message from Bernice other than the one from a long time ago telling them we were camped out in the neurobiology building waiting for Dr. Nelson to come down from his office. I dash out a quick response.

> Harleen: At Dr. Nelson's house. He locked me in the wine cellar. HURRY

I think about how Sloane is in danger and how I have no idea where Bernice is right now. What if she came in after me and he's got her locked away somewhere too? I add one more message.

Harleen: SEND POLICE

As I ease open the door to the wine cellar, my knife in one hand, a terminal bottle of Riesling in the other, a shadow fills the doorway. Before I can gasp/lunge/attack, the shadow hugs me.

"Oh thank goodness," says Bernice.

"Are you all right?" I ask, breathlessly hugging her back. "I have no idea how long I was down there. I'm so sorry. Bianca and Jasmin are on their way, but for now—"

"It's just us," Bernice says. Her face looks a little strange.

I follow her through the kitchen.

"Are you okay?" she asks.

I nod. Something doesn't make sense. She's not whispering or sneaking around or anything. Does that mean—

"Bernice, did you take down Dr. Nelson yourself?" She's so petite, it's hard to imagine. But I always knew she was more badass than people gave her credit for.

That strange look again, almost detached. "You could say that."

We come to the dining room doors, now wide open again. The first thing I see is Sloane, her feet hanging off the end of the dining room table. She doesn't look entirely conscious. I rush in to check on her, and that's when a movement near the fireplace draws my eye. Dr. Nelson is standing on a stool in the corner. There's a noose around his neck.

"What the hell?!" I look at Bernice, but before she can say anything—

"Help! Harleen, please!" he screams.

It is then that I realize there's not just a rope, but a system of pulleys . . . connected to a can of whatever it was he sprayed in Sloane's face.

"Did you . . . do all this?" I look at Bernice like I'm seeing her for the first time. This isn't just stuff she found lying around his dining room. The pulleys. The black cable. The mechanism for dispensing that spray. This took planning.

"I got the idea from when we went night rappelling," she says quietly.

I take a closer look at the design. It's unbelievably clever. If he moves, he gets squirted with the spray, which, based on the way Sloane looks right now, will probably make him go all limp on the stool, and—

"Harleen!" Dr. Nelson calls out again, this time more urgently.

I ignore him and go back to checking on Sloane. Let him worry for a minute. Her body lies completely still on the dining room table. Awake, though. She's definitely awake. Her eyes that were trained on the chandelier overhead fix on me as I get closer. Her breathing speeds up.

*There was some kind of weird toxin in her system.*

*Whoever killed her literally scared her to death.*

"What did you do to her?" I ask. I put one hand on top of Sloane's in hopes of calming her, but it seems to make her worse, so I pull my hand away.

"Nothing, I swear," Dr. Nelson pleads with me. His face is sweating entirely too much for someone who's innocent. "We were just having coffee and she had some kind of attack or something. Why don't you check to see if there's an EpiPen in her purse or maybe a medi-bracelet?"

"We saw you spray her," I say.

"What?" His face goes pale.

"Is that what you sprayed Kylie with?"

"Kylie Pearce?"

"I don't know, how many Kylies have you murdered lately?" I say, my voice hard.

That's when he really breaks down. Actually starts crying. "Please, I didn't mean for that to happen."

"What *did* you mean to happen?" asks Bernice, and I jump. I almost forgot she was here for a second.

He doesn't answer. Like he thinks if he stays still long enough, the question will just go away.

"It's okay. You don't have to tell us," she says. He actually sighs with relief. He doesn't know Bernice like I do. She goes out to the hallway and grabs a golf club from the bag sitting there. "I'm pretty sure I can get the answers with this."

# CHAPTER 46

I HALF EXPECT HER TO SHATTER HIS KNEECAPS, BUT IN-stead she raises the club high over her head and brings it down with a crash on the door of what looks like a liquor cabinet. It's small, with beautiful patterns in the wood. It's also padlocked. Bernice swings the club again, this time connecting with the lock with devastating force. The ancient knives and throwing stars mounted on the wall above the cabinet shudder in response. She doesn't break the lock open, but she does knock the entire handle off the cabinet, which is just as good.

"Harleen, I don't think I can stay like this much longer. *Please.*" Dr. Nelson makes a big show of teetering on his stool, even though I'm fairly certain he could stand there for a few hours when faced with the alternative.

"Yeah, yeah, in a minute," I say. "Let's see what you've been hiding."

One of the doors is still shut, so I help Bernice wrench it open.

"There's more cans of that stuff in here." I pick up one of the black aerosol cans. They look so innocent, like Axe body spray, but there's something creepy about them. I can't put my finger on it.

"Does it say what's in it?" asks Bernice.

"No." That's what it is. "There's no label at all."

I walk around the table to Dr. Nelson.

"Hey," I say gently.

"Oh thank goodness." He says in a wobbly voice. He really does look terrified up there.

"What did you put in that spray?" (Again, gently.)

*"What?"*

"The spray. You tell me how you made it, and I'll cut you down," I explain.

His forehead breaks out in a fresh round of sweat. "I have no idea. I've never made that stuff."

"WRONG ANSWER. Bernice, can you toss me that golf club? And maybe a ball too?"

She underhand lofts the club over his dining room table, and I catch it one-handed. I catch the ball one-handed too. Dr. Nelson notices.

"You like that?" I ask. "Yeah, I'm pretty athletic. Bet I suck at golf, though. Golf's a rich-people sport, and, well, I think this is the first time I've ever even held a golf club." I set the ball down a foot away from his stool. "You sure you don't want to tell me how you made that stuff?"

"I promise! I didn't—"

"Suit yourself."

I take a couple slow practice swings the way I've seen baseball players do, and then I rear back and really let that golf ball have it. It's a ridiculously ugly swing that bangs into the floor, but the ball still sails across the room and takes a satisfying chunk out of the drywall.

"Yep. Terrible," I proclaim. "But nothing a little practice won't fix. Bernice, sweetie, would you mind getting me a few more golf balls?"

She blushes. "Sure, babe."

She puts a few on the table next to me and slips a fourth into my hand, fingers brushing my wrist in a way that makes me hot all over.

"Thanks," I say.

I realize Dr. Nelson is watching us. Not just looking, but all hungry and male gaze-y, even in his current situation.

"Are you effing serious right now?" I ask him. (He declines to answer.)

I respond by lining three of the golf balls up, each one closer to his stool. And then the fourth one, that one I place an inch inside one of the legs. There is no winning that game of Jenga.

"So," I say. "The spray."

CRACK.

I slam the first golf ball across the room and it ricochets off a chairback.

"What's in it?"

CRACK.

The next ball takes out a windowpane. Oops, hope the neighbors don't hear.

"You really should—" I take a wild swing as I'm talking, which (A) totally misses the golf ball and (B) completely splinters the nearest corner of his dining room table. Dr. Nelson nearly wets himself. I couldn't have scared him more if I missed on purpose. Which, honestly? Is kind of funny, so I start laughing and can't stop.

"Wow, that was awful," I say, wiping my eyes. "Can you imagine if that had been your stool leg? Ah, well, let's give it another go!"

I rear back again, this time even more erratically, but before I can take a swing, he yells out, "Stop!"

Just like I knew he would.

"Please, okay, look. I swear I don't know what's in the toxin, but that's because someone else makes it. Someone at Arkham. Please don't hit another ball." He is practically sobbing by the end of his little speech, but a lot of people can fake stuff like that.

"That's awfully convenient," I say, balancing the club on the tip of one of my fingers.

"I think he's telling the truth," calls Bernice from over by the cabinet.

"Wait, really?" I drop the club, but it doesn't matter anymore.

"Check this out." She slides a padded envelope across the table. It's addressed to the R&D division at Arkham Asylum, but there's no name.

"Huh. So, there really is an Arkham connection." I narrow my eyes at Dr. Nelson. "Who?"

Fear sparks in his eyes. "I don't know. He always wears a mask. I don't have a name. I've never even seen his face."

"Why?"

"Why haven't I seen his—?"

"WHY IS A RANDOM PERSON SENDING YOU CHEMICALS IN CREEPY UNMARKED CANS?"

"That's our deal," he whimpers. "He sends me the drug

he developed—half sedative, half fear toxin—and I send him blood samples."

A fear toxin. What the effing hell? So, the whole point of it was to terrify these girls as part of some sick experiment?

"That's what you did to Kylie." The realization almost undoes me. "Making her have a"—I choke on the next words— "heart attack. With some toxin just so you could get a blood sample."

"Kylie was different. She didn't react right when I dosed her. She tried to attack me."

"Imagine that."

"It's almost like she knew it was coming. I managed to lock her in the dining room and ran to get a spare can. But she was banging on the door the whole time, like—like an animal."

That's how she got the scrapes on her knuckles. It's probably when she wrote that note on her ankle too.

"I panicked," he continues. "I sprayed her until the can was empty. She died an hour later. You have to understand, I didn't mean to do it."

"No, you just meant to do whatever you did to Stella."

I think back to the police photos of Kylie's body. Of how quickly they let me go after the coroner gave them new information. He said a fear toxin *and* a sedative. So the girls couldn't move, no matter how scared they were.

"What did you do? Tell me what you did to her!"

"You have to understand—"

"WRONG. ANSWER."

My eyes are drawn to his display of vintage hunting knives or whatever they are. I grab them two by two and splay them across the table in front of me, suddenly reminded of playing darts with his picture at Bianca's apartment. I fling two of the knives across the room and then a third. They go zipping by him and lodge themselves in the wall all the way up to the hilt. He jerks, trying to avoid them, but he can't move too much or he'll get blasted in the face with fear spray. The fourth one nicks his arm, and he screams, but not as much as he's going to. I grab the fifth—a particularly gruesome machete—and lunge across the room, ready to kill him. I am made of air and fire and vengeance as I leap onto the table in front of him. I hold the machete right up to the thin skin of his neck. My chest heaving. Hair crackling like sparks of lightning. I wait for the imaginary scene to fade.

But it doesn't.

Because this time I'm really doing this.

## CHAPTER 47

"WHAT THE—?" I LET GO OF HIS SHIRT. SCARED. SHOOK.
Overwhelmed. This is real. Every time this has ever happened
in the past, it was all in my head. It *felt* real, but some part of
me knew that all I had to do was wait, and the darkness would
disappear. Is this it? Have I hit the threshold? The place where
the darkness looms so big that I don't have the power to hold it
back anymore? I almost killed someone. And I didn't even have
any control over it. The anger drains out of me, siphoned off
in every direction. It leaves me weak, and I try not to let him
see me shake. My limbs don't seem to want to work anymore.

Dr. Nelson opens one eye first and then the other, relieved by whatever he sees or doesn't see in my face.

"Who is giving you the toxin? Who are you sending the
samples to?" I ask evenly.

He reacts with a terrified head shake. "You'll have to kill
me, because what he'd do is even worse."

"Well, you heard the man," says Bernice in a voice that is
uncharacteristically cold.

Has she been leaning against the wall the whole time? Was she really going to let me do it?

I jump down from the table, barely sticking the landing. "The police'll be here soon."

I need to end this. And I need to do it in a way that doesn't destroy me or the only girl I've ever loved.

Bernice clearly disagrees. "Are you kidding me? After all he's done? We can't let him walk. If you won't do it, I will."

She holds out her hand for the knife. I don't give it to her.

"Fine," she says. She walks over to the wall behind him and starts wiggling the handle of the one that is poking out the most.

"Bernice, please don't do this. You're not the kind of person who kills people." I think about my dad dying and that prowling, restless rage that still won't go away, even when I took to the night with my baseball bat. "When my dad died— It's not going to make you feel the way you think it will."

I say it softly, hoping that it will make her listen to me. That invoking my dad's name when I've barely spoken about his death up until now will have some kind of power over her. I've already calculated what the future will look like—in one day, two months, a year. If she does this, her life will be over.

Bernice jerks the knife out of the wall with one final pull, almost falling backward, almost crying, almost everything. "I don't care about how I'll feel. Think about how we'll feel if we let him go and he does this again. Because you know he will. *Look.*" She stumbles around to the other side of the table, drunk off emotion, and grabs something out of the cabinet and shoves it at me. It's a rack of glass vials, I realize.

Each one containing what looks like a lock of hair. Each one labeled with a name.

Remy.

Amaya.

Kylie.

Stella.

I pick up the vial that says REMY. The hair inside is pink, almost the same shade as my pigtail tip. I try not to throw up.

"Think of how many more girls he'll hurt in Metropolis if we don't stop him." Bernice is sobbing now. Can barely hold the knife.

"I agree that he's disgusting and a monster, but we don't get him *and* Gotham U. We have to pick." I come around to her side of the table and try to put a hand on her shoulder.

And she completely unravels. "I don't care what happens to me after! I don't care if I live or die! As long as he dies too."

"Whoa, whoa, whoa, I care, okay? I care about you." Seeing her like that—it makes the darkness inside me shrink. I squeeze her elbow. Look her right in the eyes. "He's not worth ruining your entire future over." I can't let her become a murderer. She's not like me. She's too good of a person for that.

She shakes me off. "We're supposed to do this."

I've got to make her understand. *"Bernice."*

She hands me the knife, and for a second, I'm relieved that she's not about to do something she'll regret.

Then her eyes lock on mine. "You're meant to do this."

Her certainty startles me. "What?"

"This is who you're supposed to be. It's who you already are. I switched the samples."

I drop the knife on the table. "I don't—"

"For your epigenetics assay. That day you ran The Joker's sample and one of the controls was twice The Joker and you thought it was Dr. Nelson? It wasn't."

I don't understand. What would be the point of switching my samples? To cast doubt on Dr. Nelson? And how would she even know to do it? That was my first time running the assay.

"Why would you do that?"

"Dr. Nelson had me rerun an earlier SV1 experiment just to be safe, and I saw that you carried the villainous version of the gene, and I figured you might have high levels for the epigenetic assay too, so I switched your serum sample with Dr. Nelson's."

If she switched my sample with his, then that means—

"You're the one who's twice The Joker."

Her words land like a sucker punch. So, I'm what? A killer? A bad guy? Do I even have a choice in what happens next? Of course I do. It's not like SV1 determines a person's fate. I think of the plots and schemes and violence. How good it felt to shoot those guys with the Dissent Cannon. I think of the darkness that creeps in around the edges. The things I see myself doing. The things I only just stop myself from making a reality.

It's all so clear now. *I'm* the villain. Even when I'm fighting for what I think is right. Good people don't fight the way I do.

I gaze down at Bernice, now completely unmoored. What does she think of me?

*It's only a matter of time until you destroy her.*

She grabs my face in her hands. "Hey. I know what you're thinking, and just stop it." She kisses me fiercely. "I love you. I will always love you. Do you understand me?"

I manage to get out one word. "Okay."

If she can find a way to love me despite all this, maybe things really could be.

She gets this gleam in her eye like she could swallow me whole and it wouldn't be enough. "Do you love me?"

Something about the way she says it scares me.

"Of course."

She takes the knife from the table and puts it back in my hands, her own hands cupped around mine, her eyes shooting electricity through me. "Then finish this. Think of Kylie. Think of Stella. If you really love me, you'll do this."

"I want to." Oh, how I want to. He deserves it. And Bernice, she's everything to me. But everything up until now has been kiss who I want, hurt who I want, set fire to the system. Maybe it's time to control my darkness instead of letting it control me. I picture myself sitting on the couch in the apartment, Montoya telling me about my dad. That terrible, restless feeling threatening to take over. I imagine this fall, not in college but in handcuffs. A lifetime of work turning to ashes in the snap of a finger. "But I can't."

There's a rustling noise from the corner, and I realize we haven't exactly been paying attention to Dr. Nelson and also that he is doing a decent job of running his zip tie over the nearest knife sticking out of the wall.

"Hey!" I yell.

Right as the word leaves my mouth, there's a knock at the door.

"OPEN UP. POLICE."

My heart swells with relief.

Until I see Bernice run across the room.

# CHAPTER 48

IT ALL HAPPENS AT ONCE.

Bernice, kicking the stool out from under him.

The front door being bashed in.

Dr. Nelson, twisting/gasping/fighting to stay alive.

Me, snatching a throwing star from the wall and flicking it across the room so it severs the rope.

Him, hitting the ground.

The police rushing in.

It all happened at once.

I never had time to think about if I was trying to save Bernice from becoming a killer or myself from losing my entire future.

This is what I tell myself, at least.

# CHAPTER 49

I RUB THE SKIN AROUND MY WRISTS AFTER OFFICER MON-
toya removes my handcuffs. Across Dr. Nelson's yard, Bernice is still wearing hers. No one shows any signs of removing
them, which isn't totally surprising. I hear one of the cops
say something about bringing her in.

"Can I at least say goodbye?" I ask Montoya.

She gives me a long-suffering sigh but tells me to go
ahead.

I'm crying before I even get to her. She's crying too. The
cop nearest her moves to separate us when I get close, but
Montoya stops him with a quick shake of her head. I'm not
sure why she's being so nice to me, but I'll take it.

"I'm so sorry," I tell Bernice. For trying to stop her? For
saving him? For not doing it myself? Because of the situation
we're in? I don't even know.

Bernice looks at me, her eyes pleading. "Everything I did
is because I love her, and I love you."

"I know."

I can see the relief flare inside her that I'm not mad at her, that I understand where she's coming from, and it only makes me cry harder, and she looks so damn beautiful, more than a person has any right to with their wrists in handcuffs and tears streaming down their cheeks. I kiss her. I take her face in my hands and try to send everything that's in me—the best parts of my heart and the darkest parts of my mind—through that kiss.

"All right, that's enough." Bernice's cop can only take so much. He pulls us apart.

"Oh! Take care of Bernie for me, okay?" she says.

And despite the predicament we're in, I almost laugh, because only Bernice would be worried about who is going to care for her taxidermized, mortal secret–guarding beaver right now.

Across the street, Dr. Nelson is getting shoved into a police car. They already took Sloane away in an ambulance.

"I hope you go to jail and never come out," I whisper.

But what if he doesn't? What if he does it again and I have to live the rest of my life knowing I could have left that throwing star on the wall?

*Don't think about that.*

I glare at him through the window until the last possible second.

I see Jasmin and Bianca sitting in Bianca's car a couple driveways away. I already sent them a message telling them not to come in, to leave, that there was nothing they could do. I don't want to give the police an excuse to arrest them too. They stayed, though. They stayed and they haven't taken their eyes off me and Bernice, and Bianca especially looks like the lack of action might make her spontaneously combust. It means a lot.

And then Bernice is the one being put in a car (much more gently). The officer who has a sworn duty to prevent kissing starts up the car, and another cop raps on the trunk as it drives away.

"She looks so sweet for an attempted murderer," he says to the guy next to him.

He nods. "This one's going straight to Arkham."

I think about telling him Bernice didn't seem crazy to me—giving him my whole rant on women and hysteria and labels—but seeing her in that car makes me feel so dang tired. I watch them take her away like I've watched so many kids in my neighborhood. I've been tearing myself up so much about the decision to kill him or not that I didn't realize for sure it was the right one until just now—as I watch Bernice get taken off to prison, knowing I still get to go to college. This almost cost me my whole future.

I shake my head. I saved him because I love Bernice and I didn't want her to become a killer. It wasn't because it would blow my scholarship, I tell myself.

I almost believe it.

"Hey, you okay?" Montoya asks.

I nod.

"We'll probably have to ask you some follow-up questions, but it's okay if you go home for now. Why don't you let me give you a ride?"

I think about taking the subway after a day like today. "Thanks," I say.

We're pretty quiet on the way to my apartment, but as she pulls the police car into the alley, she stops and looks at me.

"You showed real bravery today, Harleen. I have a feeling you're the reason a file of complaints ended up on my desk too. Aaron Nelson will probably go away for a very long time, and it's largely because of you."

I'm almost embarrassed under her praise. "Thank you."

"Hang on, I'm not done yet." Her face gets that steely look. The one that makes me feel like I've done all kinds of bad things even if I don't know what they are yet. "I think you've figured out that I was tasked with investigating the Reckoning."

My heart speeds up. Can she see it? Can she hear how it thumps in my ears?

"As of today, I'm closing that investigation."

Wait, what? I don't know what to say, so I just say, "Um," in what I'm sure is a really intelligent and capable way.

"In my report," she continues, "I'm going to state we have every reason to believe that the Reckoning ended with Ms. Watkins and Ms. Pearce and no reason to believe there will be any continued activities. I don't want my report to be wrong. Are we clear?"

My eyes dart from side to side. Is she asking what I think she's asking?

She raises her eyebrows. (So, yes.)

I think about how much of myself, of my rage, I poured into the Reckoning. It became my family. I'm not even sure I know who I am or what I'm going to do without it. But then I think about Kylie dead and Bernice gone and college starting in the fall and how close I came to losing everything.

"Yes, ma'am."

# EPILOGUE

THE DOORWAY INTO MY FIRST-YEAR DORM MIGHT AS WELL be a portal into an alternate universe. The building itself is made of some kind of gray-and-white stone with a marble placard reading ELLIOT HALL. Even the leaves on the trees look glossy, like they've been freshly buffed. It's weird to be doing all this without Bernice. I take a deep breath and walk up to the folding tables out front.

"Hi, I'm Alli! What's your name?" A girl in a Gotham U T-shirt, her brown curly hair in a ponytail, smiles an adorably chipper smile at me, and I can't help but smile back.

"Harleen," I say. And then I add, "Quinzel," because she starts scanning the list in front of her. I set down one of my bags so I can brush the blond hair out of my face. No more pink and blue—I cut off the ends of my pigtails last week. I'm going to assimilate. Be one of them. Belong here.

"You're on the bottom floor with me!" She beams that smile at me again, and I beam it right back. "We call it the Pit, but don't worry, it's not so bad. I'll be your RA this year.

If you have any questions, just let me know. We'll have a floor meeting at eight o'clock. Do you need help moving in the rest of your stuff?"

I don't want to tell her it's just the two duffel bags I'm holding, so I say, "I think I've got it. Thank you, though!"

She hands me my room key and a folder of information, and just as I'm trying to figure out how to hold all that plus my bags, a well-muscled frat boy in a bright green shirt that says GREEK MOVE-IN appears at my elbow.

"Hey, let me get that for you."

He grabs my bags like they're weightless, and a girl in the same T-shirt hands me a flyer for Panhellenic recruitment as she opens the door for us.

"Are you thinking about joining a sorority?" she asks.

My stomach flips when I see the name of Kylie's sorority on the list.

I cover it with a quick smile. "Maybe."

And then I step into the foyer, and my dorm completely takes my breath away. There is a giant room to my left with stained glass windows and wood paneling and a freaking grand piano. Gorgeous stone fireplace. Enough couches for thirty people, at least.

"That's the parlor," he says when he sees me gawking. "There's one in every dorm for hanging out and social activities and stuff."

*Parlor.* If that ain't the richest rich-people word I ever heard. We take the elevators down to the Pit, and I try not to act like such a slack-jawed hick.

Before I know it, Muscle Tee is gone, and I'm in my room alone, and there's a crappy set of bunk beds and light streaming through the window, and is this what hope feels like? Because I don't think I've ever felt this way before.

I unzip a duffel bag and start putting away my socks. No one can hurt me now. Not my dad, not Dr. Nelson, not anyone. I can put aside being the Reckoning. I don't have to be that person anymore. More than that, I shouldn't. It could ruin my entire life. So, I tuck the costume Bernice made me into the bottom of a drawer and I make a vow.

*I'm going to be better. I'm going to be the best. And I'm going to make all As. And I'm going to be a doctor someday. And I'm going to show all these rich, preppy Gotham City sons and daughters that I deserve to be here just as much as them.*

I go around and write XOXO, HQ on all the girls' marker boards on my floor. Have pancakes with my roommate. Walk around campus and figure out where my classes are. I can't believe I have a scholarship that pays for all this. Computer and books too. I am the absolute luckiest— No. I worked hard. I earned this.

I head down to the quad to sign up for clubs. It's weird how much time I spend alone here, even with all these people around. There may not be anyone to hurt me, but there's also no one left to look out for me anymore either. I'm on my own.

I weave through the club sign-ups. There are tables for everything—equestrian club, volleyball, robotics, LARPing. As I walk past the table for sorority rush, Kylie's Little Sis, Sophie, waves me over.

"Harleen!" She wraps me in a hug. "I'm so glad to see you. You're gonna do recruitment, right?"

I find myself signing up, 90 percent because of that hug. I miss being part of a group of girls. The Reckoning was like my home, and now? Bianca and Jasmin are still my friends, but we don't really get together and DO stuff anymore after what happened and after my talk with Montoya. For a second, I let myself imagine Kylie standing beside Sophie at the sorority table, waving girls over with her dazzling smile and impossibly perfect hair. I imagine Bernice signing up for every science and visual art club Gotham U offers, instead of rotting in jail, waiting for her trial. Only for a second, though. I can't think on it too long because if I do, I'll start thinking about Dr. Nelson and all those girls and whoever it was at Arkham that was giving him that drug, and for what purpose?

*Don't pull that thread, Harleen. Leave it alone.*

I'm so up in my feelings, I don't notice the girl in front of me until I've run smack into her and am wrapped around her like a koala.

"Ohmygosh, I'm so sorry," I say, trying to untangle myself. "I didn't—"

I gasp, actually gasp. That's how beautiful this girl is. *Real smooth, Harleen.*

But she just sweeps her long red hair out of her face and gives me a half smile. "No worries."

She takes a step forward, and I realize she's standing in a line. I glance at the sign on the table. GREENER EARTH SOCIETY.

*Helping make the world a better place. I like it.*

I sneak a look when she signs her name, Pamela Isley, and then I try extremely hard not to watch her walk away. *Gymnastics table, Harleen. Focus.* But I find myself drawn to an entirely different extracurricular table. I'm not doing this because of Kylie, I tell myself. I've got the devil locked in a closet, and I'm going to throw away the key and leave her there. Because I am strong. I'm a survivor. I am made of electricity and laughter, and no one will ever hurt me again.

The boy in front of me moves away from the table, and I write my name underneath his on the sign-up sheet.

### Arkham Asylum Volunteer Program

Harleen Quinzel

# AUTHOR'S NOTE

I'm thrilled I got the chance to write this series. For the obvious reasons (writing Harley is a dream and a career highlight and the coolest thing ever!), and because I'm a neuroscientist, and getting girls interested in STEM is a lifelong passion. But honestly? STEM fields are some of the worst in terms of how women are treated. We don't just need to get girls excited about science. We need to make science a place where it's okay to be a woman. I loved being able to write about this brilliant, impulsive young woman who, under all the pressures of academia and the patriarchy, snaps and becomes a vigilante dedicated to taking down the whole system.

Some of the things that happen in this book were inspired by actual events in the STEM community. For example, you may have noticed the phrase *distractingly sexy*. That comes from a Nobel Prize–winning male scientist who once said at a conference that the "trouble with girls" is that "three things happen when they are in the lab: you fall in love with them, they fall in love with you, and when you criticize them, they cry." In response, women scientists posted pictures of themselves running experiments in the lab and in the field (many wearing things like full hazmat suits) with the hashtag #distractinglysexy. They also posted pics of labs with added signage that read NO CRYING and NO FALLING IN LOVE and containers of liquid labeled LADY SCIENTIST TEARS.

Another moment from the book that was inspired by real events was Professor Perry's grossly named conference, Breaking Observations in Optogenetics and Brain Stimulation (or BOOBS). It seems ridiculous. How could something like that happen? No one would be able to get away with it! And yet . . .

A popular artificial intelligence conference was named Neural Information Processing Systems (or NIPS). It's possible this conference was named innocently, but the result prompted attendees to make increasingly more inappropriate jokes, with women feeling increasingly more uncomfortable at the meeting. There was even a preconference event called . . . Well, I'll just let you look that up on your own.

But despite these setbacks, there's good news too. NIPS changed its acronym to NeurIPS in 2018, largely because of articles and petitions and work done by women in the machine learning community and their allies. The number of women in STEM is increasing, and the amount of research performed on gender inequality in STEM fields is increasing too. Mentorship programs are being created. People are reevaluating how we review scientific journal articles and how we nominate scientists for prestigious awards. And women scientists are changing the world. We have Covid-19 vaccines because of women like Dr. Katalin Karikó, who has spent her entire scientific career studying messenger RNA, and Dr. Kizzmekia Corbett, who helped design the vaccine and whose preclinical studies and assay development paved the way for clinical trials.

These are the things that keep me going. We need to

keep working for real change for women in STEM, particularly women of color. Because after all is said and done, we can make a difference.

So I'm not going to stop fighting. Harley certainly wouldn't. ☺

XO, Dr. Rachael Allen

*Rachael Allen*

# ACKNOWLEDGMENTS

It always feels like a magical and nearly impossible thing to create a book out of nothing, and that goes double during 2020–2021. A million thank-yous to my Legion of Awesome:

To my phenomenal beta readers, Dana Alison Levy, Alina Klein, Mayra Cuevas, Debra Driza, and Jamison Ousley: I'm so lucky to have you as friends. You all deserve the power of flight—or, at the very least, glittery capes. Special shout-out to Kate Boorman, who is a diabolical plot genius. This book would be a hot mess without you.

To Terra, Dana, Maryann, Lauren, and Jenn, thank you for helping me polish this proposal until it shone, for brainstorming off-the-wall things with me, and for being a combination writing/friendship/emotional-support-to-get-each-other-through-a-pandemic group. Also for personalized queso on tables spread six feet apart and adorable garçons.

To Jillian Bates and Noam Segal, thanks for being my make-Harley-sound-like-an-actual-teen consultants!

To Meera Modi, thank you for science help!

To Alpha Gamma Delta, because I'm still best friends with my sisters from college. Thank you for providing the inspiration for every supportive girl-gang story I ever write.

To this amazing writing community that I get to be a

part of, especially these little pockets, thank you for being my people and for loving stories as much as I do: the MoB, the Drafted Tavern, High School English but with Wine, the Korner, the incomparable LBs, the Not-So-YA Book Club, and my Atlanta writer crew. To Little Shop of Stories and Brave + Kind, two of the best local bookstores anyone could ask for, and to all the librarians, bloggers, teachers, and book people who make kid lit awesome.

To my agent, Susan Hawk, who my husband has long proclaimed is actually a superhero named LadyHawk. Thank you for being the kind of person who, when I said, "I'd love to write a scientist girl superhero book!," was like, "Yes! Let's do this! I will figure out how to make that happen!" I'm continuously grateful to be working with someone so talented and passionate (and sharky!).

To my editor, Sasha Henriques, I couldn't have done this without you. Thank you for a million phone conversations, and for suggesting I watch *Promising Young Woman*, and for caring so much about giving girls the Harley Quinn they deserve. Working with you has been an absolute joy, and I am a better writer for it. To Sara Sargent, Lois Evans, Ben Harper (who seemingly keeps every detail of the DC Universe in his head all at once!), Janet Foley, Barbara Bakowski, Regina Flath, the Random House Books for Young Readers marketing and publicity teams, and anyone else at PRH or DC who worked on this book in any way: Y'all are superheroes. Or supervillians. However you identify. ☺ Also, Jen Bartel, thank you for creating this gorgeous cover that looks exactly like how I imagine teen Harley in my head. I get excited every time I look at it.

To my family, especially Mom, Mica, Dennis, Maxie,

Bekah, and Little Zack: I could not have made it through the past two years without you. I love y'all.

To Zack Allen, thank you for always encouraging me to follow my dreams, even (especially?) when the world is a scary place. To Ansley and Xander, thank you for being my hope and laughter and for being so excited that your mommy is writing a Harley Quinn book that you tell everyone you know. I love you all to the moon and back.

And to some of my favorite women scientists, Holly, Becca, Bethany, Katie, Sara, Lisa, Jeanne, Debra, Callie, Lucy, Terrell, Kalynda, Brittany, Ming-fai, Meag, Leah, Pat, Kristen, Kate, Monica, Seema, Bushra, Katherine, Heather, Hannah, Elizabeth, Erin, Machelle, Katie, Erica, Danielle, Bailey, Jenny, Cara, and Amber: You're brilliant. Don't stop fighting.

# ABOUT THE AUTHOR

**RACHAEL ALLEN** is a scientist by day and kid lit author by night. She is the winner of the 2019 Georgia Young Adult Author of the Year Award, and her books include *17 First Kisses*, *The Revenge Playbook*, *The Summer of Impossibilities*, and *A Taxonomy of Love*, which was a Junior Library Guild Selection and was among the 2018 Books All Young Georgians Should Read. Rachael lives in Atlanta, Georgia, with her husband, two children, and two sled dogs.

rachaelallenwrites.blogspot.com

— **DC ICONS** —

She is made of electricity and laughter . . .
and no one will ever hurt her again.

Check out the next breathless installment in the
Harley Quinn trilogy:

Coming Spring 2023

# CHAPTER 1

The roaring crowd in the makeshift arena didn't set her blood on fire.

It did not shake her, or rile her, or set her hopping from foot to foot. No, Selina Kyle only rolled her shoulders—once, twice.

And waited.

The wild cheering that barreled down the grimy hallway to the prep room was little more than a distant rumble of thunder. A storm, just like the one that had rolled over the East End on her walk from the apartment complex. She'd been soaked before she reached the covert subway entrance that led into the underground gaming warren owned by Carmine Falcone, the latest of Gotham City's endless parade of mob bosses.

But like any other storm, this fight, too, would be weathered.

Rain still drying in her long, dark hair, Selina checked that it was indeed tucked into its tight bun atop her head. She'd made the mistake once of wearing a ponytail—in her second street fight. The other girl had managed to grab it, and those few seconds when Selina's neck had been exposed had lasted longer than any in her life.

But she'd won—barely. And she'd learned. Had learned at every fight since, whether on the streets above or in the arena carved into the sewers beneath Gotham City.

It didn't matter who her opponent was tonight. The challengers were all usually variations of the same: desperate men who owed more than they could repay to Falcone. Fools willing to risk their lives for a chance to lift their debts by taking on one of his Leopards in the ring. The prize: never having to look over their shoulders for a waiting shadow. The cost of failing: having their asses handed to them—and the debts remained. Usually with the promise of a one-way ticket to the bottom of the Sprang River. The odds of winning: slim to none.

Regardless of whatever sad sack she'd be battling tonight, Selina prayed Falcone would give her the nod faster than last time. That fight . . . He'd made her keep that particularly brutal match going. The crowd had been too excited, too ready to spend money on the cheap alcohol and everything else for sale in the subterranean warren. She'd taken home more bruises than usual, and the man she'd beaten to unconsciousness . . .

Not her problem, she told herself again and again. Even when she saw her adversaries' bloodied faces in her dreams, both asleep and waking. What Falcone did with them after the fight was not her problem. She left her opponents breathing. At least she had that.

And at least she wasn't dumb enough to push back outright, like some of the other Leopards. The ones who were too proud or too stupid or too young to get how the game was played. No, her small rebellions against Carmine Falcone were subtler. He wanted men dead—she left them unconscious, but did it so well that not one person in the crowd objected.

A fine line to walk, especially with her sister's life hanging in the balance. Push back too much, and Falcone might ask questions, start wondering who meant the most to her. Where to strike hardest. She'd never allow it to get to that point. Never risk Maggie's safety like that—even if these fights were all for her. Every one of them.

It had been three years since Selina had joined the Leopards, and nearly two and a half since she'd proved herself against the other girl gangs well enough that Mika, her Alpha, had introduced her to Falcone. Selina hadn't dared miss that meeting.

Order in the girl gangs was simple: The Alpha of each gang ruled and protected, laid down punishment and reward. The Alphas' commands were law. And the enforcers of those commands were their Seconds and Thirds. From there, the pecking order turned murkier. Fighting offered a way to rise in the ranks—or you could fall, depending on how badly a match went. Even an Alpha might be challenged if you were stupid or brave enough to do so.

But the thought of ascending the ranks had been far from Selina's mind when Mika had brought Falcone over to watch her take on the Second of the Wolf Pack and leave the girl leaking blood onto the concrete of the alley. Before that fight, only four leopard spots had been inked onto Selina's left arm, each a trophy of a fight won.

Selina adjusted the hem of her white tank. At seventeen, she now had twenty-seven spots inked across both arms.

Undefeated.

That's what the match emcee was declaring down the hall. Selina could just make out the croon of words: *The undefeated champion, the fiercest of Leopards* . . .

A thump on the metal door was her signal to go. Selina checked her shirt, her black spandex pants, the green sneakers that matched her eyes—though no one had ever commented on it. She flexed her fingers within their wrappings. All good.

Or as good as could be.

The rusty door groaned as she opened it. Mika was tending to the new girl in the hall beyond, the flickering fluorescent lights draining the Alpha's golden-brown skin of its usual glow.

Mika threw Selina an assessing look over her narrow shoulder, her tight braid shifting with the movement. The new girl sniffling in front of her gingerly wiped away the blood streaming from her swollen nose. One of the kitten's eyes was already puffy and red, the other swimming with unshed tears.

No wonder the crowd was riled. If a Leopard had taken that bad a beating, it must have been one hell of a fight. Brutal enough that Mika put a hand on the girl's pale arm to keep her from swaying.

Down the shadowy hall that led into the arena, one of Falcone's bouncers beckoned. Selina shut the door behind her. She'd left no valuables behind. She had nothing worth stealing, anyway.

"Be careful," Mika said as she passed, her voice low and soft. "He's got a worse batch than usual tonight." The kitten hissed, yanking her head away as Mika dabbed her split lip with a disinfectant wipe. Mika snarled a warning at her, and the kitten wisely fell still, trembling a bit as the Alpha cleaned out the cut. Mika added without glancing back, "He saved the best for you. Sorry."

"He always does," Selina said coolly, even as her stomach roiled. "I can handle it."

She didn't have any other choice. Losing would leave Maggie with no one to look after her. And refusing to fight? Not an option, either.

In the three years that Selina had known Mika, the Alpha had never suggested ending their arrangement with Carmine Falcone. Not when having Falcone back the Leopards made the other East End gangs think twice about pushing in on their territory. Even if it meant doing these fights and offering up Leopards for the crowd's enjoyment.

Falcone turned it into a weekly spectacle—a veritable Roman circus to make the underbelly of Gotham City love *and* fear him. It certainly helped that many of the other notorious lowlifes had been imprisoned thanks to a certain do-gooder running around the city in a cape.

Mika eased the kitten to the prep room, giving Selina a jerk of the chin—an order to go.

But Selina paused to scan the hall, the exits. Even down here, in the heart of Falcone's territory, it was a death wish to be defenseless in the open. Especially if you were an Alpha with as many enemies as Mika had.

Three figures slipped in from a door at the opposite end of the hall, and Selina's shoulders loosened a bit. Ani, Mika's Second, with two other Leopards flanking her.

Good. They'd guard the exit while their Alpha tended to their own.

The crowd's cheering rumbled through the concrete floor, rattling the loose ceramic tiles on the walls, echoing along Selina's bones and breath as she neared the dented metal door to the arena. The bouncer gestured for her to hurry the hell up, but she kept her strides even. Stalking.

The Leopards, these fights . . . they were her job. And it paid well. With her mother gone and her sister sick, no legit job could pay as much or as quickly.

The bouncer opened the door, the unfiltered roar of the crowd bursting down the hall like a pack of rabid wolves.

Selina Kyle blew out a long breath as she lifted her chin and stepped into the sound and the light and the wrath.

*Let the bloodying begin.*

THE NIGHTWALKERS
ARE HUNTING GOTHAM CITY'S ELITE.
BRUCE WAYNE IS NEXT ON THEIR LIST.

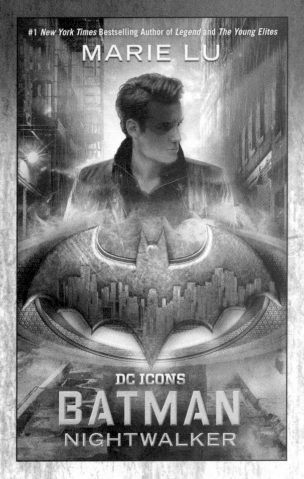

#1 *New York Times* Bestselling Author of *Legend* and *The Young Elites*

MARIE LU

DC ICONS

BATMAN
NIGHTWALKER

TURN THE PAGE TO SEE HOW
BRUCE'S ADVENTURE BEGINS
IN THE BESTSELLING DC ICONS SERIES!

As Bruce rounded another bend, the wails suddenly turned deafening, and a mass of flashing red and blue lights blinked against the buildings near the end of the street. White barricades and yellow police tape completely blocked the intersection. Even from here, Bruce could see fire engines and black SWAT trucks clustered together, the silhouettes of police running back and forth in front of the headlights.

Inside his car, the electronic voice came on again, followed by a transparent map overlaid against his windshield. *"Heavy police activity ahead. Alternate route suggested."*

A sense of dread filled his chest.

Bruce flicked away the map and pulled to an abrupt halt in front of the barricade—right as the unmistakable *pop-pop-pop* of gunfire rang out in the night air.

He remembered the sound all too well. The memory of his parents' deaths sent a wave of dizziness through him. *Another robbery. A murder. That's what all this is.*

Then he shook his head. *No, that can't be right.* There were far too many cops here for a simple robbery.

"Step *out* of your vehicle, and put your hands in the air!" a police officer shouted through a megaphone, her voice echoing along the block. Bruce's head jerked toward her. For an instant, he thought her command was directed at him, but then he saw that her back was turned, her attention fixed on the corner of the building bearing the name BELLINGHAM INDUSTRIES & CO. "We have you surrounded, Nightwalker! This is your final warning!"

Another officer came running over to Bruce's car. He whirled an arm exaggeratedly for Bruce to turn his car around. His voice harsh with panic, he warned, "Turn back *now*. It's not safe!"

Before Bruce could reply, a blinding fireball exploded behind the officer. The street rocked.

Even from inside his car, Bruce felt the heat of the blast. Every window in the building burst simultaneously, a million shards of glass raining down on the pavement below. The police ducked in unison, their arms shielding their heads. Fragments of glass dinged like hail against Bruce's windshield.

From inside the blockade, a white car veered around the corner at top speed. Bruce saw immediately what the car was aiming for—a slim gap between the police barricades where a SWAT team truck had just pulled through.

The car raced right toward the gap.

"I said, *get out of here!*" the officer shouted at Bruce. A thin ribbon of blood trickled down the man's face. "That is an *order!*"

Bruce heard the scream of the getaway car's tires against the asphalt. He'd been in his father's garage a thousand times, helping him tinker with an endless number of engines from the best cars in the world. At WayneTech, Bruce had watched in fascination as tests were conducted on custom engines, conceptual jets, stealth tech, new vehicles of every kind.

And so he knew: whatever was installed under that hood was faster than anything the GCPD could hope to have.

*They'll never catch him.*

*But I can.*

His Aston Martin was probably the only vehicle here that

could overtake the criminal's, the only one powerful enough to chase it down. Bruce's eyes followed the path the car would likely take, his gaze settling on a sign at the end of the street that pointed toward the freeway.

*I can get him.*

The white getaway vehicle shot straight through the gap in the barricade, clipping two police cars as it went.

*No, not this time.* Bruce slammed his gas pedal.

The Aston Martin's engine let out a deafening roar, and the car sped forward. The officer who'd shouted at him stumbled back. In the rearview mirror, Bruce saw him scramble to his feet and wave the other officers' cars forward, both his arms held high.

"Hold your fire!" Bruce could hear him yelling. "Civilian in proximity—*hold your fire!*"

The getaway car made a sharp turn at the first intersection, and Bruce sped behind it a few seconds later. The street zigzagged, then turned in a wide arc as it led toward the freeway—and the Nightwalker took the on-ramp, leaving a trail of exhaust and two black skid marks on the road.

Bruce raced forward in close pursuit; his car mapped the ground instantly, swerving in a perfect curve to follow the ramp onto the freeway. He tapped twice on the windshield right over where the Nightwalker's white vehicle was.

"Follow him," Bruce commanded.

DAUGHTER OF IMMORTALS.

DAUGHTER OF DEATH.

THEIR FRIENDSHIP

WILL CHANGE THE WORLD.

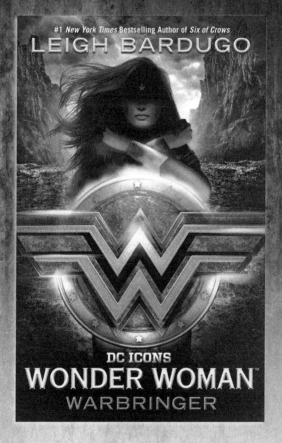

#1 *New York Times* Bestselling Author of *Six of Crows*

# LEIGH BARDUGO

DC ICONS

# WONDER WOMAN
## WARBRINGER

TURN THE PAGE TO SEE HOW

DIANA'S BATTLE BEGINS

IN THIS DC ICONS STORY!

*You do not enter a race to lose.*

Diana bounced lightly on her toes at the starting line, her calves taut as bowstrings, her mother's words reverberating in her ears. A noisy crowd had gathered for the wrestling matches and javelin throws that would mark the start of the Nemeseian Games, but the real event was the footrace, and now the stands were buzzing with word that the queen's daughter had entered the competition.

When Hippolyta had seen Diana amid the runners clustered on the arena sands, she'd displayed no surprise. As was tradition, she'd descended from her viewing platform to wish the athletes luck in their endeavors, sharing a joke here, offering a kind word of encouragement there. She had nodded briefly to Diana, showing her no special favor, but she'd whispered, so low that only her daughter could hear, "You do not enter a race to lose."

Amazons lined the path that led out of the arena, already stamping their feet and chanting for the games to begin.

On Diana's right, Rani flashed her a radiant smile. "Good luck today." She was always kind, always gracious, and, of course, always victorious.

To Diana's left, Thyra snorted and shook her head. "She's going to need it."

Diana ignored her. She'd been looking forward to this race for weeks—a trek across the island to retrieve one of the red flags hung beneath the great dome in Bana-Mighdall. In a flat-out sprint, she didn't have a chance. She still hadn't come into the fullness of her Amazon strength. *You will in time,* her mother had promised. But her mother promised a lot of things.

This race was different. It required strategy, and Diana was ready. She'd been training in secret, running sprints with Maeve, and plotting a route that had rougher terrain but was definitely a straighter shot to the western tip of the island. She'd even— well, she hadn't exactly *spied*. . . . She'd gathered intelligence on the other Amazons in the race. She was still the smallest, and of course the youngest, but she'd shot up in the last year, and she was nearly as tall as Thyra now.

*I don't need luck,* she told herself. *I have a plan.* She glanced down the row of Amazons gathered at the starting line like troops readying for war and amended, *But a little luck wouldn't hurt, either.* She wanted that laurel crown. It was better than any royal circlet or tiara—an honor that couldn't be given, that had to be earned.

She found Maeve's red hair and freckled face in the crowd and grinned, trying to project confidence. Maeve returned the smile and gestured with both hands as if she were tamping down the air. She mouthed the words, "Steady on."

Diana rolled her eyes but nodded and tried to slow her breathing. She had a bad habit of coming out too fast and wasting her speed too early.

Now she cleared her mind and forced herself to concentrate on the course as Tekmessa walked the line, surveying the runners, jewels glinting in her thick corona of curls, silver bands flashing on her brown arms. She was Hippolyta's closest advisor, second in rank only to the queen, and she carried herself as if her belted indigo shift were battle armor.

"Take it easy, Pyxis," Tek murmured to Diana as she passed. "Wouldn't want to see you crack." Diana heard Thyra snort again, but she refused to flinch at the nickname. *You won't be smirking when I'm on the victors' podium*, she promised.

Tek raised her hands for silence and bowed to Hippolyta, who sat between two other members of the Amazon Council in the royal loge—a high platform shaded by a silken overhang dyed in the vibrant red and blue of the queen's colors. Diana knew that was where her mother wanted her right now, seated beside her, waiting for the start of the games instead of competing. None of that would matter when she won.

Hippolyta dipped her chin the barest amount, elegant in her white tunic and riding trousers, a simple circlet resting against her forehead. She looked relaxed, at her ease, as if she might decide to leap down and join the competition at any time, but still every inch the queen.

Tek addressed the athletes gathered on the arena sands. "In whose honor do you compete?"

"For the glory of the Amazons," they replied in unison. "For the glory of our queen." Diana felt her heart beat harder. She'd never said the words before, not as a competitor.

"To whom do we give praise each day?" Tek trumpeted.

"Hera," they chorused. "Athena, Demeter, Hestia, Aphrodite, Artemis." The goddesses who had created Themyscira and gifted it to Hippolyta as a place of refuge.

Tek paused, and along the line, Diana heard the whispers of other names: Oya, Durga, Freyja, Mary, Yael. Names once cried out in death, the last prayers of female warriors fallen in battle, the words that had brought them to this island and given them new life as Amazons. Beside Diana, Rani murmured the names of the demon-fighting Matri, the seven mothers, and pressed the rectangular amulet she always wore to her lips.

Tek raised a blood-red flag identical to those that would be waiting for the runners in Bana-Mighdall.

"May the island guide you to just victory!" she shouted.

She dropped the red silk. The crowd roared. The runners surged toward the eastern arch. Like that, the race had begun.

Diana and Maeve had anticipated a bottleneck, but Diana still felt a pang of frustration as runners clogged the stone throat of the tunnel, a tangle of white tunics and muscled limbs, footsteps echoing off the stone, all of them trying to get clear of the arena at once. Then they were on the road, sprinting across the island, each runner choosing her own course.

*You do not enter a race to lose.*

Diana set her pace to the rhythm of those words, bare feet slapping the packed earth of the road that would lead her through the tangle of the Cybelian Woods to the island's northern coast.

Ordinarily, a miles-long trek through this forest would be a slow one, hampered by fallen trees and tangles of vines so thick they had to be hacked through with a blade you didn't mind dulling. But Diana had plotted her way well. An hour after she entered the woods, she burst from the trees onto the deserted coast road. The wind lifted her hair, and salt spray lashed her face. She breathed deep, checked the position of the sun. She was going to win—not just place but win.

She'd mapped out the course the week before with Maeve, and they'd run it twice in secret, in the gray-light hours of early morning, when their sisters were first rising from their beds, when the kitchen fires were still being kindled, and the only curious eyes they'd had to worry about belonged to anyone up early to hunt game or cast nets for the day's catch. But hunters kept to the woods and meadows farther south, and no one fished off this part of the coast; there was no good place to launch a boat, just the steep steel-colored cliffs plunging straight down to the sea, and a tiny, unwelcoming cove that could only be reached by a path so narrow you had to shuffle down sideways, back pressed to the rock.

The northern shore was gray, grim, and inhospitable, and Diana knew every inch of its secret landscape, its crags and caves, its tide pools teeming with limpets and anemones. It was a good place to be alone. *The island seeks to please,* her mother had told her. It was why Themyscira was forested by redwoods in some places and rubber trees in others; why you could spend an afternoon roaming the grasslands on a scoop-neck pony and the evening atop a camel, scaling a moonlit dragonback of sand dunes. They were all pieces of the lives the Amazons had led before they came to the island, little landscapes of the heart.

Diana sometimes wondered if Themyscira had called the northern coast into being just for her so that she could challenge herself climbing on the sheer drop of its cliffs, so that she could have a place to herself when the weight of being Hippolyta's daughter got to be too much.

*You do not enter a race to lose.*

Her mother had not been issuing a general warning. Diana's losses meant something different, and they both knew it—and not only because she was a princess.

Diana could almost feel Tek's knowing gaze on her, hear the mocking in her voice. *Take it easy, Pyxis.* That was the nickname Tek had given her. Pyxis. A little clay pot made to store jewels or a tincture of carmine for pinking the lips. The name was harmless, meant to tease, always said in love—or so Tek claimed. But it stung every time: a reminder that Diana was not like the other Amazons, and never would be. Her sisters were battle-proven warriors, steel forged from suffering and honed to greatness as they passed from life to immortality. All of them had earned their place on Themyscira. All but Diana, born of the island's soil and Hippolyta's longing for a child, fashioned from clay by her mother's hands—hollow and breakable. *Take it easy, Pyxis. Wouldn't want to see you crack.*

Diana steadied her breathing, kept her pace even. *Not today, Tek. This day the laurel belongs to me.*

She spared the briefest glance at the horizon, letting the sea breeze cool the sweat on her brow. Through the mists, she glimpsed the white shape of a ship. It had come close enough to the boundary that Diana could make out its sails. The craft was small—a schooner maybe? She had trouble remembering nautical details. Mainmast, mizzenmast, a thousand names for sails, and knots for rigging. It was one thing to be out on a boat, learning from Teuta, who had sailed with Illyrian pirates, but quite another to be stuck in the library at the Epheseum, staring glazed-eyed at diagrams of a brigantine or a caravel.

Sometimes Diana and Maeve made a game of trying to spot ships or planes, and once they'd even seen the fat blot of a cruise ship on the horizon. But most mortals knew to steer clear of their particular corner of the Aegean, where compasses spun and instruments suddenly refused to obey.

Today it looked like a storm was picking up past the mists of the boundary, and Diana was sorry she couldn't stop to watch it. The rains that came to Themyscira were tediously gentle and predictable, nothing like the threatening rumble of thunder, the shimmer of a far-off lightning strike.

"Do you ever miss storms?" Diana had asked one afternoon as she and Maeve lazed on the palace's sun-soaked rooftop terrace, listening to the distant roar and clatter of a tempest. Maeve had died in the Crossbarry Ambush, the last words on her lips a prayer to Saint Brigid of Kildare. She was new to the island by Amazon standards, and came from Cork, where storms were common.

"No," Maeve had said in her lilting voice. "I miss a good cup of tea, dancing, boys—definitely not rain."

"We dance," Diana protested.

Maeve had just laughed. "You dance differently when you know you won't live forever." Then she'd stretched, freckles like dense clouds of pollen on her white skin. "I think I was a cat in another life, because all I want is to lie around sleeping in the world's biggest sunbeam."

*Steady on.* Diana resisted the urge to speed forward. It was hard to remember to keep something in reserve with the early-morning sun on her shoulders and the wind at her back. She felt strong. But it was easy to feel strong when she was on her own.

A *boom* sounded over the waves, a hard metallic clap like a door slamming shut. Diana's steps faltered. On the blue horizon, a billowing column of smoke rose, flames licking at its base. The schooner was on fire, its prow blown to splinters and one of its masts smashed, the sail dragging over the rails.

Diana found herself slowing but forced her stride back on pace. There was nothing she could do for the schooner. Planes crashed. Ships were wrecked upon the rocks. That was the nature of the mortal world. It was a place where disaster could happen and often did. Human life was a tide of misery, one that never reached the island's shores. Diana focused her eyes on the path. Far, far ahead she could see sunlight gleaming gold off the great dome at Bana-Mighdall. First the red flag, then the laurel crown. That was the plan.

From somewhere on the wind, she heard a cry.

*A gull,* she told herself. *A girl,* some other voice within her insisted. *Impossible.* A human shout couldn't carry over such a great distance, could it?

It didn't matter. There was nothing she could do.

And yet her eyes strayed back to the horizon. *I just want to get a better view,* she told herself. *I have plenty of time. I'm ahead.*

There was no good reason to leave the ruts of the old cart track, no logic to veering out over the rocky point, but she did it anyway.

The waters near the shore were calm, clear, vibrant turquoise. The ocean beyond was something else—wild, deep-well blue, a sea gone almost black. The island might seek to please her and her sisters, but the world beyond the boundary didn't concern itself with the happiness or safety of its inhabitants.

Even from a distance, she could tell the schooner was sinking. But she saw no lifeboats, no distress flares, only pieces of the broken craft carried along by rolling waves. It was done. Diana rubbed her hands briskly over her arms, dispelling a sudden chill, and started making her way back to the cart track. That was the way of human life. She and Maeve had dived out by the boundary many times, swum the wrecks of airplanes and clipper ships and sleek motorboats. The salt water changed the wood, hardened it so it did not rot. Mortals were not the same. They were food for deep-sea fishes, for sharks—and for time that ate at them slowly, inevitably, whether they were on water or on land.

Diana checked the sun's position again. She could be at Bana-Mighdall in forty minutes, maybe less. She told her legs to move. She'd only lost a few moments. She could make up the time. Instead, she looked over her shoulder.

There were stories in all the old books about women who made the mistake of looking back. On the way out of burning cities. On the way out of hell. But Diana still turned her eyes to that ship sinking in the great waves, tilting like a bird's broken wing.

She measured the length of the cliff top. There were jagged rocks at the base. If she didn't leap with enough momentum, the impact would be ugly. Still, the fall wouldn't kill her. *That's true of a real Amazon*, she thought. *Is it true for you?* Well, she *hoped* the fall wouldn't kill her. Of course, if the fall didn't, her mother would.

Diana looked once more at the wreck and pushed off, running full out, arms pumping, stride long, picking up speed, closing the distance to the cliff's edge. *Stop stop stop*, her mind clamored. *This is madness*. Even if there were survivors, she could do nothing for them. To try to save them was to court exile, and there would be no exception to the rule—not even for a princess. *Stop*. She wasn't sure why she didn't obey. She wanted to believe it was because a hero's heart beat in her chest and demanded she answer that frightened call. But even as she launched herself off the cliff and into the empty sky, she knew part of what drew her on was the challenge of that great gray sea that did not care if she loved it.

Her body cut a smooth arc through the air, arms pointing like a compass needle, directing her course. She plummeted toward the water and broke the surface in a clean plunge, ears full of sudden silence, muscles tensed for the brutal impact of the rocks. None came. She shot upward, drew in a breath, and swam straight for the boundary, arms slicing through the warm water.

There was always a little thrill when she neared the boundary, when the temperature of the water began to change, the cold touching her fingertips first, then settling over her scalp and shoulders. Diana and Maeve liked to swim out from the southern beaches, daring themselves to go farther, farther. Once they'd glimpsed a ship passing in the mist, sailors standing at the stern. One of the men had lifted an arm, pointing in their direction. They'd plunged to safety, gesturing wildly to each other beneath the waves, laughing so hard that by the time they reached shore, they were both choking on salt water. *We could be sirens*, Maeve had shrieked as they'd flopped onto the warm sand, except neither of them could carry a tune. They'd spent the rest of the afternoon singing violently off-key Irish drinking songs and laughing themselves silly until Tek had found them. Then they'd shut up quick. Breaking the boundary was a minor infraction. Being seen by mortals anywhere near the island was cause for serious disciplinary action. And what Diana was doing now?

*Stop.* But she couldn't. Not when that high human cry still rang in her ears.

Diana felt the cold water beyond the boundary engulf her fully. The sea had her now, and it was not friendly. The current seized her legs, dragging her down, a massive, rolling force, the barest shrug of a god. *You have to fight it*, she realized, demanding that her muscles correct her course. She'd never had to work against the ocean.

She bobbed for a moment on the surface, trying to get her bearings as the waves crested around her. The water was full of debris, shards of wood, broken fiberglass, orange life jackets that the crew must not have had time to don. It was nearly impossible to see through the falling rain and the mists that shrouded the island.

*What am I doing out here?* she asked herself. *Ships come and go. Human lives are lost.* She dove again, peered through the rushing gray waters, but saw no one.

Diana surfaced, her own stupidity carving a growing ache in

her gut. She'd sacrificed the race. This was supposed to be the moment her sisters saw her truly, the chance to make her mother proud. Instead, she'd thrown away her lead, and for what? There was nothing here but destruction.

Out of the corner of her eye, she saw a flash of white, a big chunk of what might have been the ship's hull. It rose on a wave, vanished, rose again, and as it did, Diana glimpsed a slender brown arm holding tight to the side, fingers spread, knuckles bent. Then it was gone.

Another wave rose, a great gray mountain. Diana dove beneath it, kicking hard, then surfaced, searching, bits of lumber and fiberglass everywhere, impossible to sort one piece of flotsam from another.

There it was again—an arm, two arms, a body, bowed head and hunched shoulders, lemon-colored shirt, a tangle of dark hair. A girl—she lifted her head, gasped for breath, dark eyes wild with fear. A wave crashed over her in a spray of white water. The chunk of hull surfaced. The girl was gone.

Down again. Diana aimed for the place she'd seen the girl go under. She glimpsed a flash of yellow and lunged for it, seizing the fabric and using it to reel her in. A ghost's face loomed out at her from the cloudy water—golden hair, blue gaze wide and lifeless. She'd never seen a corpse up close before. She'd never seen a boy up close before. She recoiled, hand releasing his shirt, but even as she watched him disappear, she marked the differences—hard jaw, broad brow, just like the pictures in books.

She resurfaced, but she'd lost all sense of direction now—the waves, the wreck, the bare shadow of the island in the mists. If she drifted out much farther, she might not be able to find her way back.

Diana could not stop seeing the image of that slender arm, the ferocity in those fingers, clinging hard to life. *Once more*, she told herself. She dove, the chill of the water fastening tight around her bones now, burrowing deeper.

One moment the world was gray current and cloudy sea, and

the next the girl was there in her lemon-colored shirt, facedown, arms and legs outstretched like a star. Her eyes were closed.

Diana grabbed her around the waist and launched them toward the surface. For a terrifying second, she could not find the shape of the island, and then the mists parted. She kicked forward, wrapping the girl awkwardly against her chest with one arm, fingers questing for a pulse with the other. *There*—beneath the jaw, thready, indistinct, but there. Though the girl wasn't breathing, her heart still beat.

Diana hesitated. She could see the outlines of Filos and Ecthros, the rocks that marked the rough beginnings of the boundary. The rules were clear. You could not stop the mortal tide of life and death, and the island must never be touched by it. There were no exceptions. No human could be brought to Themyscira, even if it meant saving a life. Breaking that rule meant only one thing: exile.

*Exile.* The word was a stone, unwanted ballast, the weight unbearable. It was one thing to breach the boundary, but what she did next might untether her from the island, her sisters, her mother forever. The world seemed too large, the sea too deep. *Let go.* It was that simple. Let this girl slip from her grasp and it would be as if Diana had never leapt from those cliffs. She would be light again, free of this burden.

Diana thought of the girl's hand, the ferocious grip of her knuckles, the steel-blade determination in her eyes before the wave took her under. She felt the ragged rhythm of the girl's pulse, a distant drum, the sound of an army marching—one that had fought well but could not fight on much longer.

She swam for shore.

As she passed through the boundary with the girl clutched to her, the mists dissolved and the rain abated. Warmth flooded her body. The calm water felt oddly lifeless after the thrashing of the sea, but Diana wasn't about to complain.

When her feet touched the sandy bottom, she shoved up, shifting her grip to carry the girl from the shallows. She was eerily light, almost insubstantial. It was like holding a sparrow's body between her cupped hands. No wonder the sea had made such easy sport of this creature and her crewmates; she felt temporary, an artist's cast of a body rendered in plaster.

Diana laid her gently on the sand and checked her pulse again. No heartbeat now. She knew she needed to get the girl's heart going, get the water out of her lungs, but her memory on just how to do that was a bit hazy. Diana had studied the basics of reviving a drowning victim, but she hadn't ever had to put it into practice outside the classroom. It was also possible she hadn't paid close attention at the time. How likely was it that an Amazon was going to drown, especially in the calm waters off Themyscira? And now her daydreaming might cost this girl her life.

*Do something*, she told herself, trying to think past her panic. *Why did you drag her out of the water if you're only going to sit staring at her like a frightened rabbit?*

Diana placed two fingers on the girl's sternum, then tracked lower to what she hoped was the right spot. She locked her hands together and pressed. The girl's bones bent beneath her palms. Hurriedly, Diana drew back. What was this girl made of, anyway? Balsa wood? She felt about as solid as the little models of world monuments Diana had been forced to build for class. Gently, she pressed down again, then again. She shut the girl's nose with her fingers, closed her mouth over cooling mortal lips, and breathed.

The gust drove into the girl's chest, and Diana saw it rise, but this time the extra force seemed to be a good thing. Suddenly, the girl was coughing, her body convulsing as she spat up salt water. Diana sat back on her knees and released a short laugh. She'd done it. The girl was alive.

The reality of what she'd just dared struck her. All the hounds of Hades: *She'd done it. The girl was alive.*

And trying to sit up.

"Here," Diana said, bracing the girl's back with her arm. She couldn't simply kneel there, watching her flop around on the sand like a fish, and it wasn't as if she could put her back in the ocean. Could she? No. Mortals were clearly too good at drowning.

The girl clutched her chest, taking huge, sputtering gulps of air. "The others," she gasped. Her eyes were so wide Diana could see white ringing her irises all the way around. She was trembling, but Diana wasn't sure if it was because she was cold or going into shock. "We have to help them—"

Diana shook her head. If there had been any other signs of life in the wreck, she hadn't seen them. Besides, time passed more quickly in the mortal world. Even if she swam back out, the storm would have long since had its way with any bodies or debris.

"They're gone," said Diana, then wished she'd chosen her words more carefully. The girl's mouth opened, closed. Her body was shaking so hard Diana thought it might break apart. That couldn't actually happen, could it?

Diana scanned the cliffs above the beach. Someone might have seen her swim out. She felt confident no other runner had chosen this course, but anyone could have seen the explosion and come to investigate.

"I need to get you off the beach. Can you walk?" The girl nodded, but her teeth were chattering, and she made no move to stand. Diana's eyes scoured the cliffs again. "Seriously, I need you to get up."

"I'm trying."

She didn't look like she was trying. Diana searched her memory for everything she'd been told about mortals, the soft stuff— eating habits, body temperature, cultural norms. Unfortunately, her mother and her tutors were more focused on what Diana referred to as the Dire Warnings: War. Torture. Genocide. Pollution. Bad Grammar.

The girl shivering before her on the sand didn't seem to qualify for inclusion in the Dire Warnings category. She looked about the same age as Diana, brown-skinned, her hair a tangle of long, tiny braids covered in sand. She was clearly too weak to hurt anyone but herself. Even so, she could be plenty dangerous to Diana. Exile dangerous. Banished-forever dangerous. Better not to think about that. Instead, she thought back to her classes with Teuta. *Make a plan. Battles are often lost because people don't know which war they're fighting.* All right. The girl couldn't walk any great distance in her condition. Maybe that was a good thing, given that Diana had nowhere to take her.

She rested what she hoped was a comforting hand on the girl's shoulder. "Listen, I know you're feeling weak, but we should try to get off the beach."

"Why?"

Diana hesitated, then opted for an answer that was technically true if not wholly accurate. "High tide."

It seemed to do the trick, because the girl nodded. Diana stood and offered her a hand.

"I'm fine," the girl said, shoving to her knees and then pushing up to her feet.

"You're stubborn," Diana said with some measure of respect. The girl had almost drowned and seemed to be about as solid as driftwood and down, but she wasn't eager to accept help—and she definitely wasn't going to like what Diana suggested next. "I need you to climb on my back."

A crease appeared between the girl's brows. "Why?"

"Because I don't think you can make it up the cliffs."

"Is there a path?"

"No," said Diana. That was definitely a lie. Instead of arguing, Diana turned her back. A minute later, she felt a pair of arms around her neck. The girl hopped on, and Diana reached back to take hold of her thighs and hitch her into position. "Hold on tight."

The girl's arms clamped around her windpipe. "Not that tight!" Diana choked out.

"Sorry!" She loosened her hold.

Diana took off at a jog.

The girl groaned. "Slow down. I think I'm going to vomit."

"Vomit?" Diana scanned her knowledge of mortal bodily functions and immediately smoothed her gait. "Do *not* do that."

"Just don't drop me."

"You weigh about as much as a heavy pair of boots." Diana

picked her way through the big boulders wedged against the base of the cliff. "I need my arms to climb, so you're going to have to hold on with your legs, too."

"Climb?"

"The cliff."

"You're taking me *up the side of the cliff*? Are you out of your mind?"

"Just hold on and try not to strangle me." Diana dug her fingers into the rock and started putting distance between them and the ground before the girl could think too much more about it.

She moved quickly. This was familiar territory. Diana had scaled these cliffs countless times since she'd started visiting the north shore, and when she was twelve, she'd discovered the cave where they were headed. There were other caves, lower on the cliff face, but they filled when the tide came in. Besides, they were too easy to crawl out of if someone got curious.

The girl groaned again.

"Almost there," Diana said encouragingly.

"I'm not opening my eyes."

"Probably for the best. Just don't . . . you know."

"Puke all over you?"

"Yes," said Diana. "That." Amazons didn't get sick, but vomiting appeared in any number of novels and featured in a particularly vivid description from her anatomy book. Blessedly, there were no illustrations.

At last, Diana hauled them up into the divot in the rock that marked the cave's entrance. The girl rolled off and heaved a long breath. The cave was tall, narrow, and surprisingly deep, as if someone had taken a cleaver to the center of the cliff. Its gleaming black rock sides were perpetually damp with sea spray. When she was younger, Diana had liked to pretend that if she kept walking, the cave would lead straight through the cliff and open onto some other land entirely. It didn't. It was just a cave, and remained a cave no matter how hard she wished.

Diana waited for her eyes to adjust, then shuffled farther

inside. The old horse blanket was still there—wrapped in oilcloth and mostly dry, if a bit musty—as well as her tin box of supplies.

She wrapped the blanket around the girl's shoulders.

"We aren't going to the top?" asked the girl.

"Not yet." Diana had to get back to the arena. The race must be close to over by now, and she didn't want people wondering where she'd gotten to. "Are you hungry?"

The girl shook her head. "We need to call the police, search and rescue."

"That isn't possible."

"I don't know what happened," the girl said, starting to shake again. "Jasmine and Ray were arguing with Dr. Ellis and then—"

"There was an explosion. I saw it from shore."

"It's my fault," the girl said as tears spilled over her cheeks. "They're dead and it's my fault."

"Don't," Diana said gently, feeling a surge of panic. "It was the storm." She laid her hand on the girl's shoulder. "What's your name?"

"Alia," the girl said, burying her head in her arms.

"Alia, I need to go, but—"

"No!" Alia said sharply. "Don't leave me here."

"I have to. I . . . need to get help." What Diana needed was to get back to Ephesus and figure out how to get this girl off the island before anyone found out about her.

Alia grabbed hold of her arm, and again Diana remembered the way she'd clung to that piece of hull. "Please," Alia said. "Hurry. Maybe they can send a helicopter. There could be survivors."

"I'll be back as soon as I can," Diana promised. She slid the tin box toward the girl. "There are dried peaches and pili seeds and a little fresh water inside. Don't drink it all at once."

Alia's eyelids stuttered. "All at once? How long will you be gone?"

"Maybe a few hours. I'll be back as fast as I can. Just stay warm and rest." Diana rose. "And don't leave the cave."

Alia looked up at her. Her eyes were deep brown and heavily

lashed, her gaze fearful but steady. For the first time since Diana had pulled her from the water, Alia seemed to be truly seeing her. "Where are we?" she asked. "What is this place?"

Diana wasn't quite sure how to answer, so all she said was "This is my home."

She hooked her hands back into the rock and ducked out of the cave before Alia could ask anything else.

BEFORE HE CAN SAVE THE WORLD,
CLARK KENT MUST SAVE SMALLVILLE.

Award-Winning and #1 *New York Times* Bestselling Author

# MATT DE LA PEÑA

The *New York Times* Bestselling Series

## DC ICONS

# SUPERMAN
## DAWNBREAKER

TURN THE PAGE TO SEE HOW
THE BESTSELLING DC ICONS SERIES
CONTINUES WITH CLARK KENT!

# CHAPTER 1

The storm came with little warning. A flash of lightning lit up Clark's glasses as he huddled beneath the Java Depot awning with three former football teammates, all of them watching the sudden deluge pound the streets of downtown Smallville. The whipping rain had forced them elbow to elbow, and if Clark exercised a little amnesia, it almost felt like old times, back when he and the football squad were thick as thieves.

He doubted they would ever be close like that again.

Not after he had quit on them.

Clark had always marveled at the power of thunderstorms, which put even his own mysterious strength into perspective. For others, the storm was nothing more than a nuisance. An older businessman, holding a briefcase over his head, sprinted toward a silver SUV, where he beeped open his door and dove inside. A drenched calico slunk beneath an industrial trash bin, looking for a dry place to wait out the downpour.

"We can't just stand here all day," Paul shouted over the roar of the rain. "Come on, let's make a run for the library."

Kyle shot him a dirty look. "Dude, this shit is, like, biblical. I'm not going *any*where."

"I guess we could just do this here." Tommy glanced back at the closed door of the coffee shop before turning to Clark. "Cool with you, big guy?"

Clark shrugged, still wondering what "this" was.

And why no one else could be within earshot.

He had been more than a little surprised when Tommy Jones, a lumbering offensive lineman, approached him at school wanting to "hang out." He'd been equally surprised when Tommy then showed up at the coffee shop with star running back Paul Molina and full-back Kyle Turner. After all, they'd wanted nothing to do with Clark for the better part of two years—since the day he abruptly left the freshman team midseason.

Now here they all were, kicking it on Main Street again.

Like nothing had ever happened.

But Clark knew there had to be a catch.

Tommy raised the brim of his baseball cap and cleared his throat. "I'm guessing you know our record this past season," he began. "We sort of . . . underachieved."

"That's one way of putting it," Kyle said, and Paul shook his head in disgust.

Clark should have known. This meetup was about football. Because when it came to Tommy, Kyle, and Paul, *everything* was about football.

"Anyway, us three have been talking." Tommy slapped a big, meaty hand onto Clark's shoulder. "We'll all be seniors next year. And we wanna go out with a bang."

A massive clap of thunder echoed overhead, causing the three football players to flinch. Clark had never understood that reaction. How even the bravest people he knew could get so spooked by a little thunder. It was yet another example of how different he was from his peers. The guys tried to play off their jumpiness by checking their phones and studying their drinks.

That's when Clark noticed something odd.

About thirty yards to his right, a wire-thin man in his early twenties was standing in the middle of the road, holding out his arms and staring up into the pouring rain. He had a tight buzz cut, and he was dressed head to toe in brown. Brown long-sleeved shirt. Brown pants. Brown combat boots. Clark had an uneasy feeling about the guy.

"Look at *this* freak," Paul said, noticing him, too.

"Who?" Tommy asked.

"Over there." Paul pointed, but a slow big rig rumbled by, blocking their view. When it had passed, the man was gone.

Paul frowned, scratching the back of his shaved head and scanning the empty street. "He was standing out there a second ago. I swear."

Clark searched for the man, too. Random strangers dressed in all brown didn't just appear on the streets of Smallville, only to disappear seconds later. Who *was* he? Clark glanced back through the Java Depot window, where a dozen or so people he recognized were sitting at little round tables, drinking coffee and talking. Doing homework. Taking refuge from the storm.

He wondered if any of them had seen the guy.

As swiftly as the storm had begun, it now slowed to a quiet sprinkle. Steam rose off a drenched Main Street. Heavy drops fell from the trees. They streaked down the windshields of parked cars and zigzagged down street signs. The road was a sea of puddles.

"Let's walk," Tommy said, and they set off toward the public square, Clark still looking for the man dressed in brown.

The four of them had to veer around a series of orange cones blocking off yet another construction zone. A surging local economy had led to a serious transformation of downtown Smallville over the past several years. Gone were all the boarded-up storefronts and dilapidated buildings of Clark's youth. In their place were trendy restaurants, real estate offices, a luxury condo development, and two shiny new bank branches. Multiple construction projects seemed to always be under way now, including the future headquarters for the powerful Mankins Corporation. But there was no work being done this afternoon. The storm had turned Main Street into a ghost town.

"Look, Clark," Tommy said, attempting to pick up where he'd left off, "we all know how much better we would be with you in the backfield. I mean, there's a reason we were undefeated in the games you played freshman year."

"Yeah, before he bailed on us," Paul scoffed.

Tommy shot Paul a dirty look. "What'd we talk about earlier, man? This is about moving forward. It's about second chances."

Clark shrank into himself.

Two years later and he still couldn't stomach the idea that he'd let the team down. And then lied to them. He hadn't quit football to concentrate on school, like he told everyone at the time. He quit because he could have scored on just about every play from scrimmage. And the urge to dominate—wrong as it seemed—grew stronger with each passing game. Until one day he ran over Miles Loften during a tackling drill, sending him to the hospital with fractured ribs. And Clark had only been going about fifty percent. After practice, he'd climbed the bleachers and sat alone, long into the night, contemplating what was no longer possible for him to overlook—just how drastically different he was. And how bad it would be if anyone found out.

Before leaving that night, he'd decided to hang up his cleats.

He hadn't played an organized sport since.

When Tommy stopped walking, everyone else did, too. "I'm just gonna come right out and say it." He glanced at Kyle and Paul before turning back to Clark. "We *need* you."

Kyle nodded. "Come back soon and you'll be able to reestablish yourself before summer workouts. Shit, Coach would probably even make you a captain."

"What do you say, Clark?" Tommy play-punched him in the arm. "Can we count on you?"

Clark wanted so badly to come through for these guys. To put on the pads and get back to work. To feel like he was a part of something again, something bigger than himself. But it was impossible. Injuring teammates and scoring seven touchdowns a game was bad enough when he was a freshman. Imagine if things like that happened on *varsity*. With everyone watching. He just couldn't risk it. His parents had warned him how dangerous it could be if the world were to discover the depths of his mysterious abilities. And the last thing he wanted to do was bring trouble to the family. Kids at school already teased him about being too good. Too perfect. It was the reason he'd started wearing glasses he didn't actually need. And mixing in a couple of Bs on his report card.

Clark adjusted his glasses, looking at the sidewalk. "I really wish I could," he told Tommy in a lifeless voice. "But I can't. I'm sorry."

"See?" Paul said. "Told you he didn't give a shit about us."

"Unbelievable," Kyle added, shaking his head.

Tommy turned away from Clark. "Easy, fellas. We can't *force* the guy to be loyal—"

The man in brown turned a corner and cut right through the four of them. He forcefully bumped shoulders with Tommy, causing him to fumble his iced coffee to the ground.

Clark and his ex-teammates were struck silent for several seconds, until Kyle kicked the plastic cup across the sidewalk and called after the guy, "Hey, asshole! You need to watch where the hell you're going!"

The man spun around and shouted something back at Kyle in Spanish. Then he spit on the sidewalk and held up a small blade, as if daring them to say anything else.

"Yo, he's got a knife!" Paul shouted.

When Clark stepped in front of his friends, he saw how jittery the man's bloodshot eyes were. And he was mumbling under his breath.

"What's he saying?" Kyle asked Paul, who was Mexican and spoke Spanish at home.

Paul shook his head. "I don't know. Something about getting back to Metropolis."

Clark wondered if the guy might be on drugs. What else could explain his bloodshot eyes and the way he'd been standing in the pouring rain? And he wasn't just staring at Clark now. He was staring *through* Clark. "Let's leave him alone," Clark said, focusing on the knife in the man's left hand. "There's something off about the way he's acting."

"Screw that," Kyle said, elbowing past Clark. He pointed at the man, shouting, "Nobody slams into my teammate like that without apologizing. You think I'm scared of that little bullshit switch-blade?"

The man lunged, swinging the knife violently, the blade grazing Kyle's forearm, before quickly retreating.

Kyle looked at the blood trickling down his arm. He looked at the man.

Then all hell broke loose.

Clark bounded forward to kick the knife out of the guy's hand, sending it skittering under a parked car. Tommy and Paul threw their backpacks into the street and charged. They tackled the man onto the hard, wet pavement, but he managed to scurry out of their grasp, leap to his feet, and retreat.

Kyle made a move to join the fray, but Clark pulled him back. "Hang on!"

"Oh, hell no! He just cut my ass!" Kyle took a wider angle this time and joined Tommy and Paul as the three of them stalked the guy, backing him into a row of parked cars.

Clark knew how lopsided the fight would be. The man was wild-eyed and showed no fear, but he was clearly no match for three hulking football players.

Clark's instinct was to rush in and break everything up before anyone got seriously hurt. But things had gone horribly wrong the last time he'd used his powers in public. It had been winter. He'd been walking to the library when he spotted a big rig careening across a large ice patch on Highway 22. Without thinking, he'd sprinted over and used his strength to grab hold of the massive truck before it could flatten the Alvarez Fruits and Vegetables stand at the side of the road. Only he'd somehow overcorrected the big rig's momentum, toppling the heavy trailer, spilling dozens of oil drums out onto the two-lane highway. Oil had gushed everywhere.

Clark would never forget helping the driver from the wreckage. The man's face had been as white as a sheet, his leg twisted grotesquely. Would he have even been hurt if Clark hadn't stuck his nose in things? The question haunted Clark, and he'd promised himself to stop and think before physically intervening like that again.

But he could use his voice.

"Let him go, guys!" he shouted at his ex-teammates. "It's not worth it!"

The man in brown backed right into an old truck before slipping between parked cars and scurrying away.

Tommy turned to Kyle, grabbing his bloody arm and studying the cut. Paul huffed into the middle of the street to retrieve his backpack.

Clark cautiously followed the man in brown down the next block. He had to make sure he was really leaving, so no one got hurt. He stopped in his tracks when the guy began pounding his bare fists against the side of a beat-up white pickup truck while the driver cowered at the wheel. Clark stood there watching, absolutely baffled. What was wrong with this guy? And why was he beating on this one particular truck? It had just been innocently idling there at the side of the road. And the man was attacking it with a shocking ferocity, bloodying his fists in the process.

He turned suddenly and stalked back the other way, in the direction of Clark and the football players. Clark made a move to cut him off, but the man lunged toward the silver SUV instead, the one where the gray-haired businessman was waiting out the storm. The man in brown flung open the driver's side door, threw the businessman onto the street, and climbed in to start the engine.

Clark's eyes widened with panic when the SUV lurched out of its parking spot and then sped forward, seemingly headed directly toward Paul, who was still kneeling in the street, zipping up his backpack.

"Look out!" Clark shouted.

Paul looked up when he heard the screaming engine.

But he was still just kneeling there, a sitting duck.

Then came the familiar weightlessness of Clark reaching warp speed.

His skin tingling and raw.

His throat closing as he bolted soundlessly into the street, eyes fixed on the SUV barreling down on Paul.

Clark instinctively calculated his angle, the speed of the SUV, and the potential for destruction, and then he dove at the last possible second. And as he tore through the air, he peered up into the crazed eyes of the man gripping the steering wheel, and he saw how lost the man was, how bewildered. In that instant, Clark understood this was an act that ran far deeper than he or anyone else could know.

Then came the bone-crushing impact.

Dinah Lance's voice is her weapon, and in a near-future world where women have no rights, she won't hesitate to use everything she has—including her song—to fight back.

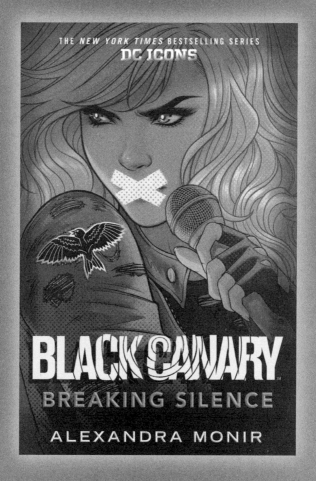

Don't miss Black Canary's story in the bestselling **DC ICONS** series!

The weeds climbed from soil to sky on all sides of Robinson Park, shrouding the abandoned grounds from the rest of Gotham City. Dinah Lance had grown up driving past this stretch, watching the once-flourishing park fade over the course of her childhood. The greenery had been the first to go, shriveling up and turning the color of mud. An army of vines came next, emerging from the ground and crawling up every bench, slide, and swing, until soon the whole space was too overgrown to see through. It used to be just another grim sight Dinah passed on her way to school, a reminder of all the ways the Court of Owls had failed their city. But today was different. Today she knew what was hidden inside.

"Please tell us you're not serious about this." Dinah's best friend, Mandy Harper, shuddered as she stared across the street. "That place looks like a hangout for serial killers."

"Yeah, it's clearly been shut down for a reason," Ty Carver, the third member of their trio, said with a grimace. "And traipsing around a sketchy old park was *not* what I had in mind for our second-to-last day of summer. Especially when we could be at Natasha Wycliffe's party right now."

"You guys can chicken out if you want, but I'm going in," Dinah said, striding ahead of them. "What we're about to uncover easily beats some party that—I hate to break it to you, Ty—we're not even invited to."

"Wait." Mandy gripped her arm. "What if someone sees us? Is your plan really worth the risk of—"

"Rotting in Arkham Asylum?" Ty finished her sentence. "Um, of course not. C'mon, let's go."

Dinah paused midstep. She couldn't exactly blame them for their reservations. Trespassing on closed government property was, technically, a crime against the Court—one that could warrant the Owls' favorite punishment. A prison sentence at Arkham used to be reserved for the most dangerous, deranged criminals in the city, but these days there was an entirely different group behind bars. The Court had "repurposed" Arkham, warping it into a torture chamber for anyone who dared to oppose them. It was a place where roles were reversed, with known criminals running the show and would-be heroes languishing in their cells. The kind of place you tried to avoid at all costs.

Still . . . Gotham City's rulers had far bigger fish to fry than high school students poking around a run-down park. Dinah hadn't heard of anyone their age winding up in Arkham—yet. Getting caught was a long shot. And for better or worse, her want was greater than her fear.

"It's totally deserted. No one's going to know we were ever there, much less throw us in Arkham over it," she said. "And if we did somehow get caught, I would be the one to take the blame anyway."

She looked back at the two of them as a beam of light from a streetlamp crossed their faces, highlighting Mandy's gold-flecked brown eyes, dark brown skin, and wary expression and Ty's pale skin and light blue eyes, jittery behind his glasses. Dinah felt a twinge of guilt for talking them into this.

"You don't have to come with me if you really hate the idea."

Mandy gave her a wry smile and pulled a tiny can of pepper spray from her skirt pocket.

"I mean, we're obviously not going to let you go in there alone."

"We're not?" Ty cracked. Dinah wouldn't have been surprised if he was only half kidding. As much as he cared about her, Ty also happened to be the furthest thing from a risk taker.

"This just better be worth it," Mandy added.

"It will be." Dinah grinned at her two oldest friends, looping an arm through each of theirs as they crossed to the darker side of the street.

The towering curtain of weeds rose up to meet them. It surrounded the park's perimeter, blocking every entrance.

"What are we supposed to do now?" Ty asked, raising an eyebrow.

"Just . . . follow me."

Dinah took a deep breath and slid sideways into the weeds, feeling them part just enough to let her through before swallowing her up in stems and leaves. They scratched at her skin as she elbowed her way forward, toward a half-buried entrance gate. A tangle of bare branches poked through the gate's iron bars, like spindly arms pushing her away. Still, Dinah moved closer.

The latch was rusted shut after so many years untouched. Dinah cringed—this wasn't going to be pretty, especially in her mandatory Gotham City girls' uniform. A starched white button-down and knee-length wool skirt weren't exactly made for fence jumping.

She tied her blond hair into a ponytail and backed up a few steps before breaking into a run, leaping up onto the gate. Her skirt snagged on the bars, and branches clawed at her bare legs, but she managed to hoist herself over to the other side, landing knee-deep in brittle, browned grass. And for the first time, Dinah was inside Robinson Park.

It looked wild, feral, in the twilight. Dead leaves and twigs littered the path ahead, ivy snaked around every surface, and even the trees drooped to the ground, as if hiding their heads in shame. Still, there were hints of the happier place this used to be. A pair of swings creaked as the breeze rattled their chains. A paint-chipped carousel swayed in the same wind, sending its porcelain horses on a slow turn they would never get to finish. Dinah stepped up to the horse nearest her, a gray Thoroughbred with a cracked white mane. Its mouth was open in an expression meant to be a smile, but time had reshaped it so that the horse now appeared to be baring its teeth. Dinah shivered, stepping back.

Just then Mandy came hurtling over the gate, landing with a flying leap. She actually managed to make it look graceful, even in her constricting uniform, and Dinah couldn't help but clap as her friend's feet hit the ground.

"Think of the gymnast I could have been," Mandy joked, dropping into a playful bow. It was a running gag between her and Dinah, albeit not a very funny one: remarking on all the different things they could have done or become if they had just been born a generation or two earlier—back when girls were allowed to be athletes.

Mandy's smile fell as she took in the scene around them. "Yikes. It's even more of a dump than I imagined."

A loud thump sounded behind them as Ty tumbled to the ground, glasses flying off his nose.

"Why is it that I always seem to wind up bruised whenever we follow one of your plans?" he complained, fumbling through the grass for his glasses.

"Sorry, T." Dinah reached out to help pull him back up to his feet. "But I promise—if what I overheard is even half true, you'll be thanking me for dragging you here."

"If you say so." Ty shook his head at her but then fell into step as Dinah led the way.

For a while, the only sound was of their shoes crunching leaves—until Mandy stopped abruptly and elbowed Dinah in the ribs. *"Look."*

Dinah glanced up and drew in a sharp breath. An old stone monument loomed ahead of them, like a temple plucked straight out of ancient Greece. Its front facade was bordered by twelve statues and, half buried among the leaves, twelve ornamented gravestones.

"The Forum of the Twelve Caesars," she murmured as they approached it. "That's what they used to call this—this mausoleum. I remember reading about it."

"Okay, well, you forgot to remind us there's a freaking *graveyard* in here," Mandy said with a gulp. "I vote we turn back now."

"I second that," Ty said quickly, but Dinah was already crouching to brush the leaves off the first headstone.

"Martha Wayne," she read, a pit forming in her stomach.

And she knew, without looking, who lay in the surrounding graves: Bruce and Thomas Wayne, James Gordon, Renee Montoya, and the rest of the heroes from Gotham City's past. These legends were the reason the Court of Owls had left Robinson Park to rot as soon as they took control of the city.

Suddenly, a sense of movement in her peripheral vision jolted Dinah from her thoughts. She could have sworn she had just seen a shadow flitting between the graves across from them. Dinah blinked, telling herself it was nothing, or that she'd imagined it—until she heard Ty jump.

"What was that? Did you see it?"

"Yeah, let's get out of here," Mandy urged her. "Now."

"You guys, chill," Dinah said, standing up and trying to ignore her own nerves. "We are in a wild park, after all, which means there's probably a dozen squirrels or other harmless creatures scurrying around. That's nothing to be afraid of. C'mon, we're so close."

She could hear Mandy and Ty muttering under their breath behind her as they advanced deeper into the park, passing a thicket of oak trees and a reservoir-turned-swamp along the way. Her eyes continued to scan the forest, alert for any signs of life that could threaten their presence. And then, finally, she found what she had come here in search of. It rose from the weeds like a decaying palace: the centuries-old Gotham City Opera House. A white marble outsider in a city of gray.

Fresh yellow police tape surrounded the building, its bold black letters shouting, NO TRESPASSING—GOV'T PROPERTY—DEMOLITION AHEAD. It was the only hint in this entire park that another human being had recently set foot in here.

Dinah ducked under the tape and gazed up at the structure in awe, as if she had just stumbled upon a holy relic. This opera house was built and run by a *woman*—back in the days when women still had the power to sing. When they had any power at all.

"Rumor has it there's a vault in there," Dinah called over her shoulder to Mandy and Ty, both of them lingering a few feet away from the police tape. "A Vault of Voices, where recordings of the old classical singers are hidden. *Female* singers." Her heartbeat sped up at the thought. What she would give to hear them . . .

"If that's true," Mandy said skeptically, "then wouldn't the Court have destroyed this place by now?"

"Apparently no one even knew about the vault until the police got an anonymous tip," Dinah replied, remembering the phone call she'd overheard between her dad and one of his fellow officers—the call that had led her here. She'd thought of little else since then.

Of all the things for her to dream of, to love most in the world, of course it had to be music—something she would never be allowed to pursue. Women were barred from singing or playing instruments, and yet there was nothing else in her entire life that had ever stirred her senses the way a song could. Playing one of her mom's old records was like slipping into a fantasy; the only thing missing was the female voice. To find those lost recordings, and get to hear what the women singers actually *sounded* like, would be the greatest historical discovery of her generation.

She just wished it didn't have to be.

"Well, that would explain the sudden demolition plans," Ty said darkly.

"And why we have to get in there before they do." Dinah quickened her pace. "Aren't you dying to hear it? A girl's voice, *singing* . . ."

Of course, it wouldn't technically be the first time Dinah heard the impossible, though she'd given up trying to convince anyone else that her childhood memory of hearing a girl sing was real. Her dad and her friends had all written it off as an eight-year-old's dream, which was no surprise. The idea of girls being able to sing, or do *anything* so powerful and free, was pure fantasy in the world they were living in. A world taken over by the Court of Owls, who ruled Gotham City as a patriarchal dictatorship while spreading their influence like a virus across the globe.

Dinah pressed her hands against the glass of a first-floor window and gasped as another world materialized inside: one with cobwebbed chandeliers, a sweeping staircase, and painted murals covering every inch of wall space. There was more color in this one room than she'd seen before in all of Gotham City.

Mandy and Ty joined her at the window, their interest finally piqued, while Dinah rifled through her crossbody bag for the lock-picking kit she'd "borrowed" from her dad. She hurried to the front entrance and got to work, angling the sharp pick into the keyhole. Just when she felt the pins in the lock start to budge, her eyes caught another flash of movement in the shadows. Goose bumps prickled a warning across her skin. And then—

A body leaped down from above, landing on the ground behind her with a nearly silent whisper of sound. A scream lodged in Dinah's throat as she recognized one of the unmistakable figures of Gotham City's nightmares. One that, until now, she had only ever seen in books and pictures—but never in the flesh.

The towering body was nearly seven feet tall, with muscles bulging beneath his black suit of armor. A chilling mask gave the twisted appearance of something half man, half avian, with a jagged beak where a nose should be and enormous, piercing yellow eyes. He lifted his hands to reveal the telltale steel-plated gloves, fingers ending in the sharp claws that gave this feared creature his name: *Talon*, faithful assassin of the Court of Owls.

And he was lunging straight toward her.

"Run!" Dinah shouted to Mandy and Ty before turning on her heel and breaking into a sprint behind them. Mandy tore off toward the maze of trees, gripping Ty's arm to keep him at her speed, but before Dinah could catch up to them, a gloved hand shot out and closed around her ankle. The Talon's claws dug deep into her skin, using the momentum to spin her roughly toward him. The breath left her lungs as Dinah looked up into those enlarged yellow eyes.

"Please, I didn't mean any harm," she managed to choke out. "I wasn't doing anything. Please just let me g—"

Instead of answering, the Talon gripped her neck with one steel glove and used the other to slide one of his claws from her chin down to her chest, drawing blood. Dinah opened her mouth to scream, but the Talon dug his fingers into her windpipe, and she couldn't make a sound. *He's going to kill me. He's going to kill me right here, right outside the place I've been dreaming of, and no one will hear me die.*

The pain from his roving claw seared through her till she could no longer think; all she had left was instinct. And it was instinct, coupled with years of Sandra Wu-San's training, that drove Dinah to reach up and seize the Talon's wrists in one lightning-quick move.

Her body acted on its own, ignoring her fear, ignoring the threat of retaliation, as she twisted his arms around her back in a standing arm bar. She wouldn't have stood a chance against him if not for the element of surprise. Girls weren't supposed to fight back—they weren't even supposed to know how. And so the Talon was caught off guard, roaring his fury as she yanked him toward the ground and then let go, sending his body falling backward.

Dinah shot forward, racing for the trees. But just when it seemed that she might actually make it, that she could have somehow succeeded against the odds—another monstrous figure pounced to the ground in front of her, and then one more. She was surrounded by Talons now, circling her with blades extended, eyes glittering with the promise of blood. Her amateur jujitsu skills were futile in the face of these three. Dinah squeezed her eyes shut, bracing for the end while silently praying for Mandy and Ty to make it out of there alive.

And then came the blare of a siren.

Dinah's head snapped up in surprise, just in time to see the police car come crashing through the gates. Even before the two officers jumped out, she knew her dad would be one of them. As Detective Larry Lance flew onto the scene, his gun aimed straight ahead, Dinah didn't know whether to feel relieved or even more afraid.

"Gentlemen—Talons—thank you for catching this intruder. The Gotham City PD will take it from here," Larry called out, feigning confidence. But Dinah could see the fear written across his face. Fear for her.

The Talons turned their attention to Detective Lance and his partner, blades curling in their direction now. Larry caught Dinah's eye and gave a slight nod toward the trees. But she couldn't run away, *couldn't* leave him alone with the Talons. Everyone knew they loathed the police and considered the GCPD far beneath them. It was the Court, not the GCPD, that had the authority to dump "offenders" in Arkham Asylum, the worst of Gotham City's prisons. Which meant one wrong move, and the Talons could make her dad their newest inmate—or their latest victim.

*Now,* Larry mouthed, eyes fierce. She forced herself to move, darting away from the Talons as her dad stepped closer, pulling their focus from Dinah. *If anything happens to him* . . . Dinah shook her head violently to rid herself of the thought. She had to find Mandy and Ty.

Dinah raced to the dark pocket of trees they had disappeared into, eyes scanning in every direction. Panic bubbled in her stomach as she combed through the weeds, growing more desperate the longer she looked, until—

"*Psst!* In here."

She whirled around. Her eyes welled up instantly at the sight of Mandy and Ty, huddled in the trunk of a split-open tree. They pulled Dinah in with them.

"I'm so sorry," she whispered.

She never should have dragged them into this; she knew that now. It was so easy to overlook the risks when she'd never encountered them in real life before, but now, at the thought of what could have happened, her chest was tight with guilt.

Mandy nodded. "It's okay. Let's just get out of here."

"My—my dad." Dinah swallowed hard. "I don't know

how they knew we were in trouble, but he and his partner are there right now, surrounded by Talons. I can't leave
until—"

"They'll be okay," Ty said gently. "They have guns, remember?"

"But the Talons have something else. Something just as
lethal."

Dinah shivered as the fabled word flew into her mind.
*Electrum.* An elusive, highly conductive alloy that the Owls
had controlled and hoarded for years, injecting it into their
Talons to give them enhanced strength and instant healing
capabilities. What chance did an ordinary pair of cops have
against that?

Mandy wrapped an arm around her shoulders.

"Your dad just gave us an opportunity to escape, and the
last thing he would want is for you to stay here and not take
it. He knows what he's doing. Please—let's go."

Dinah forced herself to follow as Mandy and Ty climbed
out of the tree trunk. The three of them crept back through
the park with their hands clasped, holding their breath. The
carefree energy that had propelled them over the gates just
an hour earlier felt foreign now, as if it had been three entirely different people who entered Robinson Park. Dinah
kept turning her head to listen in the direction of the opera
house, but the quiet was even more chilling than the sound
of Talons descending. If the unthinkable happened, she could
be going home an orphan. And it would be her own fault.

Mandy cleared the gate first, followed by Ty, whose
sweating palms kept causing him to slip off and into the dirt,
until Dinah finally helped push him over. And then it was
her turn. She could feel her muscles protesting, her adrena-

line nearly spent, but she managed to give it one last hurdle over to the other side. When they finally emerged past the barrier of weeds and back onto the street, they were bruised and bloodied, their clothes torn by brambles and muddied by the forest. But they were alive.

"You were right about one thing, at least," Ty said to Dinah as they walked in a huddle toward the residential side of Gotham City, hidden in the shadows of the sidewalks and alleyways between buildings. He draped his jacket over her and Mandy to cover their frayed skirts, and they kept their heads down, trying their best to blend in.

"What's that?" Dinah asked numbly.

"The rumor must be true—about the Vault of Voices. Because whatever is in that opera house was obviously important enough to be guarded by Talons."

Dinah stopped in her tracks as another realization hit her.

"And it's something they haven't found yet. The Court must still be searching for the vault. Otherwise . . . why would the opera house still be standing?"

Mandy and Ty looked back at her with wide, uncertain eyes. And as they made their way home, the questions in her mind grew louder with every step.